The Bismarck . . .

Part 3

"Redemption"

Or

Hood's Gambit

by

Alexander Kemp

It is strongly recommended that you read books 1 & 2 first.

Acknowledgements

Many thanks to those who helped shape the story as it evolved. I include the United States of America and the People's Republic of China as well as various members of my family who all wanted their 'two penneth'.

Particular thanks to my Electro-Technical Officer son for the heads up on the high voltage and my Deck Officer son for general advice. Thanks also to my editor Catherine for her patience and skills. Big thanks to my father in law, Peter Nurding, for his constant encouragement and keen interest in my work.

Alexander Kemp, 2017

Foreword

I wrote the first two books in this series out of duty. Duty to dead and injured comrades let down by a procurement system, long ago. They were my soapbox pieces to moan about the lack of just one little point defence gun system which could/would have prevented the loss of so many sailors lives thirty five years ago, and which cost so little itself.

Yes I was there back then and I confess I put myself in the Falklands chapter I wrote. It felt odd to be having a conversation with an imaginary character about real events in that setting. Job done though.

This one is almost for fun, it would be totally fun were it not for the very serious real-time power-plays going on out there in the Far East, where more ordinary sailors are at risk.

I mention America and China in the acknowledgements for a good reason. They are currently engaged in an exceedingly dangerous chess game, at least the US thinks it is chess, not sure about the Chinese though, could be 'Go' they are playing.

China and the Chinese are pretty opaque to most in the West, so different are their ways, their thoughts and their methods, but mostly their concept of time. It always seems to me, as someone who lived in Hong Kong before the handover, that America just doesn't quite get it when it comes to China. They want to apply their rules to a game which unfortunately only China has the rule book for. This could be as dangerous to China as it could to America but I'm not thinking world or even regional war, I'm thinking 'spats', 'incidents'. These spats will however cost the lives of young men and women on both sides.

But clearly there are other oriental minds out there with long memories desirous of taking China down several pegs, and who are very able to interpret Chinese plans and policies in the correct context.

Heart of Oak

Come, cheer up, my lads, 'tis to glory we steer,
To add something more to this wonderful year;
To honour we call you, as freemen not slaves,
For who are so free as the sons of the waves?

Heart of Oak are our ships, Jolly Tars are our men,
We always are ready: Steady, boys, Steady!
We'll fight and we'll conquer again and again!

William Boyce, and David Garrick 1860

The March of the Royal Navy

Acronyms:

ADCAP	Advanced Capability torpedo
AIS	Automatic Identification System. Ship based transponder.
A/S	Anti-Submarine
ASROC	A Rocket boosted Mk 46 torpedo for ASW.
ASuW	Anti-Surface Warfare as opposed to
ASW	Anti-Submarine Warfare
CG	Guided Missile Cruiser
CHOPs	Chief Petty Officer Operations
CMS	Combat Management System
CNO	US Chief of Naval Operations
DDG	Guided Missile Destroyer
Dog	Name for a lever which is engaged to secure an armoured hatch
DShKM	Russian made heavy machine gun
ECDIS	Electronic Chart Display Information System
ESM	Electronic Support Measures. Listening for emissions
EMCON Alpha	Refers to shutting down all electronic emissions
FACM	Fast Attack Craft [Missile]
GMDSS	Global Maritime Distress and Safety System
IMO	International Maritime Organisation
LAMPsIII	Light Airborne Multi-Purpose System. US desig for MH-60R helo
LCAC	Landing Craft Air Cushion
LiDAR	Light Detection and Ranging
MGCC	Main Gunnery Control Centre
NVG	Night Vision Goggles
OS	Operating System eg. Windows 10
QRF	Quick Reaction Force.
Q-ship	Vessel which appears to be a merchant but is armed
Papa, Flag	Universal flag recalling crew to a ship about to proceed to sea
PE	Pre-Environment. Interrupts OS boot sequence
POL	Petrol Oil Lubricants. General term for liquid stores inc fuel
RHIB	Rigid Hulled Inflatable Boat
ROE	Rules of Engagement
ROV	Remotely Operated Vehicle
SAG	Surface Action Group. Flotilla of warships with no carrier.
Sail/Fin	Term used for a submarine's conning tower USN/RN
SecDef	US Secretary of Defence
SSK	Ship Submersible Conventional
SSBN	Ship Submersible Ballistic Nuclear
SSGN	Ship submersible Guided Nuclear
SSN	Ship Submersible Nuclear
STANAVFORLANT	Standing Naval Force Atlantic. Cold War NATO ASW group
SWAG	Scientific Wild Ass Guess
VLS	Vertical Launch System.

September. Foreign & Commonwealth Office, London, England.

The old mantle clock ticked away in the background and became a source of irritation to Myers as he sat in the chair opposite his boss's antique desk, whilst the worthy man quietly read the dossier he had prepared.

Finally with a sort of 'hurrumph' sound, Sir Edgar Portlington finished the last page, smoothed them all down then closed the folder. Then he looked up and pinned Myers to the chair with his gimlet eyes.

"Let me summarise for you Myers. You have, for reasons unknown at the moment, taken department time and resources to compose this dossier without being tasked to do so. In addition you have appropriated resources from our overseas colleagues in various embassies to 'dig the dirt', to use the modern vernacular, on one Jonathan Henry König. Specifically, in regard to the operational activities of his specialist maritime security division."

He paused, well into his Sir Humphrey Appleby mode and enjoying it. Steepling his fingers he considered the man in front of him. Best described generously as a hard worker, but mostly as a nonentity according to his personnel file, he was under the misapprehension that Sir Edgar was unaware that König had gone straight over Myer's head to the Foreign Secretary before that dreadful business in the Caribbean.

Spiteful little creature thought Sir Edgar. After all König was a distinguished former officer in the Royal Navy and is now by any standards, a wealthy and influential business leader; most importantly an esteemed member of Sir Edgar's club, the Naval Club which as a former RN Captain, he visited regularly. He returned his attentions to the problem at hand.

"I see you have catalogued events and incidents as clearly as you were able Myers. By your own words you allege König's security staff to have taken the lives of as many as one hundred and fifty pirates. And these self-same 'victims' have probably, you say, been responsible for the deaths of six hundred and fifty crewmembers of various nationalities worldwide. But their catalogue of mayhem doesn't end there," he said looking over the top of his spectacles, "they appear to have murdered policemen in various countries and a sprinkling of intelligence operatives as well as undisclosed 'others' over the last decade." He continued with ice entering his tone. "Also, presumably when bored with hijacking and murder at sea, they partake of human trafficking. In addition you claim these pirates were responsible for the theft of over one point four billion pounds worth of goods, some ransomed back, numerous ships stolen and ransomed, with eight hundred million pounds paid out in ransom. There are various ships still missing suspected to have been renamed, repainted and sold on and some simply sunk."

Sir Edgar placed the folder back on the desk in his precise manner.

"You also state in your appendices that global piracy, according to IMO, has dropped by seventy two percent during the time König has been operating, declining more steeply towards the present day. That this has had the knock on effect of reducing transit premiums for various customers of Lloyds of London insurance by virtue of drastically reducing the pay outs for loss, thus making the Lloyds 'Names' lots of money and improving the profit & loss accounts for a variety of shipping companies."

Myers jiffled a little in his seat, not daring to lean back lest he gave the impression he was comfortable, or horror of horrors, in case the chair back which seemed fragile, gave way. This wasn't going quite how he expected it to go. Sir Edgar appeared not to be filled with the fires of righteous indignation and the desire to personally hand König to the jailors at Wormwood Scrubs. On the contrary Sir Edgar was actually turning around all of his anti-König points and making them sound, well... positive.

"Pray tell me Myers, is there a downside to Mr König's activity that I have missed somewhere?"

Myers gulped. There was the proof, it had all gone wrong. His plan to have the Foreign Office launch an official investigation into the activities of this partly British company was in tatters. He still burned with the humiliation of König's treatment of him eighteen months ago when he'd been dismissed as just another flunky.

"But they are murdering people Sir, without due process of law. They are committing crimes against humanity."

Myers watched as Sir Edgar's left eyebrow rose to an impossible height, seemingly about to detach itself and fall on to the blotter.

The Whitehall Mandarin drew a large breath then slowly let it part way out as he considered a response to Myers silly politically correct objection.

"Myers, the people guilty of crimes against humanity listed here, are the ones who murdered and tortured their way through six hundred plus people including law enforcement officers, in order to line their filthy pockets. They were then, and any remaining now, are scum. Nothing more and nothing less. Even our liberalised government won't be too upset to learn of their demise since so much of the nation's wealth still travels by sea. The only kind of people who would see this as something to be concerned about are those such as that shyster lawyer chap who was struck off for hounding British soldiers, and the likes of Mrs Blair! Lastly, and it had better be lastly Myers, you have no evidence. Nothing. All conjecture and assumption. Nothing that would stand in even a civil court, where the burden of proof is somewhat less than its criminal opposite."

Sir Edgar removed his glasses, rubbed the bridge of his nose with thumb and forefinger then fixed Myers with his intense gaze again meanwhile adopting a more fatherly tone –the very last thing he felt towards this simpering fool.

"A word of advice Myers. I will overlook this breach of departmental protocols and the waste of resources, but just this once. I suggest you allow me the dubious privilege of consigning this rubbish to the incinerator or we'll have to consider an internal disciplinary tribunal. Well I'm waiting. What's it to be?"

Myers looked down. Utter defeat and the prospect of a disciplinary hearing should he object. He sighed.

"Yes Sir Edgar."

"Yes what Myers?"

"Err, you destroy them Sir."

"Thank you Myers, now get out and get on with the work you are supposed to be doing, I will speak to Mr Carmichael about your workload, clearly too light."

"Yes Sir." Was the dejected response.

September. Lloyds of London, 1 Lime Street

The subject of Myer's incriminating folder was at that moment in London and at a meeting of his own. Jonathan Henry König sipped his coffee and savoured the exquisite flavours, not from a capsule or jar of instant for sure, he decided. The other gentlemen and one lady in the meeting room stared at him as if he were the man from Del Monte about to pronounce on this year's crop.

"Excellent." He said at last.

They waited. Clearly these highly paid brokers of marine insurance were not interested in his appreciation of their coffee.

König sighed, but not loudly.

"I have explained Gentle...err, people." He nodded to the solitary lady in the room. "I have explained that operating conditions in that area have become very challenging in the last three months and very much more so even more recently. But I see I must explain further. There is a power play in process. Given the principal but by no means only protagonists, China and the USA, this is not something that has just started and nor will it be finished this time next week. China is partway through one of its long term plans which appear to be aimed at appropriating the South China Sea for its own mineral exploration and exploitation. It also seeks to deny the right of freedom of movement across the same area. By doing the latter they reinforce the former. It is a convoluted and long term goal of theirs and no one really knows what they are prepared to do to enforce their claims. They tend to move slowly, hoping no one will notice or won't bother to object as piece by piece they implement their objectives. I have to caution however that in my opinion there will be times in the near future when the passage of ships of any kind through the South China Sea could be, well...stopped."

The five men and one woman looked at each other and leaned in for a muttered conference. The sole female, Mrs Sarah Barnes-Barker spoke for them.

"Surely Mr König, you exaggerate the dangers. With so many warships of various navies in the area there should be a reduced risk to commercial traffic. Perhaps an increase in your contract fees would help?"

Jake refused to be insulted. He knew they were simply business people and thought that money would or could solve the problem.

"Mrs Barker, I assure you the fees for this contract, should I take it, are not my issue. The safety of my ships and their crews are my biggest worry. The recent exchange of fire between a US destroyer and a shore battery in the Spratlys may have caused everyone to back off for now but I don't think the game has ended yet. The danger I was referring to was not from pirates, but from national navies. Anyway, I'll let you know as soon as I can, within the week if we are fortunate, a little longer if not. There will be no charge for this pre-investigation. If we come up with any clues as to the missing vessels or their cargoes, then and only then, will we consider whether we can operate in the area, after that, as I say, I will be back in touch. Anyway, those are my terms, if you are happy I'll get going and start organising my teams?"

Barker looked at the others who nodded, puzzled in part that this somewhat enigmatic man had firstly chosen to respond to their request in person, but secondly hadn't been interested in pushing the price up.

"We are agreed Mr König, we will await your response."

Jake nodded and stood up.

"I'll take my leave then and thank you for seeing me."

They nodded in unison and he left, wondering if there were puppet strings somewhere out of sight. He looked round as he was escorted off the floor, 'the inside out building' was rightly named, he wasn't prone to vertigo himself but he wasn't sure he'd be happy working in one of the buds on the outside of the building. Bit late to object if the architect screwed up.

The Naval Club, 38 Hill Street, Mayfair, London.
Later that evening.

Jake settled into a chair and sniffed appreciatively at his balloon of Croix de Salles 1922. A ridiculous amount of money to pay for a drink but as money was no object to him he allowed himself the indulgence since this particular Armagnac was his favourite.

A superb meal, then a retreat to the ground floor bar in the company of some old navy friends whom he hosted. The inevitable wide ranging and stimulating discussions coupled with a good belly laugh was just what he needed to distract him. Apart from the company of his beautiful wife, off gallivanting somewhere in Uruguay of all places, or his children, James now twenty and Helen nineteen, both studying at maritime colleges in the UK, he could want for no finer company.

Relaxing now, having said good night to his friends, he let his mind run over the events of today.

He had on occasion done work for Lloyds before both on commission and inadvertently –by killing pirates. He wasn't sure just how much money they had paid out recently in losses but it must have made those particular 'Names' squeal loudly for them to want his company to investigate.

What he needed now, he decided, was a Captains conference along with Andy Evans, his ubiquitous Security Chief, and his deputy Arkady Zotov. He considered the logistics of gathering them all in one place and where to do so.

Bismarck was currently operating in the Gulf of Guinea acting as a base of operations and radar picket as well as drone base, for several smaller units engaged in anti-piracy work for the Nigerian oil industry with permission of the government. According to Reiner, still Captain of Bismarck, the nearest they'd come to any action was when they intercepted a boatful of pirates fleeing one of the company RHIBs about a mile offshore, literally intercepted he emphasised.

Reiner, not noted for his humour had found it highly amusing when the pirate vessel, slowly being overhauled by the RHIB and clearly aiming for a thick bank of morning fog, had simply run into Bismarck's side when they entered the same fog bank that Bismarck was already occupying. The wooden vessel had disintegrated having hit the side of the titanium alloy ship at about thirty knots. Everyone on board it, comically looking aft at the approaching armed RHIB when Bismarck had suddenly loomed out of the fog.

Given that the stunned survivors offered no resistance and the average age of the occupants was about fourteen, they were arrested and handed over to the Nigerian authorities, who, no doubt would administer a serious beating at the very least.

Reiner had contented himself by lining them up on the quarterdeck under the outward pointed guns of turrets Caesar and Dora, and through his interpreter delivered a blistering rant about actions and consequences and how close they'd come to death. The frightened 'wannabee' oil thieves had quailed under his harsh guttural voice as all the while the muzzles of numerous assault rifles were locked onto them. DNA samples were taken and the threat issued that should they ever be caught again, there would be no second chances. The only downside, he said, had been when the prisoners were off loaded at Port Harcourt and the local dignitaries had insisted on a tour of the famous Bismarck, victor of the Caribbean battle the year before.

Hood was still operating off the Gulf of Aden and making a severe dent in the operations of the Somali, Eritrean and now Yemeni pirates in the area. Her new

Captain, the recently retired Captain Jon Roby DSO RN, was having a wonderful time playing with all the gadgets and generally becoming a pain in the ass to the local pirate warlords. So said his newly promoted First Lieutenant, Julius Kopf former Gunnery Officer of Bismarck.

Roby's old friends still serving in the RN and other navies were quite happy to pass on pirate spotting intel to him, knowing he wasn't restricted by the same conventions in his dealing with the scum that preyed on merchant ships. This had allowed Roby on a dozen or so occasions to intercede at a crucial moment, destroying the attacking pirate vessels and their larger mother ships with a few well aimed volleys and little fuss.

Twice they'd arrived as a security detachment on board the stricken ship, usually two or three men, was reporting being boarded. On one occasion the security detachment had scared away one boat but was boarded at two other points. Hood's timely arrival and the swift, noisy destruction of the distant mother craft had quickly turned the tables. Two of the three fast boats had been destroyed by shellfire as they sped away, the third Roby had let go, turning Hood full broadside so they could see who their nemesis was. He presumed the remaining three pirates in their fast boat, speeding away from the ship with so many guns, were expecting destruction all the way until out of sight. He wanted to put the fear of Hood, not God into them, said Julius happily.

The third ship in his anti-piracy squadron, the highly successful Q ship Ocean Guard, was operating near the southern islands of the Philippines but not with their permission as such. There had been a recent rash of barbaric incidents involving piracy, mass murder and mutilation. Simon McClelland the Captain of Ocean Guard and former First Lieutenant of Bismarck, was trolling the waters for pirates using his special ship as bait, but well outside of territorial waters.

One daring buccaneering come drug running gang -and sometime Islamic State rebels- had boarded an inter-island ferry en-route between Zamboanga and Lamitan. They had stripped the passengers of their money and any possessions they fancied. Four passengers had objected and been immediately hacked to pieces in front of the rest by pirates clearly off their heads on something sniffed, smoked or injected.

President Duterte had vowed on national TV to personally hack them to pieces when they were caught. Simon didn't have the heart to tell him that Ocean Guard had already taken care of business for him, but instead of being hacked to pieces they had been reduced to their component parts by the 30mm AK630 guns hidden in the deck housing. Subsequent searching of wreckage and photography of pirate corpses had revealed a match to the leader. Jake would be the one to drop the word to the President quietly and without the fuss the media would like. Thus he would ensure favourable consideration, in the event of any problems which occurred whilst operating in an area of Philippine economic interest.

This buccaneer had been a fool and let his face be photographed and his actions recorded on a hundred smart phones, so identity wasn't an issue. A 'sometime' fighter for the *Maute* group, he was obviously short of a few 'readies' and decided to appropriate some when he had attacked the ferry.

Simon's meeting with the pirate's flashy high speed boat, purloined from another raid, had amazingly taken place in broad daylight not fifty miles from the scene of his atrocity; clearly the man was either taking his own drugs or thought he was invincible since the Philippine Navy were looking for him too.

Simon's methodology was different from either Bismarck or Hood as Ocean Guard encouraged attack by pirates rather than doing the attacking. This of course was precisely what she had been designed for. There were no known survivors of an armed encounter with Ocean Guard, simply because the pirates were always overt in their use of weapons and therefore became easily justified targets within company rules. The self-same rules that the European Parliament had obliged Jake to write into company policy after the law suit in 2016, gave him not just the right but the obligation to defend his ships. The lack of survivors also kept her as a surprise package if opened by any 'wannabee' pirates in the future.

In all incidents for all three ships, every effort was made to capture data which justified the use of each vessel's weaponry and a strict event log kept. Subsequently this was reviewed by Jake himself. If he required any clarification he would seek it directly through the relevant Captain, but in almost all incidents so far they had been open and shut cases. The culprits were guilty of piracy on the high seas and killed in the execution of their criminal acts, pardon the pun Jake thought. The penalty for piracy to him was singular, death by whatever means and sentence to be carried out immediately, there would be no more Willy Van Plasterks if he had anything to do with it.

Once Jake had reviewed the incidents, all the evidence was destroyed, completely, utterly and irretrievably. Physical evidence was incinerated; electronic evidence was erased and over-written and erased, re-formatted, overwritten and erased. One of the geeks in his anti-cyber warfare division had written an erasure protocol which it was said even the NSA retrievalists could not unravel. The only person who would ever end up in the dock was going to be Jake himself and he'd just be saying 'prove it'.

Pirates usually had little desire for witnesses to their acts and that was all too often their undoing when faced by Simon and his Q-ship.

So given the respective locations, all in all the best place to meet would probably be somewhere like Goa in India. That could not be though. He had closed all his business interests in India and would not even employ an Indian national for the moment, since the arrest and imprisonment of the crew of a privately owned security vessel of American origin. They had been taken, so say, having strayed into Indian waters whilst on anti-piracy patrols. Jake's real bug bear was that the only people on board who could be rationally held responsible for any navigational offence were the ship's master and or the watch officer at the time of the incident. To keep in prison for years all thirty five crew including the cook and six Britons all formerly British soldiers, on the trumped up pretence that they had been unlawfully in possession of firearms was too much.

Because of weak UK government protestations and little consular assistance, these men had resided for years in Chennai prison. So no, he would have nothing to do with India until those men were pardoned and compensated. The US company which owned the vessel was also derelict in its dealings on behalf of the men, an utter waste of time, said one when Jake had visited them on the quiet.

So, Oman then. He was due there in three days anyway to meet a delegation from the Japanese petroleum company Sainex and Hood was going to be there for that meeting to demo its advanced weapons and surveillance systems, so they'd just tag this Captains conference on to the end. Sainex were looking to engage König Marine Security for defence and anti-piracy protection. This was required to look after the new oil field they had a significant share in, off the Islands of the Comoros. The Comoros Government had awarded Sainex the seventh and last block for exploration in 2014. Thought to be the least promising location, Sainex had at first been reluctant to commit, however preliminary results had exceeded all expectations. The downside had been Mozambique interference both official and unofficial.

Sainex's exploration, and now *exploitation* block, was right on the border of their economic zone, adjacent to Mozambique's. Mozambique of course claimed the area **after** the find. In their usual prevaricating, bumbling, unhelpful and tardy way, the UN had failed to immediately support the government of Comoros thus encouraging official and unofficial interference with Japanese exploration units operating in the area.

Hence the need for proper security since the Japanese had complained that their installations had been ordered to move by a Mozambique patrol boat, which had pointed its bow mounted cannon at the exploration unit. Subsequently a helicopter with visible weapons on pylons had then buzzed them. Recently, a night visit from a fast vessel which had machine gunned the accommodation area and other parts, was the last straw.

The Japanese wanted to bring in full drilling, piping and all the paraphernalia of processing but baulked at there being no protection for them. Comoros had no navy to speak of just two old former Japanese coast guard vessels which didn't even possess a deck gun. König Marine Security was therefore in with a chance at the contract.

Before any get together he needed to confidentially inform all three Captains what was in the air so they could do their own research. So if he then sent his company jet on to Zamboanga to pick up Simon and another to Lagos for Reiner they would meet after the Japanese delegation had left. Andy and Arkady needed to do some serious snooping and intel gathering prior to the meeting so they all had a fighting chance of making an informed decision.

Simon had furthest to come and he would need to adopt his official Caymans identity to dock at Zamboanga, then pick up the company jet. That would mean suspending operations for a while, but it would be a good opportunity to meet up with the supply ship and do an early crew change, he thought.

All those employed for special sea duties on board Hood, Bismarck and Ocean Guard, were protected as much as possible from any kind of external scrutiny. Their identities were closely guarded. This meant that as far as possible all relief crews were exchanged at sea during regular replenishment cycles, they then sailed back to Little Cayman in the replenishment ship and went on leave to wherever, from there. So, all that an external observer would know is that in some capacity they worked for König Marine which also did oceanic survey, rig support and plain cargo carrying with a base facility and repair yard locally. In effect they became part of a crowd.

In any event Andy Evans, had a permanent presence at immigration in the main airport on Grand Cayman and there was constant close liaison with the Island's own security through the Interior Minister Sandiford Roche who was only too well aware that there were still people in their part of the world who would want revenge on some of these crewmen.

So a meeting in five maybe six days then, but plenty of pre-meeting work for himself and Andy's security people beforehand.

September. Khasab, Oman.

Jake stood next to the three Sainex executives under a specially erected sunshade and watched as the Hood swept past the outer mole and turned to starboard, almost bows onto them. He'd already cleared this visit with the Omani customs and Naval authorities but it was still polite to include the locals, you never knew when cooperation would be needed and toes which had been stood on, noses that had been bent out of place, could make for awkwardness at a later date. So he nodded, shook hands and thanked the Omani customs officer who was clearly only too happy to return to his air conditioned office further along the harbour.

The heat was almost a physical thing even under the shade but the three Japanese executives appeared unaffected and Jake wondered if they had some new super small air conditioning unit built into their immaculate pin striped suits. He was melting in just a polo shirt and cream slacks and deck shoes. The driver of their large Mercedes had the best of the deal, Jake decided, glancing towards the car parked next to a warehouse just off the Khasab coastal road; engine running and the aircon going full blast no doubt. He turned back to see Hood commence her final turn to end up broadside to the waiting observers.

A tray loaded with glasses and a cooler full of iced unsweetened lemon tea beckoned Jake. He asked if anyone wanted a drink but they all politely declined, eyes fixed on the sleek and warlike vessel whose bow wave now fell away to barely a thin white moustache as she slowed, ready to anchor. Her business like Atlantic grey paint contrasted starkly with sand coloured rocks of the outer breakwater and the majestic Omani mountains that rose up behind her as she made her final turn.

The Finnish Steerpods and the bow thruster easily turned the three and a half thousand ton vessel to its final bearing as she came to a halt and the bow and stern anchors ran out noisily and simultaneously. Before the echoes of the first splash had died away the Caymans national flag broke out from the jack staff in the bows and the Caymans Naval pennant broke out from the mainmast starfish alongside the Omani Naval pennant as well. At the stern the Caymans Naval ensign also appeared, as if by magic. The dozen sailors in dress tropical white, who had formed the deck party, disappeared only to return seconds later with awning canvas for both the fo'c'sle and quarterdeck. Using fastenings on both B turret and X turret to stretch them, a large part of the wooden planking could be quickly shielded from the sun.

Smartly done, thought Jake, as the Hood was now properly 'dressed', awnings spread and a companionway lowered all within five minutes of dropping anchor. One of the Japanese executives turned to Jake and bowed slightly.

"A creditable display Mr König, the vessel was well handled and smartly clothed." He added, in flawless English but with the wrong vernacular for the last word.

Jake bowed slightly also and answered in fluent Japanese –he hoped it was fluent anyway.

"Her Captain is a former Royal Navy Officer of great experience and very insistent on smartness." Not how he wanted to say it but...he hoped that his own vernacular worked, he didn't use Japanese much nowadays and so he was very rusty. Fortunately he'd decided to bring Tetsunari, a Japanese and one of his security team, and had been speaking only Japanese for the last forty eight hours. Not enough though to feel comfortable with nuance and nuance was an oriental speciality without any doubt at all.

Even as they concluded the brief conversation a RHIB had been lowered by one of the midships derricks and was speeding towards them.

"If you would come this way gentlemen." Said Jake, leading them toward the steps down to a floating jetty.

The second he'd stepped into the direct sun light the heat soared and a rash of perspiration sprang out on his forehead. Without his sun glasses he doubted he would be able to see through the glare to make out the steps down.

The boat was manned by an officer and rating in blue working dress and as the boat turned neatly to kiss the jetty pilings, the rating jumped ashore and made fast.

The officer closed the throttle and shouted over to Jake.

"G'day boss." The unmistakeable twang of Kiwi McLean, Lieutenant and Gunnery officer of the Hood who now turned to the rating.

"Parksy, get these gents set up with a life jacket mate and we can be off before we bleedingwell melt."

Jake smothered a grin as the leading hand started dishing out life jackets to the Japanese and himself.

As the speeding RHIB neared the Hood's companionway the side was manned and the senior rating on board, a big Hamburger and former *Oberstabsbootman* or Master Chief in the German Navy, used a bosun's whistle to expertly pipe their boss, Commodore Jonathan Henry König, aboard, along with the three Japanese executives.

Jake stepped on board and immediately turned to salute the Caymans ensign hanging limply at the stern, Captain Jon Roby stepped forward and offered Jake a salute followed by a handshake.

Then Jake introduced each of his guests. The awning covering the entry port was a great blessing as the formalities were concluded. If the Japanese thought the whistles and salutes were odd they gave nothing away. In point of fact the senior of them had served in the Japanese Maritime Self-Defence force for some years and was impressed with the respect and etiquette displayed.

Below decks at last and in the spacious wardroom with the air conditioning going at warp speed, Jake relaxed a little and chatted lightly whilst iced drinks were served.

The plan was to spend a few moments here to cool down before Jon Roby led them on a tour of the OPs room, engineering spaces and drone preparation hanger before visiting the upper deck again to have a closer look at the various armaments carried.

Later they would sail out and through the Straits of Hormuz to a live fire range off Limah in the Gulf of Oman. Then there would be a demonstration involving two RHIBs towing targets for the main and secondary batteries to shoot at and a drone demonstrating the reconnaissance and surveillance capability. Viewed variously from the Bridge and the OPs room Jake hoped the technical demonstration would put the cap on the deal.

All went according to plan and Jake was sitting in the wardroom during the passage back, answering any remaining questions when the action stations alarms sounded for surface action –without the prefix 'For Exercise".

He calmly stood, gave a slight bow and excused himself explaining that he needed to see what was happening.

Walking calmly out of the wardroom Jake put two dogs on the Zulu marked hatch as per the announced condition 1 X-Ray which was an order to close all below waterline hatches and openings and then ran forward. He paused briefly debating whether to go to the bridge or OPs room, the bridge won and he legged it up the next ladder.

Someone raised their voice and announced 'Commodore on the bridge.' Jon Roby turned in his command chair and smiled at Jake.

"We have company Sir." Jake gave him the look and he modified it.

"We have company Jake." Old habits die hard, said his lifted eyebrow.

Jake moved forward and looked at the nearest magnified viewer. Two, no three, fast moving light craft. He zoomed further on to the nearest of them. Standard DShKM 12.7mm heavy machine gun in the bow with 'grab bars' and big engines.

"Anything on channel 16, VHF, FM or even radio 2?" Jake asked.

"Nope. Nothing. What do you want us to do bossman?"

"Well the standing ROE orders are fire if fired upon, or if you think the ship will be placed in danger if you don't fire, whether shots have been fired at you or not. The ship is at action stations, I presume that includes loading appropriate munitions?" He got a nod. "In this case then I think we just ignore them, don't even bother with the radios, they know exactly where they are and how close we are. Keep your course and take no evasive action, if you do it will only encourage them."

Roby looked a little uncomfortable and raised his right eyebrow once more.

What is it with eyebrows that speak a thousand words? Jake thought.

"Problem Jonno? Not used to being able to take appropriate action without lengthy signals, conferences, umming and aahing from politicians etcetera?"

"Something like that I suppose. Do you really want an incident if they get too close or something; Iran has a lot of weird kit and a lot of small attack craft. What if they whistle up some friends?"

"OK. Just sound the foghorn five times then ignore them. If they start a fight, we will finish it. Other than that they need to abide by the rules of navigation, failure to do so may result in injury or death I think it says in a health and safety manual somewhere." He added. "You've been sinking small craft for the past few weeks, should have thought you'd got it weighed off by now."

Jake continued in a less assertive tone.

"Jonno, we have no beef with them, we aren't American or British, so no reason to suppose they're doing anything other than playing while setting up to ambush the smugglers this evening."

Roby still looked a little perturbed.

"OK, you're the boss."

"Yep. Now I'm going back to keep our guests happy. Ignore them, they'll keep out of our way, oh and no one on the upperdeck, just in case.

Fifteen minutes later Roby watched as one of the Iranian craft, possibly pissed off with the lack of response, got too close and caromed off the bow. The small vessel immediately capsized, helped by the foaming bow wave, and dumped its crew in the water.

Their two squadron mates immediately turned to offer assistance. Roby shrugged, at least its warm water. The helmsman was looking askance.

"Stop the pods until they are past our stern then resume previous speed and stay on course helm, they have plenty of helpers. Make sure the external camera footage is uploaded at the next opportunity, I want to be able to prove he was an idiot, if necessary."

Hood continued on its way and docked an hour later. By then Roby had almost forgotten the silly incident as more immediate concerns took precedence, like getting rid of the boss and his guests, having a check round all departments and getting a diver over the side to check whether the very expensive radar absorbing paint had been damaged. Even a small amount of bare metal significantly increased the ship's standard radar cross section.

Later that evening, the duty OPs supervisor brought in the 'good' news from various sources. Iranian news agencies carried the story on the evening bulletin. He read them all.

'NATO warship caused the capsize of a peaceful Iranian vessel in Iranian territorial waters, and didn't stop to assist in rescue efforts. Protests have been lodged'. And the ever bloody helpful BBC he noted reported 'In what the Iranians call a provocative incident, an unknown warship transiting the Straits of Hormuz has collided with and sunk an Iranian warship. NATO states it wasn't one of theirs.'

Bugger, sighed Roby, they lie like they breathe. Iranian territorial waters my arse. This is probably not the last I'll hear of this, he decided. Better make out a draft report in case.

In the hotel not a mile away, Jake had also been notified and had read the reports. He had a brief conversation with his sort-of Commander in Chief, his old friend Andrew McTeal, Prime Minister of the Cayman Islands.

"Yes Andrew, in international waters, unprovoked and highly dangerous manoeuvring, something not at all uncommon out here. They collided with us and simply capsized." He listened carefully for a few seconds. "Yes I spoke to Jonno, they could see the survivors bobbing next to the hull and the two remaining Iranian craft heading straight for it. No. They didn't want to hang around in case the Iranians got snotty. You know how volatile they can be, worse than an Italian sailor after a pint of Chianti." He chuckled at McTeal's response. "Will do Andrew. Sorry for the nausea but they can be silly buggers at times. Yes, yes, fully support Roby's actions. Will do." He closed the

32

conversation and looked up at Andy Evans sitting calmly across the table.

"Trouble Jake?" Andy asked, mentally reviewing his assets in the area.

"Hope not. You can never tell with Iranians though. Kipper's dad was at Ganges back in the 70's when we used to train them there. Big buggers, he said they were, quick to take insult and quick to get into a punch up, he added. Of course that was before the revolution. Now they're even more stroppy because they're all God botherers now." He shook his head.

"I think when we have our Captains meeting we'll sail from here and move back into the Gulf of Oman, round to Muscat, a lot more friendly there. Besides I'm sure Reiner and Simon will want to have a good look at the kit that Jonno gets to play with every day."

"Sounds like a plan. Don't like being this side of the Straits, them buggers all seem to have piles if you ask me, the way they're always going around having an 'issy fit'...about anything. I reckon half the time it's all show just to put reasonable folk on their back foot."

"You're probably right Andy. Anyway, now that we have the Japanese contract we can leave here. It seems Mr Tackai, their boss, was impressed that we didn't mess around and play softy when they attempted suicide by battleship."

Andy Evans, laughed and polished off his Lagavulin.

"Right boss I'll see you in the morning then. Night."

"Night Andy."

*

Jake watched as the Gulfstream taxied into a slot near the terminal building, he waited patiently for Simon to disembark and clear the formality of the customs. Simon

33

was waved through with his small 'grip', sailor-speak for overnight bag, and moved quickly into the air conditioned 'coolth' of the terminal building.

They shook hands then walked back towards the exit and the waiting Mercedes.

"Lot of fuss the Iranians are making about Hood."

This was his opening gambit and Jake knew of old that Simon was as up to date as he was.

"That and the ridiculous over reaction of the Iranians to Andrew McTeal's brief public apology, which of course included the fact that the Iranians were behaving in a dangerous and provocative manner in international waters. I told him not to apologise and I told him to show the footage of the Iranian boat too. At least he did one out of the two. I suppose it was an apology in name only when accompanied by the vid and what he said. Everyone could see what a dick the Iranian had been. If I were them I'd demote him, he's not fit to be in charge of a ship's tender."

Simon laughed. He always enjoyed Jake's somewhat unvarnished approach to things. He brought new meaning to the old saying 'Calling a spade a fucking JCB'.

"Well in light of the shit it's caused we are going to leave with the smugglers this evening just before dark and do a fast transit in case the silly buggers want round two."

"Right." Said Simon calculating how that would affect things for getting back to his ship and wondering about the reference to smugglers. It would probably be easy enough to get a flight out of Muscat, he decided, but the smugglers reference didn't become clear until later.

It seemed unusually crowded on Hood's bridge that evening, it might have been something to do with all the Captains and Commodores etcetera, thought Jon Roby as he sat relaxed in his command chair waiting for the evening spectacle to take place.

There was a lot of activity over at the Iranian smugglers jetty as boats were prepped for the return journey across the straits, no goats this time just fags, booze and perfume. They all knew there was a risk of being caught, but it was small. This was for three reasons. Firstly, small wooden or fibreglass boats are not easy to see at night and have poor radar returns if they have no added reflectors. Second the people who are tasked with catching them had only to do so every now and then to avoid being under suspicion of not making the effort, and finally if you paid the right people the searches would all be in the wrong places.

There were around twenty boats readying for the journey and some of the officers on Hood's bridge were sucking teeth and tutting at the over loading of a few of them. But these fellows were hopefully going to be a distraction as Hood slipped quietly around the neck of the straits, always within Omani territorial waters. The consensus at the briefing earlier was that with Hood's low radar cross section and being close to the shore against the backdrop of the tall Omani mountains, they had little chance of accidental discovery and should pass without problems. The key word was 'accidental' of course.

Jake stood on the seaward side using a viewer on low light setting to scan the sea in the direction they would take in a little over twenty minutes. Sunset was around 18:20 tonight with nautical twilight until 19:10. The peculiar Omani customs system allowed for a visit during the day but boats must leave by sunset or....what? Jake thought. Did they get arrested or impounded or something? He'd forgotten to ask. It didn't matter right now though. His political and tactical antenna had been quivering all day. The speed with which the Iranians had muted their outrage and then gone quiet over the confrontation the day before yesterday made him suspicious, if not actually worried.

You could normally rely on them to be in 'Allah ul Akbar' mode for a week at least when their feathers were either ruffled or they thought they'd been ruffled. They'd probably be burning Caymans flags in public squares if they could find any. To fade away within forty eight hours made his nose itch. He'd said as much in the briefing and all there had taken note, clearly some not seeing it his way. He recalled Julius Kopf nodding sagely and making notes so at least the First Lieutenant was a believer in the potential for problems.

Jon Roby, chairing the briefing, while not dismissing Jake's twitchy nose didn't feel the threat to the same degree. He'd sailed in these waters on numerous occasions over the last thirty years or so and yes the Iranians could be a pain but usually if you didn't take the bait they'd go and play elsewhere. Only occasionally did they present a problem.

He recalled the poor showing of HMS Cornwall's boarding team in 2007 when they'd been taken by Iranian revolutionary guards without a shot being fired, by the ship or the team. They'd just left a Dhow they had searched when a group of Iranian light craft ambushed them. Quick thinking from the officer in charge of the boarding party was clearly lacking. In a battle of wits and the measuring of risk, he was a failure. He was obviously paralysed by the audacity of the Iranian commander who showed a greater ability to think quickly and control a situation on the fly. Roby's opposite number in Cornwall had finished the farce totally handing the initiative to the Iranians, by asking for MOD advice instead of taking action. In Roby's opinion a strong demonstration by the Lynx and a rapid return by the boarding party to the ship they'd just left, would have led to a stand-off. He seriously doubted the

Iranians would have opened fire unless fired upon. Then with the initiative back in British hands the Iranians would have eventually stood down since British forces in greater numbers were not far away. In addition, taking over the Dhow and steering it towards the Cornwall would have meant that for every yard of progress the safety margins increased. He knew the area and was certain Cornwall could have got significantly closer too, despite the reported shallowness of the water. Besides, the Aussies had done the exact same thing a couple of years before with great success.

Lack of quick thinking, paralysed by indecision and the seeking of higher authority, were symptoms of officers poorly trained and equipped for the job. Everyone knew it but few dared to say it in a country dominated by the Blair PC years. By giving in so easily they simply encouraged the Iranians to play the game and keep pushing to find the line they could not cross. He smiled, up until a couple of days ago they had never been reined in even by the Americans who were generally less reticent about keeping small boats at bay –with good reason. There had been a number of incidents recently where the Americans had fired warning shots into the water ahead of the approaching Iranian craft, maybe the Iranians were working up to something?

Perhaps Jake's political instincts were more finely tuned than his own, he decided. He resolved to go to actions stations from harbour stations, immediately after clearing the harbour.

Roby checked the time and almost simultaneously the roar of a number of powerful engines starting up over at the smuggler's jetty broke the quiet of the evening. It echoed back and forth from the hills behind the small town making it sound like many more vessels were present.

All of the Hood's company who could see a viewer were fascinated by the spectacle of this nightly smuggling ritual, as one by one the heavily laden boats cast off, revved up and proceeded out of the harbour, increasing revs as they passed the outer mole.

Slowly the engine noise diminished until once more only the sound of the ship's air conditioning and systems were audible. By habit Roby checked his watch rather than look at the monitor for the time. Sunset was 18:20, in just a few minutes. They'd then pull their hooks up and quietly leave harbour only picking up speed and increasing the noise level as they headed away. If they rammed the throttles to the stops the gas turbines would wake camels and goats for forty miles around.

Canvas awnings were taken in and stowed, the companionway recovered and stowed with the anchors aweigh a low rumble became audible as the engines began station keeping. The gyro-stabilised systems of the Hood kept her still while the final preparations for leaving were made. With the anchors washed and stowed in the hawse pipes the upperdeck parties returned below.

Roby looked across to Jake who nodded.

"Starboard Steerpod ninety degrees to port, bow thruster to starboard. Minimum revolutions."

"Aye Sir. Starboard Steerpod port ninety and bow thruster to starboard. Minimum revs." Answered Geordie Moore, the helmsman.

Roby waited until the Hood's head had come round, knowing that the eyes of three other captains were critically observing his every move and command. Unfazed he gave the orders to take them out.

"Stop bow thruster, stop Steerpod, starboard Steerpod fore and aft."

"Aye Sir, both stop, and return pod to fore and aft."

He waited another few seconds for the ship's head to finish its glide across the outer mole and begin to slide across open water again.

"Both ahead slow helmsman, keep us between the buoys."

"Aye aye Sir." Responded Geordie, he needn't repeat the rest since they'd be on the rocks if he didn't stay in the channel.

Roby waited until Hood was half a mile clear of the outer mole before he switched the Tannoy to his console and gave his next commands.

"Secure from harbour stations." A pause then. "Action stations, action stations. Assume condition one X-Ray. EMCON Alpha. Not a peep people, we are not here." Then almost as an afterthought, which it was. "We shall be darkening ship when we are five miles out. No nav lights and all scuttles closed tight above deck too." Then he turned his attention to the OPs staff.

"OPs." Click then.

"OPs aye."

"Start IR, low light and ESM sweeps, I'd like to know who's out there if anyone, before they find us."

"Aye aye Sir." Answered Lieutenant Bianchi the senior OPs officer.

Warrant Officer Crause prowled the ship making sure every section was on the ball, he had briefed everyone on the night's plan when he'd done his pre-sailing inspection an hour ago so the people were up to speed on the night's fast cruise into less potentially hazardous waters further around the coast.

Even though it was sort of routine, going to action stations never failed to get the pulse up a few notches thought Jake as he made his way into the OPs room.

The layout was very similar to that of Bismarck, with the work stations and the advanced holographic display table giving an observer an 'at a glance' picture of what Hood's sensors could see. The table at this moment, Jake noted, was set to display everything out to seventy five miles. This covered both sides of the Omani peninsular and a good chunk of the Iranian coast. AIS showed them all the civilian traffic that was out there squawking their ID, including aircraft, but it wouldn't of course tell them if there were people out there wishing to do them harm. Their own AIS was off.

He was tempted to get Roby to slow and launch a drone but recovery at night using the new catcher system was fraught to say the least and using the old 'land then recover' system was out of the question in this part of the world, they'd have to buy it back bit by bit from the nearest souk. They were bloody expensive too. So he got himself a coffee and slumped in a vacant chair with his eyes roving over the hemispheric holograph bubble in front of him, while in the background the three duty OPs personnel went about their job, locating and identifying where possible, every peep, chirp and burst of radar and radio traffic. Slowly the plot filled and Jake used the filters to remove everything civilian more than twenty miles away.

Reiner Krull stood on the bridge talking in a low voice to Jon Roby. They were discussing recent anti-piracy operations on opposite sides of Africa and had included speculation on the new contract with Sainex off Mozambique. Both thought it would be a doddle with so little in the way of official opposition, but there was the question of how many unofficial players there might be in the game and how far they'd go to disrupt the Japanese oil extraction operations.

Both men were keeping a weather eye on a screen with the 2D representation of what Jake was looking at down in the OPs room. The bridge wing doors were open so any non-ambient sounds would be heard over the noise created by their progress through the sea.

Distant lights were mentally matched to AIS markers on the screen and ticked off all the while the conversation continued at low volume. These two men had much in common, not least the command of two of the most advanced armed vessels in the world today.

Simon McClelland the fourth Captain currently on board, was deep in conversation with Kiwi Mclean up in the somewhat cramped Main Gunnery Control Centre or MGCC, above and behind the bridge.

These systems were almost identical to Bismarck's too but they were one upgrade more advanced. Bismarck had yet to have the software upgrade for the Sea Giraffe radar and Combat Management Systems which were being adapted and de-bugged by Hood's crew on this trip. Simon's Ocean Guard had a smaller less capable version of the system which helped them identify and track pirates from a long way away.

Of course the primary reason for the system was control of the guns and Simon looked out over the fo'c'sle noting Hood's forward battery, a pair of turrets each sporting twin 5.1" guns of Russian origin. They discussed the secondary and tertiary weapons too. It had been somewhat problematic fitting secondary guns since the original Hood had mounted twelve single 5.5 inch guns spaced along the shelter deck on either side, but these had all been removed in 1940 and replaced with seven twin 4 inch dual purpose mounts but no smaller AA guns.

The compromise that Jake had finally approved was to have four of the AK630M2 twin Gatling mounts as used on Bismarck but modified to superficially resemble the 4 inch originals. The final three emplacements were three twin 3" turrets, one on each beam and one centreline aft, behind X turret. Privately Simon thought Jake was wasting his money, the chances of there being another engagement like those in the Caribbean were remote.

Anti-piracy work was against mainly low tech opponents and very occasional rogue officials moonlighting, as in China in the 90's when senior officers would bimble down from Beijing for the weekend and take a patrol boat out to hunt a few freighters off Hong Kong, and impound them. Then of course they'd effectively ransom back the ship, the crew and the cargo under the guise of being a customs tithe. Sometimes the owners wanted to pay for just the former and the latter and then the crews were released after a few months. Such things were rare or non-existent now so that made both Hood and Bismarck somewhat over powered for the job. He wouldn't of course say so to Reiner, Jonno or Jake, but he knew his own Ocean Guard was the most viable of the three.

Down in the OPs room and twenty minutes into the fast transit around the top of the Omani peninsular, Jake became aware that the OPs room had chilled a few degrees. The relaxed atmosphere on sailing, had been exchanged for one of increasing alertness and muttered conversations between the operators. He checked the Holo plot and noted a new 'racket' designated sierra 1, to the north east and he also took in a series of past and very recent rackets to the east designated sierras 2 through 7.

The Senior OPs watchkeeper was Lieutenant Alfio Bianchi and Jake could see him stiffen up and become alert. What was happening?

He picked up a spare ear piece and mike then turned his attention back to the Holo plot. Bianchi was replaying tracks and rackets for the last five minutes or so, in a speeded up loop. Immediately Jake could see the pattern. The brief transmissions must be 'On station' reports. There appeared to be a line of them across their intended path.

He zoomed the view with the Hood's track included and now could see that there was a line of ...of 'somethings' forming between the islands of Bu Rashid and Jazirat Salami, almost exactly at their closest approach point to Iran and where they would begin their turn to starboard for the run down to Muscat. The gap between the two Omani islands was only about five and a bit miles it seemed looking at the scale and plot image.

He listened in as Bianchi reported the anomaly to Roby. To his credit Jonno didn't quiz or doubt the information and announced he was on his way down from the bridge.

Jake continued to study the plot and looked further to the north and east of their current position, then zoomed a little. The racket that appeared periodically with a single radar sweep already designated sierra one was interesting. The radar was listed U/K unknown, which simply meant the CMS had never come across it and identified it before. Suspicion rose in Jake's mind as he manipulated to holo display to run a loop of just the unknown radar and the unknown radio transmissions with the date-time reference visible. He ran it fast then slow.

Jon Roby entered the OPs room at a fast clip and instead of going over to his command station he stood behind Lt Bianchi who pointed out the anomalous radio transmissions.

"Jonno." There's something else Jake announced. "Have a look at this."

Jake explained what the loop was showing.

Jon Roby rarely swore but now he used some serious 'old sailor' words and headed for his command chair.

"What do you think Jake, ambush?" He asked, having settled himself in and brought up his own ESM picture.

"That's my reading of it Jonno. That character to our north and east is the Commander. He receives a radio confirmation that each unit, whatever they are, is in position. But he doesn't quite trust them so he wants to make sure they are where they say they are. Hence the single radar sweep to confirm."

Jon Roby nodded slowly, rubbing his rather pointed chin between forefinger and thumb, a habit Jake recalled from years ago when Jonno was confronted with a sticky problem.

"So he's setting someone up, probably us. OK. My guess is that the boat to the north is a shooter then. Maybe one of the small missile craft. Not sure why they need a line of others across the path, searching for us maybe? Why aren't they just lining everyone up East West, half a dozen shooters maybe one spotter?"

"Buggered if I know. But that line between the two islands suggests something else is going on." He included the OPs Officer. "Alfio, how long before we are in sight of that line across our path?"

"Fifteen minutes at current speed will put us three miles from them Sir." Bianchi answered promptly having been listening to these senior commanders exchange ideas."

Roby nodded again and spoke into his mike.

"Bridge." A click followed.

"Bridge aye." Answered Steve Sharp, Officer of the Watch."

"Slow to fifteen knots immediately. Report any lights ahead unless from AIS identified contacts."

"Aye, aye Sir, slowing to fifteen knots." Answered Sharp.

"Good idea Jonno, gives us a few more minutes to work out what the fuck is going on. Be a good idea to get Simon and Reiner in on this. No point in having all the brain power aboard if we don't use it."

Jonno nodded and spoke into his mike again.

"Main broadcast." Click.

"This is the Captain. Captain's Krull and McClelland please join me in the OPs room."

It was less than thirty seconds before both men entered and Roby waved them over to the holo display and indicated the spare chairs.

"Join us gents. We have a developing situation. And our good Commodore has just joined two of the pieces together."

Roby quickly brought them up to speed and Jake replayed the loop recording of the radar and radio contacts.

"So gentlemen," Jake began, "does anyone believe these are unrelated events and pure coincidence? And is anyone NOT suspicious?"

Reiner and Simon both studied the plot. Reiner was first to speak.

"I see the relationship between the contacts but cannot understand why they are forming a line across our path. I would have expected them to have one or two vessels spotting for a number of missile shooters spread east-west."

"My point exactly Reiner. Something is clearly going on but I can't quite work it out. We have about another twenty five minutes or so before we run into this line." Added Jon Roby.

Jake looked over at Simon and a spark of hope flitted through his mind. Simon was one of the brightest warfare officers that Jake had ever met or worked with. His ability to think sideways and upside down if required, was legendary and during their Caribbean battle he had demonstrated this on several occasions, he was next to speak.

"As you have all noted this is not a logical way to set up a missile trap. That means it probably isn't one. The Iranians know that their small craft ahead will all be spotted at the same time and probably before they spot us.

Head on attack with missiles is not a sensible way to come at us either if they are missile boats. They really could not stop our passage through that gap if we forced the issue so why are they there? What do they think we will do when we find them there? That is what we need to think about."

Jake smiled. Instead of trying to fit a theory into the available data Simon was trying to reverse engineer the problem. My turn now, thought Jake.

"OK. Thanks for that Simon, spot on. What would we normally do? Slow down of course, maybe even stop to assess things or try to communicate or even lower a RHIB."

Reiner smiled grimly.

"In all of those cases we will be very slow at the least or stationary, and apparently vulnerable. But to what? We don't need to be slow or stopped for a missile shooter. I don't understand."

Simon was still looking thoughtful and addressed Jake.

"What will we do when we get there Commodore? Are we going to risk another incident in the papers? It will look like we are going out of our way to insult the Iranians, no one will bother that they are in Omani waters."

Good question, thought Jake noting Simon had used his rank not his name. What am I going to tell them to do? This *IS* my responsibility after all.

"If we go active we could get a clearer picture of what's out there BUT of course they will know exactly where we are. If there's more than one missile shooter out there lying doggo, or if there's a line of them all on EMCON Alpha bar this one on the end," he ticked his points off on his fingers, "then we can standby to receive any number of incoming missiles." They waited expectantly as he paused.

"I did wish to avoid it but I think we are going to need a drone up. We'll have to work out where will be the best place for recovery and try to be there first. OK? Then we will have more info to go on." He turned to Roby.

"Captain, please reduce speed further, seven or eight knots ought to give us the time we need to work out what's happening."

They all nodded. Nothing dramatic, just more info gathering. A drone with a recon package using high resolution Lidar should be able to literally map the area without putting any 'noise' out. That coupled with its sensitive infra-red and low light cameras should at least tell them what was out there if not what it was up to.

"Drone control." Click.

"This is the Captain launch a recon drone as soon as possible please, oh and arm a second with a mix of flechette and thermobaric please."

"Drone control aye Sir. Launch bird with recon package and prep second with mixed munitions, aye Sir."

The broad Glaswegian accent of Chief Petty Officer Stuart McKenzie came through the headphones clearly. He was an absolute star with the combined technologies of remote control, programming and electrical engineering needed for these technical marvels. The original Hood did not have a seaplane catapult in her final configuration around 1940 so they had created one which emerged from a recess in the shelter deck and then retracted after use, no big deal but it solved the problem of how to launch the drones. These drones, unlike the ones on Bismarck which resembled the old Arado 196s had no pretence about them; they were a modified version of an Israeli Hermes 450. Jake had bought ten of them and his technical people had modified them all to include the stealth LED lighting system used successfully on Bismarck's Arados, which effectively made them invisible from below. That they could also be readily adapted for catapult launching from a ship with a rocket assist had been another big plus. Hood's catapult track could be elevated up to 20 degrees to facilitate a launch, depending on payload.

Ten minutes later the drone was in the air and circling slowly as it climbed. McKenzie programmed it to circle up to five thousand feet then head north and finally east. It would take up to seven or eight minutes to reach its operational altitude but all the while it would be using its sensors to look north and east.

The OPs room was quiet as the holographic display was continually updated by the drone as it climbed and then finally turned north.

The first thing that became apparent was that there was no line of missile shooting boats spread out waiting for them in the north. The Identity of the 'racket' over there was confirmed by the CMS database as being a C-14, China-Cat class FACM. So they now knew the likely maximum number of missiles they were facing, not the type though but they were pretty sure that this craft was limited to small and medium sized anti-ship weapons. The smaller they were, the more they could carry though. The drone would have a good set of images of the vessel's upperdeck soon and that would likely fill in the missing puzzle pieces.

It now headed east and then began a racetrack pattern, continually updating the picture. The line of blocking boats, six of them, were hard to track and refine because none were showing lights, of those, three had very low IR signatures. Not all of them appeared to be moving. Half seemed to be almost stationary and were it not for the computer generated track an observer would be forgiven for thinking that they were not moving at all, so slow was their westward progress.

Around the plotting table there was much head shaking and chin stroking as well as major volumes of coffee disappearing. The Hood continued on her way at eight knots, now only seven miles from the slowly approaching barrier, if that's what it was, thought Jake as he studied the situation.

He, like the rest no doubt, was mentally creating a scenario then feeding the known data in to see if there was a match or near match, but he had to admit he was pretty stumped at the moment.

What the missile boat was waiting for? Maybe some sort of signal? What were the slowly advancing light craft aiming to achieve and how? Were they were coordinated or not, and how? So many questions no answers.

Simon intently studied the so called 'blocking boats', continually bringing up the images in loop on his data pad. These he thought were the answer to what was planned. These were the pieces that were out of place. These were the bits that didn't fit. Not because they were small attack craft, you could see the big 12.7mm machine gun on each bow, but because of the way they were behaving. They were clearly combing or sweeping forward looking for contact with Hood. That was one of their purposes, but what then? They knew she was armed, they knew she had very sophisticated and powerful sensors. He went back to the IR images and something fluttered at the back of his mind.

Reiner too was concentrating on the line of craft. Three of them seemed to be sweeping behind the other three, repeatedly crossing their wakes at low speed while three advanced very slowly and inexorably towards Hood but steering a straight course. What did that mean?

"Sir." Lt Bianchi's voice interrupted the thought processes of those gathered around the Holo plot table.

"What is it Alfio?" Asked Roby, not taking his eyes from the plot.

"A cleaned up image of the northern racket Sir, on main viewer now."

The Forward bulkhead screen was 84 inches of multi-mega pixel LED, the very highest definition money could buy. Displayed on it now was a compiled rendition of the vessel to the north. The image rotated in three dimensions to give an all-round view. It was immediately obvious that this wasn't a standard configuration for a C-14 China-Cat, images of which appeared on the left of the screen.

"No missile bins." Noted Jon Roby pointing. He jumped up and quickly walked to the screen.

"What the hell is that thing down the starboard side?" He pointed to what appeared to be a single tube which extended from near the stern almost to the bow.

"How large is its diameter?" Asked Reiner.

"I'll check Sir." Answered Bianchi. A pair of red dots appeared on the screen then rotated, became a circle and then a scale stood next to it.

"Computer estimates between 520mm and 540mm Sir."

Then everything went haywire.

"Racket bearing 355 degrees. Designated sierra eight. Very strong signal. It's close. Computer identifies as standard military band VHF radio. Estimate less than a mile." Reported the OPs number two, Petty Officer Hogarth.

"Shit we've been spotted." Added Jon Roby, unnecessarily.

"The blocking boats have all speeded up Sir. *Madre Dios*, they were quick off the mark. Three still steering straight ahead and the others still weaving behind them."

Simon suddenly exclaimed.

"Three of them are bombs. Full of explosives, the other three are the remote controllers!" He pointed to the IR images of the two groups. No people on three of them, bugger I should have seen it sooner!"

Before anyone else could comment or react Bianchi shouted out another warning.

"Sonar contact. On the same bearing as contact sierra one. Contact classified as cavitation noises." He added with a puzzled tone, as if doubting the report himself.

All the Captains looked at each other then Jon Roby exclaimed.

"It's a *Hoot* for fuck's sake! Bianchi override helm control. Emergency all ahead full! Start the clock!"

Reiner and Jake waited for the explanation as even in the sound proofed OPs room, the sudden whine of the two gas turbines reached audible level. "Go active now Bianchi."

The OPs officer switched the radar from passive to active and within seconds they were getting the full picture on the Holo plot. Roby turned to them and pointed to the plot and all the new information being displayed

"He wants us to be stopped or slow so they can use one of their ultra-fast ex-Russian torpedoes. They have no guidance as such and need a slow or stopped target. Thing is they move at 200 knots by using a rocket propulser unit and super-cavitation."

"Shit, yes. Heard of them some years back." Said Jake. Thought the Russians gave up on them, the *Shkval* or something they called it. So have the Iranians worked out how to use them?"

"I read something about tests in this area a couple of years ago which is where I got the name from, I sort of found it funny, a *Hoot*, until now."

Roby looked at the speed indicator and the bulkhead clock which had started a timer as he asked. He quickly interrogated the plot for the range to the northern target sierra 1. Three miles give or take a few feet. At 200 knots that would be…..48 seconds…ish total time.

"Range to sonar target?"

No one spoke or interrupted him as he was clearly calculating furiously.

"One mile Sir."

"Fifteen seconds to impact. We haven't got time to decide whether he's got guidance or not."

The clock clicked around to 30 seconds and the speed indicator was nudging 28 knots. Roby let out his breath.

"Emergency port Helm, come left to 350 degrees, add in the bow azi-thruster too." He spoke into his mike.

"Main broadcast." Click then.

"Brace, brace, brace."

Then he turned to Jake.

"Permission to engage the torpedo shooter in case he has guidance?"

Jake thought for a second.

"Yes, permission to engage both sets of targets. Make sure we're recording all of this. The shit will hit the fan for sure gents and we need an umbrella to stay clean."

"Better it's our shit hitting them I think than the other option." Added Roby with a grimace.

He spoke into his mike.

"McClean. Click.

"Guns, kill targets designated sierra 1, 3, 4 and 5. Sierra 1 first. Begin now."

"Aye aye Sir! Killing targets sierra 1, 3, 4 and 5. Number 1 first." Answered the surprised voice of Kiwi McClean, up in the MGCC.

Roby watching the clock counter as it seemingly raced towards 48 seconds, then added to the OPs room at large.

"The torpedo shooter was in charge of all this business wasn't he? He asked in a rhetorical manner. "And using modern vernacular, he deserves a good kicking for starting it all. If we destroy the remote controllers, there will be three boatloads of explosive evidence left Commodore."

Hood steadied on her new course and then all hell let loose.

Turrets A and B trained over the port bow and commenced firing. The crack, crack, crack of the guns as they chugged out 5.1" high explosive shells was clearly audible even though with flashless powder there wasn't the bright, night vision destroying light, that Hollywood showed on the films. There was still the smoke though. With each crack the smoke momentary showed dark against the last remnants of twilight before it was whipped away by Hood's greater than forty miles an hour forward speed. The barrels were alternately thrown back as the recoil was used to power the loading of its turret twin. At the same time the twin 3" guns on the starboard side and the pair overlooking X turret began pumping out high explosive rounds at the widely gyrating remote controller boats to starboard. They were difficult to hit and Mclean added in two of the AK630M2 batteries to make sure. These fired in one hundred round bursts of just over a second for each of the Gatling mounts, the sound very much like tearing sheets. The Sea Giraffe fire control system silently plotted the outgoing rounds against the positions of the targets and corrected the aim several hundred times a second using linked data from the drone and the ship based radar so there was no doubting the outcome.

The first pair of 5.1" shells arrived at the stationary C-14 China-Cat, unmissable at three miles range, it ceased to be in that instant. The explosion was clearly visible to all those on the bridge and those watching monitors throughout the ship, and probably thirty miles around, as fuel and ammunition for its other weapons cooked off in an instant. McClean turned his attention fully on to the other designated targets.

"Sonar contact has passed to port Sir!" Reported a relieved Lt Bianchi.

Jon Roby watched the Holo plot intently as the secondary and tertiary armaments homed in on the three boats controlling the three bomb vessels.

"Helm come left about. Steer 135 degrees. Slow to twenty five knots."

The Combat Management System noted the change in bearing to the remaining targets and began spooling up the port side AK630's and the twin 3" mount on that side in preparation for a seamless hand off from the starboard guns and a constant flow of 3" and 30mm high explosive shells on to the targets.

First one then quickly a second ran into either a 3" shell or the shredding effect of hundreds of 30mm rounds, the watchers couldn't really tell which. The last boat zigzagged wildly as it sought to evade the death that marched towards it across the sea. Instead of the ambusher and hunter, they were now the prey.

The end when it came was a simultaneous hit from a 3" HE shell and a stream of 30mm heavy bullets from the other side.

The noise ceased and in the near darkness three boat loads of high explosive slowly went off course and without correction began to veer in three different directions.

"Christ those bleeding bomb boats will be the death of us yet!"

The voice of Kiwi McClean came clearly over the now linked MGCC, bridge and OPs room broadcast system. It raised a few chuckles.

"He has a point." Noted Jake. "Unless those things have got some sort of failsafe timer we will have to destroy them before they run into someone else. Get the drone to do some low sweeps over them on high magnification, record it all, confirm we have the images, then destroy the boats."

"Aye, aye Commodore." Answered Roby with a smile and gave the necessary instructions to the drone controller.

Jake sat down again at the Holo plot table and gestured for everyone else to do so too. They'd all stood to watch the action on the main viewer on the forward bulkhead.

"Now while I have your undivided attention gentlemen I want to organise our meeting schedule regarding the Lloyds contract. I doubt it will be as exciting as tonight but we have to cover all bases. We shall be early into Muscat so I suggest we convene at 10:00. That OK with everyone?"

A chorus of nods.

"Right I'll leave you to it. Jonno, can you forward all of the visual data to me and send both the visual and all the other records to Sandiford Roche. He's going to love me for giving him more work to do. Meanwhile I'd better get on the phone to Andrew and explain that we've just compounded the shit he was getting from everyone about poor defenceless Iran two days ago. Someone else who's going to love me." He sighed and stood to leave. "One more thing gentlemen. The Iranians demonstrated some serious lateral thinking here. If you have friends still in national navies, I suggest you explain how close we came tonight. I do believe that my former comrades would still be waiting for answer from MOD when the *Hoot* hit them, closely followed by three exploding boats. The only thing the Iranians hadn't factored in was that we aren't chained down by the very disadvantageous rules of engagement imposed upon most national navies."

Reiner watched him go. He was in a contemplative mood now. Of course the very nature of the job meant that he was more likely than not to see small scale actions when hunting pirates, but *this* sort of thing really was the domain of national navies. On the other hand he knew Jake was on the mark when he said a national ship would have still been sitting there waiting for orders from home, since under their usual rules of engagement they'd be hard put to justify opening fire until it was way too late. Either the *Hoot* would have hit or one of the explosive packed boats would have got close enough to detonate. He wasn't aware of any ship as manoeuvrable as either Bismarck or Hood, except perhaps some of the littoral warfare ships.

Simon went up into the MGCC to find Julius Kopf, the First Lieutenant, already there reviewing the weapon systems performance.

"Hi Simon, just about to batter the three bomb boats, all three are over a mile away now." Then he held up his hand for quiet and began giving audio instructions to the gunnery system.

"Target. Sierra two, sierra six, sierra seven. Three inch, HE. Rate, thirty. Continuous. Commence, commence."

There was a distant sounding lighter crack, crack, crack than with the main guns, the 3 inchers could kick out up to 130 rounds per barrel per minute, but they'd soon overheat if they did so they were on a steady thirty rounds each for the moment.

The guns quickly found the range and the three explosive laden vessels disappeared in spectacular fashion, all recorded for posterity's sake.

"Better send this feed down to the bossman as well. Certainly proves they were packed to the gunwales with explosives." Added Julius with a frown.

"What about the racket that piped up just before it all kicked off?" Asked Simon.

Julius considered a second and mentally translated 'piped up' into German then put it back in English nautical vernacular where it belonged.

"Drone control." Click.

"Chief what happened to the 'racket' that became active just before the action?"

"Wait one Sor!" Answered the drone controller while he quickly went back through the images.

"Can't find it Sor. Do you want me to re-task and find it?"

Simon just shrugged.

"No Chief, forget it." Julius looked puzzled.

"Could have been a small tethered PIR type unit or something, strapped onto a preconfigured transmitter, I'd guess." Simon speculated.

An hour later, still in Omani waters and slowing from a very fast sprint out of the Straits of Hormuz, they entered a bay near Ra's Da'aliq and recovery of the drone commenced. The problem with them had always been recovery. Even Bismarck's seaplane shaped drones were problematic if the seas were above state three. So for Hood they'd tried a new system which was to be retrofitted to Bismarck if trials went well.

The receiving ship would turn into the wind like a carrier recovering aircraft does. The returning drone would behave to all intents and purposes, as if it were about to touch down onto a flight deck, i.e. nose up flaps down and throttles most of the way back. Out to either port or starboard would be deployed a boom raised to 60 degrees and another horizontal. Between them a net, like conventional nylon webbing, was deployed but not pulled taught, and weighted so as to droop. Effectively it formed a cup into which the throttled back drone was flown by the operator.

Being pusher propeller driven these drones had little in the way of external projections to break off or suffer damage, the trick was to chop the throttle at the last second so it almost fell into the net. That meant being high enough and slow enough. Like all such things practice was the key and Chief McKenzie had spent hours on the simulator program doing just that. Now with all the ship's company watching he carefully guided the expensive drone straight into the catcher's mitt as the American's would say. As soon as it landed the horizontal boom was raised a little, then both rotated towards the boat deck where the drone was then disentangled and moved onto a deck lift to be taken below, refuelled and have all its systems checked.

Just as the drone was brought inboard Jake finished a difficult conversation with Andrew McTeal and Sandiford Roche in the Caymans. The upshot being that both men had reviewed the data Jake had sent and concluded that had they not acted when they did, either Hood would have been lost or severely damaged. They both commended Captain Roby's quick responses and skilful manoeuvring.

Then the serious stuff started. Half an hour later Jake, exhausted by the conversation, had disconnected with his brain in a whirl. The fact that Hood was operating as a private Man O' War when the incident occurred meant that McTeal's support could really only be confined to objecting to an attack on a Cayman flagged merchant vessel. He wasn't sure in his own mind what difference that made because the merchantman in this case was armed to the teeth. He presumed there was some legal aspect which centred on which flag was being flown at the time. The remainder of the conversation had been about damage limitation and mitigation and of course the approach to be taken with the media.

No one from Hood would comment at all McTeal ordered, which Jake thought was not only sensible but what he preferred anyway. Andrew McTeal had then insisted over a reluctant Jake and Sandiford Roche, that the data package Jake had sent them should be shared with the US, Russia, China, the UK and Saudi Arabia – intact. Usually certain elements would be removed, these would identify a vessel's capabilities and a variety of other information about it. But he had been insistent. To be wholly believed, they needed to be transparent with these five big players. Sandy had wondered whether or not to include the UN and the EU if they were handing out this information anyway, but McTeal had declined to go that far since both organisations had more leaky bureaucracies than anything he could think of. May as well tell the press direct if we do that had been his final point.

So the Cayman's government would handle all the media and Hood would try to stay out of trouble.

Next morning, 07:00, Off Muscat, Oman

Jake rolled over and peremptorily answered the persistent buzzing of the intercom.

"König."

"Officer of the Watch Sir, we have an Omani Coast Guard vessel approaching and the Captain suggests that your presence will be required."

"Why?" Jake wasn't a 'morning' person but even so, why the hell did he need to get up for this?

"Err, we had a conversation with them on channel 16 Sir, we have been denied permission to remain in Omani waters and are not allowed to dock at Muscat."

"What? Fuck it. What next?" He grumped angrily and then his brain started to wake up. "Hang on a minute. Then why do I need to come up?"

"I was just about to say Sir, there is an Omani diplomat aboard her and he wishes to speak to you in person."

Steve Sharp, OOW, wanted to end the conversation as quickly as possible. He'd had a much more exciting watch than expected before midnight then a few hours kip and was now back on duty again. This 'Morning' watch looked as though it was shaping up to be a pain as well. At least he would be off in an hour and not back on duty until the second 'Dog' watch' that evening and he'd already been anticipating breakfast and a nice comfy bed when this shit started.

"Very well, make sure we have a side party and Warrant Officer Crause with his pipe. Oh and tell Captain Roby, I'm sure he'll want to be there." Jake added maliciously knowing full well that Roby would be there anyway as any Captain would be when receiving foreign diplomats.

"Another thing Sharp, ask chef to prepare and deploy some sort of Omani type breakfast stuff if he has any please, and strong coffee too, you know 'spoon standing upright in the cup' strong. OK?"

"Yes Sir, I'll pass that on."

Jake sat on the edge of his bed and wondered what the fuck had been happening overnight. He put on his ear piece.

"OPs." Click.

"OPs, Langford." Answered the duty OPs senior, one Petty Officer Langford, who Jake recalled was now called 'Ringbolt Langford' by the ship's company. This new epithet was earned after apparently having too many beers on their last night in Djibouti, tripping over a ringbolt on the dockside and thereby falling into the harbour. He loved to hear all these little tales and his personal steward, 'Granny' Smith who travelled with him everywhere, was the most common source. Smith himself was now known more commonly as 'Headbanger' Smith since after Bismarck's action in the Caribbean he'd been smacked on the forehead by a suddenly training 3" gun barrel. This apparently because the speakers on that side of the ship were still out of commission and he never heard the warning.

"PO have there been any communications from either head office or the Caymans overnight?"

"Aye Sir, I was just putting them in a folder to be brought down to your cabin at 07:30 as per standing orders."

"Think you'd better bring them down here pronto, I suspect this ship will feature quite prominently in them. How long before the Omani boat is alongside?"

"Will do Sir, and it does Sir. The Omani boat will be alongside in about fifteen minutes."

"Right. Bring that stuff down now then PO."

"Aye aye Sir." Ringbolt Langford clicked off and began to gather the communications he'd printed off earlier. The boss wasn't going to be too happy that was for sure, the shit had well and truly hit the fan after last night's little firework display. The duty OPs staff acted as the communications specialists too on Jake's ships, they simply hadn't the need for a separate section, usually, which was why Langford had read everything Jake was about to read.

A knock on his cabin door announced the arrival of both Granny Smith with a pot of tea and some toast and PO Langford with the communications folder.

Just looking at the thickness of it told Jake that he'd been sleeping while a shit storm gathered elsewhere and he groaned inwardly. He'd already discovered to his cost that the truth had little to do with international affairs, perception was all that counted.

He quickly showered and then got down to speed reading the communications folder. Having gone all the way through once, he let it percolate while he buttered some toast and poured a cup of tea. Then he went back through the folder.

Iran had issued a statement condemning the Cayman Islands registered vessel as the aggressor and its owners and commanders as war criminals, although they didn't say which war, they demanded the ship be impounded and the officers sent to Iran for trial. They stated that the vessel known as Hood had opened fire indiscriminately on Iranian customs vessels conducting an anti-smuggling sweep in international waters. They further stated that the Hood had opened fire without any prior communications with the Iranian vessels, the only true bit, thought Jake. Lastly the loss of life was put at thirty six customs officers and this could rise as some were in critical condition.

The UN had condemned the loss of life but said little else.

The EU had condemned König Marine and himself personally for displaying a reckless disregard for life, international law and anything else they could think of, no surprise there.

The Americans had stated they would wait for further information before making a formal statement but on the face of it, it seemed that Iran's history of dangerous provocations in the very busy shipping lanes of the Hormuz area had finally resulted in fatalities.

Russia lamented the loss of life but it too would wait for further information. It did add that freedom of navigation was an important tenet of international law and no country should seek to impinge on that right.

The Chinese stated that the events took place in internationally disputed waters and urged all parties to show caution and behave with sincerity. They also objected to the arming of merchant ships.

The UK offered no statement at all preferring to wait for further information Whitehall sources revealed.

Saudi Arabia, though not through the Gulf Cooperation Council, issued a statement of outrage, declaring that the Iranian version was a lie from start to finish and they should be condemned for using such weapons in the Hormuz area but most of all, within the territorial waters of an ally. That ally remained remarkably mute however.

The Cayman Islands vigorously protested the unprovoked and foiled attack on their vessel. They further lambasted Iran's cavalier attitude towards other states territorial waters stating that the failed ambush took place in recognised Omani waters and was in effect a declaration of war.

So what was being said but not said, Jake mused as he sipped his tea? They all had the facts they needed so why the reticence to condemn Iran? Jake thought it through. The US, had more or less pronounced 'foul' on the Iranians without upping the ante. No surprise really, they didn't want any more complications added to their already strained relationship with Iran but clearly felt the Iranians needed to know that they *KNEW* what had actually happened.

Back channel contacts at the Pentagon however, were apparently exceedingly grateful for the 'heads up' on this new Iranian methodology. Russia and China both sold massive amounts of their second class armaments, export grade, to Iran, so it was obvious that they would be cautious and would not outright condemn a customer, hence their muted response which would still annoy Tehran for that reason alone. The UK was still extricating itself from the EU despite the March 29 deadline having passed and negotiations were almost at the point where the UK would pull up the stumps and go home, so it was rumoured. So clearly HMG wanted nothing to do with another situation and would remain mute as long as they could.

The Saudi condemnation was automatic and vocal but the issues with the Qatar and Omani relationship with Iran prevented a coordinated Gulf Cooperation Council response. Israel had surprisingly stated that the Iranians were clearly in the wrong, firstly by being in Omani waters and secondly by attempting to ambush the Hood. Jake concluded from that that Israeli intelligence was also in possession of the data.

Israel's supporting statement meant that there would be no further supporting statements from any Gulf state that was for sure, or any follow up from the Saudis. Glad the Israelis waited until last, he thought.

Then the media folder.

Well this was always going to be negative Jake decided in advance. European media was wholly against them defending themselves, it appeared they would much rather wax lyrical over their corpses. Most of the digests were the usual drivel churned out by media groups which had long since failed to provide news, but simply told readers what to think. US media was as usual divided in that Fox and one or two others bothered to analyse the two stories and were so accurate in their assessment at some points that Jake concluded they too had some inside lines on the information. The others, both TV and print, were apparently variously calling for action against him, his company and the ship. New international rules about arming vessels were demanded and a shedful of other rubbish. MEPs were kicking off in the European Parliament and churning out 'this is why merchant ships should not be armed' drivel, thereby neatly ignoring the fact that Hood was attacked by national ships violating another's territorial waters. Perhaps something else to blame on Brexit?

He was mindful though that whilst Andrew knew the facts of the case, there could come a point where he considered their relationship had run its course despite the debt he owed Jake's ships from the battle in the Caribbean. The media, as usual, were like packs of dogs howling after people, baying for his blood. What many leaders clearly either did not understand or were not yet aware of, was that the media was no longer trusted by very large sections of the public at large and therefore not as important an indicator of voter sentiment as it had been when a credible source. Dozens of 'talking heads' were wheeled out, many former naval officers in a variety of countries pontificated over events. Those who came down on the side of the Hood were only seen once whilst those who went along with the media agenda were shown time and again. Nothing new there then.

Still, it cannot have been comfortable for Andrew's media people Jake thought sympathetically. Locally of course in the Caymans, the media were given facts which they reported and allowed the readers to draw their conclusions. A novel approach? Or perhaps they hadn't caught up with the modern way, which was usually to start off with a conclusion and work it back, depending on who was paying you, ignoring any contrary evidence if possible. Not to mention the ridiculous headlines which seldom bore any relation to the body of the article and merely drew your attention. Anyway at least according to the news digest from the Caymans, they were still heroes and being unjustly accused and attacked. Nothing from Oman though, nothing at all.

Jake finished his tea and toast, completed his dressing and made his way up to the starboard boat deck where preparations were proceeding to receive the visitor, all the while thinking about how much he despised the press, even more now than most politicians and lawyers, which quite surprised him.

He spoke briefly to Roby as they waited in the shade of the superstructure and Hood's Captain spoke immediately into his headset.

"Bridge." Click then.

"Bridge Aye Captain." Steve Sharp's voice sounded tired, Roby thought.

Position us twelve point one miles from the nearest Omani land mass please Mr Sharp."

"Aye Sir. Twelve point one miles it is."

The Hood changed direction slightly as she slowed awaiting the visitor.

"OPs, Captain and Commodore."

Jake nodded and Roby responded.

"Listening."

"Approaching vessel is the *Haras1* of 1,850 tons gross, Omani Police slash coastguard patrol vessel."

"Acknowledged."

"That's their newish shallow draft multi-hull I believe, we'll see in a second or two. 'Big Wigs' only get to commandeer that one I think." Roby commented.

Hood swung to its final bearing pointing to the south east and away from Omani waters. The Haras1 came alongside in a seamanlike fashion and given the very calm waters managed to gently kiss the fenders that WO Crause had positioned himself; two of Hood's seamen reached out to steady their visitor and ensure no mishaps occurred.

Jake's humorous but irreverent thoughts about how they would deal with the diplomatic incident occasioned by either dunking the fellow or squashing him between the hulls, never reached his face as he waited for the business suit clad gentleman to step onto his deck. Give him his due, thought Roby standing next to Jake as they watched the somewhat dumpy but agile envoy, he's light on his feet. Then he stepped forward to greet the man.

Jassim Bin Dinar Bin Murie al-Shanfari, as he was so named, took in the smart sailors and the very presentable and powerful looking warship he had just boarded.

This would not be a pleasant visit though and it grieved him that his message from the Sultan would not be welcomed by the man to the right of the Captain who greeted him. He had met Jonathan Henry König once before some years ago in Dubai he believed, long before his latest venture into marine security and anti-piracy work. Long before the new odd looking warships he had constructed had tasted the water, and most certainly before the great battles in the Caribbean. The man had a penetrating gaze, an almost physical pressure being applied as he himself was scrutinised and assessed. The tall Captain with his slightly stooped posture looked to be no mere lackey either. We shall see how this goes, he thought.

"Welcome aboard Sir, I'm Jon Roby, Captain of this vessel and this is Commodore Jonathan Henry König, the owner."

Jake shook the hand offered him and found it dry and firm.

"Would you come this way please Sirs?" Announced Jon Roby, in his best Dartmouth 'plummy' voice.

He led the way down a deck to the spacious wardroom area where their Lebanese chef had laid out various sweetmeats, pastries and a large coffee pot. Now it begins, he thought.

"Do you wish me to be present Sir?" He addressed König directly not even glancing at his guest.

"Please stay Jonno, I'm not doing the full formal bit and I will be pleased to have your opinion on our guest's message."

They all sat and an uncomfortable silence began which lasted until Granny Smith coughed politely from behind their guest asking if he would like coffee.

Jassim nodded and began his discourse.

"I appreciate you receiving me at such short notice gentlemen."

He said it in perfect English with almost no accentual traces at all, probably UK educated, Jake decided, and it's not as if we had a choice in the matter was the thought kept totally from his face.

"Not at all, it is always an honour to receive a representative of Sultan Qaboos bin Said al Said. I trust he is in good health? Would you avail yourself of something to eat?"

Jassim helped himself to a small plate and took a sample of each of the offerings. Neither Jake nor Roby took either coffee or snacks.

Jake continued when the diplomat had taken a bite.

"I apologise for my impolite and brief courtesies but how may we be of service to the Sultan?"

Jassim was a little taken aback at the brevity of the introductory discourse but like the professional diplomat he was, nothing was given away on his face or in his eyes. He chewed the tasty snack briefly allowing him time to finalise his Sultan's message.

"My Sultan sends his good wishes Sirs, but he wishes me to explain why it is necessary for you not to stay in Muscat as previously agreed."

Jake nodded for him to continue.

"You will no doubt be aware of the long and profitable relationship my country has with its neighbour across the straits. It is to that relationship that my master alludes."

"I see." Said Jake with a frown. "It must be the infringement of your territorial waters last night which causes the Sultan distress. I understand completely, it was a flagrant breach of international law and I am most distressed that my ship had a part in this but pleased we saw off your trespassers."

Jassim looked surprised for the briefest of moments and covered it by taking a sip of the extraordinarily good coffee.

"Very nice coffee Mr König, my compliments. I rarely enjoy coffee not prepared the Arabic way, your steward is to be commended."

"Thank you. I will pass your remarks on to him. As I was saying, this infringement of your territorial waters is merely the latest in a long line of dangerous provocations originating from the other side of the straits. I consider myself fortunate in being able to render a service to the Sultan in acting as a deterrent to future possible incursions," before Jassim could reply, Jake pressed on, "..and I am at your service if you feel that we can be of more assistance."

Jassim nearly choked and covered it by coughing gently.

"A crumb in the wrong place. Err, the problem Mr König is that our friends across the water see things in a slightly different light. Especially in regard to last night's….erm, events."

Jake jumped in.

"Yes I am sure, I'm only too pleased that we were able to fill the slot most commonly occupied by one of your own naval vessels, since this is one of your regular patrol areas is it not?"

Jassim knew he was being played now and sat a little straighter.

"Mr König, the reason for the absence of our patrol vessel has yet to be determined but I can assure you, it was certainly not something countenanced by the Sultan." He brushed imaginary crumbs from his immaculately tailored trouser legs.

"As I was saying your actions have caused the Sultan great distress. He appreciates that on this occasion the naval vessels of the Islamic Republic appear to have strayed across into our waters. He regrets the attack on your vessel but cannot publically say this for risk of offending those across the straits. In order to return things as quickly as possible to the situation ante-bellum he asks that you move out of our waters and do not return until such times as we are certain that no reaction will come from across the straits."

Jake nodded slowly.

"So an attack on a guest vessel, in your own territorial waters is greeted by banishment for the victim, not the aggressor?"

"Victim? I suppose it depends on your perspective but you destroyed seven Iranian vessels and killed thirty something sailors."

Jake pounced.

"All of whom were trying to kill me and my crew, and yes *victim*; simply because their intended target was able to defend itself effectively does not remove the appellation 'victim' from us Sir!" His last tone was a little higher than before and was noted by Jassim.

"Very well. I concede the point. However in order to put this particular genie back in its bottle Mr König, the Sultan believes it is best that you leave our waters for the time being. That is all I came to say. In this part of the world it isn't a matter of siding with brothers, for they are not Arabs, it is a matter of maintaining a peaceful co-existence with a people who, shall we say, are somewhat more volatile and prone to take offence very quickly. I'm sure you understand."

Jake stared him in the eye.

"I do, as it happens, fully understand. I just wanted to make sure that the Sultan was aware of the true nature of last night's events. I would also appreciate greatly if he could relay such to my government and I do understand that his position requires him to take 'no position'. We will continue on our way to Djibouti. Oh and good luck discerning the reasons your patrol boat was absent."

Jassim was a little ruffled at the last sentence but had delivered his message. Not one to mess with this König, he decided.

"I am grateful for your understanding Sir and I will convey your request to his Majesty. I wish you fair winds and good sailing Sir. Now I must take my leave. You will leave Omani waters soon?"

"We are not in Omani waters now Sir."

"Aah, thank you."

"Captain Roby would you escort our guest to the side?"

"Certainly Sir. This way Sir." He stood and indicated the exit before leading the Omani away.

Roby and Jassim Bin Dinar Bin Murie al-Shanfari left the wardroom leaving a deeply thoughtful Jake now munching on the snacks set out for his former guest.

"Granny!" He shouted.

"Yes Sir." Answered Granny from the Steward's pantry where he had been listening to his boss box nimbly round the Arab fella.

"Coffee please, the kind that the Captain and I can drink. Oh and see if you can get Captain's Krull and McClelland along with Mr Evans and Mr Zotov up here in the next half hour or so please. Oh and tell chef 'excellent'."

"Aye aye Sir, no sooner said than done."

Jake went back to ruminating whilst he waited first for Roby to return and then for his other Captains and the security chiefs. As the others arrived he glanced at the trip screen and noted that the journey would take three days at their high cruising speed of twenty knots, plenty of time for a full on discussion of the Ps and Qs of the Lloyds contract, and wondering whether Lloyds themselves were regretting their offer. No. They were pragmatic not emotive, he decided.

Andy and Arkady had been working out in the ship's gym and so after a quick shower were ready for work and a bite to eat. Reiner and Simon were early risers by nature and had merely stayed out of the way while the visitor had been present.

Jake had moved over to the wardroom table with Granny's new pot of coffee and a couple of the snacklets that he must ask Adnan about; delicious whatever they were, sort of nutty fruity things, damned tasty.

The others arrived, Roby first sat down and ordered his breakfast, Andy Evans and Arkady Zotov were next and the smell of Jon Roby's bacon and eggs was enough for them to order a plateful each. Simon arrived last with an armful of papers and a laptop, declining anything other than Earl Grey tea, black no sugar.

"Right gentlemen, a summary of my recent meeting with the Sultan's representative. Not an accredited diplomat in this context, rather an unofficial official if you see what I mean."

Jake reached for another snack but discovered the last had gone, he looked up to see a smiling Arkady Zotov put the last piece in his mouth.

"Thanks Arkady, I'll remember that….git."

"No problem boss, you got to watch your weight, I ain't going to live long enough to get old and fat." The big Russian responded with a wide grin, seeing the smiles from the other guests as he ribbed his boss who was as lithe and wiry as he had been twenty years before.

"Any more of that and I'll have my Security Chief throw you overboard to swim back, you peasant." Jake shot back.

"Right boss." Answered Arkady. "He's too old and fat for that as well."

"Not if I shoot you first and use a derrick." Added Andy Evans.

Jake smothered a grin.

"Right you lot. Business. Our guest basically said that the Sultan had been pressured by Iran's potential reaction to revoke us porting facilities. They are aware of the truth regarding the attack but for political reasons they choose to say nothing about it and allow themselves to be pressured by Iran. You might not think much of them for bowing down to that pressure but consider they could have gone all the way and vocally supported Iran's version of events. They didn't though which will not go down well with the Ayatollahs."

He picked up his coffee cup and went for a refill. The jug was empty.

"Bloody vultures you lot." He turned towards the steward's pantry and waved the cup. Granny Smith always watching and listening, appeared as if by magic with a new jug of coffee and another plate of snacks. He took the cleaned plates away along with the empty coffee pot.

"Thanks Granny." Said Jake pouring a fresh cup.

"Right so we're off to Djibouti to deposit Reiner and Simon. Transit time at this speed, just over three days. Head Office are organising your flights as we speak, tickets will be at Ambouli airport waiting for you." He paused a second then changed subject.

"I want to go round the table and get your feedback on the proposed Lloyds operations in the South China Sea. Don't duplicate each other but if you have anything to amplify, fine. This will be a preliminary discussion, we've plenty of time and a good satellite connection if we need any other info. Start with you Jonno." He said, looking left.

"It is quite a while since I've visited the South China Sea but I can recall a number of navigation advisories if you are not on the beaten path so to speak. I find it amazing that with all the traffic over the centuries we still occasionally discover an uncharted pinnacle. However I rather think it unlikely that all of these vessels found a hitherto uncharted rock pinnacle. Anyway, I've looked up all of the ships that have been reported as missing whilst transiting the area during the time frame given. None of them got off a GMDSS call. Not one, which means surprise was complete. I've charted their last reported AIS positions, their cargoes, port of sailing, port of destination," Roby ticked them off his fingers as he talked, "crew composition, nationality of owners, flag of convenience or otherwise, weather slash storms etcetera, and I've plotted them out."

He rotated his chair slightly and pressed a button on the remote laying on the table. On the forward bulkhead a few feet away, the sixty inch LED screen flashed to life and Roby tapped his mike and spoke.

"Show Roby image 1.1." He loved this technology, when it worked. His headset location told the computer which screen to display on in order to comply with the request. The screen changed to show a large scale map of the whole South China Sea incorporating China and Taiwan in the north, Philippines to the east, Vietnam to the west and Sarawak with Brunei to the south.

"Zoom one and centre. Down a little. Stop." The screen zoomed in one level, moved down and now showed the Paracel islands in the north and the Spratlys in the south. In between the two island groups were a number of coloured tags.

"If you were looking at this from historical piracy perspectives, these tags are in the wrong place." He tapped his headset ear piece again. "Show overlay one." The image changed to show fifty years of piracy locations according to the key.

"The vast majority as you can see are located in the peripheries of this water mass, places like the Sulu sea and between the Riau islands, both sides, and of course the Malacca straits." He tapped again. "Show overlay 1 on overlay 2."

This now showed the recent spate of attacks against the background of historical attacks.

"Now you can see without any effort that the ones we are talking about have occurred in areas which are not commonly pirated if at all. I also cross referenced the other mentioned factors to see if there were any commonalities. Sorry, there were none that I could see. I did think at the start that perhaps there was some sort of inside job going on, you know, crewmembers as part of the 'gang' setting their ships up but if that's the case then they are a multi-national corporation not a gang, given the variety of recruitment sources and nationalities involved. I can only suggest a painstaking search of the area since none of these vessels have shown up again for sale, that we are able to determine that is."

Jake nodded.

"Thanks for that Jonno. Any questions?" There were none.

"OK. Reiner what have you got?"

"Very little more I'm afraid. I did think the stolen cargoes would be quite relevant and I pursued that even though one of them was bulk material like blast furnace slag for the cement industry. There were also two ships taken that were in ballast on their way for long term repair or maintenance. I was clearly heading in the wrong direction and a friend in Interpol checked for me that none of the listed cargoes of a trackable nature i.e. anything with a serial number, have turned up on the recovered properties lists. So, no, I have nothing much of a clue to offer and concur with Jonno about the systematic search, because these vessels have to be somewhere."

"Thanks Reiner. Mystery piled on mystery. What about you two?" He motioned across the table to Andy and Arkady.

"We have squeezed our contacts in the piracy industry until they squeaked. As you know we have been developing intelligence assets in both the Philippines and Malaysia to try to get the jump on pirate activity. No one has heard a damned thing. They are all aware of the missing ships and apparently the known pirate groups have discretely been in touch with each other to see if there was a way of getting in on the action, having assumed it was a rival group doing the hijacking. Again they came up with nothing. Then, like Reiner, I went for the cargoes but unlike Reiner I reversed engineered it offering good money for listed items which I knew were on these ships, putting out commissions and orders for them. Nothing that was offered me was on the list. In my opinion the goods on these ships have not been sold on the black market. Not only that, no ransoms have been demanded for crew. There are a number of negotiators who've been contacted by relatives worried about their missing family members but even the negotiators have been unable to get a genuine response since no ransoms have been issued and all their enquiries came up blank, no one to negotiate with. No boss, I'm stumped at the moment, I've still got the bids out there, but given that the earliest one we are looking at was taken a year ago, I really just haven't a clue. Oh, just one other thing, there appears to be a slow increase in frequency." He tapped his mike.

"Show security overlay 1."

A Graph appeared showing slow but steady increase in the rate of ship losses.

"Sorry but that's about it for me."

"Thanks Andy. Simon, any luck with you?"

Simon took a breath then paused as if unsure, then shrugged and started speaking anyway.

"As usual I have looked at this in a different way. I concur with all that Jonno and Reiner have said, did the same stuff myself. Then I put my warfare hat on and had a think about things from the perspective of the two largest protagonists in this area."

He paused again.

"We know that all the bordering nations have objected to and resisted China's claim to the South China Sea but China has gone ahead and even conferred a 'government status' on the land masses in the disputed territories. I understand they have given the Paracel and Spratly Islands prefecture status, with the prefecture being called Sansha and the capital being on Woody Island aka *Yongxing Dao* in the Paracels. This has upped the ante in the area. Add in a Chinese long term plan regarding control of access to the South China Sea. Then add reports of underwater activity in the nature of cable laying in certain areas where cables have no need to be laid ...by Chinese vessels." He tapped his mike.

"Show McClelland overlay 1."

The screen flicked to a larger scale map again similar to Jon Roby's.

"This activity has been reported in areas to the west of the Riau Islands, to the south east of them, to the north of Palawan and to the south east of it as well as in the Bashi channel and close to the Luzon strait. These reports are sourced from a variety of places including near miss reports from ships transiting the area." He let that sink in a second or two.

"If you were into anti-access or area denial you would need to monitor traffic in the area of concern. The former Warfare Officer in me says that they're laying a sonobuoy chain like the Americans had SOSUS in the North Atlantic during the cold war. With this cover they could at some point in the future close off the area to assert their claim." He rushed on seeing the puzzled looks.

"What if these ship disappearances are somehow connected to China's long term plans for the area? They certainly all occur in the disputed area. None of the ships are Chinese flagged or owned or registered −which I find an anomaly-and, they are all within a thousand tons the same unladen tonnage, and very similar in length and draft too. They are all US, British or Japanese owned or flagged vessels of a similar size. Now that's a hell of a coincidence."

Reiner was shaking his head.

"So what are you saying Simon? That China is stealing these ships? To what end?"

"I don't know Reiner, I just look for patterns and connections; but if I was partway through a masterplan to take uncontested control of an area like this I'd certainly be wanting to know exactly what goes in and comes out, under and above water, where and when. Another thing. This area is a mixture of mostly relatively shallow water and in the centre a bit of seriously deep water. Ideal hunting grounds for SSKs and it just so happens that there's the world's largest concentration of such submarines in that area. China has ten improved Kilos, more than Russia itself. Vietnam for some reason, has six improved Kilos. These as you will recall are quieter than the grave at 5 knots and below, hard to find with sonar in shallow water passive or active, and also possess a variety of modern wire guided torpedoes and anti-ship cruise missiles." The others were listening intently now.

"If I were planning to do some anti-access area denial work in shallow seas, I'd choose Kilos over almost anything else except our former Upholder class boats." Simon referred to the RN's replacement for the 'O' class diesel electric boats. The Upholder class were big boats, not as big as an SSN but much more stealthy. After the cold war, the RN facing cuts went just for nuclear submarines and the Upholders were laid up and eventually sold to Canada.

"I remember talking to a classmate who'd gone to boats some years later, he said that SSNs hate operating in shallow water i.e. anything less than 750 feet deep, places like the South China Sea are perfect for submarines which thrive in just those kind of conditions, Kilos are about the same size as Upholders and damned deadly by all accounts, especially now they can have the export version of the Klub 3M54 missile with the supersonic terminal sprint. Don't know if the Chinese have them or their own variant?"

Jake decided to draw him in a little.

"So Simon, clarify or give us a hint where you're going with this please?"

"Sorry boss. I cannot say for sure but my instincts tell me this is all connected to the 'Nine Dash Line'." He spoke into his mike. "Show McClelland 1."

Onto the screen popped a picture which showed the South China Sea but had a number of green lines added at various points.

"I'm certain you are all aware of this map showing the extent of the Chinese claims to the area and the parts where it conflicts with other claims. Anyway, to get into the SCS, if you were a submarine, you have to go into shallow water. To enter via the Bashi Channel and Luzon Strait you need to go over a ridge into shallow water and that's one of the areas where cable layers have been seen. The Riau Islands north and south are in relatively shallow water leading to deep water further in, same with the SCS side of the Sulu Sea, shallow. I think someone is putting in place systems which mean they can monitor submarine activity in all the access points to this sea. Add that to the other events like the recent exchange of fire between one of the Chinese placements and the US destroyer, the continuous program of creating land where there was none before, all strategically located....and it just becomes a linked pattern. I just don't know how the missing ships of similar size fit into this unless they are being kept somewhere for some reason and the facility has size limits. Sorry boss, I'm off on one. I just know there's a pattern here."

Jake smiled.

"Whilst you have not provided us with a solution Simon, you've given us one hell of an update on the geopolitical status of the area. I think it means whoever operates in there needs one eye on the Chinese, one on the Americans and one on the seabed...oops! Just done a Diane Abbott!"

The British attendees laughed and the others just looked puzzled.

"Never mind I was just making a UK specific political joke. Anyway it was enlightening Simon, and now all of us here have got that information percolating around, maybe it will link to something else we find. There is something else. Given what you've just said, those who will be working in the area if we go, will be in an unusually active submarine environment. While you were talking Simon, I asked for intel on current dispositions of those ten Kilos. It appears that eight, according to our sources, are operating in the SCS. In addition the Vietnamese have six of the same all in the area, however the Viets have taken the Russian weaponry as well. That is a shitload of Kilos in a relatively small area of the ocean. In view of this all of my ships will be receiving some new kit. You will be aware of 'upgrade space' in the OPs rooms."

Three nods accompanied that statement.

"I never envisioned operating in an area where there might actually be a submarine threat since obviously weaponised submarines are owned by nation states, no privately owned shooters that I know of. I do however have an active hydrographic section in our ocean survey division. Now they have been working on a few things that might help in this area. They've been doing a lot of research on the blue/green lasers. Basically they want to use drones to map seabeds and harbours etcetera. I won't bore you with the problems they've had selecting wavelengths but the issue has always been about penetration of the water, red lasers are quickly absorbed but not so Blue/green. The second problem they had was the weight issue. How could they generate enough power to do it without it being the size of a London bus and requiring cooling that a reactor would be envious of."

They were all listening closely now, naval officers and security experts alike are avid gadget users and all like the latest tech.

"Well I recall seeing a memo recently about a breakthrough in both areas, almost simultaneous in fact. They now know which wavelengths to use –more towards the indigo end of the spectrum- and how to get the required power into a small package -by using millisecond bursts with a microsecond pause for cooling. Fascinating I know. The third piece of the puzzle is the data analysis side, the number crunching. Now that the processing power is available on the mother ship so to speak, the drone can simply fly around mapping the area to a high degree of accuracy whilst sending data back for processing. Well I'm going to do a bit of checking but something one of the scientists flippantly added was that they could watch Moby Dick wandering around under the water now. You can see where I'm going with this?" Again the nods and then Reiner spoke.

"Isn't this a rather dangerous arena to be moving into Jake? There's a lot of people out there who want to track submarines and not have anyone able to track theirs, if you see what I mean."

"Thanks Reiner. Yes I do take that point, so we shall all be tight lipped about it, except for one thing. I need you to check your OPs staff on the QT to see if we have anyone with an anti-submarine background; we might have some new kit for them to play with. Allied to that and quite possibly complimentary, we have the underwater ROVs ready for all three ships."

"Oh excellent." Said Simon, gleefully rubbing his hands.

All three ships were designed with a hull mounted recess from which ROVs could be launched, a sort of cigar shaped moon pool which had been hitherto unused and it also had a docking bay with all the power and data connections. The original concept had been that underwater searching could be part of the tasking for these ships and Jake, never one to miss an opportunity, had insisted that the ships had the ability to survey as well as search, not quite the same thing. There was a big market for accurate charts of some quite obscure places, now used as cruise ship destinations as well as high end get-aways for those with super yachts.

As he sat delivering the news another thought popped into in his head. Would they be able to mount a blue laser on the ROVs? Cooling wouldn't be quite as much of an issue now would it?

The rest of the meeting consisted of discussions relating to the visit to Djibouti. It was decided that although the president of Djibouti supported Saudi Arabia in various things including the Qatar dispute, that they would try not to make too many ripples on the pond at this time.

Jake, Reiner, Simon, Andy and Tetsunari would go ashore in a RHIB keeping Hood just outside the twelve mile limit. The President could then deny, if necessary, that they'd been there.

Jake summarised.

"We'll coordinate it based on external flights. Having all checked in with customs and immigration at the dock, Reiner and Simon will make their way to the airport whilst Andy, Tetsunari and myself are going to wander over to my local agent's place and see what's cooking; after that we're off to the airport ourselves to take a scheduled flight back to London and meet with the Lloyds lot. That is of course assuming they still want us to pursue this for them after last night's little bust up. Meanwhile, we've a couple of days to burn so everyone have a re-think in the light of what has been said."

Jake closed the meeting and went back to his cabin. A note was on his desk asking him to contact Prime Minister McTeal; apparently it wasn't urgent. Good job they added that last bit thought Jake, wouldn't look too good if you were too busy to ring your boss now would it?

"Hello Mr Prime Minister." Jake said formally when he was connected. "Are we switching to video?"

"Hi Jake, yes if you please." There was a pause as the encryption at both ends shook hands and decided they were OK with each other. "Right there you are Jake. How are you?"

"Well Andrew. I won't ask the same of you after all the hassle I've dumped on you in the past few days. Really sorry, but none of this was of my choosing."

"I know, I know." McTeal let out a big sigh. "I could do without it but I know you don't start things, heaven knows I'm just pleased you step up when the chips are down if you'll pardon the mixed metaphor."

The allusion to the battles of the previous year was a reminder to them both that they had been through worse times.

"OK headmaster, now that I know I'm not in for six of the best, what can I do for you old friend?"

McTeal laughed his big rumbly laugh, a bit like a volcano, you didn't know if it would develop into a full blown eruption. It subsided after a few rumbles and he smiled widely.

"I should talk to you more often, I need a good laugh every now and then." His frown deepened briefly. "Emily could always get me laughing, mostly at myself of course." Another sigh.

Jake was suddenly aware of how lucky he'd been to get his wife back alive, not so for Andy Mac, as he used to call him.

McTeal continued.

"I just thought I'd let you know the gist of a public statement I'm about to release covering last night's mess. It goes along these lines. 'I will not apologise to the world for being attacked. I would ask that the aggressor be told to apologise but you won't tell him to, because you are all afraid to upset him. Iranian ships behaving like playground bullies in some of the most congested shipping areas of the world and you blame us for defending ourselves? Well I am not afraid to call him out on this. Does Iran condone its naval units deliberately entering into the waters of a friendly country and setting up an ambush for a visiting ship? They were not customs vessels as Iran claims, you will see this from the images to be released after my announcement. When all the information is out there to be seen, people will know who attacked whom. That the consequence of their irrational action has caused the loss of more young men for no sensible reason will be apparent to everyone. I call upon Iran to behave in a civilised manner and to review and clarify who is in charge of the military over there, because surely this naked aggression towards a tiny Caribbean nation cannot have been endorsed by the leaders of that great nation?' How does that sound Jake?"

"Wow! All those diplomats who hide behind thousands of words that say sod-all must love you, especially when you speak so plainly. I suppose it's that legal brain at work. I recall you made plenty of speeches while at the bar but I don't seem to recall flattery and obfuscation in the mix. Clearly you'd make a crap diplomat Andy."

Another big guffaw from McTeal.

"Thank you Commodore." He said with a twinkle in his eye. "And when shall you grace our Royal presence again?" He added with a self-mocking hand flourish.

"Not long actually. I should be home in a day or so. I have to sort out a few things in Djibouti first since whichever of our ships is operating off the Gulf of Aden needs a resupply port and somewhere the boys can have a beer or two in relative safety. I know there has been the occasional attack there but for the most part it is just what they need after few weeks at sea. I need to feel out whether we'll be welcome or unwelcome. Then on to London for a meeting with the Lloyds 'Names' that I mentioned before, finally a company jet home."

He paused a second.

"Why don't you come out to the Island for a couple of days Andy? Have a drink and a laugh and some good food, you look positively skeletal. Sophie will be home in the next few days or so as will my globetrotting offspring. Looks like it will be quite a gathering. We'd all want you there, really. Your BBQ prowess is legend and James says Uncle Andy's courtroom stories are brilliant."

McTeal looked thoughtful but then shook his head.

"No, you have your family time Jake, make the most of it."

"OK, Andy, you leave me no choice. As soon as they get back I'm setting Sophie and Helen on you. I'll send a plane with them in it to fetch you!"

McTeal cracked a big smile, his own wife and children, killed by narco-terrorists several years before, had left him bereft. He simply poured himself into his work leaving no time for brooding.

"You play dirty Sir!"

"Yup. I'll let you know when I get things nailed down. I'd really like you to come Andy, its ages since we had any quality time together without someone trying to take over the islands or blow me up."

"OK, I'll see what I can do. I doubt the Caymans will sink into the abyss if I have a weekend away. Sandy is now officially my deputy. He can have the reins for the weekend; give him a shot in the big chair."

"Now you're talking. I guess I'd better not invite him as well then." They both laughed knowing that the very last thing in the world that Sandiford Roche enjoyed, was socialising; he'd have been sat in the corner in the shadows or a darkened room if possible, watching everyone.

"OK Jake, stay safe. Be in touch."

Jake noted the smile was still in place as Andrew McTeal disconnected. Good. Now he needed to enlist Helen and Sophie as well as James to ensure he kept his word.

The passage along the coast of first Oman and then Yemen passed quickly. Roby took the ship out to eighty miles from land to avoid the ongoing conflict in Yemen and any chance of Hood getting involved in another unwanted fight.

Over the two and half day passage he'd quizzed Jake more and more about the possibilities that green/blue lasers could unlock for underwater object detection. As a former RN Captain he was well versed in anti-submarine warfare a field where surface ships, referred to simply as targets by submariners, were at an almost permanent disadvantage. Like most Captains he had had the occasional success but having an SSN surface two hundred yards behind you and signal 'Bang!' by lamp was a much more likely result.

So he was very curious and intrigued, pestering Jake to have some of the schematics sent out so he could look at them, same with the ROV. Roby saw the huge potential of using a drone to pick up the wake of a submerged boat and then using a ROV to refine its position. The clever thing about using the water penetrating lasers was the way the information was processed. The aerial part of the team was all about detecting the thermal disturbance that an underwater wake would cause. Apparently the Australians had been trialling a version for mapping harbour mouths and had had problems with a school of porpoises crossing the survey area which was how the idea of using green/blue lasers for moving underwater objects had come about. But for the underwater ROV it would be a direct line of sight detection and better still the other fellow would not know they had been detected. Food for thought.

Jake worked at organising a quick drydocking for all three ships with the kit to be flown out, escorted by a pair of Andy Evans' security staff, to each of the ports. The easiest was for Simon and Jon Roby for whom he chose the LSE shipyards on Labuan Island, Malaysia. It was the obvious choice because Hood's passage to the SCS would take them past it, unless Lloyds pulled the plug, and it wasn't far for Simon's Ocean Guard to go. So both of his ships in the SCS would have their ROVs and the laser attachments for the drones before they started operating in that very same area.

Another good thing about the LSE shipyard was that they had experience of both commercial and military vessels so whilst Hood could never be seen as an ordinary naval vessel it wouldn't be the shocker that would occur in a purely commercial port. LSE also had the capacity to drydock or work dry two ships simultaneously. They either drydocked for a quick turnaround or lifted the ship out via the drydock and moved it on to land; the site was cleverly designed, he recalled.

Bismarck would be a bit more problematic however the Shipside drydock at Port Harcourt in Nigeria appeared to be a possibility. The drydock was 120yds long with a 5000 ton limit which would just fit Bismarck, but he needed his agent in Lagos to check the place out first, anyway Bismarck wasn't as high priority for this refit as the other two.

Djibouti, two days later.

The late afternoon sun sat shimmering behind the land mass as Hood glided slowly to a point 12.1 miles from the nearest land mass, that being Djibouti City.

The water had a peculiar liquid coppery look to it with a lazy swell. The unusual offshore wind at this time of day was probably the start of a Khamsin Roby thought as he watched the RHIB being prepped from the bridge wing. This wind brought the usual mixture of smells from the nearby land, a fusion of exotic spices and other nebulous ingredients unique to Africa.

The RHIB kissed the sea as gently as the crane driver could possibly manage, being mindful as he was of all the bosses on board it. Reiner, Simon, Jake, Andy and Tetsunari were passengers with WO Crause at the wheel and AB Scouse Smith on the lines. Crause had detailed himself off for this trip, a little entertainment to liven up a dull day even though he wouldn't be landing himself. He could practically wave to his favourite restaurant 'The Melting Pot' and he salivated at the thought, remembering the Camel steaks and the amazing fish dishes he'd had last time.

"Cast off Smith." He ordered having checked that his valuable cargo was settled and kitted out properly.

"Aye aye Sir." Acknowledged Scouse Smith as he quickly made his way back aft having stowed the bow line; the livid scar on his arm from last year's action on Bismarck still clearly visible, a badge of honour. Still an AB in Jake's Navy as the lads called it, he'd declined an offered promotion. He had actually been a Petty Officer seaman in the Royal Navy but was quite content as an AB amongst these professionals.

The big engine rumbled as Crause expertly moved the RHIB away from Hood's side without a single bump. He waited until it was well clear.

"Achtung. Halten sie an engen Gentlemen. Hold on tight please Gentlemen." He added in English, unsure as to who spoke what language other than English.

Then he gunned the engine and the RHIB responded, momentarily causing everyone to lean back as it swiftly accelerated.

Jake had always enjoyed RHIB rides and the fresh ocean air combined with the thrill of high speed travel over water left him with a big smile on his face as he switched his view left and right continuously, old habits die hard, he laughed at himself.

Crause saw the smile and understood his bosses' feelings. Such trips as these were quite liberating which was why he took every opportunity to make them. He had worked for König Marine, Ship Security Division, for over a year now and in that time had seen more action, albeit small scale, than in the twenty three years of his service to the Deutsche Marine. Not only that but hitting back at the low life who terrorised ordinary sailors was satisfying. He felt for once that his contribution to things was worthwhile and of course completely justified in the light of the predations of these scum who only thought of money.

The miles passed swiftly and in no time the RHIB was approaching the port. Crause turned them in towards a small boat marina area and brought the RHIB alongside with a minimum of fuss.

The passengers disembarked and returned all their safety gear to the RHIB before waving it goodbye as Crause, no longer restricted by having his boss aboard, was looking to break the record on the way back.

Hood had communicated with the Port Authorities the day before and since no goods were being landed there were no customs in this duty free port, and immigration was a formality.

Jake had had to get one of the company jets re-tasked to come and pick up both Simon and Reiner since there were no scheduled direct flights to either Manilla or Lagos and it would have taken over a day to fly them there via several other stop offs first. He, Andy and Tetsunari would have to fly business class Air France to Paris, because there were no first class places for some reason, and then on to London after an overnight there. However the flight wasn't scheduled to take off until 22:40 so they had time to sort things with the local agent as well as having a bite to eat in one of the local restaurants, Crause had recommended his favourite. Two cars were waiting on the jetty as ordered. Even though the sun was sliding down into the hills behind the city the temperature was still in the thirties and as soon as they stepped on the jetty everyone except Tetsunari broke into a sweat. They were all wearing shades and light tropical traveling clothes except Tetsunari who wore his trademark dark business suit cut perfectly for him to allow maximum comfort and flexibility. He always took his work seriously and now scanned everything in sight with a jaded eye looking for potential danger.

Jake wondered if he had a little aircon of some kind inside his suit too, just like the Japanese at Khasab must have had, as he was seemingly unaffected by temperature too.

They all carried their own bags up the jetty and the drivers of both vehicles jumped out to assist as soon as they were in sight. The two groups parted and Jake wished his Captains a safe journey before climbing in with Andy and Tetsunari.

The cars parted company at the Rue de Venice as Simon and Reiner's turned right towards the airport and Jake, Andy and Tetsunari headed left toward to the

Bankouale district. The aircon was going full blast as they moved off and Jake took out his phone, waited for a local network, then dialled his agent. No answer. Puzzled he tried again, same result. He gave the driver the address and wondered whether he was dialling wrong or whether there was an issue with the network or what?

On instinct he told the driver to pull over when they were still a quarter of a mile away. Jake pulled up a Google map of the area and put in the agent's address. He waited while his phone got used to his current location and then zoomed in a little. He looked outside and the name on the corner of a cross road gave him the location.

"I fancy stretching my legs gentlemen. Join me?"

He turned back to the driver and told him to pick them up from 'The Melting Pot' in three hours' time.

Tetsunari became alert but not in an observable way, however he went mentally to Defcon1 at the sound of the pre-arranged code words Jake just used. Andy Evans too mentally went into 360 scan mode and prepped himself without a clue as to what was going down.

They alighted from the car and Jake passed the driver a $20 dollar bill so he was more than happy to drive off with the promise of more later.

"Either of you armed?" Jake asked nonchalantly.

"No." Said Andy.

"No." Echoed Tetsunari, scanning everywhere. "Is there a problem Mr König?"

Jake had never managed to persuade Tetsunari to drop the 'Mr' and call him Jake. That would be unprofessional as far as Tettas was concerned, he decided.

"I am unable to reach Mr Ashuff at his office. I have tried twice and I'll try again now. He has never ever not answered when he's expecting me to call. Never."

"You think there could be something wrong with Ashuff?" Andy added, discretely stretching muscles, flexing joints and scanning, always scanning looking for disruption to patterns. Looking for something that didn't quite flow and fit.

"I don't know." Answered Jake, still getting no answer from the Agent's number. "There are a thousand possible reasons why he hasn't answered but after the Omani experience with someone tipping off the Iranians and that patrol boat going walkabout, I'm a little paranoid. Bear in mind we had to notify our intent to arrive more than 24 hours in advance along with ETA, numbers etcetera. Add to that the Omanis knew we were heading this way as well and add to that, the Hood has been making itself a bloody nuisance not far from here. It is possible that they, whoever they are, have had three days or so to organise a reception."

The three of them were walking slowly down a fairly quiet street with commercial offices one side and large imposing residential properties the other. Trees dotted the boulevard on both sides. There were no parked cars and only the occasional person seen in the distance.

"What do you wish to do Mr König?" Asked Tetsunari, slowly rotating his head like a turret training, sifting the input for disturbances and things that didn't quite fit.

"If we keep heading this way Ashuff's office is a left at the next crossroad and on the right hand side, set back a few yards as I recall." Answered Jake consulting his phone again.

They began walking along the pavement on the right side, Andy and Tetsunari flanking Jake, one slightly ahead the other slightly behind, both discretely but constantly checking the shadows, but not overtly alert; to all intents and purposes a jovial conversation passing between them is all that could be observed.

"Furtive movement to our eleven o'clock. Unsure of any details." Came the slightly sotto voce comment from Andy on the left, with a big smile and a laugh.

"Same at one o'clock." Intoned Tetsunari, punching Jake lightly on his right deltoid and causing instant numbness.

"Fuck's sake Tettas." Said Jake, rubbing his shoulder and causing an outburst of genuine laughter from Andy Evans.

They walked on another hundred yards.

"OK we'll increase speed slowly." Said Jake.

Without any apparent fuss or hurriedness they gradually began to move faster making it very difficult for people paralleling them to keep up without sprinting, and thereby giving their furtive movements away. How on earth did anyone know we'd be getting out the taxi here he wondered?

Sure enough there were at least four separate shadowy figures keeping pace with them. Can't phone the police because nothing has happened, Jake thought, can contact the ship but they couldn't do anything in time anyway. He started examining the buildings more closely, where were the Asdas and Tescos when you needed them most?

They reached the intersection crossed over and turned left on to the deserted avenue D'Esperey.

"This is the embassy district, surely they'd have more police in evidence down here." Said Andy, looking at his Google map noting a sign for the Russian embassy on the right and behind them now, along with one for the Japanese embassy, ahead and to their right; although neither of them could actually be seen.

"There. Ashuff's is just ahead set back from the road." Said Jake without pointing. They looked ahead and saw a property fronted by several trees with a semi-circular in and out driveway.

"They still with us?" Asked Jake.

"Haven't seen any on my side for a minute or so." Answered Andy.

"Me neither." Added Tetsunari.

"OK, I read that as they knew where we were going anyway. In we go." Said Jake

"I will lead the way." Stated Tetsunari in a tone which brooked no opposition, and he took the lead walking swiftly to the door of the building. There was a brass plate on the wall and writing in both Arabic and French. 'Monsieur A.Ashuff. Agent Maritime.' Read the French version.

Tetsunari yanked on a bell pull on the right side of the door of the colonial era building. A tinny ringing could be heard from within. No one came to answer. He tried again, no answer.

Then he slowly turned the knob on the door and pushed gently inwards, the door gave way. They entered and let their eyes adjust for a few seconds. The hallway was dark but it led to what appeared to be a reception desk. No one there.

Andy took up station by their entry door while Tetsunari pressed on down the darkened hall. He approached the reception desk slowly but even before he arrived he could see a pair of legs poking out from behind the office style chair behind the desk. Moving with care he stepped forward to examine the body while Jake took post watching the corridor ahead and the doors leading off.

Tetsunari leant carefully over the desk disturbing a few flies which buzzed away angrily. The woman, wearing a full Burka, had had her throat cut and then head bent forward to stop the spray, he presumed, since the front of the black dress was completely sodden but there were no blood sprays visible around her. He picked up a long stiletto letter opener from the floor next to her with dried blood on it, which unusually was sharpened, and then signalled to the others that she was dead.

Moving beyond Jake, Tetsunari walked slowly and quietly, listening to the house, checking for patterns out of synch. He came to a door with a similar brass plate to the outside wall, it was slightly ajar. Moving the paper knife to his right hand he placed his left on the door and pushed. When the door had swung to its limit he stepped in quickly and to the right. Not much light in here either, he thought, noting the blinds were drawn. He flicked the light switch behind him and watched while the room was poorly but fully illuminated. Clearly not the man's reading light, he decided as he began to explore the room.

It was quite a large rectangle with what looked like wooden panelling on two walls, the third had the bay window and bookshelves lined the fourth. He approached the desk which had a large anglepoise lamp on it, and then stopped. There was a hand on the desk near the right side, it was gripping the edge, clearly in death. He moved so he could see the body that it must be attached to and even his case hardened mind rebelled at the sight.

This must be Ashuff. He looked at the pitiful figure kneeling on the floor, where the fingers of his left hand should be were bloody stumps. The fingers themselves lay scattered around randomly where they fell. A pair of pliers he noted, sat on the desk, the wire-cutter blade edge slickly black. Poor man, thought Tetsunari, they had tortured him and when satisfied had killed him with what looked like a matching letter opener pushed down into his ear canal.

"Boss."

"On the way." Answered Jake, as he quickly crossed the dozen steps to the office door. Jake entered and walked straight over to the desk.

"Oh for fuck's sake. Ugh. The poor bastard. Right I'm ringing the police now." He took out his phone and was about to begin dialling when there was a whistle from the front door that took him back into the hallway.

Tetsunari snatched the second letter opener from the corpse of Ashuff and turned to join his boss in the hall.

"Bad guys coming from the road. Four of them, must be the buggers that were tagging us. They're armed, I can see barrels poking out from the hem of their robes."

Recalling the few seconds it took him to adjust his eyes to the gloom Tetsunari wondered if there was a slight advantage to be had.

"Are they together Andy?"

"No, two up and two hanging back. One of them is watching the road with his weapon hidden, the other closer."

"OK. I will kill both of the closest with these letter openers from here. As they fall, drag them in and get their weapons."

If Tetsunari said he would kill them with the letter openers then that was what was going to happen decided Jake and Andy simultaneously. They stood either side of the small porchway waiting for the door to open again.

Tetsunari stood four square to the doorway in plain view of anyone entering, but only once their eyes had adjusted.

The door opened a crack, then there was a pause, a Keffiyeh covered head quickly poked around and then withdrew. Then the door was pushed open and two men, one behind the other, stepped in with the first holding his rifle before him.

Tetsunari threw. The blade flew through the air with hardly a discernible sound and buried itself in the chest of the leader. Without even a gurgle he began to crumple to the ground, a heart shot. The second man had heard and seen nothing but suddenly his partner appeared to be crouching down.

He leaned over him.

"Abu what are you doing you fool, move on we can't stay here." His Arabic was understandable to all three of them. He took hold of his partner's shoulders and shook him. Then watched in disbelief as he slowly slumped forward. The man stood suddenly alarmed and began reaching for the AK47 slung over his shoulder. Thud. The second letter opener arrived and Andy closely followed by Jake grabbed a body and yanked them inside whilst pushing the door to; hoping those outside would not see them.

They retrieved the pair of AK47s, inspected their condition then checked the magazines. Andy noted these were really old rifles without the slanted muzzle break, the stocks were worn like old mahogany.

"Stick it on single shot Jake." Andy said adjusting his own rate selector. "And don't forget it will climb up and to the left if you repeatedly press the trigger."

Tetsunari calmly retrieved the two letter openers, wiped them on their victims and stood to the side looking out the front window to observe the remaining attackers.

"Now what?" Said Jake. "The other two won't wait long before coming to investigate."

Andy Evans pulled the Keffiyeh from one of the dead men, sniffed it, wrinkled his nose and then looked down at the owner. Nope, nothing like me, but in shadow……

He pulled on the headdress then tore the sleeve from one of the white robes and pulled it up his arm.

"Right, get ready. I'll open the door, signal them to come in then close it again. Same game Tettas?"

Tetsunari grimaced at his truncated name, he usually only allowed Winston to call him that, but Winston was still not fit for work. After the Caribbean beating Winston had needed three operations on his legs so far. He missed him.

Tetsunari simply nodded and went to stand back where he'd been before.

"Right. Here goes."

Andy pulled the door open slightly put his head in view, hissed then used the sleeved arm to beckon. The nearest bad guy just looked and shrugged. Andy hissed again and beckoned again then closed the door. The reluctant adversary shrugged again in a way more eloquent than words, threw his hands up in the air then walked towards the door muttering loudly, this was clearly not part of the agreed plan.

Once again the door opened and a figure outlined himself by the door. This time there wasn't any whispering just a loud mouthful of unrecognisable guttural Arabic. The robed figure walked in closed the door loudly behind him and again raised his voice whilst gesticulating with the arm not carrying the now slung AK. Tetsunari's blade flew through the air once more, this time it took the target in the throat and he sank to his knees gurgling until Andy Evans appeared and pushed the blade in further, whilst wiggling it about.

"Die you twat." He muttered impatiently.

One left.

"We going to try again?" Asked Jake.

Andy Evans sighed.

"No boss, the best thing to do now is to all of us pick up an AK then go stand outside the front. He'll shit himself and run off. Then we can get the fuck out of here in the opposite direction and let the coppers try to work out what happened after we're gone. Like we were never here. The last bandit ain't going to be complaining about his mates is he?"

Jake thought for a second or two. Part of him wanted to leave at warp speed in any direction to get away from this charnel house, but Ashuff and his receptionist deserved better. The problem was it could take days or even weeks to establish the facts of what happened, then the grind through courts, possibly. But if they left now there would only be the driver of the car who knew that there'd ever been anyone intending to visit Ashuff. He thought it unlikely that the driver would want to get involved with the police. He marched over to the reception desk and swivelled the diary. His appointment was in there for this afternoon but nothing afterwards. Without hesitation he picked up the book stuck it in his hand luggage and turned back to the others.

"OK, I hate to leave this sort of shit behind but I agree with you, Andy we should get the fuck out of here and….wait a minute. What if…" He paused again.

"We could leave and then go to 'The Melting Pot' for a meal as we had planned, what could be more natural? If we lock the door on the way out clean our prints off and if asked we could say we were unable to make contact with Ashuff by phone or knocking on the door and left. We'd have to be the world's most daring or stupid murderers to then go on down the road and sit in a restaurant wouldn't we?" The flight's not until 22:40, we only need be there an hour or so earlier. Additionally, the driver is a witness that we were at the restaurant as planned. Clearly *he* wouldn't, and no one else *would* expect us to remain close by the scene of a murder we'd just committed. What could be more natural? We could even make sure something is overheard by the restaurant staff and tip hugely, they always remember the big tippers!"

Andy and Tetsunari looked at each other and nodded. The boss was making sense. To flee would not be the smartest move.

"OK boss, let's go do the 'Gunfight at the OK Corral' bit then."

They looked out on to the street. No movement, just the last bandit leaning against a tree watching the road and occasionally turning their way. Andy led the way quickly walking out of the door and standing to the left. Tetsunari was next walking to the right and Jake followed standing in the middle. Unsurprisingly the last bandit just did a runner as predicted.

Jake went back in, collected the AKs, wiped them and laid them next to their owners while Andy made their hands grip the weapons and then left them. They all walked out. Jake now locked the door wiping the handle with a hanky he then twisted the key in the lock and put it in his pocket. It would magically disappear before they got to the airport.

Then swiftly, but not hurriedly, they returned to the road and carried on down it towards 'The Melting Pot', and according to Crause, the finest camel steaks in Djibouti.

An hour and a half later the driver arrived at the restaurant to collect them. They'd heard no police sirens or any indication of alarm. Jake had explained in his near perfect French that their meeting with Monsieur Ashuff had not happened. He had then embellished the story a little but stuck closely to the chain of events, obviously leaving out the fate of the three bandits.

"Anyway," he said by way of explanation, "the restaurant had come highly recommended by one of my men so I was pleased at least that part of the afternoon had gone to plan."

With much nodding, bowing and declarations of enjoyment along with a huge tip and promises to return, they were ushered into the car for the journey to the airport.

As they sat in the otherwise empty Air France business class, relaxing with a drink and some nibbles, Andy suddenly cracked out laughing. Tetsunari and Jake both turned to stare.

Andy composed himself for a second or two.

"Sorry, but the look on the last bandit's face, it was classic, worth a mint. There he is watching the road then he glances back and there are three armed guys standing in front of the door. He looks back at the road not registering then Bam! His head spins back at warp speed to look at us. Like a Tom and Jerry moment, eyes out on stalks etcetera, then he's gone and all you can hear is the sound of his slapping sandals."

Jake joined in with the laughter and even Tetsunari raised an eyebrow which was as close to a smile as the others had ever seen.

Mid-September. Hood, Indian Ocean, Maliku Kandu channel,
aka Eight Degree Channel

After Jake had returned to London, the agreement with the Lloyds Names had been signed without any hesitation. Of course there had been the slightly awkward moment when he was asked what happened in the Straits of Hormuz. By this time, having repeated the story many times, he was somewhat brisk in the retelling but as things had seemed to quieten down on the international stage it was a brief summary.

With the contract in the bag Jake now actioned all the dockyard requests and sent signals to his vessels. Bismarck would complete her refit then sail to the Comoros to take over from Hood, and both Hood and Ocean Guard would then make their way to Labuan for their refit. Meanwhile he returned to the Little Cayman and managed to get some time with his family and had even successfully prised Andrew McTeal out of his self-imposed prison for a couple of days.

From his office he checked the AIS position for all of his ships using the coded lettering only available to him, now he was near content. Hood would take another week and a bit to get to Labuan and Ocean Guard should arrive the day before them.

*

Lt Alfio Bianchi, Hood's senior OPs Officer, looked over the shoulder of PO OPs, 'Ringbolt' Langford. They were studying a recent 'racket' or electronic transmission. This was the third time they'd picked it up and it was clearly from a system heading in their direction. The advanced CMS or Combat Management System, which looked after the entire multitude of data inputs for the Sea Giraffe radar, had a databank which compared and contrasted signals with known sources. It was unendingly added to as new signals were either identified or remained unclassified but archived. Periodically each of Jake's ships would upload their latest database extract and download the contributions of the other ships. At the moment their only radar emission was in the single frequency navigation mode. The other 'emitter', clearly airborne, would note that too, *if* it was as they thought, a military platform.

At the moment Hood was cruising along at seven knots through the wide channel which separated the Maldives from the southernmost atolls belonging to India. It was a peaceful part of the planet very little in the way of disputes but the Indians were very keen to prevent non-official traffic between Minicoy, the southernmost Indian island and Thuraakunu, the northernmost part of the Maldives, despite the ethnic ties between the two. So there were likely to be occasional sea and air patrols. Hood had a drone up at the moment and it had just sent back images of Minicoy and its lighthouse, then the 'racket' had begun.

Whatever it was, this radar 'racket' was flicking through frequencies and scanning for very short periods; the topics of discussion were twofold. Did it have them as a contact or were they just a 'racket' to it as well? Given that the signal was getting stronger it was likely that it would have them as a small fishing boat sized contact before long even if it hadn't now. The Nav mode on the Sea Giraffe had an emulator so they could appear to be something they were not. At the moment they were emulating a Furuno DRS12A, a navigation radar fitted to small and medium merchant vessels around the world. In other words innocuous.

Both men were also aware that Hood was more visible than usual because some of the anti-radar paint on the funnels was being replaced. It was clear that at high speed in the tropics, the temperature on the outside of the twin funnels was a little too much for the existing paint so Lt Louis Braime, recently promoted after his Bismarck escapades, had requested that the existing paint be stripped, and replaced. Since each gas turbine effectively had its own funnel, he was in the process of shutting down each one in sequence, replacing the paint and at the same time adding an extra level of copper cooling units inside the base of the funnels to try to bring down the exhaust temperature further. He was pretty certain there was sufficient room but only actually fitting them would reveal the truth of the matter. It was something the design crew were going to have to look at back on Little Cayman, the same thing but not to the same degree had happened on Bismarck when she was in action in the Caribbean. So in times of need they started to lose their stealthiness, which wasn't a good idea.

With the analysis complete both men arrived at the conclusion that this was a military transmission, possibly one of the Indian AWAACS. It had an Israeli AESA radar sat on top of an Llyushin 76, heavy lifter body. It was reckoned to be a pretty advanced system too.

They were in international waters approximately 30 miles south of the nearest land mass so it wasn't as if there was any territorial issue. The 'racket' was now close enough to get a good return on Hood and they could roughly estimate that it was within one hundred miles, very tricky with that frequency hopping AESA radar and without another platform to triangulate it.

The racket now turned parallel to them and over the next ten minutes it became apparent that it was in racetrack mode performing figure of eights in the sky.

Time to tell the Captain.

Roby wasn't unduly concerned and just told them to maintain a watch on the assumed Indian AWAACS movements and ordered the drone chief to change the patrol station of the 'up' drone. He was naturally a cautious man.

He spoke into his mike.

"Drone control." Click.

"Drone control Aye." Answered the drone number two operator, Steve Hayward.

"Move your 'up' bird to cover our northern flank and prep a second bird please, recon package, use it to scan ahead. How long left for bird one?"

"Wait one." A pause. "Seventy five minutes Sir."

"Fine keep them rotating until further notice."

"Aye Sir."

Roby paid a visit to the bridge and spoke to Kiwi McClean who was on watch, had a quick scan around with one of the bridge viewers, then headed back down to his cabin.

"Chief Engineer." Click.

"Captain?" Came the somewhat out of breath answer.

"Awkward moment Chief?"

"Not really Sir, the copper fins in this cooling unit needed a bit of extra plumbing in is all; a bloody awkward space to get to." He knew what his Captain wanted to know. "Aft funnel is painted and drying, nearly finished the copper work, I estimate half an hour max before we switch over. We've done a little maintenance while number two was down which will save time later. It will be another four hours before number one funnel is finished, less if we have an extra body or two to help with the painting."

"I'll speak to number one and get a couple of spare hands rigged up with sprayers or rollers if necessary. Good work Chief."

Braime closed the connection and sighed. He'd spent half his working life getting to be a Chief 'Tiffy' or Chief Petty Officer Artificer, then when I get promoted to Lieutenant everyone calls me Chief again…..

Roby headed for his cabin and the pile of technical data on his desk. Jake had been as good as his word when he got back to the island, and had the boffins send the schematics for the ROV that would be fitted when they got to Labuan drydock. The only real drawback he'd seen so far was that it would still be attached to Hood by an umbilical cord which would carry the data back to the ship and supplement the power needed when the Laser was in use. Apparently there was just no way around it given the wattage needed to pump out enough laser energy, despite using near indigo spectrum lasers. Even then it was likely to be limited, depending on turbidity, to around a one kilometre range. He sighed, wondering how long the umbilicus would be. A one K range was so near they could practically throw stones at any submarine which got that close. Still, it will be fine for finding sunken ships which is what it is really for, I suppose.

He had the desire, a legacy from being just a target so many times, to have the ability to spot a submarine before it spotted him. Not for a while yet, he decided.

Reading through the specs for the package which would be attached to the underbelly of the drones, he perked up a bit. It seemed highly likely that they would pick up the thermal disturbance of a submarine wake at depths up to and including a thousand feet. Basically shallow water for submarines, but pretty normal when operating in large parts of the SCS. They would also spot large metallic objects, rather like a posh MAD he decided, thinking back to the days when everyone had had such high hopes for Magnetic Anomaly Detectors when searching for submarines. With this it was something to do with the type of return such lasers received from large ferrous objects not magnetism of course, but same effect really.

"OPs, Captain." Came the crisp voice of Lt Bianchi.

"Sir the drone has detected an Indian naval vessel approaching on what appears an intercept course. Must have been directed by that AWAACS earlier, in my opinion. We have had a 'racket from that direction, two in fact. We believe the ship is communicating with a helicopter. The ship has been identified as a *Saryu* class patrol vessel. One 76mm and two AK630 CIWS plus one helicopter a Druv 3, possibly armed with rockets or anti-ship missiles and or a 20mm chin gun."

Roby thought for a second.

"Right, go active with the full array. Let's see what's out there. I'll be along in a minute."

Roby made his way to the OPs room in less than a minute and took his command chair. The full CMS picture had the helicopter at forty miles on a near intercept course, with the ship about fifteen miles behind. The Bogey will have visual on us in a couple of minutes he estimated, that'll be a surprise for them. They would have been expecting a merchie and intending a simple customs check to make sure it wasn't smuggling, he surmised.

He continued watching his own screens.

You could tell when the Druv spotted them. First there was a change of course to a more gentle closing angle, then a series of radio transmissions.

About five minutes later there was a call on channel 16 from the helicopter which had closed to a range of about three miles by then.

They wanted an ID. Langford answered with the ship's phonetic id and asked the same, the response was a little unclear but sounded like the phonetic for *Sunayna* but it was difficult to be sure. Then there was a pause of a minute or so.

The next bit was a bit of a surprise for all concerned. The Sunayna ordered them to heave to and stand by to be boarded as part of a customs inspection.

Roby nearly choked on his coffee. "What the hell?"

"Langford, ask for Captain to Captain and put it through."

"Aye aye Sir. Then he nodded as the link was made.

"This is Jon Roby, Master of the Caymans ship Hood, how can I help you?"

"Captain you will please heave-to and prepare to accept a boarding party, we have much smuggling in this area and need to check your ship."

"Sorry Captain, I can't do that for several reasons, mostly because we are in international waters and actually secondly because simply I don't actually want to."

"This water is Indian economic zone, all activity in this water is controlled by Indian government. You will comply."

"We are not engaged in any commercial activity, we are merely in transit. You have no authority to interfere with a vessel in international waters. However if you wish to come aboard for a cup of tea and a guided tour, you will be welcome."

"Captain you must comply with my lawful instructions or there may be consequences."

Roby, paused for a second a deep frown on his normally affable face. This guy was just being a jobsworth and fast becoming a pain.

"Captain, your instructions are not lawful, you have no right to stop, search or board my vessel, and the only consequences will be directed at yourself if you persist. You must know this is an **armed** Merchant Protector vessel and all that entails. I repeat my invitation, come aboard for a cup of tea and a chat."

By this time the *Sunayna* itself was just visible from the bridge and was duly reported as such over the command open line.   Next second everything changed as the *Sunayna* fired a warning shot over Hood's bow.

"Persistent bugger isn't he?" Roby addressed the OPs room in general while he watched through a viewer as the column of water fall back into the sea.

He switched back to the open channel.

"It was unwarranted for you to fire a warning shot Sir, I will not reply in kind because to do so would reduce me to your level. However I must warn you that if you do fire **at** my ship, I will authorise a response."

He switched to on-board comms and the open command line.

"Sound action stations please Mr Kopf. Mr McClean, are you in your eyrie?"

"Yes Sir."

"Right, if this pillock does fire at us I want you to march four main battery shells 100 yards in front of him, another four 100 yards off his starboard side in a line and four more 100 yards to his stern. No hits, understand? His popgun can't hurt us so we'll be more patient than he deserves."

"Yes Sir, four in front, four down his side and four astern, all in line. Aye, aye Sir."

McClean grinned while he began programming the shoot; the Hood's fire control system would find this an easy task he thought, waste of bloody ammo though.

The helicopter had taken station astern of Hood, hovering at about 500 feet a mere three hundred yards astern.

Roby noted the helicopter.

"Langford. Program the aftermost AK630s to follow every movement that chopper makes, that should unnerve him a bit. McClean, you may train the main battery." That should be visible too, Roby thought as he tried to avoid yet another diplomatic incident. For fuck's sake, why don't people leave us alone he groaned inwardly. The eight slim barrels of the 5.1 inch guns rose and trained to port, tracking the target which had closed to six miles.

Nothing happened for another five minutes, ESM picked up more transmissions, probably doing an ET, thought Roby, phoning home to see what the boss wanted. Be a bit over his pay grade to actually open fire on another ship in these circumstances especially when he was suicidally out gunned. We might expect a visit from aircraft though if they get really uppity, was his grim thought.

"Captain, Chief here. We've completed cooling additions on both funnels and the paint is just drying out on the forward funnel. So we are ready whenever you are Sir."

"A timely intervention Chief. Give me the Steerpod equivalent of revolutions for twenty eight knots please."

"Already Sir?"

"Yes Chief, we have a silly situation here which could be remedied simply by being somewhere else." He was looking at details of *Sunayna* on his computer app of Jane's Fighting ships. She could only do 25 knots. And the copter wouldn't be able to stay up forever. Now that the AWAACS had done his thing he'd left so it was just the three of them.

"Well when you put it like that Sir, I can only say the paint will dry quicker."

Hood accelerated like the thoroughbred she was and there was swiftly a great white moustache at her bow as she came up to speed, with a good seven or eight knots in hand if needed. One last call to the Indian skipper.

"I'll leave now, repairs are complete. But that wasn't very friendly and it was utterly unnecessary. Bad manners in fact."

"Hood Captain, it was bad manners of your boss to criticise India regarding the criminals that were held in Chennai. We will meet again."

"So that's what this is all about. You keep innocent people under lock and key for years with some sort of sham trial on very dodgy grounds and you think I'm being impolite? Well if we do meet again, I caution you against firing at ships which could sink you in less than a minute if they were so inclined Sir. It isn't very prudent. Goodbye." He disconnected without waiting for a response.

"Secure active radar. Remain at this speed for ten more minutes then slow to twenty five knots and then after thirty minutes resume 'high cruising' and stand down from action stations. I'm going back to my cabin." He announced to the OPs room at large.

Silly buggers, he thought as he marched back along the corridor, I can do without that sort of foolishness. With roughly three and a half thousand miles to cover before we get to the dockyard, I wonder how many other pillocks I am going to run across? Best call Jake and let him know the Indians didn't appreciate his support for the Chennai six.

*

Jake switched off the video call and sat back in his chair. He was at the house on Little Cayman, still hosting the Prime Minister and still enjoying his family time. The Indians were being foolishly peevish, but since they'd been being foolishly peevish about the Chennai six anyway, then at least they were being consistent.

His phone vibrated. The security detail. Now what did they want?

"König."

"Sir we have a game fishing boat entering the harbour. We've waved them off several times but they just keep coming. He's heading for the jetty nearest security anyway Sir. There's a white guy up on the top deck waving a hat to all and sundry like he's some sort of Pope."

"OK. I'm on my way down there anyway. Detain but no violence. Search the boat with caution and identify the intruders."

"Will do Sir."

Jake was more bemused than worried, they'd had several visitors in the three years since the base's construction, usually out of fuel or needing something, utterly unaware of the high powered hardware watching their every move.

He jumped into the golf cart and made his way to the jetty, in the distance he could hear raucous laughter from the tennis courts where James and Helen were taking on Andrew McTeal and Sophie. It was nice having his family around him again and nice too to get Andrew some much needed R&R. The three man MPP security detail he'd brought with him could almost relax too. They were on an island this end of which was about as secure as it could get, since Jake's own security were watching everything and making sure everyone was safe.

He stopped the cart next to the security office on the dockside and walked in hearing a familiar voice as he did so.

"Miles Carlson, as I live and breathe. What the hell are you doing gate crashing the party? You'd be welcome through the front door!"

"Hey Jake long Story." Said a smiling Miles Carlson, former US based senior CIA Operations Officer, now currently serving out the last few months of his banishment to the Far East.

"You got somewhere private we can have a chat? No offence guys." He added gesturing to his former captors.

"Who's on the boat Miles?"

"Just a local guy, he's OK, I use him when I'm this side of the world."

"Right." Answered Jake taking in the crewman laid on cushions in the stern with what looked like a newspaper over his head.

He indicated the golf cart and they both got in.

"OK, my friend, happy as I am to see you, I'm not foolish enough to think this is a social call."

"Just on vacation Jake, you know I like game fishing, used to come here a lot before I was sent to the Far Eastern Alcatraz."

"Try that on the local cops Miles, this is me you're talking to."

"OK, OK. Pour me some of that Lagavulin and I'll tell you anything."

Jake laughed out loud as they pulled up at the main house.

"Ah it pleases me to convert heathens and take them away from that dreadful Jack Daniels petrol that most Americans seem to think is whiskey."

Once in Jake's study Miles brought out a small piece of electronic gadgetry and wandered around the room fixedly staring at a digital display of some kind while Jake sat there sipping his Lagavulin with a bemused smile.

"God you're just like one of those Hollywood spies or something. Miles, you know very well Andy Evans has this place swept every other day and every time after visitors of any kind."

"Yeah, yeah. Man's got be sure for himself. Not many people I'd trust as far as I could throw them after half a bottle of this stuff."

He sipped appreciatively at his own glass while intently studying the screen on his device. Then he snapped the cover closed and with a big smile sat down opposite Jake.

"You guys could be headed into someone else's war again Jake."

"Really? How come Miles?" Jake was rapidly sifting through possibilities. It had to be Far East for Miles to be interested, so that ruled out Nigeria and Mozambique but left the Philippines and South China Sea in the frame.

"You guys picked up a contract with some Lloyds Names. Search for traces of twelve ships listed as missing etcetera. All in the SCS, all in a disputed area. You're sending two of your ships to have a poke around."

"Well informed as usual. I hope the leaky end is in London and not my end."

"Sure. You're hot news again after you kicked the shit out of those Iranians when they tried to dice and slice you. I have news items mentioning you and your company flagged on the system discretely so I get a look at what you're up to."

Then he turned serious, like a light switching on and off, thought Jake.

"Some serious shit going down in the SCS at the moment and that's in addition to the missing ships and there's the highest concentration in the world of high quality SSKs out there."

"I know, Simon was batting on about them not long ago."

"Well just to be sure, there's sixteen Improved Kilos able to access that little pond, so that makes it the valley of death to surface ships. You know about the USS Nathan Allen incident a week and a half ago, right?"

Jake nodded, marvelling at the way Carlson dispensed information in discrete packages.

"Only the basics. She was doing one of your freedom of the seas parades through an area the Chinese 'think' is within their territorial waters and the Chinese launched half a dozen anti-ship missiles at it from one of their 'new' islands, having repeatedly warned her off."

"Yeah that about sums it up for the Allen. They shot down all but one and it impacted near the hangers causing a big fire, killing seven and injuring twelve. She responded with six TLAMs wiping out that battery, and two others. No idea what the Chinese casualties were because they aren't saying. But as you can guess the shit has hit the fan in major quantities and it is still simmering out there. Now between you and me there will be other examples of us exercising our right of freedom of navigation in the near future. So it could get pretty hairy out there. Don't think it will escalate beyond local but you never know."

"That's all Miles? You could have put that on a post card and sent it me."

"Yeah I know. There's some other shit going down but truly I ain't sure what yet. The local boys are so puzzled they've scratched their bald heads raw. It probably has something to do with your missing ships too. There's something real smelly about this whole thing. I know it's my job to be paranoid but even I'm feeling paranoid about this. We're going around second guessing our second guesses at the moment, there's just something that don't add up. Could be there's another player in the game we don't know about yet. But when I go add the figures up it either comes to 101 or 99. It should be 100, no variances."

He passed Jake a business card bearing an innocuous sounding company name and a telephone number.

"That goes through about 97 cut outs and filters and God knows what else but if you get anything you can't work out or any of your boys do find something interesting, let me know using that number. It may just be you uncover something none of the rest of us has yet. When that something is added to what we know, it might just get us a glimpse of what the fuck is happening in time to do some clever shit and stop it dead."

Jake turned the card over, blank; then put it in his trouser pocket, there was a thoughtful expression on his face.

"That's the lot now? Do I need to whistle up a few of Andy's heavies and squeeze you a bit? Or have you actually delivered the entire message this time?" Jake was alluding to Miles Carlson's interventions in the Caribbean.

"Ouch. You don't play fair. Truly that's all we have at the moment." He said, lying with his most honest face.

"If there was anything else I'd tell you. Come on Jake you know I can't always be 100% up front but I'm telling you the truth, we don't know what's going on."

Jake smiled. He should have been a politician, the choice of words meant that there could be more information but he wasn't going to let it slip, however the only 'truth' bit was that they don't know what's going down.

"OK Miles. No worries. I'll pass this on through Andy and his boys so that anyone with a big question mark will filter it through me. And I, if I think I need to, will let you know. Now that the business is over, why don't you come and meet everyone else, they're over on the tennis courts. Andrew McTeal is here too."

"Love to but I've got a hot date with a lady Marlin, besides that McTeal fella can see through me like I'm transparent, makes me nervous not having secrets."

"OK Miles. Thanks for the heads up on this. I'll drive you back down to the jetty."

"Great. Give my best to the others, better still don't. Maybe I wasn't here after all." He added with a laugh.

Jake dropped him off at the jetty and watched as he kicked the deck shoes of his "Skipper" who languidly sat up and stretched before walking to the flying bridge. Two of Jake's men stood by with the mooring lines whilst Miles, showing an agility which belied his increasing girth, first took in the stern line then scurried forward to accept the bow line as the big diesels chugged astern until well clear of the jetty. It then turned nimbly with the stern digging in as the big engines went to full power propelling it forward with a roar before swerving past the two moles and out into the Caribbean proper.

Jake watched the diminishing boat thoughtfully for a moment or two before climbing back into the golf cart and returning to his house part way up the hill. As he parked up he heard again the sounds of his family having fun and mentally cursed the timing of Miles' visit. He had so wanted to spend time with them, but now he needed to sit still for a few minutes and rewind what Miles had said – literally. Jake had installed a recording device as part of the process of setting up his office. Years of naval and business discussions had taught him that people very often forget or fail to take in, huge amounts of information because partway through a dialogue they pick up on and fixate over a particular point. When this happens the next few pieces of information are just not hoisted in. So having too much to lose nowadays, he recorded everything in order to pick up on these often innocuous but sometimes devastatingly important tit bits of information.

The reason Miles's fancy device did not pick it up was simply that it was not 'power connected' at that point. Only when Jake sat down having poured the whiskey, did he push the button which engaged the power adapter thus activating the device. The device itself was simply voice activated when it had power.

Now he sat listening to Miles, looking for what wasn't said as well as what was hidden in plain sight. That was the thing about spooks, they couldn't say 'hello' without putting more than one word into it along with a thousand meanings.

He didn't spot anything that he hadn't already cottoned on to, but there was that niggle in the back of his mind that he'd missed something important. In the background and beyond his attention the tennis game came to a riotous finish and the protagonists made their way back for some well-earned refreshments. Jake stared at the wall, the clock ticking away unnoticed as he tried to grasp what may not even be there.

With a frustrated sigh he mentally put the problem to bed resolving to get Andy Evans' opinion on it, and went out to see what the result of the tennis tournament was.

He made a voice note to push the boffins for some more data on their underwater object detection software or UODS for short. It apparently showed some serious promise. With the hardware in place very soon, it would be down to the tweaking and manipulation of this software as to whether they turned up anything or nothing.

He was about to get up and join his family when he brushed across a letter waiting for his signature. He read it again. It was to the Police Service in Djibouti, they were inquiring into the events that led up to the death of Mrs & Mrs Ashuff on or about the 9th of September. Could he shed any light on the subject and would he and his companions be prepared to offer up witness statements and answer any questions raised?

Jake had written a statement covering the main points of the day, obviously leaving out that they had entered the building. He included reference to several telephone calls he'd made trying to contact Mr Ashuff, they would of course be verified as not having been answered, and that he was sincerely sorry that they had not arrived sooner since it is clear now that the crime had already been committed by the time they knocked on his door. No harm in stating the obvious.

Jake put his reply down, he had been greatly saddened to learn that Ashuff had a son of fifteen who was now clearly an orphan. In duty to the dead man who had been a very efficient Agent over the years, he had paid from his own accounts into a trust fund set up for the boy's education. He had also engaged a local solicitor for this to be properly administered. There was nothing at all to be gained by explaining what really happened, Ashuff was dead and that was all there was to It.

He reflected that Jon Roby's generosity in not killing all of the pirates on that one occasion, and also showing them the ship that had killed the rest, may well have contributed greatly to the attack in Djibouti and Ashuff's death. He wouldn't tell Jonno though, he'd be mortified.

The last thing he did before joining the family was to instruct his cyber team manager to penetrate the Malaysian Immigration Department and when the ships had left Labuan, to delete the passport details. He didn't want anyone at a later date paying some baksheesh to get his men's identity from some lowly immigration clerk. He had absolutely no qualms about doing this, it was after all, for the benefit of the men who worked for him, and he'd run barefoot over broken glass for his crews.

Labuan Island, Malaysia, Late September

The Malaysia Airlines flight from Kuala Lumpur touched down on time and taxied in. Piet Magrun, Chief Engineer for the ROV project stood up and stretched his large frame. He and the twelve others in the team made their way to the luggage carousel and did what everyone worldwide does. They stared fixedly at a hole in the wall. The yellow beacon light came on after five minutes or so, the conveyor belt started and the fixed staring became more intense. There were some expensive but not delicate tools in some of the luggage and if they didn't all arrive there was a possibility of delay while replacements were found.

The big South African turned as a shadow fell across him and his even bigger Zulu deputy stood beside him.

"Christ man, I thought the bladdy sun had set then."

Ayize Mopantokobogo smiled at the jest revealing a large number of slab like white teeth, and he rumbled a response.

"How's the 'bwana' like the heat here? Bit cool for my liking."

He looked down on the six foot six white South African who was clearly not liking the humidity.

"I'll fucking melt soon, how is it not affecting you for fuck's sake? We come from the same place!" Piet looked like someone had thrown a bucket of water over him.

Ayize gave out another rumbling laugh which had nearby Malaysians looking around worriedly. Compared to them he *was* a giant at seven feet four inches, heavily muscled and ebony coloured he was every bit the dictionary definition of a giant.

"It's because I'm black man. We're just naturally cool."

Piet laughed and then spotted their bags emerging from the hole in the wall.

"Well if you're so fucking cool grab them, I reckon if I move I'll be straight on my arse since I'm standing in a puddle *of* myself. Bladdy place, like being in a bladdy bath all the time."

Ayize Laughed again, like rumbling summer thunder, and casually leaned over the two Malaysians in front, said 'S'cuse' with that deep rumbling voice and plucked the two heavy bags straight upwards and over the top of the terrified couple.

"Come on you melting white fart, hold my hand in case you slip."

"Fuck off you big ape, stop blocking the sun, I need to dry out."

The pair, long-time friends, ribbed each other unmercifully as they made their way to immigration, a gaggle of somewhat smaller engineers and technicians trailing them. No one would have guessed they'd been to the same university and studied marine engineering together years before. Piet had got Ayize an interview when he had begun work for König Marine, because Ayize was damned good and he needed someone he could trust. Sometimes they ended up in some pretty shitty places and having him there meant no one with anything resembling a brain would fuck with them. Then there was the fact that Ayize was able to straight lift weights that normally needed a block and tackle or a small crane. He also had a fantastic insight into the art of marine engineering and what one didn't know the other usually did and gleefully announced it. They were an unlikely pair but the very best of friends.

A Mini bus was waiting for them when they got out into the collection area, along with König's local agent a wiry little man with a big beaming smile. He's only smiling thought Piet, because of the wad this little excursion will pay him. He grunted as he passed his bag into the back of the bus and took his place beside the driver. If everything goes well then he didn't care that the guy got plenty of money for his service, but if things weren't up to scratch the little runt had better standby, he thought, as he mopped his forehead with a soaking handkerchief and directed the vents for the aircon, including the driver's, straight at himself. He was already stuck to the plastic seat. Fucking place. It also smelled like a Rhino's backside, worse in fact, maybe a Hyena's.

They arrived at the LSE yards where the agent, Piet and Ayize got out. The others headed to the hotel for a shower and a bit of downtime. Work was due to start on preparing the ROVs next day, Ocean Guard should arrive the day after and then Hood two days after that, well that was the plan anyway.

The Agent marched importantly into the LSE yard manager's office and proceeded to spout out what both Piet and Ayize heard as a torrent of unintelligible gibberish. It seemed to do the job though because the tiny Malay secretary seemed to vertically launch herself from the chair and fly into the main man's office without apparently touching the floor. Piet and Ayize looked at each other with raised eyebrows, but said nothing.

More 'Warp 9' gabbling but in a deeper voice and the yard manager himself emerged from his office and waved them inside. The agent now acted as interpreter as first introductions were made, then formalities exchanged before the offer of refreshments. Finally Piet got to ask whether the ROVs had arrived yet as well as the other equipment needed for installation. The agent whose name sounded like Witch-it Somkand, and was they later discovered, a Thai not a Malay, received the manager's reply and informed them that the boxes had arrived and had been passed through customs but were still at the airport waiting collection.

Piet bit back on a 'What fucking use are they over there' and asked when they'd be delivered to the yard for inspection by the team. The answer seemed to puzzle the agent so Piet took charge.

"Tell him I want them here today and I will personally inspect them when they arrive. Tell him not too late because we want to be up early and start work on systems testing."

Ayize chipped in before he could translate the request. He leaned over the desk just a little and his voice rumbled, the water in the glass on the desk seemed to ripple when he spoke.

"Tell him the boss gets antsy, irritated, if things aren't how he likes them, then he asks me to sort it."

The yard manager was staring at Ayize and oscillating between awe and terror. The translation occurred and the yard manager gulped and immediately summoned the flying secretary and issued a series of instructions.

Wichit Somkand smiled and looked up at Ayize shyly.

"You have a great influence on the decision to immediately dispatch two lorries to collect the boxes Sir."

Ayize reached out one massive shovel like hand to the yard manager's proffered hand and gently squeezed it.

"Thank you. We'll go to the hotel now."

The yard manager just nodded several times and gulped again.

"Wichit, that was good work man." Added Piet, when they were outside again. "You OK for an early start tomorrow? We need to check out our gear before the ships arrive and the sooner we start the sooner we finish."

"I am fine Mr Piet. The yard manager has ordered his own car and driver to take us to the hotel. Tomorrow I will arrive with the minibus at whatever time you tell me. Mr König told me to spare nothing in assisting you."

Wichit sat in the front seat next to the driver of the Toyota Avensis as it cruised the mile or so to the hotel. He had been awed when both Ayize and Piet sat in the back of the large saloon car and the front lifted noticeably along with the rear sinking closer to the ground. He just hoped there were no bumps on the way as Ayize had had to bend his neck to the right and almost put his head on his knees just to get everything in the car and he didn't want to think about this now friendly giant, with a sore neck and head. Being on the same side as him made Wichit feel very safe and secure for some reason.

The Dorsett Grand Labuan was on the opposite side of the river to the yard. A big hotel run along traditional lines it was clean, airy and the rooms were large and well appointed. Piet and Ayize had adjacent suites on the fifth floor, with the rest of the team all on the floor below them. Ayize as deputy, didn't want to be herding team members from too many different floors, not that anyone would be silly enough to oversleep.

Piet stepped on to his balcony which overlooked the wide estuary and Victoria Harbour. Almost directly opposite he could see the drydock and slipway areas of the shipyard they'd be working in for the next however long. Hopefully just a week at most, he thought.

"Nice view Piet." Came a familiar rumble from his right.

Without looking over Piet answered.

"See that dockyard. It's very open. Any fucker could just bimble up in a skiff, load up and fuck off. Hope Hood has some security boys with her or they'll pinch anything that's not nailed down."

"You know this how? We haven't been here before." Ayize rumbled in reply.

"Well you remember that bladdy repair job in that Chinese place, what was it called Luoyuan or something?

They nicked everything but the crew. That one where they berthed us next to some rust bucket that we had to walk over to get ashore? Coming back at night after a few beers you needed fucking sonar to find all the fucking holes the bastards had cut in the decks without so much as a fucking warning sign. Talk about near death experience, man what a place."

Ayize let out another rumble before chipping in with his own memory.

"Hah and the stuff floating by in the river fuck me, I expected to see human bodies as well as the animals. Remember the floating fish farms on either side of the channel? Christ what a life those poor buggers must lead. Wonder what they're like in a fucking Typhoon man?"

Piet stood there shaking his head.

"Yeah but you remember why we had to be there man? That fucking idiot who cut the hole into a fuel bunker with a blowtorch has to be the luckiest man alive and not just 'cos his boss didn't kill him. When he cut through that bulkhead, straight into an empty fuel bunker, fuck, the Captain said they'd heard the bang over in the dockyard where he was talking to their agent."

Ayize stood looking over at the dockyard too remembering. It had taken two weeks to do the inspection and repairs before the ship could leave. Then it sailed straight to Singapore for a refit.

"Yeah I remember, the crew guys were real spooked. After that they had someone with a torque wrench following any of the locals armed with welding gear. Any deviation from the plan and they were to whack them first and ask questions later. What about that other idiot that set himself on fire while we were there? Kneeling on dry rags while he was welding man, wondering why they caught fire? Twice! No fucking welding masks either for fuck's sake, Health and Safety is a menu item on a fucking

Chinese Take-Away out there! Anyway these guys aren't Chinese, they're Malays, you can't say everyone out east is the same."

"Well I'm going to be watching carefully. The boss wants us to check the Steerpod alignments while they're out of the water and the ship's engineers will be doing maintenance on them too."

"Mmm, I'm going for a shower, get changed and get me some food. The smells wafting up here are making me hungry."

"You've got worms you big lunk, you're always eating. I'll join you in a minute, I just want to check in with head office. At least I won't have to search long to find a big lump like you in the restaurant, you better hope they have bigger chairs than that place we stayed in Taiwan that time. Laughed, I nearly shat when you stood up and the chair was stuck to your big black ass!"

"Fuck off white boy; they make 'em big in Zululand. See you downstairs if you can find your way."

*

The arrival of Ocean Guard caused very little interest in Labuan, just one more mid-sized tired and rusty work horse coming in for a refit, exactly as Simon wanted it. They took her into the pre-sunk Synchrolift shiplift and the thirty four hoists lifted her straight up and out of the water on her own railway trolley. Eventually when everything was lined up, the Ocean guard was moved along the slipway like a beached whale. Now the really clever bit began. They then moved her sideways still on her trolley. This would allow Hood to be brought up to the same level, so they could have a pretty secure area to watch over. The nightmare would be controlling access and entry to his ship and the Hood. He wondered what kind of reception she would get.

Jon Roby was thinking much the same thing as his somewhat unusual ship passed slowly by the elephant's graveyard of offshore oil industry rig support vessels. He wondered how long they'd been there and if they were rusting hulks maybe just mothballed waiting for sale or a new oil field to be discovered. There must be fifty or more, he decided, using one of the bridge viewers to point and mark, point and mark. He ran out of time at thirty nine and there were still plenty he hadn't marked, it was somehow sad to see them like this.

Fortunately the approach to the LSE shipyard was almost straight on and took little effort. It was early evening and just dark, all along both shores flashes were going like crazy as people spotted the unusual warship entering the floodlit yard. They quickly manoeuvred into the Synchrolift and were secured, then waited as the process of slowly raising the bed of the lift to meet the ship's hull began and went on and on and on. Fortunately the customs had been ultra-quick, the officer coming on board as soon as the lines to the Synchrolift were secured. All the passports were ready to be presented, each owner available should the Officer wish to see them. It had helped that all the names had been forwarded along with passport details by Head Office. The young man stayed on board until the ship was dry, wandering around the upperdecks, fascinated by both the ship and the lifting and moving process.

The weirdest part Roby thought, was when they were finally moved ashore and then sideways towards Ocean Guard. Simon was standing on his bridge wing watching the process. It had to be the most surreal moment of his life, standing on his own bridge wing, on a four and a half thousand ton ship being moved sideways on its own little railway, towards another ship. He took a few photos for his log.

When the stairs from each ship were in place, rather like airport mobile staircases, Roby descended to the jetty along with Crause, Julius Kopf and Arkady Zotov. They then headed over to the little deputation standing in between the bows of both ships. He thought he was seeing things for a start but standing next to a big boned engineer identified by his white hard hat, had to be the world's biggest and hardest looking black man also wearing a white hat. Roby was no dwarf at six two and Arkady the big Russian security officer was six four but he had to tip his head back to look up into the smiling face as well.

Piet introduced himself as Chief Engineer and Ayize as his deputy to the new arrivals. Having already met Simon and his seniors the day before, he asked them all now to accompany him to the offices where a conference room had been set up for a briefing. It was 04:00 but you wouldn't know by the lights, the noise and the amount of work going on.

"Thank Christ for that." Said Piet as he took his hat off and stood in front of the aircon going full blast. Everyone else was hot too but it seemed the big South African couldn't take the humidity. A beautiful Malay woman bustled in excusing herself repeatedly as she laid out jugs of iced water and then more jugs of iced lemon tea, then left in a flurry of silk and perfume.

The conversation started up again as everyone helped themselves to the very welcome refreshment then it was down to business. Piet activated a PowerPoint presentation on his laptop which detailed what was to happen, who was in charge of various aspects, what arrangements had been made for the crews and what security arrangements he was recommending.

An hour later with the light growing in the east they all filed out and went their respective ways. As they wandered across the dockyard Roby talked to Crause about taking advantage of the docking to clean any weed or muck off the hull and do a careful inspection of the anti-radar paint above the waterline. Arkady was on his radio talking to the section leader of the security team giving him the good news about their extended watches.

Piet yawned and looked at his watch debating whether to curl up on the site manager's sofa for a couple of hours or return to the hotel for a shower, a change and some of the excellent food. The shower and the food trumped everything else but Ayize decided to stay on saying he would leave earlier this evening. It would extend the engineering day that way. Too tired and sweaty to argue Piet went to find the driver of the mini bus and told Ayize he'd be back for ten.

Ayize wandered around the two ships up on their cradles, he was joined after a moment by Arkady who was now wearing all black and discretely armed to the teeth. He'd brought along his Taclite too in case there were any nooks or crannies the floodlights didn't reach.

They walked along in companionable silence for a moment or two before Ayize rumbled a question.

"We haven't worked with the Marine Security boys before, are we expecting any trouble?"

Arkady weighed up his answer carefully before stopping and staring out into the still black waters of Victoria Harbour.

"Merchant Protectors make a lot of friends. But they also make a lot of enemies. Our enemies that live through an encounter, have lots of money, as much as the boss I think." Then he shrugged.

"No Ayize." He said it slowly trying to get the correct inflection. "I am not expecting any but you understand, I am always watching for it *da?*"

Ayize rumbled a short laugh.

"Me too."

131

Then it was Arkady's turn to laugh.

"I think it would take a main battle tank to put your lights out my friend, and then it would be no pushover, I think the English say." He turned and shook hands. "I'll be watching your back so relax, I never lost anyone I was guarding yet." He didn't mention the number of corpses he'd created in order to achieve that record. Besides, he couldn't remember them all now but he didn't regret a single one so far.

*

The work progressed well though there were a few complaints by various members of each ships company as extra space had to be found directly above the ROV docking ports. They needed a cable compartment to stow the four kilometre ultra-fine titanium alloy umbilical cord. This also carried the power feed inside, made from aluminium, copper and gold alloy, as well as the data conduits to return the information and give direction to the ROV. The whole thing was less than a centimetre across.

To people unfamiliar with such things, this cable would seem slim for what it carried. But it was very thick compared to the ultra-fine wires which guided modern torpedoes for instance, and they carried data too. The difference was the power requirement for the ROV to operate the high energy blue laser, this meant that they needed the cable to carry power as well as data. But physics was physics, the 11,000 volt and 30amp current the cable carried to the ROV was changed by step down transformer to become 220 Volts and 1500 Amps for the laser in the ROV. When Louis Braime, Chief Engineer on Hood had looked at the figures his mind boggled. The generated power was used in one nanosecond bursts with a 99 thousand nanosecond pause for cooling, which allowed the laser to be rated at 11 gigawatts for that one nanosecond. This according to the data sheet would, dependant on the water turbidity and particulate content, allow a discrete laser to be maintained out to up to three kilometres.

So on a good day, if pointed in the right direction, this ROV could pick up a submerged object with sufficient clarity to allow it to be identified properly seven kilometres from the ship. It was all interesting stuff and they wouldn't need an additional generator either, they could just run it from the board on the ship.

Chief McKenzie in the drone control room was sitting with his side kick Billy Burns. They were reading and attempting to digest the data sheet for the small blue green laser package which was moulded to fit the position occupied by the camera pod on the drone. They had two packages so the question had to be whether to mount them on two drones or mount one and have a spare. They referred that to the 'Jimmy' and carried on with the sub-system testing and the fitting procedures because for sure at least one of the four drones would be used. Again the power requirement had been greatly reduced by the nanosecond burst rate and since this was a much lower rated laser the existing battery packs need only be supplemented by another two. Reducing the fuel by 20% and removing absolutely all other non-essential electronic modules had saved so much weight that its time on task was surprisingly almost the same as an ordinary drone.

They then checked and installed the accompanying software package onto the drone compartment systems which were isolated from other ship's computers with only a video feed output to the rest of the ship. If all went well they'd be ready to test the system on the way to their initial search point.

Piet and Ayize worked one on each of the two ships, customising the recesses and ensuring the torpedo like ROVs both fitted securely and had all the necessary magnet clamps functioning. The delicate task of installing the cable drums took the most time, absolutely every inch of the cable had to be checked, a single puncture of the power cable would cause a direct earth power loss and once at sea it would render the system inoperable and non-fixable.

Just after sunset on the third day Ayize was taking a break from the mind numbing cable inspection. He took his breaks by topping up with cool bottled water and wandering randomly around the perimeter of the ships as they sat on their cradles. The only local workers employed, and only as a sop to the local authorities, were doing the hull scrubbing and anti-radar paint painting. He wandered down towards the stern of the Hood and stood looking at the big Steerpod motors in their housing, the engineer in him was interested in these Finnish propulsion units and he made a mental note to ask Chief Braime about their efficiency.

He looked up as he took a swig from the bottle and noticed movement in between the two pods and then noticed the painting scaffold hanging just below the stern on the opposite side to him. Even though a very big man he moved quietly, the ship's hulls cut out a surprising amount of sound so there was little ambient noise apart from the occasional clang somewhere distant in the dockyard.

He could see someone sat on a Steerpod shaft but they weren't painting or scrubbing. His curiosity peeked, he took another step so he was almost directly under the nearest pod. The Malay, he knew he was a local because of the colour of the overalls, appeared to be scraping at the hull and while Ayize watched he produced a small disc-like thing from his work bag, unrolled, perhaps a wire, squirted something from a tube on to it then slapped it on to the hull.

Now alarmed more than interested Ayize looked around for someone or some way to get to the little bugger, because it was clear that this wasn't on the work plans, but he could see no one even at the security check point between the bows of both ships. Fuck. He had no communicator and wasn't patched into either ship's comms system.

Looking under Hood's stern he could see the trailing chain ropes from the painting platform and had an idea. He walked under and took hold of one of the chains and tested it to see if it were the one to raise or lower. He guessed right first time and now started hauling rapidly on it. It rattled and clanked as the small gears worked to bring the platform down to the ground then he picked the whole thing up and walked to a nearby stack of oil drums. He put the platform down and then lifted a forty five gallon drum up and put it on the platform, then another. Satisfied the platform was going nowhere he looked back up into the face of the saboteur or whatever he was, and smiled a big cheese eating grin. It was about twenty feet or so for the little bugger to jump so unless he was a retired para or a ninja, this guy was going to get hurt if he jumped. Ayize promised himself he was going to hurt him anyway if he was sabotaging the ship. Now he used his deep basso profundo voice to summon assistance.

"Yo. Anyone on duty here. I need assistance. Get security."

People telling the story later said the hulls of the ships vibrated when he shouted out but he knew they were bullshitting.

There was a rush of bodies to Hood's stern; two of them black clad security with the ear pieces and all the gear. A pair of powerful Taclite LED torches illuminated the intruder, like turning the sun on.

Muted conversations into microphones and strategic positioning was next on the job list and Ayize watched as the security guys took charge of the area and got everyone else back to work. Another rush of voices and feet and the shipyard's own security guys rocked up and started jabbering in warp speed Malay whilst pointing at the illuminated felon and gabbling into walkie talkie sets. Then Arkady arrived just doing up his TAC vest over a white T shirt.

He looked up and then over to Ayize, then over to the painters platform and the barrels sitting on it, and then let out a laugh whilst holstering his Sig automatic.

"Turn one of those lights off and let's get this little fucker down. I want a lifting platform so I can go and inspect what the piece of shit has been up to. Then we need check, Ocean Guard as well."

He wandered over to Ayize while his men carried out the instructions. He smiled as they struggled to move the two drums from the platform and gave up. Just how strong is this guy next to me? He wondered.

In no time a better light appeared courtesy of the security watch supervisor who was gabbling, no doubt to his boss at home, into his cell phone. The lifting platform like those for street light maintenance, with two of Arkady's boys on it, was manoeuvred into place as close as it could get to the guy clinging on to the Steerpod stem. One of the black clad men holstered his weapon and offered a hand to the limpet like Malay, while the other covered him with a weapon with underslung Taclite. The guy hesitated then realising the futility of just hanging on, took the proffered hand and was immediately plasti-cuffed and put on his knees. The lifting platform was moved back out and then lowered.

Then it got difficult as the home security team wanted to take custody of the man and Arkady wanted him on Hood. Since the Malays spoke only very small amounts of English and Arkady's guys zero Malay, there was a serious language barrier and he wished Wichit was there to translate.

Arkady, through gestures and the usual speak slowly and quite loudly routine, finally got the security supervisor to allow them five minutes with the miscreant before he was handed over.

Ayize walked over and parted the crowd with a big hand then he reached over and picked the guy up by the front of his overalls, straight arm lifting him up to face level. He then grinned.

Arkady thought the bloke was going to shit himself, he did actually pee himself and it ran down the inside of his leg dripping on to the dock.

Ayize shook him gently and just said 'Talk' in a loud voice just a foot from the guy's face. He then marched him to the boarding platform and still holding him off the ground with one arm, proceeded to walk up the steps and on to the ship.

Arkady speed dialled Wichit Somkand and asked him to get over there, now! He knew they wouldn't have long with the bloke but they wouldn't need long with the way he was looking at the enormous Zulu holding him like a rag doll.

Ten minutes later Wichit, still wearing pyjama bottoms, hurled himself up the stairs onto the Hood.

He found Arkady, Ayize and one of the security detail in Hood's security room just staring at the prisoner.

The man brightened as he saw a fellow Asian face but quickly lost hope when he turned into an interrogator. Arkady fed the questions and Wichit asked them. Any hesitation was met with a movement or stiffening of Ayize who was watching carefully. This usually cured the problem of reticence immediately as the guy was clearly terrified of the giant Zulu.

It was fifteen minutes before they allowed the local security to take him away to presumably hand him over to the local police.

Arkady conference called the Captains and First Lieutenants of both ships. So Jon Roby, Julius Kopf, Simon McClelland and Martin Turner all got their sleep interrupted by a simultaneous bleep message to dial a certain number for an urgent conference call.

Arkady put them in the picture up to now and explained that he had ordered both hulls to be examined carefully but expected any additions to be in the same position on Ocean Guard. He was only concerned at this point because of the potential, however remote, of explosives of some kind being deposited on either or both hulls. He also added that local workers were now banned from site and would not be needed for future work. If that wasn't acceptable to the local authorities then it was his recommendation that the work be terminated and carried on elsewhere. The man said he was paid just to stick the two discs on to the ships and glue the antenna wire on afterwards.

"At this point gentlemen I see no reason for you to return to your ships before morning, I will make use of available crewmembers to secure the area and wait for daylight before a full examination and removal are carried out. I have already signalled head office and asked for another security quartet to be despatched from the quick reaction unit and they will arrive later today on a company jet bringing in extra security equipment. So sorry to wake you but that's the standing order."

If he could have seen the four weary officers he would have remarked they looked a bit stunned, Jon Roby was first to break silence.

"Err, thanks for the brief Arkady, you say it was that huge Zulu chap who spotted the intruder?"

"Yes Sir. He then picked the fellow up with just one hand and carried him aboard."

"Well I'll be damned. Well as there's nothing more to say or do until morning I'll bid the rest of you good night."

Simon was next.

"Do you mind if I tag along when you do your examination and removal Arkady, I confess miniaturisation is a fascination of mine. I presume once the object has been determined as safe it will be shipped back to Little Cayman for in depth analysis?"

"No problem with you joining me Sir, and I plan to keep the company jet here until whatever objects are ready to be taken away; they can take it/them back without any of the panic you'd get if you tried to ship it commercial with an honest declaration of contents."

"OK. See you in the morning."

Neither of the two First Lieutenants had anything to offer and so the call was closed. Arkady went back to ruminating over what the Chinese saboteur had said. Chinese for sure by his naming style and immigration listing as the civilian security had established. He had only been taken on in the last two weeks which was clearly coincidental with the commissioning of the maintenance work.

Someone was leaking intel from this yard or possibly other places, there would be an investigation he knew. With a 22% Chinese population, Malaysia had plenty of potential Chinese recruits that is if China was behind the sabotage or whatever it turned out to be. Then there was the Muslim aspect, being an over 60% Muslim country and König anti-piracy patrols doing away with a lot of them in the last couple of years or so, that couldn't be ruled out immediately.

He went back to Hood's security office and poured another coffee then discarded it because he needed sleep and to be refreshed without having a caffeine tremor when he was playing with whatever the little shit had stuck on the stern. The criminal hadn't known what it was he was attaching, he'd just been given instructions on how to attach it. The instigator clearly knew that Hood wasn't made of ferric metal and had therefore ordered the use of some sort of epoxy glue instead of a magnet, he theorised.

He sighed and did a last walk about outside, talking to each of the quartet on security duty. He told them to step down to two and two patrols with three hours on and three off. He was staying on board and sleeping in the security room on the couch. Back on board he headed for the security office and passed the crew galley area. The chef had put out a couple of large trays of 'nine o'clockers' for the night duty staff and so he helped himself to a pair of corned beef and pickle sandwiches before sliding the tray back into the cooler.

He lay back on the security bunk for a moment then set his mental clock for five AM, and closed his eyes. At 5:15 he awoke with a start. Clearly not Jack Reacher quality, I'm fifteen minutes out, he thought ruefully. Arkady would never admit it but he'd read every Lee Child book in the series at least twice and saw himself as a bit of a Jack Reacher character.

*

As soon as it was full light at just after 06:00, they would begin the close examination and then removal of the device on Hood. At the same time a further search of the hull would begin to ascertain if there were any other devices. Then a repeat on the Ocean Guard.

Speculation about the location of the device was especially fierce amongst the OPs and weapons electrical crewmembers with a healthy dose of guessing by the two sets of drone operators who saw themselves as the best combination of engineering, electrical and computer skills. Theories fell into two categories. The first was that it was a weapon, some sort of shaped charge which would be triggered remotely and given the locations on the steel vertical struts which held the Steerpods in place, would cause severe damage but not sink the vessels. The second category had it that it was simply a transmitter, a tracking device so the owner of the device could at a glance see where they were.

It took Arkady, the ex-Spetsnaz demolitions and explosives expert, around an hour to examine the Hood's object from every angle and with high magnification through a headset. He photographed it from every angle and auto transmitted the data through his headband action camera using 4k high resolution. Back in the Caymans, scientists and weapons experts combed catalogues and the internet for similar devices. There was a single pressel switch on the right hand side which had an etched arrow pointing upwards, above it. He had no idea what that was about except that clearly it related to the position of the very small rocker switch under the flexible cover. Arkady could see bubbles of now set epoxy resin around the edges where the device had been pushed on.

He wiped the sweat away from his forehead and after a muted conversation with the Caymans base over his mike, those down below who were watching from behind a hastily erected corrugated aluminium barrier, saw him reach for his tool belt and extract what looked like a spatula.

Arkady was sure there was no anti-tamper device but not positive. There was always a risk he rationalised, a risk coming to work in the morning, a risk going for a drive or going for a swim. This risk was better than most because there were no external influences. He picked up his portable faraday cage and locked it into place with a pair of suction clamps, then worked the spatula around the edges of the discoid object.   Looks like a sherbet saucer or a flying saucer, he thought as he manoeuvred the spatula carefully.   Unlike a pharmaceutical or culinary spatula this one had very sharp edges and he began to work it sideways under the edge, levering as he went.   If there were an anti-tamper device it would blow as soon as he released pressure.   He didn't think there was because of the way Ayize had described the guy squirting the glue over the whole thing rather than carefully around the edges.   The kind of anti-tamper he didn't want was one that would blow as he levered the disc off the hull.

Working on slowly, a little here then a little further around, he began prising the disc off being careful not to break the fine metre long antenna wire glued to the hull. He thought maybe the resin in the centre might not be set rock hard yet if it hadn't had much exposure to air and therefore the last bit would just come away like chewing gum.

After another minute where everyone with their breath held suddenly realised they needed to breathe, it popped off leaving a little dangly glue residue behind and was nestled in Arkady's large hands.

OK.   Now to get it packaged and sent back to base for a full analysis.   Just then a shout went up from Piet up near the Steerpods on the Ocean Guard.

"Another one here!"

He looked down at everyone below and pointed to the very same position as on the Hood.   Arkady strolled across and mounted the steps to the platform.   He looked carefully at the disc on Ocean Guard, not presuming it was identical to Hood's passenger.   After a couple of minutes he was satisfied that it was the same and so with less gentleness he quickly prised that one off too.

Ayize, Piet, Louis Braime and Ocean Guard's Chief Engineer Joshko, a Croatian with huge experience on the Steerpods, were all discussing the possibilities when Arkady descended the platform and came to join them handing the two discoids over for examination.

While they were still trying to work out what the damned things were there was a shout from the bow area. All clear on both hulls.

So back to work.

Off to one side Jon Roby and Simon McClelland waited for Arkady to bring the discoids to them before he sealed them in a bag for transport back to the Caymans. Simon had decided not to get in Arkady's way while he removed the offending objects, but he was keen to have a look now. He used a small but powerful monocular to examine the surface markings.

"Simon," said Jon Roby bored with the wait while Simon seemed intent on examining every millimetre, "we should get together and do some planning for the upcoming search. To my mind we're on a hiding to nothing. Absolutely no sight or sound of these ships doesn't bode well for the crews to my mind and I'm buggered if I can think of an easy or logical way to search so much water. How about you?"

Simon continued perusing the objects for a few more, moments before reluctantly looking up and passing them to Arkady with a nod of thanks, before answering.

"Yeah I know what you mean. I've done some preliminary thinking and chart plotting, I'll bring it over to you in about half an hour say? Our Wardroom area is pretty noisy with the last of the cable drum work at the moment."

"OK. See you then. Breakfast?"

"No thanks I'll just have some tea, Earl Grey if you have it?"

"One of my morning favourites Simon.   Right I'll see you then, my cabin I think."

Jon Roby sat mulling over the charts Simon had brought.   Nowadays paper charts weren't quite so common.   Simon had brought his digital charts on a USB stick and plugged it in to Roby's laptop.   He then pushed them up onto the active bulkhead display in large scale. On the chart were plotted the last AIS locations for the missing ships along with a direction of travel arrow.   The only oddity he could see immediately was that they'd all been travelling from north east to south west when they disappeared.   That meant probably outbound from either China, South Korea, Taiwan or Japan.

That fact alone meant it was deliberate, no accidental problem could ever reasonably be expected to hit traffic going in just one direction.   Next he added their port of destination as a dot if nearby like Singapore or a name at the edge if they were going further.   Then the most likely track they would have been on, given that destination.

Of the twelve, four finished at Singapore and the remaining eight carried on through the Malacca straight. When the tracks were added it appeared that the ships were just about on parallel tracks. The biggest gap north west to south east was about ninety miles.   So all had passed through a fairly narrow corridor.

"What do you make of that Jonno?"

"Mmm maybe not as big an area as I thought.   I suppose this is quite logical really, their Second Officers will be detailed off to do passage plan for the journey.   The computers on all the ships have a similar loaded program and Bob's your uncle out pop similar passage plans which is why if you were looking to hijack them you wouldn't have far to go in each direction to intercept them."

"What do you mean?" Asked Simon.

"I mean that if this were deliberate, if these ships weren't randomly chosen but selected, as if it were a military operation rather than some pirate on a binge, then you could sit astride the likely route they'd take. If you had your own AIS access, then you'd see them coming from when they left port. Simple really if you were military."

"Nice to know someone else can think laterally. Yes I agree, the more you look at where they were taken and, interestingly their size rather than what they're carrying and where, the more it begins to look like a well-planned operation rather than random predation by pirates. So where does that leave us with finding them?" Simon queried.

Jon Roby paused in his deliberations and topped up his coffee whilst preparing some Earl grey leaf tea in an infuser for Simon.

"Before we get to that, what we haven't discussed is the purpose of this 'military' operation if that's what it is."

"True. If you were a nation state why would you do this? There has to be a big prize for whoever is doing it, a very big prize because the risk of discovery increases the longer it goes on. The ship owners and insurers can't just keep writing them off as 'unknown loss', and the relatives of these crews are becoming more vocal. In my research I discovered that there are petitions in the pipeline in the UK for it to be discussed in parliament also some legal actions at The Hague." Added Simon.

"What is it achieving? What is the result of these ships going missing?"

"Increased naval presence in the area by China is one. Could that be it do you think? A Chinese operation to become more protective of the area *because of* these disappearances?"

"If it is China we are in way out of our depth Simon, we'll have to brief Jake but we can't really do anything other than tell him our speculations as we've no evidence at all."

"Well let's follow it through. China can justify an increased naval presence in there are because of high levels of 'piracy'. They are therefore reinforcing their claim to the Paracels and the Spratlys at the same time. So as far as that goes the finger of blame can point to them. Incidentally none of the missing vessels are Chinese registered or crewed. So that's another finger pointing the same way."

"Yes but it is tenuous. What if it's a false flag game? Someone going out of their way to make China look bad?"

"Well I suppose forcing a conflict between America and China locally, and it would have to be local or the roof would come down economically on everyone, could force the issue over Chinese claims to this area. If China came out worse off, and it should despite Obama's defence cuts, then maybe their claim to the area goes away for a time. Such a train of thought suggests another player though; clearly it isn't something China would wish since they have done so well out of a 'softly softly catchee monkey' approach for so long."

"Yes, I see what you mean. From that particular angle if the Chinese were the culprits they'd be shooting themselves in both feet with a reload to make sure, as it would simply draw world attention to this area. Their best hope long term is that the US just gives up on this, folds their tents and goes home, and the world's media is helping towards that since America's foreign policy has been so clearly shabby for a long time with invented reasons for invading various places. It's like crying wolf for them, nobody believes them. America tries to draw attention to the bad boys and gets slated for more imperialist aggression BUT even though China's predations in the SCS *are* a genuine threat to freedom of navigation they now have difficulty pointing this out without being accused of yet *more* aggression in the name of oil or whatever."

Simon removed the infuser from his cup and sipped at his perfect tea.

"Unfortunately as you say America has blotted its copybook somewhat over things like the Iraq war and supporting so say moderate terrorists in Syria –if that isn't an oxymoron I don't know what is- as well as systematically engineering regime change all across North Africa as well. So now, when there is something that people ought to be very, very, concerned about, no one wants to know."

"Right what I propose then is this. We sail up through the SCS avoiding treading on Chinese toes, up to the point where the most northerly ship was taken, then you sail back down the median line in Ocean Guard, trailing your coat as it were. You are after all near the low end in size and if whoever is doing this is still active, then you fit that criteria at least. We can post a false AIS image with you having sailed from Japan in one of your other identities. You could be loaded with electronics for Singapore say, British owned but Panama flagged, rate of advance about eight or nine knots should do it. What do you think?"

"Works for me. We should wait to change ID when we are close to a group of ships all heading this way, then we'll be part of the clutter as we reverse course and slow down. I looked at AIS this morning and it strikes me that there are plenty of ships coming through now in groups of three or four, almost like in convoy given they stay within ten or fifteen miles of each other. One wonders if a few ship's masters have been chatting to each other. Ocean Guard ostensibly travelling alone might be quite a tempting target. Where are you going to be?"

"No more than fifteen miles away. AIS off, just listening quietly in the background, hopefully close enough to intercede if required, or hot pursuit if they do a runner."

"OK, let's get ourselves afloat again, feels odd being on a ship that doesn't rock even slightly."

*

With no further incidents work was completed the following day and both ships were manoeuvred back to the Synchrolift and down into the water again over a twelve hour period. Ayize stayed on Ocean Guard to cover for the trials period and train up the ROV operators on the control software. He would move between Hood and Ocean Guard as required, most could be achieved through show and tell live video-casts between the two ships as they headed north east through the South China Sea. However as with every new piece of complex equipment certain things could only be done well actually on site. Arkady stayed on Hood with an extra quartet of his men, just in case. Piet and the rest of the engineering crew watched from the dock as the two ships sailed, before heading to the airport for the long journey home.

Hood and Ocean Guard had a leisurely transit with stops to test the ROVs in action and the fine tuning of the lasers in the drones. Four days after sailing from Labuan they heard the results from the examination of the objects back in the Cayman's. One had been deconstructed very slowly and carefully to expose the components. Then these were examined minutely to ascertain their function. Finally the theories were tested on the intact discoid.

In the final analysis the objects were determined as low frequency transmitters giving out a response at 100khz, which would have easily been detectable for hundreds of miles. They were to be triggered by perhaps aircraft, ships or even submarines. An activation signal from the interrogation unit would trigger a response from the object allowing for triangulation from multiple receiving units or bearing only if interrogated by a single unit. The message it gave out was a simple Morse grouping repeated five times but not a word as far as they could tell. There was a single Morse letter difference between the two units thus identifying the two individual ships. It was that simple. Guesstimates suggested that the small Li-ion batteries present would have lasted for quite some time dependent really on how frequently they were activated. There was no firm indication of ownership but unsurprisingly very nearly all the components appeared to be of Chinese origin. That of course didn't mean China was the culprit.

As the days went by, usually with at least four hours of both ROV and drone practice, the various crews began to really understand their charges. Each ship carried four drones, two were fitted with the new laser packages and two for general surveillance work.

As time passed the crews became good at using the drones to spot a likely object for inspection and then getting the ROV down on it to have a look at what had been found. There was a surprising amount of identifiable ship debris but none of it recent.

Competition between the two crews was intense. The Ocean Guard's crew felt they were more the James Bond types and that this cloak and dagger stuff was their bread and butter. They thought the Hood was all posing and bling.

On the other hand of course, Hood's crew thought the Ocean Guard was just what it looked like, a shabby work worn freighter with none of the Hood's abilities and good looks.

In the last day or so as they had begun to examine the potential for detecting moving underwater objects, the competition had intensified. Under the guidance of Ayize, the drone operators learned how to program herringbone search patterns so that vast swathes of sea could be searched with little chance of anything slipping through the net; vital for seabed surveying and more so for detecting underwater moving targets.

Meanwhile the ROV operators scaled up the competition even further as they were alternately used for moving underwater targets, each crew trying to detect the other's ROV wake with their drones. Simon and Jonno smiled as each ship took turns being blue force or orange force and following up the drone sightings with the 'blue' ROV closing in to take images of the other as proof of what had been detected. The after exercise debriefs were often hilarious, competition they both knew was usually a positive force if managed well.

On the third day of practice, Hood was the current blue force trying to detect Ocean Guard's ROV as it wriggled left and right, up and down attempting to avoid detection. This was the last full day of exercises as they were nearing their turning point before the real searching began. All was proceeding as usual when Hood's drone operators detected a wake which wasn't the Ocean Guard's ROV. It was right at the edge of the search pattern and had nearly been dismissed as an artefact, but true professionalism is when you check things even if your mind is halfway or more to taking the easy route and ignoring it.

This was a real wake. As in, that it didn't belong to either ROV. Then things got seriously exciting. Both ships had a pair of laser equipped drones up and they began to work the wake, which was when all the previous practice localising the ROVs for exercise came into its own.

The method of determining direction of travel was to move a drone ahead and behind the first point crossed, waiting until the readings either showed increasing temperature differences or diminishing differences. Obviously the less the temperature differed from the surrounding water, the older the track. Since they'd been practicing with objects only five metres long, to have one as big as the one they'd just found made life very much easier.

All the off duty crew and the dutymen who weren't actually engaged in the tracking process, crowded into various messes where the wall screens were turned on and linked to what the ROV saw as it moved towards the target. Travelling at twenty knots but using the same kind of pump jet technology that submarines use themselves, meant that the ROVs were virtually silent and unless a submarine went active the ROVs would remain invisible.

Excitement mounted as the countdown distance in the top left corner of the screen reached zero and the words 'extreme visual' popped up in the other corner. The computers were translating the laser returns into digital images on the fly and first a dark splodge appeared in the centre of the screen and then it began to grow more distinct as the ROV hummed in behind it. At this angle it was virtually impossible to determine what it was so the ROV was guided to the port side and moved parallel.

Gradually the shape became distinct and the classic elongated cigar shape of a modern submarine became visible. Once they were amidships the speed was matched and the laser swivelled on its gimbal to take a side on picture.

It would not have mattered if the boat's name had been written in red fluorescent paint on the side for the laser could only see what was being bounced off the sub's hull and not what was written on it. The ROV carefully moved ahead diving a little underneath and above also, to get a comprehensive set of images from which identification by the Hood's battle computers brought in a not wholly unexpected result.

This was an improved Kilo class submarine, length two hundred and seventeen feet bar a whisker, height from keel to fin top twenty six and a bit feet, diameter of main hull almost twenty three feet. She was travelling at seven knots in a north westerly direction; it looked like she was heading for the relatively shallow water. Then a major shock. It was being followed.

The second ROV was launched and slotted in behind the trailing submarine close to a kilometre behind the Kilo, it was clearly deliberately following the Kilo as it had matched speeds and course changes.

The identity of the tracker was revealed as the ROV moved left again and ran up alongside. A Seawolf class, unmistakably. This was a true leviathan of the deep with eight torpedo hatches a massive three hundred and fifty four feet long, the same size as themselves, and seventy nine feet from keel to fin top, all measured precisely by laser. The Seawolf was, until the Astutes came along, the most advanced submarine in the world. It was still the most deadly even if its detection systems were a little behind Astute. The damned things are huge, Simon thought as he watched in fascination.

Awesome doesn't cover it thought Jon Roby as he watched on the screens in the OPs room. All through his twenty eight years service in the RN he'd wanted to have the drop on a submarine, and the only times it had happened had been more good guess work than any other reason.

"Are you seeing this Simon?" He said into his mike.

"Yes." Came back an awed voice. "Didn't believe it would ever happen."

"Yeah, me too. You do realise we've just written a page for ourselves in the history books. Not only that but we've just made everyone's submarine based nuclear deterrent redundant."

"The thought had crossed my mind. Silly arses in Britain are going to buy a weapons system that is no longer undetectable. They'll spend upwards of a hundred billions of taxpayers money on a system that was already obsolete before we even did this. Now they are double idiots."

"Criminal springs to mind, what with our old service having fewer ships at sea than there has ever been since it was first called the Royal Navy and they want to waste money on the last war's weapons."

"How are we going to deal with this Jonno. Almost everyone on both ships has seen these pictures. It can't be kept secret and folks all over the world will want this technology -and kill to get it."

"I know. I'm going to send this recording straight up the line and mark it 'Eyes only' Commodore König." He sighed. "I hate passing the buck but this is the very hottest potato since some chap in the 30's said 'I wonder how big a bang I can make if I smash these two hemispheres of U235 together.'"

Both ships had been stationary for some time when they first detected the two submarines, they didn't have to be stationary, it was just a precaution whilst they were getting used to deploying, recovering and using the ROVs and drones in a networked manner. Eventually both submarines passed out of range for the ROVs and the two of them were recalled along with the drones. After an hour's wait they started engines and began to move north east again. The wait was to make sure neither submarine heard them start up and move away. Just a precaution in case anyone started wondering.

Speculation amongst both ship's companies was rife as to whether the Kilo knew about the Seawolf following it, best guess was that it was blissfully unaware, like in Jaws when you want to shout 'Look behind you!' to the swimmer. Those who had been submariners, and there were a fair sprinkling, were positive the Kilo hadn't got a clue. At seven knots a Kilo is barely audible but the advanced filters in the passive sonar system on the Seawolf would have latched on to it as, by luck, it had passed inside detection range and her skipper would be doing what he loved best, sneaking up on folks unawares.

All the while he'd be recording the specific acoustic signature of this boat, it would be classified as a Kilo but not with a specific ownership tag –unless it had already been recorded in the past. The signature would be passed to all US submarines worldwide to be held in their databases for future reference, a digital fingerprint.

October, Early. König Marine HQ, Little Cayman, Cayman Islands

Jake doodled with his pencil whilst sitting at his desk in deep thought. Damn, what have I done? The message from the South China Seas yesterday and the accompanying video recording was heart stopping in its implication. He had never felt so alone, such a weight of responsibility. He'd never intended to get involved in anything nation state oriented, never wanted to take sides. He'd failed on all counts so far. Naïve doesn't quite cover it, he decided.

He and his 'funny' ships and their advanced systems had been like a brick dropping into an international pond that already had plenty of similar sized objects plopping in all over. That was 'copeable' if not desirable. But this, this was not a brick. To use the same analogy, it was an entire building dropping in a very small pond.

As the circle of those in the know got wider, the possibilities of a leak became exponentially greater. Impossible to manage basically. If he passed the info to NATO, it would be common knowledge outside NATO within five minutes. If he passed it to Andrew McTeal it would put him in the most outrageous position imaginable. Possession of a technology but no way to benefit from it, whilst at the same time being aware of what a game changer it was and that everyone else wanted it.

If he passed it to Britain, they would use it and pass it to America. If he did it the other way the Americans may eventually pass it to Britain. Passed to both and it would put them in a position of almost ridiculous power over Russia, China and anyone else who possessed either SSBNs, SSNs or SSKs.

Was that desirable? What about the old Soviet argument that went 'We now have a narrow window of opportunity. We either attack now or lose our parity'. This had been the logic when NATO began the installation of cruise missiles in Europe during the cold war, and then when NATO precision bombing and missiles were so accurate they could cause the damage of a nuke without using one.

Game changers, all of them but nowhere near as big as this. In one fell swoop the ability to detect these underwater leviathans with their intercontinental ballistic missiles, meant NATO forces would have to adopt the same tactic as Russia when it discovered that its SSBNs were being routinely followed by US and British SSNs. They ended up keeping them in an enclosed sea that had a single entrance through which nothing passed without being checked. Additionally there were submerged defences, mines and patrols by their own SSNs outside.

Same with China, UK and France, the other nations with SSBNs. He wondered if given a choice, whether these nations would prefer for nobody to have this technology at all and to what lengths they'd go to prevent it becoming known?

He sipped at his cold coffee and considered further. No, it was obvious really. Avarice or power trip, the chance to be one up would mean they all would move heaven and earth to obtain the technology whilst simultaneously attempting to prevent anyone else getting it. All very James Bond.

Oh fuck, what have I done? The possibility that his ocean bed searching ROVs and the drones with their sea bed mapping ability would actually be able to detect submerged submarines had not been the prime motivator or even on the list.

The reason he'd pushed forward on them had been because he believed that somewhere in the South China Sea there was a ships graveyard that the Lloyds people needed found to prove what was going on.

He moved the file on to a USB stick and deleted the main file. He knew it was still trackable but that was one less copy. He then sent eyes only messages to Roby and McClelland. Just one sentence 'Delete all copies and reprogram to ignore moving objects.' It wasn't going to hold things forever but it was a block in the way while he decided what to do.

Then he went looking for his wife, the only person he knew he could trust without reservation on any subject under the sun.

Unusually it wasn't roasting hot outside and there was a distant rumble of thunder. He made a mental note to look at the met forecast, maybe a late season hurricane brewing out there?

Sophie was in her office in the main house a little way up Weary Hill. He came in behind her and stopped. She was clearly away somewhere else, hair pinned up, pad on the desk covered with notes and pencil tapping gently against her lip as she considered whatever the problem was. Beautiful, beautiful outside and beautiful in her heart. God I'm so lucky, he thought as he coughed slightly and went on in.

"Get you a drink darling?"

She turned quickly and a smile broke out spontaneously.

"Gosh I'm honoured. A lime cordial with ice please Sir."

He wandered out to the back and the kitchen area. Granny Smith was sitting there reading a book as he walked in.

"Get you something boss?"

"Err, yes Granny. Thanks. Two lime cordials with ice please."

"On the way Sir. Where to?"

"Aah, the office of 'she who must be obeyed' I think."

"Roger that Sir, right on it."

Jake wandered back to Sophie's office and walked over to the sofa and sat, a big frown returning to cloud his features. She finished the notes and looked up as Granny arrived with a tray and two glasses. They both thanked him and he disappeared.

Sophie was no one's fool and she knew Jake like no one else. Must be bad if he's come here to unload, she mused.

"What's on your mind husband of mine?" She asked in a gentle way before taking her drink.

"That obvious eh?"

"Well I think you could surf those eyebrows if they were water hun."

Then it all came out, everything. Exhausted after getting it off his chest he picked up his glass now with nearly melted ice in it, and sat back to wait.

Sophie was stunned. She immediately grasped the situation.

"How long before Hood and Ocean Guard hit port again? Do the crews have internet access at sea?"

"Sage questions. Maybe three weeks before port and yes they do have internet access."

"Well you are going to have to come clean. You're going to have to tell them the danger they would be in if they were to let this story out before you've worked out what to do. Tell them it won't be just them in danger, their families, shipmates, friends everyone will be potentially in harm's way."

"Mmm, OK. That sounds like a start but again like my messages to Jonno and Simon, it only buys time."

"Yes darling but we need to buy as much as possible for now. You are not going to like what I think you should do next."

"Really? Try me. I've thought of nothing else since the message came in and still can't see a way forward."

"I didn't say it was forward dearest, just that you wouldn't like it. You then need to brief Andrew in person and alone. Then when he's stopped panicking you have to do something else."

"Pray tell, what will that be oh wise one?"

"You have to tell everyone what you have discovered and why you are telling them. Then, as you know I don't swear often, then the shit-storm will hit the fan. When they've all stopped having issey fits and declaring you a traitor to everything under the sun, they will perhaps allow that you had little choice but to do what you have done. That not to do so would in fact be far more destabilising than breaking the discovery to selective governments."

"Wow, let me think about that for a second or two. That wasn't anything I had in mind. Nothing close. I've been trying to think of ways to eliminate the information without eliminating the people."

"Yes and no doubt going around in circles because like they say the genie is out of the bottle and you can't un-invent something."

"OK. I'm starting to think you may have something but timing is going to be crucial. I cannot announce it whilst I have two ships in the South China Sea using the technology. They would instantly become targets but also crucially, whoever is knocking off these ships will know too and I still have high hopes that the technology will find those missing ships and maybe just maybe, what happened to the crews."

"OK. You may need to pay a visit in person then to ensure the message gets across to your crews and just hope that none of them have a greater loyalty to their first passport colour than to their friends on board the ships they now serve on. Meanwhile the internet may have to 'break' and then the announcement could come later when you have all the pieces in place. I know it's a little deceitful but I'm hoping they'll forgive you trying to protect them. Perhaps there could be security reasons or what do you call it EMCON?"

"Clever girl. I'm sure I can get a reason together to switch off outside comms."

Jake stood up and walked across to his seated wife, gently he pulled her up kissed her on the lips and hugged her gently.

"I do love you." He stepped back and smiled, then headed off, presumably back to the offices she thought.

Jon Roby read Jake's message on his monitor, hit the delete button and sat, thoughtfully, as his ship moved at thirteen knots into ten foot rollers with a little drizzle splashing on the bridge windows. He stared out over the graceful bows as they dipped into the waves with a freshening wind whipping the tops off them and the spray from the bow itself.

"McClelland." He spoke into his mike.

Click, then.

"Yes I got one too, you beat me to the button."

"I have known Jake for more than twenty five years. He's not stupid, senile or foolish. Ergo he knows this is not an answer and is out there looking for one. He's buying time to line his ducks up I think."

"Concur. We should do as he orders but with a slight mod. The program needs an option menu built into it instead of simply overwriting the algorithms. Something innocuous that maybe only you, me and the two who make the changes will understand."

"Why?"

"Well I don't know about you but I think the next few weeks are possibly going to get a little exciting at times. Now whilst you can cover air and sea, sub-sea has never been an issue until now. I think we need a boot menu option something as if it were a standard re-boot option for back up. Something that maybe comes up as 1. OS, 2. PE. Now most geeks know there's a Windows pre environment, it's been part of recovery software for ages, no one would think it odd. Then we get to keep the detection ability. One leads to the newly cleaned OS that cannot detect moving objects, two leads to the existing program which can."

"Devious git aren't you. I like it though. My WEPs is a bit of a boffin on this sort of stuff I'll have to brief him if he hasn't worked it out already, then I can send you a patch that puts it in. Thank God the controlling PCs for this aren't networked. Also we need to curb our boys enthusiasm for sending long, loving letters home. I think we need EMCON state changed now that we're approaching our turnaround point."

"Call me devious? Look at you. OK, let's get on before someone sends an electric 'Bluey' with some partial recording attached or something."

Roby laughed. Blueys used to be free Airmail letters that servicemen and women could send from their place of foreign duty free of charge, in the days before Facebook and the internet.

"Roger that, I'll get my WEPs down to the cabin."

He turned to the bridge at large.

"Officer of the Watch, set EMCON Alpha. I want no emissions gentlemen other than Link. We are about to turn and Ocean Guard is going to trail its coat and we don't want any bugger to know Hood is about. Cool us down as well please." He added, referring to the pre-wetting system that effectively cooled them to the same temperature as the surrounding seas and made it that much harder for anyone to get an infra-red fix.

Then. "WEPs." Click.

"Williams here?"

"Bungy, I need a word. Can you visit my cabin in three?"

"Aye Sir, no problem." It always made him smile when he heard his old navy nickname, he wondered why civvies never did the nickname thing.

Three minutes later Lt Pete Williams arrived at Jon Roby's cabin, ten minutes after that he left wearing a big frown and went down to his domain. Anything electrical on the ship was technically in his domain, now including the engineroom. But weapons and radar systems were his primary reason for being there and his skills included programming in several different languages.

Fifteen miles away Simon, on the bridge of Ocean Guard waited until the clock ticked down to the pre-arranged time before issuing the command to shut down their AIS system remove the current module and insert the replacement. At the same time the ship turned 180 degrees to its new course and became another vessel entirely. The new AIS module began passing out its details every few minutes as usual to the watching world. The ship was now the MV Ocean Leader, British registry, 18,000 tons, left Yokohama three days before, arriving in Singapore in four days' time. If anyone checked the manifest they would find microchips and integrated circuits along with a variety of general cargo from Japanese *shoyu*, or soy sauce, to *senbei* rice crackers and industrial printers. After Singapore she would sail to the UK for refit with whatever cargo could be arranged.

Hood turned almost in tandem. The intent was to be at ten miles in the seven o'clock position. Only the ship to ship datalink from Ocean guard to Hood was transmitting

162

outside the normal navigation emissions expected for such a vessel, but since these were almost undetectable, to all intents and purposes Ocean Guard was the Ocean Leader now, even if somewhat smaller in reality.

They each had a drone up coordinating the search of the surface ahead using a standard recon package along with the blue laser fitted drone peering down under the sea, sometimes as far as one thousand feet in crystal clear water.

Simon studied the charts of the water over which they would travel. In the first few days it was relatively deep, sometimes twelve to fourteen thousand feet, excellent SSN country, but at the bottom end nearest Singapore, for the last five hundred miles it shelved quite dramatically rising to three or four hundred feet in most places, definitely a place where SSN skippers would sweat a lot and avoid if possible. Over to the east the channels from the Sulu Sea were shallow too and the places where a one hundred thousand ton carrier would feel safe were few and more to the point, well known. The straits to the north between Taiwan and the mainland the Bashi channel, was quite shallow too, even more shallow than the Singapore end. He moved the digital chart over to the north east between Taiwan and the Philippines, this was the only area where there was a deep water entrance or exit to the South China Sea, and this was where the reports of cable laying had originated, what a coincidence.

Around him the business of working a ship continued. His crew were used to him staring at the charts or going off into 'think mode' as they called it and they left him to it unless they really needed his input. They already called him 'Data' behind his back, alluding to his computer like concentration skills and his ability to work through massive amounts of information. They were also seriously happy to have a Captain with such ability.

So there he was frozen in time while the watch officers changed and the now off duty crew went to get something to eat and relax a little. Simon's ever attentive steward removed the cold coffee twice, took away a plate of now curling sandwiches and replaced them this time with a cling film cover.

He was oblivious. His tactical mind looked at the problem of isolating the SCS from the rest of the world through a Chinese perspective, south west no problem, shallow water, mines and SSKs spread around; SSNs would **not** want to hunt there. Likewise the Sulu Sea entrances, the channels were few and well mapped and easy to seed with mines if you only allowed the Philippines twelve miles of territorial waters.

He considered that point. The Philippines could be key and recently, the American liberal press had systematically slated President Duterte for his crack down on druggies and Islamists. They had their own agenda and Simon marvelled at their ability to ignore the massive contradictions of their own foreign policy and then cast their support for so say *moderate* Islamists which truly was self-deception. Then there was their stoic defence of the human rights of the drug gangs which mercilessly dragged people down into crime, prostitution, violence and murder, while Duterte scorned the need to give them any rights because of their crimes against his people. The people of the Philippines had voted in this tough and eccentric former city mayor, knowing full well he was going to war against the drug barons, it was a democratic decision. You would also have thought, given how unorthodox he was, that he'd be big pals with President Trump, but no, Trump had continued the Obama era negative rhetoric for some reason.

More time passed, Martin Turner, now OOW made a comment to Simon about tests on the ROV but got no answer. He looked over at his boss staring down at an electronic chart of the South China Sea; he seemed not to have moved in over an hour; such concentration. Martin let him get on with it, Simon's tactical ability was legend and Martin hoped one day to learn enough from him not to be embarrassed by his own apparent lack of such skills.

Simon was unaware even of Martin's presence.

Cause and effect. After the slating from Obama and then Trump the Philippine President had shocked them all by telling America to get stuffed and had started talks with China.

Simon considered the type of deal that might come about. So, what if the Chinese did a deal with the Philippines? Perhaps something like, you get our support, you can buy our military hardware, new stuff, not American cast offs, and we will veto any UN sanctions and keep the Americans out of your hair. In return you get a smallish slice of the revenues from any oil and gas but have to give up your claims to the Scarborough reef area. Then we tell everyone we're simply cooperating.

Martin jumped as Simon suddenly straightened and walked out on to the bridge wing closing the door behind him. He's scary sometimes, he thought, as he slowly shook his head from side to side then concentrated on the ECDIS again.

Simon sucked in the warm and fragrant air; the band of rain squalls had passed and left the air clean and energising.

Cause and effect. Part of the deal would be no objection from the Philippines if China laid a sonar buoy network in the Bashi channel, it would have to include that. Clearly Taiwan would never agree to turn a blind eye to Red Chinese activity though. He then recalled that under high magnification the Bashi channel wasn't all deep water. If the Chinese had a very quiet SSK to the north say, placed just south of Taiwan fifteen miles or so and maybe another a further thirty miles south, they would effectively block SSN access at that end since it was quite shallow with a hump in between the proposed locations for the two SSKs.

With that part of the puzzle seemingly sorted he took another deep breath and returned to the bridge and the electronic chart display, absently taking a sandwich and a swig of his lukewarm coffee before returning his attention to the next part of the strategic riddle.

He noted that further south in the Bashi channel, in fact for the next hundred and thirty miles or so, any detection would require sonar buoys to pick up inbound SSNs.

The water was too deep for the use of conventional seabed mines, a technology in which the British had led the way with the Stonefish mine a few years ago, and the Americans had gone one further with the Captor mine which deployed a Mk46 torpedo he recalled. They weren't the random weapons of yesteryear, nowadays sea bed mines could be programmed to go after specific acoustic signatures so ordinary merchant ships would be safe – unless they were the target of course. He dismissed seabed mines for a moment as they'd really only be used in the shallow water. The ones he would use in the Bashi channel would be the modern suspended mines. They were designed to sink to a predetermined depth say two hundred feet or more, and wait for activation. They could be fed up to date acoustic signatures, for instance some newly detected contact picked up by the conveniently close sonar buoy network. The problem was they could only be deployed in the few days preceding the closing of the channel, otherwise their station keeping propulsion batteries would be drained.

These types of mine were the most dangerous of all being able to target a specific vessel or class of vessel, submarine or surface, by deploying a homing torpedo from relatively close range. The Chinese he'd read, were big on mine warfare and regularly exercised deployment from either planes ships or submarines. Ironically the Western navies had cut back massively on mine counter warfare vessels despite knowing their potential adversaries thought these weapons were wonderful, cause and effect? They ignored the lessons of the Gulf War and Iraq's notable success with a limited number of primitive mines. Typical, Simon fumed, the UK government would rather have four useless black slug SSBNs than vessels which could and would keep Britain's sea lanes open.

Over on Hood Jon Roby looked down at Simon's recently sent analysis of local conflict potential. The mines, if used, would be a real threat for sure. The mine warfare aspect could also work for small nations with small navies though, it was a force multiplier of considerable potential. A lucid analysis, he thought, but the question at the top of his list was what would set the ball rolling? Another more serious spat with America? Were the Chinese that desperate to obtain full and complete control of the SCS that they'd risk war? He knew that Vietnam and China occasionally shot the crap out of each other's fishing boats but this was on a different level, he just couldn't see how it was going to help China's case. Most puzzling of all was how would making ships disappear fit into a plan to control the SCS? Not clever really because it simply shone a spotlight on the area and begged for external scrutiny –like us for instance? So, are these pieces of information actually connected?

Jake had signalled the intel from the visit by Miles Carlson and the 'heads up' regarding further American naval efforts to exercise their right of freedom on the seas and Roby wondered just what the Americans were planning. The presence of that Seawolf yesterday was significant, those were perhaps just about the most deadly vessels ever to deliberately sink beneath the waves, true hunter killers with the ability to fire and control eight independently targeted torpedoes over tremendous distances. He couldn't remember off the top of his head what the range of the ADCAP torpedo was but something over thirty miles he recalled depending on the speed setting, wire guided until the terminal phase, a real beast. But the Chinese had been developing a series of weapons called the *Sha Shou Jian* literally meaning 'killing, hand club', he'd been told. The series included space weapons, a ballistic missile designed to kill carriers and their state of the art suspended sea mines. All apparently using advanced technologies.

The OOW informed him of the AIS switch and that Ocean Guard had now turned and become Ocean Leader. He set aside his thoughts on Simon's analysis and acknowledged the report. He then ordered the course and speed changes that would bring Hood around to their 7 O'clock position at ten miles range. He just hoped that was both far enough away so there was no association but close enough if they needed to intervene. He ordered the pre-wetting cooling to be carried out every hour before leaving the bridge and heading for the OPs room for a good shufty at the complete air/sea picture available to them.

21st October, Sulu Sea, USS Nimitz Carrier Task Group 11.1

Rear Admiral James Summers commanding the Carrier Task Group 11.1, flag USS Nimitz, was all too aware of Chinese cunning and Chinese technology. He wasn't one of the folks who still thought that China's major export was rubber dog shit either. He thought that the fools who only rated Uncle Sam's technology as good, were missing some vital brain cells.

Summers knew it was his job to be paranoid, paranoid and damned careful on this mission. There was no doubt there would be surprises in store for everyone, including the Chinese. The powers that be were sending *his* task group into the South China Sea because it was the oldest carrier in the USN. He knew that, he also knew it wasn't expendable by any means, however if the US was to lose one, this would be the one they'd prefer to lose if they had to.

It was going potentially into harm's way because Uncle Sam had the only navy left big enough to pull off a freedom of navigation exercise in the South China Sea. All he was going to do was pass pretty close to some places that China had pissed on and then decided that was now home turf. If they tried anything like they'd done with the USS Nathan Allen he would fuck them over properly all the while watching out for their uppercut to go with the left cross. Then they would make a stately withdrawal through the Bashi channel and on to Japan for an almighty party and possibly another star for his collar.

He had a full air wing with plenty of firepower in the sky by way of F18C Hornets, the E and F Super Hornet squadrons and E2D Hawkeyes watching over them from above. On the sea he had a beefed up escort of two

Ticonderoga class CGs and six Arleigh Burke II class DDGs, all of them loaded for anti-air which gave his task force around eight hundred surface to air missiles, just in case things got hairy. One of the DDGs was going to be detached early to see what was happening down south where he couldn't take the carrier. In addition, out of sight but not out of mind, he had two new Virginia class SSNs which were working ahead of the group, sanitising the area before they got to it, lastly the awesome Seawolf itself even further ahead looking out for potential trouble.

The Nimitz group was going to stay in deep water, well away from the kiddy swimming pool down at the bottom of the SCS or in the far north, but the boat skippers were going to make sure nothing came over the rim into the deep water undetected. This was one of the most powerful task forces put together in quite a long time and he was proud to command it.

Right now they were heading for one of the northern channels leading from the Sulu Sea into the South China Sea, and then they'd turn to port once they'd cleared the shallow water, wander down south and west for four hundred miles or so and then turn north and east to head out through the Bashi channel.

Seawolf had come up to fifty metres earlier and streamed her LF antenna to pick up latest intel and to report finding and following two Kilo class SSKs. Nationality unknown, presumed Chinese.

Summers knew the Kilo could be a hard nut to crack on its own turf lying doggo or moving ultra-slow. It had all the necessary tools to make his life hard from advanced anti-ship missiles to heavy torpedoes that could make big holes in his ships but at least it didn't have the Set-65/76, wake following carrier killers. However he knew the Kilo preferred shallower water and the Chinese knew that his SSNs were the sharks in the deep part of the pond. So he expected them to vacate the deep water and head shallow whilst his CTG and its escorts were around. Chinese satellites had picked them up some time ago, you couldn't really hide things like carriers for very long, so they knew it was on its way.

What they planned to do about it was not within his ability to predict all he could do was guess and prepare.

22nd October, South China Sea, Hood & Ocean Guard

The last six days had been pretty boring for everyone, the only highlights were catching sight of two more slow moving Kilo class boats, one heading south west slowly, right on the edge of the deep water and the other heading almost reciprocal, again right on the edge of the deep water. They were easy for the ROVs to follow but they could have problems if they had to track something faster because their top speed was around twenty three knots.

Simon McClelland sat in his cabin thinking things through once more. A report from Jake had placed a US CTG en route to the South China Sea via the Sulu Sea. Some of Andy Evans' contacts passed on nuggets like that for a few dollars pocket money, especially in the Philippines where that could equate to a fair amount of someone's wages. He was of course usually fishing for piracy info but every nugget helped.

As far as Simon could see this CTG could be a provocation too far for the Chinese, coming so soon after the Nathan Allen incident, but they were quite a bit to the north east and hopefully would head the other way. He checked his watch, night was coming soon and with the typical rapidity of the tropics, it would be full dark very quickly. He had rounds to do; the chances of a contact had just gone up considerably when they arrived in this area.

Yesterday they had entered the shallow waters of the south western South China Sea and their route now took them on a gentle weaving course which would be pretty standard for such a vessel heading towards Singapore. Merchant ships wouldn't contest the freedom of the seas they were commercial vessels, so their course avoided the hotspots.

With the water being so shallow the drones had no problem seeing all the way to the bottom and he thought there could be some serious commercial prospects for the drone technology at least. The advanced computer systems were able to give a superb 3D rendering of the sea bed, accurate to centimetres rather than feet. With such units harbours where the sand bars moved continuously could be mapped regularly and accurate readings for more rarely visited areas could be had at a price, providing the water wasn't too murky though and that was the real drawback to the technology with most light being reflected in turbid water.

The ROVs had proved their worth for submarine hunting but not yet for bottom searching, that would change soon. He'd been doing some extrapolations based on the approximate times and dates the ships had disappeared. Given they were all at night he thought he'd cross check with sunrise and sunset times to get an idea of how far the captured vessels might get if they were just travelling at night. He looked at the ones which occurred earliest and drew his circles denoting maximum travel distance at the high and low speeds of the vessels which had disappeared. He then added in the later ones and drew his circles again. There seemed to be an overlap, roughly hour glass shaped, in an area between twenty five and thirty five miles SSE of Cừ Lao Thu Island which belonged to Vietnam. This was what the rest of the world called international water and what the Chinese called home turf. On high resolution there were a number of small Cays or Atolls or whatever they were called around here. The degree of correlation was quite high. He sent it via the link to Jon Roby for an opinion and then got up and went to do his evening rounds.

Out on the upperdeck the last hints of light were fast disappearing ahead of them. In company with his First

Lieutenant Martin Turner, he did the rounds to ensure Ocean Guard still looked like and displayed the lights associated with Ocean Leader, the ship it was impersonating. The deck fittings and structures were as close as they could get to Ocean Leader's silhouette but of course this ship was half the size. That wouldn't matter because people saw what they wanted to see and judging size at varying distances was very difficult especially at night.

They checked the access panels which were closed in front of the AK630 Gatling guns in the aft superstructure and ensured the ladders which would normally allow access to the bridge were in their raised and locked positions. No one could go up to the next deck even if they somehow managed to get past the guns. The two aft gun positions could sweep the decks and the water in an arc of 140 degrees with a 20 degree overlap at the stern, getting close into the lee of the hull wouldn't help either as the gun mounts were on platforms which rose up and gimbals which allow them to tilt. Ocean Guard's crew also contained a permanent security quartet whose job was to deal with whatever happened that they hadn't planned for.

They moved on to the midships area which could either emulate a very low freeboard or a normal freeboard depending on who they were tempting and which plates were in position. Again the guns here could cover good arcs especially when certain panels and plates were slid back to expose more deck area. They were killing grounds for people who attacked ships and slaughtered crews on a whim. They all knew the work they did would be criticised by do-gooders the world over if it were known. But people in units like the SBS, SAS or Delta and the SEALs also knew that if what they did and how they did it were widely known, they too would come in for massive criticism from the same people. They didn't care. They lived in reality, the do-gooders lived in an imaginary utopia where people were always nice to each other and if for some reason they weren't nice, then a quick explanation of what they were doing wrong would solve it.

Martin had in fact been on a ship in the Gulf of Aden which had been attacked by Somalis in three boats. The crew used hoses to wash the first boarders off and then the others in the boats started firing their AKs at whatever they fancied, which included the bridge windows, injuring the Second Officer and a Filipino helmsman. Martin himself had grabbed a couple of heavy metal hatch cover bars and run to the side where he thought the boat had hooked on, then popped up and dropped them into it. The weight had taken them straight through the bottom and with much warp speed gabbling from the crew, the sinking boat had sped away towards the mother ship with two of the crewmen bailing frantically. The other boats had hauled off to look for easier prey. Martin had recounted how the Second Mate had died two days later, his chest wound had proved more serious than initially thought and he drowned in his own blood after a sudden coughing fit.

People forgot how many merchant seamen had lost their lives due to enemy action, piracy and a thousand other causes over the years. His own Grandfather had been a Mate on a petrol tanker during the WW2, on the dreaded Russia convoys. The old man had never been able to talk about it even when Simon had been a naval officer, all he would do if the subject came up, was to tear up and go silent. Simon could not imagine the terror and the horror of those convoys; at war with the elements and a determined enemy in one of the most inhospitable places on the planet, winter in the Arctic. Worse though was the reception the survivors received at the other end.

Satisfied all was ready for the night they walked to the front of the aft superstructure and used a coded entry pad to gain access through the armoured door. Up on the bridge finally, the OOW, Captain and First Lieutenant went through the procedures and watches for the night then checked the charts of the area they'd be sailing through. The two seniors left, one for his cabin the other for the OPs room. Simon checked in with Jon Roby ten miles away and then got his head down after a quick bite to eat; he had the middle watch between midnight and 0400, not the worst, that one followed his, but bad enough.

Hours later another uneventful night watch was just about to end, it was 03:55 and his relief, Martin Turner had arrived yawning, getting ready to take over the watch. Suddenly the OPs room repeater pinged drawing their attention. There was an object astern about two hundred yards back. They both grabbed viewers and swivelled them to point dead astern. Nothing. Simon switched to low light half a second before Martin and could not believe his eyes.

With just its conning tower visible was a submarine, it was difficult to see properly, the fin appeared much bulkier than he thought it should. Then he realised why, it was carrying a conforming pod aft of the sail. He knew what that was for too.

"Shit, we have a part surfaced boat behind us with a Special Forces pod on its back. Who the fuck are this lot?"

Martin didn't answer immediately instead he opened the combat comm lines linking OPs, bridge and security on an open channel then chipped in.

"Trouble boss, there's one, no, two RHIB type boats being deployed, one either side."

"Security are you seeing this?" Asked Simon.

A voice answered immediately.

"Aye Sir, we are on the way up now."

The security section leader arrived on the bridge wearing a helmet mounted NVG unit and carrying his weapons; he immediately stepped out onto the bridge wing.

"Fuck. They have NVG too and the fuckers are armed to the teeth. Get the armoured bridge screens down now Sir!"

Simon leaned over, lifted a button cover and pushed the button underneath to drop the front and rear armoured screens into place, half a second later the outside view was projected on to them seamlessly. He switched it to low light then infra-red trying to find the best visual aid.

"I count half a dozen in each boat Simon." Said Martin, still using the viewer. Who the fuck are they?"

The security section leader answered.

"Well I'm ex-SBS and I can tell you that ain't no British boat and it ain't a Yank either, I know the size and shape of ours and theirs through lots of practice trying to find the fuckers at night boss. Whoever the fuck these cowboys are, they are not on my friendly list. I'd get ready to engage, we don't want them on board Sir!"

Simon was thinking rapidly as he continued to stare aft. He spoke into his mike.

"Roby."

"What's happening Si, we see a small contact astern. I'm going full ahead as we speak, be with you in a few minutes."

"It's a submarine Jon, part surfaced, just astern and it's deploying two RHIBs full of armed men."

"Shit. No id or you'd have said."

"No. One of our security bods is ex-SBS and he says it's not a Brit or a Yank."

"Have to assume its hostile Si. Yes it must be from a national navy, but they aren't behaving in a friendly way. They'll be spec forces from somewhere, you can't let them on board. You have to engage soonest."

"Roger that. We have everything on camera anyway. I hate to use our stuff on folk who are not pirates though."

"No choice Si, your men and your ship, or them. Besides they may be pirates of a different kind for all we know. Careful though, the sub may get a snot-on when you take out its boarding party. Have you seen that shoal ahead on your chart?"

Roby was looking at a high resolution chart. Half a mile ahead and slightly to starboard of the Ocean Guard the seabed heaved up to within six to ten feet of the surface in a long coral arc leading away to the right, with deeper water beyond.

"Yes. OK. Good idea." Said Simon, immediately cottoning on. "Hang on a sec Jon." He turned to the helmsman. "Full ahead. Engage the gas turbine. Steer to cross behind that shoal ahead and to starboard." He designated it on the chart with a stylus then he switched back to Roby. "I think we'll get there before they decide to shoot a tin fish at us."

"Hope so." Answered a worried Jon Roby. "Thinking out loud though, this is clandestine stuff. A missile launch would be picked up by all sorts of folk so I don't think that's likely. That Yankee carrier group has turned this way by the way, range about two hundred miles. We have two E2D Hawkeyes on our ESM, one radiating in the north the other the west. One of them would pick up the initial climb out of a missile launch since they're radiating enough to do my toast if I stick it on a fork outside. If you have anything to laser designate let me know and I'll use a few of these fancy laser guided shells."

"Right. I'll get back to you."

"Good luck Si."

"Ta. Won't need it though."

Roby hoped not. He reconsidered his actions and decided a noisy blind approach to a submarine which was likely to be uber pissed off in a minute or two, probably wasn't a smart move.

"Helm bring us to two six zero, slow to fifteen knots. OOW sound action stations."

"Aye Sir, two six zero, slow to fifteen knots."

As the action stations buzzer ran through the ship he started thinking tactically.

"Drone control." Click.

"Drones Aye."

Move our laser drone over to Ocean Guard's track and see if you can find what's following her and stay with it for when it submerges."

"WEPs."

"Williams."

"Bungy what's the maximum speed we can safely deploy the ROV at?"

"Uncertain Sir, no test data. If you wish to deploy underway I'd slow to five knots, launch then speed up again, the real danger is from the drag on the cable."

"What if we change course to follow the ROV?"

"That would reduce the cable stress to almost zero Sir especially if there were little difference in the relative speeds."

"OK, thanks Bungy. What we'll do is stay at 15knots then until we're ahead of any bad guys then turn towards Simon, and then deploy the ROV. Does that sound plausible."

"Works for me Sir. I'll stand by for your order."

Roby went back to work on the angles and speeds using his interactive chart. About fifteen minutes to get ahead at a guess, then another five steering towards the bad guys, then deploy. Refine when we get the wake data.

"McClelland." Click.

"Busy Jon."

"Yes I know. Any joy with the laser designator?"

Simon looked over to his security team leader raising his eyebrows in askance.

"Bit dicey to step out with a laser designator while these muppets are getting ready to board Sir."

"Right, forget it. Wait until we've disposed of the bad guys then we'll let Hood have a go."

He switched to Roby.

"Difficult until we've dealt with the intruders. Just as soon as we can, we'll get something up for you. I'd guess you'll need to be quick, I doubt he'll hang around on the surface after we dispose of his boarders."

"We'll be ready."

Simon turned back to the screens, the two RHIBs separated from the submarine and powered up quickly. One to each quarter, clearly not expecting any resistance, they zoomed in towards Ocean Guard's stern not realising the tapered aft superstructure was deliberately designed to facilitate the overlap of firing arcs. The hull mounted cameras on Ocean Guard recorded the moment they both sent up their aluminium scaling ladders and the first pair began climbing them. Both black clad masked intruders then took up a position where they could cover the ascent of their teammates. The supressed stubby machine pistol style weapons were clearly visible through the infrared cameras. The two cameras mounted underneath the bridge wings gave the watchers a bird's eye view of the emptying RHIBs, quickly and efficiently they were all on board except the RHIB drivers.

Then the deck lights came on. One thousand watt LED lights. Instant glare and instant negation of the NVGs the intruders were wearing. With barely a heartbeat later the covers slid back noiselessly on either side of the deck housing, and the whirring of the already spinning barrels could clearly be heard out on deck. Ten men pivoted towards the noise, ten men opened fire in the direction of it.

Then the barrels began spitting heavy bullets. The Security team operators fired in one second, sixty round bursts, skilfully moving left and right between them.

There was nowhere to hide. Nothing to hide behind, no cover to dive to except the mooring cleats and they weren't big enough. It was over in two seconds. The two RHIB drivers waited a few seconds and all they got was a cascade of blood and bits as it sluiced down around them. Five, ten then fifteen seconds passed before, with a shout, first one then the other pulled sharply away.

It was a short lived reprieve. As soon as they cleared the shadow of the ship the pair of guns tracked then destroyed them, three short bursts from each and that was that. OPs reported that no communications had been initiated by either team and therefore the submarine which was receding rapidly as Ocean Guard increased speed would be only aware of the first part of the brief engagement, the sudden illumination.

Simon turned to the Security Team Leader and pointed.

"Designate the fin. Lights out first." Then he nodded to Martin Turner.

"AIS off. Reflectors down. Stealth mode." At least they wouldn't be transmitting their position from now on and without reflectors would be that much harder to find on radar.

"Roby." Click.

"Sorted?" Came back the calm voice of Jon Roby.

"Sorted. Designating now." Answered Simon.

"Roger that. Shooting."

"Guns open fire using Lazshell single shots, please." Said Roby in an almost disinterested voice.

Kiwi McLean had been waiting for a chance to try these beauties out. Bloody expensive but bloody accurate. He only had twenty of them. Carefully but swiftly he set up the shoot so the initial firing solution was for the contact Ocean Guard had transmitted, now almost half a mile astern of her. Then he selected Lazshell, single and closed the circuit. These were a Russian direct copy of an earlier American design called the Deadeye, apart from being laser terminally homed, they used a Sabot system which of course reduced the actual shell weight but gave them a much greater range, up to thirty miles. The book said to use them with a drone designating but it didn't matter as long as the designating laser used the same coded lasing sequence. The shell would pick up the reflected laser light from the designator and the tiny fins would steer it to target.

He readied a second while he waited for a report from either the drone or the ship.

"Hit. High on the fin." Reported the Security Team leader out on Ocean Guard's bridge wing whilst still lasing the target, but now back to using the NVGs.

"Shoot!" Ordered Roby again.

Seconds passed.

"Another hit, low near the main casing. Wait. He's blowing his tanks. I hope he's got a bloody leak." Said the ex-bootneck, still lasing and hoping for another shell before the target disappeared.

"Cease fire. He won't have a bloody clue what just happened." Laughed Jon Roby over the open circuit. How far to your shoal Simon?"

"Just coming abreast now. Turning."

Ocean Guard now exceeding twenty five knots with her single gas turbine howling away, heeled into the turn as a bit of thrust from the bow Azithruster helped her around the corner too. The pair of Steerpods now receiving massive amounts of current were turning out their highest speed. Using Steerpods to turn like this reflected Simon, dabbing at his wet coffee splashed leg, should be prefixed with a 'brace' warning in future. He heard other cups hit the deck, pencils roll across the floor and more than one curse as someone tried to find a hand hold to stay upright. The result was a ship that could nearly turn right angles, even at speed.

Safe behind the protective reef he ordered the gas turbine to shut down and speed to be reduced to fifteen knots while he studied the chart and tried to think what the Chinese sub driver would do now, that is of course if it was a Chinese sub. I've just declared war on someone, he thought ruefully. Bloody pity I've no idea who. Still whoever it is they're unlikely to want to broadcast the news. Just hope the bugger goes away to get repaired and doesn't come back while we're out here. He traced a course which would take them near to their search area whilst shielding them as much as possible from any retaliation by the damaged and annoyed boat driver, then plotted it into the navigation computer.

"Helm stand down. Autopilot engaged." The helmsman sat back but continued to watch the chart and the readings the depth-finder were giving.

At just about the same time both Simon and Jon Roby realised that what they'd just witnessed was an attempted state sponsored hijack.

"McClelland." Click.

"Simon, they will be back old son, they can't afford to leave you to tell the tale so to speak. Pity we can't ask someone where they're from, did you get any living prisoners?"

"No. We have two bodies not too messed up and the security detail is going through them photographing equipment, labels etcetera. The doc is taking samples for DNA analysis. They are both east oriental looking. Afraid I can't tell the difference between a Chinese, a Vietnamese or a Japanese. About as much as we can do right now. I know they'll be back, I agree we will now be hunted but hopefully the drones will give us some advanced warning. The only options as I see it are to thin out now and whiz down to Labuan again or keep looking and hope the bastard goes home. I'd like very much to explore the area I mentioned though, otherwise safety first."

"Tricky. We don't know what their orders are or how closely they are being guided by their big wigs. We need to tell Jake soonest. Pity we haven't actually got any A/S weapons."

"Yeah what I wouldn't give for a couple of Stingrays right now."

"Well I'm going to try to get a look at this fellow, I'm going to deploy my ROV in a few minutes while you disappear and then we'll see what we are up against."

Roby closed the connection, checked his chart scribblings then ordered slow ahead, five knots and a turn to starboard. The drone had easily picked up the submarine's track and had begun following the now submerged submarine ready for the ROV to get an image of it. We ought to mount a flash camera on these things, he mused, just so we can take a visible spectrum picture. Might see some hull markings. That's worth a note to self, he said, doing just that in his electronic diary.

The Hood's ROV scooted away at twenty knots heading for a calculated intercept. It was clear the submarine had decided to follow Ocean Guard's course around that shoal but he didn't appear to be speeding. Given that the lasing drone could actually get a return the sub itself and not just its wake, they could work out its speed easily and drone control reported they were doing just four knots. Roby passed this on to Simon who increased speed slightly so that he'd make his next turn before the following sub had made the first one.

Meanwhile the ROV approached noiselessly and rapidly, moved out to port and began sending back images. It was immediately obvious this was yet another Kilo.

Like bloody Kilo-Piccadilly Circus out here, Roby muttered to himself, what was that, four they'd seen now? That's four more than I ever saw in the navy, he reflected, only ever seen pictures of the blasted things before, usually taken by some WAFU from 824 squadron, hanging out of a Seaking up in the frozen north somewhere.

He tuned back into the 'chase' as it was; it looked like Simon would make a clean getaway, these shoals had more twists than a snake's back, so what to do now? Undoubtedly there was one pissed off national navy out there, they wouldn't know for sure who was responsible but since König Marine were the only non-national navy team in the world, they might make an educated guess as to who owned the merchant ship which had just butchered their Special Forces team and put holes in the delivery sub. But what would they do? He wondered if this lot were the ones who were trying to tag them with a locator beacon back in Labuan? Not too great a leap into the dark. He'd put that in his report too.

OK. Best thing to do is to follow this geezer until we need haul the ROV in, see what he gets up to.

"Match speed with target. Let me know any changes, I'm going down to my cabin to write this up. Number one, you have the bridge."

"Aye, aye Sir." Answered Julius Kopf, who as a gunnery specialist himself, was desperate to go over the last shoot with Kiwi McLean.

Roby looked out at the gathering light over to the east and then down at his watch 05:20, part way through the morning nautical twilight, another forty plus minutes before the sun makes an appearance. He tried to calculate what time zone Jake was in over in the Caribbean, but gave up. God I'm tired, he realised.

*

Things seemed to be sliding towards a confrontation in the South China Sea, thought Jake as he read the latest intelligence digest prepared from his many sources around the world. Their new found ability to locate and track submerged submarines had revealed at least four Kilos operating in the SCS within three hundred miles of a US carrier task group. That wasn't a recipe for anything yet but it could be that the first ingredients were being placed in the bowl; he had to make sure his own ships were not in the recipe further down the page.

He flicked Miles Carlson's card over and considered the consequences of telling Miles this piece of information. It would either trigger a request for verification or be dismissed as nonsense, he thought. Miles wasn't a fool though, he knew Jake wouldn't pick up the phone unless he was certain. So it depended on how well Miles was regarded now, he supposed.

"This is Jake, message for Miles. There are at least four Kilos operating in the SCS at the moment." He gave details of detection times and locations. "Oh and your Seawolf was following the first one. One of the Kilos attacked a König ship last night, it had a Special Forces delivery pod. It is currently following one of my ships and in turn being followed by my other unit. Just in case anyone is interested..."

*

Two hours later Admiral Summers was sitting in his customary place on the Admiral's bridge when his

186

communications chief brought a message which had passed through a variety of locations before arriving on Nimitz. Unknown to him, a certain CIA officer had read an interesting message from a reliable source. The message had sufficiently alarmed him that he needed to send a private coded message to a friend in the NSA. This is when a certain Vernon Weathers NSA, decoded the message redacted and re-arranged it and then re-routed it, to disguise the origin. After that it was sent on to Admiral Summers as part of an advisory.

Summers scratched his head a little and called the Captain.

"This smells of 'spook' to me," he announced without preamble to the Captain of the USS Nimitz as he entered, "but I wish someone could explain how spooks get information out of the depths of the ocean. It sure is pretty hard to ignore. Now interestingly one of these detailed contacts gives the same info as the Seawolf signalled yesterday. Worse though, it actually says where the Seawolf was." He looked up at his next down in the chain of command. "Even we don't know exactly where the fuck she is minute by minute for Christ's sake, which tallies with Seawolf's position report from yesterday too."

Captain Henry Balfour USN, was no high-speed-low-drag collar star chaser, he was on his last commission and looking forward to his retirement. Normally he would dismiss this kind of bullcrap but something stopped him. He re-read the classified intel-digest and especially the part the admiral referred to.

"Jamie, there's a subtle difference between the stuff that comes before and the stuff that follows this bit about the Kilos and Seawolf. Almost like this bit was copied and pasted into a routine, but still classified digest." He stopped talking and sat down thoughtfully, reaching for the

Admiral's coffee pot, something that would result in a rapid transfer for anyone else.

Admiral Summers had known 'Bull' Balfour since their days at Annapolis, his 'bullish' manner belied an acute tactical mind and the ability to sift information and winnow the salient facts from the dross. Yes, the 'tone' of the message did change. Now what did that mean?

"Do you suppose that this means we have ways of tracking submerged boats now and the clowns at foggy bottom aren't telling us they can?"

Balfour nearly spoke but bit his lip, Summers smiled, the reason 'Bull' had never collected a few stars was because he usually didn't bite his lip.

"Maybe. Maybe something else too. Whatever, I think we have to treat this as being a nugget of gold in a pan of shit, which means there's a lot of sneaky bastards in our back yard at the moment. Wish we still had the damned Vikings for their range. Anyway I'll get the escort commanders on conference and give them the good news about how they are going to break records for searching ocean and using up sonar buoys. Good job we have so many helo platforms around. Is there anything else you want Sir."

Summers noted the return of formality.

"No Captain. Carry on."

*

When dawn broke the USS Simmons, an Arleigh Burke II class DDG, had been closing with one of the pieces of land that the Chinese now claimed as part of their territorial waters. It wasn't the same one that had resulted in an exchange of fire and the damage to a sister ship a few short weeks ago, this one was further north towards the coast of Vietnam but still technically right slap bang in

188

the middle of international water as far as the rest of the world was concerned.

She was at action stations because of the previous incident and had not received any notifications regarding submarine activity in the area.

Her SPY-1D(V) radar system had the littoral warfare upgrade which her owners thought would make her better able to deal with anti-ship missile attacks in and around the myriad of atolls in this part of the SCS.

The Improved Kilo was drifting almost. Just station keeping with the three knot current trying to push her back around the shoal. The two 533 mm (21") UGST torpedoes that she had fired five minutes ago were close to completing their somewhat circuitous route towards the slow moving American destroyer, the three shoals nearby made for a perfect ambush site shielding the currently slow moving torpedoes to within two miles of the target, at which point or as soon as they were detected the wires would be cut and the Kilo would drift back into cover.

A beautiful sculpted patch of seabed close by provided a four hundred foot deep hidey hole, if needed, after the attack. If it was successful they wouldn't use it anyway, they'd just head north and then home.

Tension in the control room was at fever pitch. This was an act of war, everyone knew that. The Captain let the sweat run from his face and wished for the nth time he could move and wipe it with a cool cloth but he had to set an example. So he continued staring up at the periscope head that he couldn't yet use, while standing still, as was every member of the control team. All ventilation was off along with every non-essential piece of equipment which made a noise of any kind. All crewmembers not in the control room sat on the deck wherever they were and said nothing, did nothing, no noise at all. They had been at action stations for four hours now, ever since they had first detected the approach of the American ship using their ESM mast. There had been a helicopter active earlier but it had gone now, probably landed so as not to offer the island's defenders an easy air shot.

The Captain looked over to the torpedo console and the man carefully steering the two torpedoes on their short but hopefully spectacular voyage. He said nothing, a clock in his head was telling him it was time to cut them loose. Almost by telepathy the operator looked around at that moment and received a nod. He sent the commands to the two torpedoes which would accelerate them to their top speed of fifty knots and start their own active homing, then cut the wires.

The CIC of the USS Simmons was tense but quiet, this was a worked up ship, a competent crew. They were however unintentionally conditioned to look for danger from the man-made islands eight miles away. Their radar was active and so was the Chinese radar on the island. Everyone was tense but calm, they knew the Chinese would be at the same pitch of tension and no one wanted a mistake of any kind which would result in what happened to the Nathan Allen a couple of weeks before.

So when the passive sonar picked up the high speed hydrophone effect coming from seaward, there was a natural several second delay before the alarm was raised. In fairness the two torpedoes were less than a mile away at that point anyway and there's little likelihood that the ship could have reacted in any other way. The torpedoes were travelling at almost one mile per minute in their final phase and both began active sonar pinging less than three seconds after their approach had been heard.

No one can guess what goes through the mind of a commander when he is confronted by a lose lose situation like this this. Undoubtedly he would know he'd lost even before issuing the automatic commands learned over decades of service.

The ship responded like the thoroughbred she was, gas turbines screaming as the throttles were rammed forward to beg for instant flank speed. The rudder command after a few seconds was a patiently controlled response to the building speed. The man appeared calm on the surface at least, everyone said so later. There was no time to deploy any active countermeasures of any kind. No time to report the attack. No idea where the perpetrator was hiding either.

The twin explosions lifted the stern of the eight thousand ton destroyer out of the water and then slapped it down again. Water rushed in through two great rents starboard side way aft. There were many engineers killed in the blast as they were lifted and then slammed to the deck breaking bones here, there and everywhere as the shock was transmitted directly through the steel deck to them. Others were close to the blast and died immediately or drowned in the water that rushed over their unconscious forms. The lights went out.

She was a good ship though, her crew well trained. Damage assessment began immediately but with emergency lighting only it was even harder than usual to work out what was happening. The Captain thought frantically for a few seconds before quietly ordering all non-damage control and firefighting personnel to the upper deck, bow end. He sadly gave the preparatory orders necessary to begin the procedures for an orderly abandonment of the ship if the bulkheads didn't hold and if there were likely to be any further attacks. Then he got up and went in search of information.

Hood was twenty miles away at the time of the explosions, her passive sonar sounded an alert one and three quarter minutes after the twin blasts. The OPs team had been passively monitoring the approach of an American warship, thought to be an Arleigh Burke destroyer according to the Combat Management System.

The duty team had been monitoring the destroyer's approach to a Chinese claimed set of atolls and man-made islands for some hours. Now there were no radar transmissions just a low powered VHF signal.

The OPs supervisor didn't hesitate.

"Bridge, OPs."

"Bridge." Answered a tired Julius Kopf.

"Sir you know that American destroyer we've been tracking, it's gone quiet. Sonar reports twin explosions on her bearing. Underwater explosions."

"Shit. She's been torpedoed or mined or something. I'll call the Captain."

"Drone control, bridge."

"Drone control Aye."

"Can you move our recon bird twenty miles south southeast and search for the American destroyer we were listening to earlier."

"Aye, aye Sir."

Julius moved on to the next item on his mental procedure list.

"ROV control, bridge." Click then.

"ROV control.

"How long to recall and stow the ROV?"

Sensing some urgency in the request the ROV operator thought quickly.

"Ten minutes Sir."

"Begin recovery."

"Aye, aye Sir."

"OPs, is she transmitting on channel 16?"

"No Sir, they seem to want to keep this in house at present."

Last item. He spoke into the mike.

"Captain." Click then.

"Captain. What's happening?"

"Sir the American DDG we've been tracking has gone off line. Two underwater explosions were detected on her bearing at the time she went off. There's nothing but a low powered VHF now. I've re-tasked the recon drone to that area and commenced the recall of the ROV."

"Well done Julius you've read my mind again. Right, continue ROV recovery and let me know when we have any images of the Yank. Send an advisory to Simon and HQ. I'll be up to OPs in about ten minutes after a quick shower and a slice of toast."

"Roger that Sir."

The drone quickly picked up a plume of smoke on the expected bearing and continued to close while scanning all around with its LIDAR. By the time the ROV was recovered the whole grim picture was being viewed on large screen in the OPs room and Jon Roby was munching on a piece of toast heavily coated with his favourite sharp marmalade.

"Bloody hell. She's stopped, down at the stern and on fire aft. Zoom in on the bow please Drone control."

The picture wobbled then stabilised at high magnification. Upwards of a hundred sailors could be seen near the bow, sat on the deck in their life jackets, others could be seen gathered around the life raft launching points as if waiting for the order.

"ROV recovered Sir." Piped up one of the OPs operators.

"Right. Port 30 full ahead both, and helm take us on the quickest route through these shoals. Send a message to HQ and Ocean Guard that we are now in rescue mode." Then he touched a button on the command chair. "Do you hear there, this is the Captain. There's an American warship ship in distress about twenty miles away. We're going to render assistance. We shall also go to actions stations because at the moment we are unsure as to why she is in trouble. However, underwater explosions were reported on that bearing at the time we lost standard transmissions. So we have to be careful not to become a victim as well, if there are any nasties around. That's all for now."

Hood's ship's company reacted as trained when the action stations alarms sounded, everyone was closed up and ready for whatever was down the track within in five minutes. The primary teams replaced others at their actions stations who then went off to their own action posts, damage control teams began assembling packs of shoring timber and Louis Braime had two of the portable pumps taken up to the upperdeck near the bows. The fire fighters in their fear-nought suits stood calmly watching the monitor screens which showed the boiling smoke and occasional lick of flame visible on the stricken ship.

Roby wanted to try them on channel 16 but since they weren't asking for help on that channel he didn't want to compromise them. There was also the possibility that if somehow the Chinese were responsible, that he'd be announcing to them Hood's intent to intervene.

Sod it all. OK, we stay quiet and just appear wearing Cayman's battle ensigns, then if anyone interferes with rescue or damage control they'll have more to deal with than they bargained for. He looked at the bulkhead clock, they were about half an hour away by his reckoning, a lot can happen in half an hour.

"Drone reports vessels putting off from the Chinese island Sir!"

Roby came back to the present.

"Can the drone get a closer look?"

The image shifted and the boats zoomed into view, they weren't boats though they were hovercraft, big ones like the American LCACs, two of them. What the fuck did that mean? Were the Chinese attempting to help or were they about to make a disaster into a big fucking disaster?

The hover craft were approaching fast. Then he noticed sailors and marines taking up positions along the upperdeck of the American ship on the side closest to the approaching Chinese, they were armed.

"Guns, standby to engage approaching Chinese LCACs. On my command only."

"Standing by Sir." Answered McLean, fingers racing over his keyboard.

Kiwi McLean loaded the main batteries with HE and stood by, watching the approach of the Chinese vessels. They were already in range. But it was a big, big step to start shooting at them. He sincerely hoped they would back the fuck off if the Americans told them to, otherwise the stuff was going to hit the fan in bucket loads and only some of it was going to be brown.

OPs noted that one of the Hawkeyes had moved its racetrack orbital towards the distressed ship. Roby thought it would not be many minutes before there was a permanent CAP above the ship, but help from the CTG itself was hours away.

"Smoke plume in sight off the starboard bow Sir."

"Roger bridge." Answered the OPs Supervisor.

Roby stood up.

"I'm going up."

He quickly climbed to the bridge, it was always better to see first-hand.

"Begin radiating if you please." He said as he took his seat in the command chair. He wanted plenty of warning before the first American aerial response arrived.

"Conversation on channel 16 between the Chinese LCACs and the Americans Sir. The Chinese have offered assistance but the Yanks are telling them to go away politely and warning them not to get any closer. The Chinese have acknowledged."

It was clear to Roby that the Chinese therefore were not trying to make a bad situation worse. Was this the action of people who had just deliberately attacked a ship of a foreign navy? Not unless the Chinese commander was unaware of what his head office's plans were. Unlikely though, since as the nearest target of opportunity, his lot would get the payback if there were any.

"Sonar anything?"

"Nothing Sir. Difficult sonar conditions around here Sir with all the shoals and such."

Hmmph was Roby's only reply.

"McClelland." He said into the mike.

"Jon what's happening?" Asked Simon as soon as they were connected.

Roby brought him up to speed quickly.

"Simon, is your laser drone ready yet? I need mine to see if there are any nasties hiding around here?"

"Yes, I'll get it up straight away, be about ten minutes OK? I expect we'll be able to pick up the trail easy enough, he doesn't know we're watching and isn't being evasive."

"Fine, that was my conclusion too. I'll bring ours over this way then. Since your limpet seems very attracted to you, do you want to lead it towards deeper water? It won't like that and there's always the possibility that one of Uncle Sam's big black slugs is prowling around at the edge of the deeps."

"Not a bad idea if I can do it without giving him a direct line of shot at me or even a good sonar fix. Otherwise I'm going to keep threading these islands and have a look at the suspect area.

"OK, I'll let you know what goes down here, if and when something does."

Just then Lt Bianchi joined in.

"Inbound aircraft. Two. Right down on the deck bearing zero nine five degrees range four zero miles. Speed is err.... 600 knots. No active transmissions. They will pass directly over the American ship."

A few seconds later he made the next call.

"They're climbing now and turning. Looks like they're going into contra orbit. They've levelled off at 5000 feet."

"They're transmitting." Piped up Ringbolt Langford. "We have an incoming transmission on channel 16."

"This is US Navy aircraft Mike Papa Juliet one two, vessel steering one zero five degrees at eight miles, bearing three one zero from me. Please identify."

Roby nodded to Bianchi.

"Mike Papa Juliet one two, this is Bravo Kilo Two, Merchant Protector Hood, heading towards your stricken vessel to render assistance. Pass on, we have no surface or sub-surface contacts at present but be advised there is an improved Kilo India Lima Oscar operating twenty miles north and there are others around."

"Roger that Bravo Kilo Two. Will pass on. But be advised you should not approach our ship."

"Mike Papa Juliet this is Bravo Kilo Two, I suggest you ask the skipper of your ship whether he could do with a couple of portable generators and pumps. Plus we have firefighting and damage control teams available and a medical team."

"Bravo Kilo Two. Stand by."

"They need to look us up in the book before turning down our help." Roby muttered loudly to no one in particular.

Admiral Summers looked up as Bull Balfour knocked and came in.

"Sir, one of our Hornets over the Simmons has had contact with a ship wanting to assist. It is a Merchant Protector class vessel called Hood, Captained by one Jonathan Roby RN, retired.

"Damn me, Jonno Roby. Had some serious beers with him when we both had ships in STANAVFORLANT, if it's the same fella of course. I read about another of those Merchant Protector ships in the Caribbean a year or so ago. Damn but they're feisty, like a bear with a sore ass. Can you get a patch through our Hawkeye, I'll talk to him one on one, see if he can help?"

"There's another part to the message Sir, they say there are Kilos operating in the area and they already know of one twenty miles or so to the north."

"That's too big a damned coincidence ain't it. Hot damn what are they up to out here?

"Guess we'll find out if you give him a call Admiral. The Chinese have backed off a ways now too."

"Set it up Bull."

"Aye, aye Sir." Bull wandered out listening to the Admiral chuckling about Jonno Roby."

*

"Captain." Lt Bianchi had a bemused smile on his face.

"Sir I've got someone called Summers claiming to be an American Admiral and Commander of the US task Group to our north east. Wants to know if Jonno has any more of that special rum stashed in his cabin?"

Roby let out a loud guffaw.

"Good Lord, Jamie Summers an Admiral? "Whatever next? Put him on speaker."

"Jamie you old fraud. Are they that desperate that they not only gave you a couple of stars, they gave you some ships to play with?"

A loud barking laugh came from the other end.

"They sure did Jonno, shows how low the USN has gotten nowadays old friend."

"Come on, too modest, you were always a shoo in for those stars Jamie my friend. Anyway this line is about as secure as it gets so I'd better tell you what's happening. You can't ask too much at this point because the big boss has yet to announce things. Right now, we're out here looking for some pirated or just plain missing ships, or a clue any clue as to where they might be. However there have been some bloody strange things going on the last few days. Last night our other ship was attacked by Special Forces chaps, launched from one of those conforming pods on the back of an improved Kilo, but not twenty miles away from your currently stricken ship."

"Jonno, I hate to interrupt such a great story but I think a few pieces of my own puzzle have just fallen into place. You just said an Improved Kilo dropped off SF guys to attack your ship, is your other ship like yours i.e. armed to the teeth?" He was now looking at a photo of the Hood courtesy of US Naval Intelligence.

"Err no, not quite. Oh dear, trade secrets about to come out. It's a Q ship Jamie, we usually go hunting pirates in it and it has a certain defensive firepower that your bog standard pirate couldn't compete with so to speak."

"OK, I kind of get the picture, fast forward. This Kilo attacked your ship by launching an SF attack at sea? What happened to them? Where were they from? Has to be China or Vietnam right?"

"Ah well they were repulsed with casualties. We managed to get two bodies that's all, no living ones."

"What happened to the rest?"

"Erm they kind of died a bit Jamie. A lot actually. There were no survivors from the SF team and I shelled the sub a bit and it dived. We've been following it ever since, right up until something happened to your vessel here."

"Jees, you Brits with your understatements. When you say you've been following them. What exactly do you mean?"

"Aah, now you're treading on thin ice, or rather I would be. Look suffice to say we know where one of them is at this precise moment and we've seen four so far in the few days we've been in the area. You'll have to trust me on that point. Anyway can we go and help your chaps? We have fire and rescue as well as medical. We can provide pumps and a generator."

"OK. Look forget the rest of the conversation Jonno, you go and help where you can and we'll be grateful for the assist. Hey when this is over, you and I got to get together in Japan or something. Call me if you need anything, right now you got 24 hour CAP and one of my other destroyers is currently at flank. She'll get there in less than seven hours. Oh, by the way the ship you're helping is the USS Simmons."

"Right you are Jamie, we'll get on and do all we can to help your chaps. Speak soon."

Roby turned to the OPs room.

"Right let's go. See if you can get someone with a lamp to communicate with the Simmons please."

Ten minutes later Hood moved slowly bow to bow with the Simmons and lines were passed. About ten feet of each bow over lapped with the American bow two or three yards higher than Hood. Fenders kept them from damaging each other as a ropeway and steps down were quickly established. First order of business were the generators and two pumps which were quickly passed across and the Chief Engineer plus one went with them. The Americans quickly manhandled the bulky equipment to appropriate points and began setting the generator up while the pumps quickly disappeared below. A sooty faced Lt Commander came forward and shouted across to Roby while he stood off to one side from the Hoods bows, legs apart fists on hips.

"Captain Roby I presume?"

"Yes Commander, what can we do to help? I've got a medical team here and volunteers to help the firefighting if you want."

"Michael Coveos Captain. That's real kind Sir but we've plenty of firefighters for when those pumps get into action. The generator will give us a chance to rig some of our pumps we hope too. Could you take our wounded aboard Sir? They're having a tough time out in the sunshine and some of them will need more care than we can give, the sickbay is almost in darkness at the moment."

"No sooner said than done." He turned to Warrant Officer Crause.

"Get the lads to help lift across the casualties Mr Crause. Chief Parker, get your team over to help triage and take charge of bringing back casualties. Someone tell the Doctor to prep the wardroom for casualties please."

Then he addressed the Lt Commander.

"Where is your Captain Commander Coveos?

"Ah he's missing at the moment Sir. He went to investigate the damage after we were hit, by the way it was two torpedoes, then there was another explosion near the Mk41 VLS and he hasn't been seen since. I guess I'm Captain for now Sir."

"Thanks for the torpedo tip. One moment please." He tapped his face mike twice.

"Drone control." Click.

"Drone control aye."

201

"Confirmed the ship was torpedoed Chief, make up a second laser package and get it airborne fast, then get the First Lieutenant to help you work out the most likely submarine egress routes. Assume the attacker has slipped away for now but may come back."

"Aye, aye Sir." Then he turned back to the American.

"Anything you need Captain, and it's yours if I've got it. Do not hesitate to ask."

"Thanks again Captain Roby, I'll be getting back to the shoring party now, one of the bulkheads is seeping some."

"I've plenty of shoring timber if you need any. How many casualties have you suffered?"

"Well it isn't an accurate count at the moment but I think we lost about thirty five people if we include the skipper, about the same wounded too. Be seeing you."

Roby watched him go. What a bloody mess this is. There will be all sorts of shit to pay. He crossed to the Simmons' fo'c'sle and observed his small medical team as they linked up with the Simmons' own medical staff and began moving casualties to Hood. He wandered round. A word here and a word there, he had a big bag of humbugs and offered them around. The sailors were pretty stunned most said nothing they just looked blankly out to the sea, but they smiled and looked up when the tall gangling Captain wandered around offering that most traditional British sweet.

They're in shock thought Roby as he did his best to get some animation out of them. The seniors were organising now, taking names and numbers to catalogue survivors and also asking about missing crewmembers. Chiefs are priceless, he decided, as he watched them walk among the crew and then detail off people to go and get drinks and whatever food they could scrounge up.

Julius Kopf sat with Chief McKenzie looking at the charts of the surrounding area. They'd spotted two possible places to start the search from and were working out how far out to go before starting another search. In Julius's opinion the submarine would slip quietly away having done its dirty deed. The likelihood that it was yet another improved Kilo was high and so he worked on a top escape speed of five knots, just about the fastest a Kilo could go without making noise which could be picked up by passive sonar at quite a range. Once they were singing from the same hymn sheet the drone Chief got on with programming a search pattern which would favour the two potential egress routes. Julius went back to the Hood's bows to see if there was anything more he could do to help.

It took another twenty minutes and some serious cursing before both pumps and generators were up and running. One of the Simmons' surviving engineers and Chief Braime had finally worked out how to integrate their circuits without blowing fuses everywhere and the fire was quickly brought under control. The pumps drained the compartments forward of the damaged areas but there was nothing they could do about the fully flooded areas, the holes were simply too big. The generator was now chugging away happily and providing power as needed to various sub systems.

Roby went to see if he could find their new Captain, after several twists and turns and a couple of deck changes he found him inspecting the shored bulkhead which had been giving problems.

"Ah there you are. Look my doctor says some of your chaps and chapesses need extra care or they'll either die or lose limbs. There are four on the immediate list. Do you think you could talk to your colleagues who are on their way here now and perhaps get their helo to ferry them to Nimitz?"

"Well there's nothing more I can do down here, if we're lucky and it doesn't come on to blow at all we might get a tow to a port somewhere around here. Let's go see if I can rustle up a medevac."

Five minutes later he informed Jonno that an MH-60R was leaving the fast approaching backup destroyer, the USS WS Churchill.

"Right I'll inform my lot and we'll get them prepped for winching. Do you have access to any of your flight gear for them, the ones that we can dress that is?"

"I'll find out." He looked around and spotted a Master Chief. "Chief can I borrow you a second?" Then he explained what he wanted.

"I'll get a couple of boys and see if we can get into the hanger Sir, bound to be plenty in there." The Master Chief went off shouting orders and calling for people by name.

"Look Mike, we'll hang around here until your back up arrives, can't leave you in case that bulkhead gives way and you need somewhere dry in a hurry. Thing is though we're using drones to search for the bastard who did this – don't ask," he noted the puzzled look on the American's face, "I'd have to kill you and eat you if I told you. So what I'm saying is that we'll be here but cruising around for launch and recovery of said drones. Let me have a radio handset and we'll keep it on the bridge. You can let us know if there's anything you need or if there's a problem."

The American stuck out his hand and shook Jonno's, then he quite unexpectedly stepped back and gave a sharp salute. Jonno had no choice but to follow suit.

"Righto, I'll be off, and good luck Mike."

"You too Jonno, if I may?"

"You certainly may Mike. Take care."

Back on Hood Roby went straight to the bridge to catch up.

"Anything on the search for the bastard that tinfished them?"

Julius Kopf looked up from his ECDIS chart.

"Actually you may have arrived just at the right moment Sir, drone control report they are following up a possible wake that they think is some hours old. At least they know which way to go to find a newer trace, better still we know it is the culprit because we know from where he came."

"Well that is good news for a change. I'm sure our American cousins will be most interested in that tit bit. The more I think about it the less I'm sure it is the Chinese. It makes so little sense for them to do this BUT if you were trying to get them the blame for something, might you do it this way?"

"I suppose so Sir but really that only leaves Vietnam as the owner of the Kilos, why would they be trying to set the Chinese up?"

"Good question. Short answer is that none of this makes sense when you use logic."

*

Two hours later the casualties had been winched up and were well on their way to Nimitz, which like all big carriers had a full medical team on board. Now out of the haze to the east the USS WS Churchill emerged from the morning mists and gave a light signal 'hello' to the Hood. Roby got on the VHF phone to her Captain. They quickly organised an orderly transfer of the less badly wounded from Hood before handing over the overwatch to the new arrival. Then the tricky bit began and Roby decided a face to face with the Churchill's skipper would be the best way to introduce what they knew about the attacker and where it was currently, so he invited the American Captain on board after he'd done his duty by the Simmons and her crew.

They stood in Hood's OPs room and Roby could tell the American skipper was impressed with what he saw. He showed him the 3D holo display and then brought up the current and past track of the target the drone was now following steadily. During the last five minutes the drone had actually pinpointed the moving submarine, it was now fourteen miles away from its starting point that morning. He saved the best until last.

"When we take our leave in a few minutes, we will head towards this fellow and when we're close enough will send something down to positively identify its make and class. It won't tell us the owner's name though. Then if your comms people and mine can work something out, we'll send you a picture of the bastard who torpedoed your colleagues over there. Then I'm afraid it's up to you, we have no ASW capability."

"Wow. This is phenomenal and also highly 'explosive' technology isn't it?" He waved his hands at the track readings on the hologramatic representation. "Your drones can track them?" The American Captain was no one's fool.

"A recently discovered ability in fact. So at least we'll be able to let you deal with them if you choose to." He said, moving swiftly on.

"Well I'll fire it up the chain, this one is out of my pay grade, the Admiral's too I shouldn't wonder."

With a final farewell on the signal lamp, mainly because Petty Officer 'Hughie' Green had re-discovered his love of Morse, Hood increased speed and turned smartly to port heading back towards the northerly group of atolls and the Ocean Guard.

Simon received the news with relief but changed his mind when Jonno briefed him of on the ROV's latest mission.

"Shit you sent them pictures? Jake will kill you and scatter your ashes over the seven seas Jonno. We were supposed to keep Mum about this stuff."

"Didn't see I had any choice Si, we couldn't let the bastard get away scot free could we?"

"Mmm, I hope for your sake Jake agrees or you'll be hanging from the nearest yardarm before your ashes are scattered. Anyway, we took over following our SF delivery boat and it looks like he's decided to go home. The drone followed him for a few hours and he's just sat on a northerly course, rough guess towards Hong Kong if he stays on the current track."

"This is bizarre. The Chinese on the island near to where the Simmons was hit, sent a pair of LCACs to help. Pretty sure they wouldn't do that if their own sub had just put a pair of tinfish into the Yankee now would they?"

"I don't have second sight Jonno and neither do you. Without having all the pieces of the puzzle we have no idea what is going on here except this. Whoever is steering this game doesn't give a fuck about kicking off a war between two major powers, they most certainly don't care about making us disappear permanently. I think Jake should pull us out before we get pulled in all the way, if you see what I mean." He paused to catch his breath and OK a turn to starboard before pressing on. "At the moment the attack on my ship is known only to us and the buggers that did it. I suspect they'd rather keep it that way either by sinking me or ignoring me and hoping I'll go away. Now I'm not a betting man but I'd put my pension on the incident in Labuan being an attempt to keep track of the only player in this game who is an unknown quantity and a possible fly in someone's ointment, and a very carefully prepared pot of ointment it has been. This attack on the Simmons is an escalation of extraordinary scale. There will be folks in high office in the US who want to come out and blame the

Chinese in public as well as send them a message at the end of a cloud of Tomahawks."

"That's just it Simon. I can see false flags all over this. Everything is all too convenient and points in just one direction. One thing the Chinese aren't is stupid. If they wanted to take out a US destroyer why would they do it next to one of their claimed islands? They could have done it a long way away and made it almost impossible for the Americans to pin it on them whilst still sending the message that they wanted. The US would know but not be able to prove it. This proximity to the disputed island sounds very much like 'a big boy did it and ran away'. Too obvious and the Chinese are nothing if not subtle in their 'long plans'."

"Fair points all. Changing the subject, when do you expect to re-join me."

Roby thought a minute and checked the chart.

"In time for a late lunch. Why not come across and we can have a live chat with Jake if we can find him. We can also debate the merit of checking that area you suspect or bugging out as our cousins say."

"Sounds like a plan. Oh and by the way the met indicates the weather changing round here over the next couple of days. If the seas get up they'll stir things up and we'll lose our magic submarine tracking ability or at least have it degraded in littoral waters as well as our ability to find ships sat on the bottom."

*

Admiral Summers sat brooding. This was turning out to be a major shit-storm. His orders made him responsible for the level of confidence he attached to the information and God Damn it, those incredible pictures of the Kilo. Well this one was shit or bust. If he accepted that this was the vessel which had torpedoed the Simmons he was duty bound to take it out. America just couldn't let any asshole go around 'plinking' destroyers and think they could get away without the wrath of the USN descending on them. But if he sank this Kilo and it somehow turned out to be not connected with the Simmons, he could kiss his next star and career goodbye. Minutes. I've got minutes to decide before the datum for the Kilo is too old for the Mk46s in the ASROCs to find it.

"Bull. Ask the Hood if it can keep drone contact on the Kilo until a LAMPsIII off the WS Churchill can get an active ping on the boat. Say about fifteen minutes. Get the Churchill closer but always with an island between it and that damned thing. I'll let you know to kill it when my aging mind has worked through things a little more."

"OK Admiral, I know this is your decision alone but I'm with you either way."

"Thanks Bull."

Summers went back to his ruminations. He looked at the signal from SecDef via CNO again, written by a fucking politician and no mention of the President. Someone keeping their shoes fucking polished so any falling turds slide straight off. Hell Jamie boy you're the one playing for time now. You're the one whose decision is based on the same information you had fifteen minutes ago but still haven't acted on. He gave himself a mental slap or two. Come on Summers stop sitting on your fucking hands, make a decision. Is this the boat that killed upwards of thirty American sailors and injured even more? If you're sure it is, you have to kill it in turn. He looked again at the perfect rendering the submersible or whatever it was, had taken of the Kilo, every fucking bump and barnacle but no red star on the fin to nicely advertise ownership. But did it matter who the owner was if he was certain it was the culprit.

He looked again at the Hood's trackback for this submarine. He pulled over the chart for the area and studied the seabed terrain as a submariner would. It helped that he had two such people as senior officers on this ship and they had both independently, given the same charts and the ambush location, pointed to where the boat most likely hid and the way it most likely departed the scene. They both agreed and when you marry that to Hood's backtrack and overlay all three, you get this fucker just slowly sailing away having fucked Uncle Sam over a desk end.

He reached for the intercom.

"Bull, give the order. Kill track designated Sierra one two. Issue orders to Churchill to use ASROCs and monitor with the LAMPs. LAMPs to finish off if the ASROCs are unsuccessful."

"Aye, aye Sir. Kill track designated Sierra one two."

Seconds later the VLS tubes on the USS WS Churchill kicked out two RUM-139, vertical launched anti-submarine rockets and they boosted away to the current location of the unaware Kilo as it slunk away north.

The two airborne torpedoes lost their boosters and splashed into the sea six hundred and fifty yards from the Kilo, one on either beam. Arming distance. They immediately powered up and began actively scanning with their on-board sonar turning in a descending spiral until both found the Kilo.

The drone observed the sudden increase in the Kilo's speed and it rapidly changed both direction and depth, kicking out decoys but the two Mk 46's were not deceived and it all ended with two dreadful detonations close about the stern. The LAMPs observed the two muddy humps in the water and dipped its sonar to check out whether the Kilo was fatally damaged or not. Passive sensors picked up the awful sound of internal bulkheads collapsing. It was a kill. The LAMPs marked the area with a coded nav buoy in order to be able to find the wreck again. The US would be re-visiting this wreck to identify once and for all the perpetrators of the Simmons attack.

Jamie Summers got through again to Roby on the Hood.

"I've done it Jonno, killed it and everyone on it. It won't of course bring those boys and girls back for the Simmons but such an attack cannot go unpunished. I suppose we have to wait around now until someone asks if anyone has seen their submarine. We will of course get a dive team and a heavy lifter over there in due course."

Roby heard the sadness in the Admiral's voice and knew it was genuine.

"In my humble opinion Jamie, you didn't have any choice. I just hope we find out before long why so many young people had to die. My money is an each way bet on greed or revenge."

"Look Jonno, I know you guys have got something, a box of tricks of some kind that will change a whole hell of a lot of things before long but there's a 'here and now' element in this. My cynical mind says there's more to come in this sad little saga and it may have something to do with not letting you find those missing ships. So I've decided to hang around a little at this end of the pond, a few days only though. If you have need of us and I can twist it and turn it to allow me to help, I will. Even if it's just a heads up on incoming stuff."

"That's big of you Jamie, I know how constrained you are by your masters and that we aren't formal allies so to speak. Don't take it the wrong way but I really hope I don't need to call but if I need a hand I hope you can come."

"OK. Now don't forget the night on the town in Japan."

"Oh Lord I'm not sure my liver can take that sort of punishment any more but I'll see what I can do. See you later Jamie."

"Bye for now Jonno and good hunting."

Good hunting indeed, thought Jonathan Roby. So far they'd not managed what the Lloyds people had contracted them to do, however they had managed a status quo changing discovery, helped sink a submarine owned by God knows who and aided in a firefighting and rescue mission. Variety is the spice of life I suppose.

*

It was getting late in the afternoon when they finally hove in sight of Ocean Guard and somewhat later than expected. They'd sat stationary for nearly two hours as a cable and drum malfunction on the ROV system needed divers to go down and un-tangle the mess, it had somehow jumped its runner and begun wrapping round the axle instead of threading onto the drum.

According to the CMS link between the ships, two of Ocean Guard's drones were up. Presumably a recon bird and a laser bird, decided Julius Kopf as he scanned Ocean Guard on their approach to her. She had had no contact for some hours with the Kilo that had deployed the SF team, but that didn't mean it had gone away so it had to be factored in. Looking at the pattern that the laser bird was flying and checking against the chart indicated that Simon and his team were keen to watch any and all sub surface approach channels to them in the northern part of this atoll chain. Clearly, having Hood's drones join in would widen the search area and speed things up. The only slight drawback with the laser drones was that they hadn't quite the endurance of the others, probably mostly because they operated at only eight hundred feet altitude whilst the recon birds drifted along at five thousand feet. With eight drones between them, four running laser searches and four on recon, they could safely cover quite a lot of ground and probably finish this part of the search area quickly and move further south and west, he thought. Depends on the conference with the big boss he supposed.

Simon motored over to the meeting on Hood in one of their RHIBs, he sat on the centre seat as the nimble craft sped across the surface. As they drew closer he saw Hood's profile change giving him a slow 360 degree view of that famous silhouette. She must be doing random figure of eights he decided, waste of time if he's facing wire guided torpedoes but better than a stationary target he supposed.

On board and down in the wardroom Simon waited while Roby finished talking to the OPs communication specialist about the video feed connection. At last it appeared sorted and the screen came on with a thirty second countdown.

Jonno sat next to Simon on one of the comfy chairs, he almost ordered popcorn and coke but decided the irreverence may not be appreciated.

Then a picture formed. Jake sitting on a comfy chair too in what looked to be a small office or such.

"Morning Gentlemen."

"Afternoon boss." Grinned Roby and elicited a smile.

"Amazing this real time comms stuff isn't it. Probably the very best thing ever to come out of the internet." Answered Jake. "Anyway you two have been busy stirring up a hornet's nest I see. I received all the reports and the video footage and concur with almost all of your speculations and conclusions." He paused and dusted an imaginary spec of fluff from his knife-edge creased trousers.

"Clearly Jonno you have revealed the little secret we possessed in order for the Americans to exact revenge on the submarine which attacked them. I had hoped for this to remain a secret until you had both left the region."

Jonno interrupted.

"Sorry boss but I thought the Americans deserved a pop at the fellow who attacked them, he's probably from the same mob that attacked Simon too. The Admiral in command is an old pal of mine and he says his group will now hang around for a couple of days to sort of act as sort of distant cover instead of heading north-east as they planned originally."

"Yes, I can see your point Jonno but I wish the circumstances were different; how long will your pal keep mum about our discovery?"

"Not sure, I think he wanted the enemy sub more than anything else, they lost a lot of good people. I think he'll keep it in until he sends his final report to the Pentagon and then the lid will pop off."

"Not long then. I suppose we can be grateful that China hasn't been all over the airwaves about US aggression otherwise it might be a little quicker. Simon how confident are you that the Kilo which tried boarding you is out of the area?"

"Fairly. That's the best I can say boss. I'll claim the Belgrano defence if I'm wrong and he turns around. He was on a straight course just past north north east for five and a half hours, but that coincides with a known channel for a hundred miles or so which then opens out and he could really have gone anywhere, however Hong Kong would only be a few degrees off from that direction."

"OK. I suppose that's the biggest drawback with this gear, you cannot actually identify who owns the submarine unless it is unique in shape, owner or type."

"Got an answer for that too bossman." Interrupted Roby again. "A camera to take a flash shot to see any markings at all."

"Possibly, I'll pass that on. The laser alone would be good enough to identify US and UK subs but not an awful lot of use for Kilos or plenty of German and Japanese sub types either as both are widely exported." He picked up a sheet of paper from his desk and read it again before putting it down.

"Anyway, a little bird has whispered to me that there is a Chinese SAG heading down into the South China Sea at this very moment, it sailed from Hong Kong yesterday morning. Whether it is as a result of recent activity or whether it has been long planned I don't know, but it could get a bit hairy around there if they start chucking stuff at each other. The SAG will be supported by land based air no doubt which evens things up a little and I rather expect your admiral pal will be in the picture by now."

"Do we know the composition of the SAG?" Asked Simon.

"No not as yet, a dozen ships is all I know but you can bet that the Chinese will have some of their newest units in it and they are first class."

"Let's hope they all keep their fingers off the red buttons while they are wandering in the vicinity of each other." Added Roby thoughtfully.

"Indeed. Now that brings me to the nub of this call. I need you both out of there at the latest in 48 hours, and Jonno you are now officially riding shotgun as well as search partner. I want you to ensure nothing approaches you by sea or air without you being well aware. Your ROE are as usual. Fire if fired upon or if in your opinion your ship will be endangered if you do not shoot; on the other hand I have it on good authority you'll be in for a bit of a blow after that so searching will be curtailed anyway."

"Will do Jake, I'll try to keep slow-mo here safe."

Simon bridled a bit at the description of his ship but said nothing.

"Well, when you leave you can both head back to Labuan, that should take you out of harm's way. Just be careful please the pair of you, and get out on time whether that area survey is finished or not."

"Aye, aye." They both answered and the screen went blank.

Simon waited a moment before speaking.

"He's on Bismarck."

Roby looked up interested.

"How do you know?"

"There was a watercolour on the bulkhead behind and to the left of him, I recognised it. Can't imagine a bloke as rich as Jake having a job-lot of the same piccy. Wonder if he's out there checking on the Japanese contract?"

Simon had of course been First Lieutenant of Bismarck the year before.

"Mmm, I suppose they will be starting production soonest, they seemed pretty keen to get going. Anyway I'll get some coffee, and tea for you of course, and we can finalise tomorrow's search pattern and drone activity."

A thorough examination of the charts of the area, some of which it had to be said, were a little suspect, revealed a limited number of locations where someone might 'park' ships on the seabed. There were also several atoll collections none of which were supposed to be occupied but all claimed by China.

It would be best if there weren't any Chinese on them otherwise they might object to having nearby waters searched and they also might spot a drone, or eight. They decided that Roby would search the southern end of the box, search area one, and Simon would start in the centre, and then work north, search area two. They agreed also that it was too dangerous for searching in the dark in amongst the shoals and that they would both make slow and careful passage through the night to their jump off points for a first thing in the morning start.

In addition Hood with its full OPs room and staff would monitor all the recon birds and Ocean Guard would set the search patterns for the laser carriers and review the footage, when a bird needed to re-fuel they would be handed back into control of the owning ship. The ROVs would only be launched if the drones spotted something worth investigating, otherwise the ships would just slowly travel through the area mapping the seabed for chart production.

One Week before

Jake worried. He sat in the OPs room of Bismarck as she butted through a medium chop at her fastest economical speed which was twenty one knots; the motion was slightly awkward because of an almost following sea, not quite right on the stern though. They'd need a refuel and RAS soon and the rendezvous had been agreed with their auxiliary ship. The last few days had been hectic for him and the ship's company to say the least. After his conversation with Sophie he'd set about getting closer to the action so to speak.

The Caribbean was the wrong side of the world to be making decisions where his ships and men were concerned so he'd hopped a company jet to Prince Said Ibrahim International Airport, Moroni, Comoros. On the way he wondered what sort of reception he'd get from this ninety eight percent Muslim country. They may well be Sunni, he mused, but they are Muslim first and foremost and so the spat with the Iranians of Shiite belief could have pissed the locals off to the point where the Japanese contract may have to be abandoned.

He recalled the landing and the passage through customs and immigration had gone OK until he, Granny Smith and Tetsunari were asked to accompany a man in the uniform of a police officer. They were taken to a room which belonged to the senior immigration and customs officer and there they waited for five minutes with no explanation, Granny chuntered just under the audible range and Jake could pick out the occasional non-PC description of their hosts. He was outwardly calm but inside was wondering where this might go.

In Japanese he asked Tetsunari to speak to the company jet and find out how long down time they needed before they could fly again. Having a Japanese pilot and bodyguard was a real bonus in this situation since the likelihood of the single policeman left in the room speaking Japanese was pretty low.

Tetsunari tapped his earpiece, spoke the pilot's name and connected. Jake thanked the Lord they were still in WiFi range. The answer was two and a half hours.

A minute later the door on the opposite side of the office opened and a man in a suit with a slight bulge under his left arm entered and stepped to the left, he was followed by another in traditional robes and backed by two others in suits who took up strategic positions clearly his body guards, and finally a pretty young woman also wearing traditional robes and a headscarf but no veil. Jake was quietly amused as he observed Tetsunari scrutinise the newcomers in his own inimitable style and write them off as a waste of space.

Jake had recognised the newcomer as Azali Assoumani current President of the Comoros a former Colonel in their armed forces trained by both Moroccan and French military colleges and three times President of these islands.

"Good afternoon Mr President, so kind of you to welcome me personally."

Assoumani smiled but it didn't get as far as his eyes. He spoke in French and his pretty interpreter translated.

"Mr König I presume?" Jake just nodded. "I have come here to both welcome and warn you. I am aware of your, shall we say, little mishap with the brothers in the Straits of Hormuz." He continued without waiting for Jake to comment. "So my warning is simple, please keep a low profile for you and your men while on any Comoro Island, there may be those who feel the need to seek vengeance on behalf of the fools who attacked you and failed."

Jake was somewhat reassured by the nuance of the last sentence. Perhaps as a former military man he saw that the Iranians had started something and underestimated their opponent or were simply foolish for starting something at all?

"However now I would like to welcome you privately and say how pleased I was that the Japanese showed such sagacity in their choice of protectors, truly your reputation precedes you. I have read at great length of your activities in the Caribbean and latterly on either side of the African Continent. No one with an ounce of sense condones theft and barbarity. So now I will take my leave and wish you success on behalf of myself and my people; Mr König we need the revenue from these discoveries to help us achieve greater things."

"I thank you Mr President. My people will not in any way make themselves a nuisance, you will not even know they are here. They will pass through this terminal to and from the production platforms in a civilised and polite manner, there will be no exceptions." He paused a heartbeat. "I wish you good fortune in next year's elections Mr President."

Assoumani smiled this time with genuine amusement. He nodded once more appraised Jake again and left through the same door.

Jake drew a deep breath then let it out slowly. The policeman who had been dismissed when the president arrived, returned and escorted them back in to the terminal where another Japanese waited patiently to guide them to the waiting helicopter and fly them out to the platform.

The production rig closest to the disputed area had been chosen by Andy Evans as the command post for security operations on all the platforms both production and accommodation. To that end König Marine Security had a quartet on each of the rigs with an additional QRF of eight on this platform with heavy weapons if needed. The utility helicopter they were currently flying in was one of two permanently based here, one was always to be available for QRF at five minute standby. They also had a pair of RHIBs with a heavy machine gun on a pintle mount near the bow.

While they circled and came in for landing Jake could just see a familiar silhouette near the horizon, clearly heading this way. As they landed Andy Evans himself appeared on the pad to wait for his boss.

Ten minutes later they were all sat in the Security Chief's office drinking something cold and refreshing.

"So what brings you here boss. No notice visits aren't your style?"

Jake smiled.

"Got to keep you on your toes Andy. I'm curious as to whether there's a need for one of the Merchant Protectors to be stationed here given your resources and the opposition. I mean they officially have just one attack helicopter and an old Spanish customs patrol ship. What else are you up against?"

Andy hurumphed and pulled up a digital map of the area.

"The pink dots are sightings or contacts suspected to be related to the unofficial opposition to Comoros's good fortune. The red ones are definite contacts or incidents involving unofficial opposition. The blue dots are where Mozambique official forces have been sighted."

Jake squinted a little closer, he could see a number of pink dots, maybe two dozen, half a dozen red dots located close to what he assumed were the rigs.

"I can't see any blue dots."

"No you won't there aren't any, the buggers are playing it crafty like. The Mozambique government can say with hand on heart that it isn't violating anyone's territorial waters. But someone is buying fast sports boats and kitting them out with RPGs and DShKM machine guns.

They zoom in pretty close to the platforms and let off a few rounds. The Japanese have no choice but to cease production while they are in the area, the tankers have to stop loading too. Everything grinds to a halt."

"How often?"

"At least once a day."

"That bad. We'd better pull our fingers out or the Japanese will be wanting a refund."

"My thoughts too. I've studied the contacts, times, numbers, locations etcetera. They're getting careless. There's a pattern forming. These guys know what they're doing, they know how it fucks up production."

He pointed to a rig about five miles to their south.

"If I'm right, they'll hit this one this evening between six and seven, just after sunset and then disappear in to the dark thinking they're invisible and that production will be shut down for hours because they could return at any time. So far they have reappeared just once and really that's all it needs to stop production 'just in case'."

"What are you planning to do about it?"

"I've asked for Reiner's help. We're going to spend a bit of your money. He'll have a pair of drones up watching for the buggers. They'll spot them in plenty of time to gather an intercept force. I've got the two RHIBs fitted out with a five thousand Watt LED deck light, Bismarck has her own mega searchlights, so what we'll do is scare the living shit out of them. They always approach in the twilight so the rigs with their lights and burn-off plumes are just guiding beacons for them. The RHIBS will come from the flanks and Bismarck will come from dead ahead. If we get it right everyone will illuminate them simultaneously and Reiner in his best Teutonic voice at 500db will start ordering them to close their throttles and standby to be boarded. Bismarck'll swing sideways and let them see all the guns trained on them. You'd have to be a total fuckwit

222

to even think of challenging such overwhelming force. Then we take 'em in and hand them over to the Comoros authorities for a bit of a chat."

Andy grinned at that point.

"I can imagine the Comoros boys will be well pissed off with them. Maybe a public trial. Sod knows what the Quran says about stopping oil production but I'm sure the punishment won't be nice. That should a) put us in Comoros' good books, b) reassure the Japanese that they're getting their money's worth and c) depending on the severity of the punishment, might turn 'a money for old rope job', as it used to be, into a 'not bleeding worth it mate' job. What do you reckon boss?"

Jake sat back and thought a few seconds.

"Sounds like a plan. It also makes it easier to do what I came here to do."

"What was that then Jake?"

"Actually I came to steal Bismarck."

A frown grew on Andy's usually placid face.

"Now what?"

"Not sure. We'll see what happens tonight, then if I feel it appropriate I'm going to borrow her for a few weeks."

Andy Evans was no one's mug.

"So you're heading out east are you?"

"For fuck's sake Andy are you clairvoyant or something?"

"Nah, just good at adding 2+2=5; I can see from the comms logs that you're worried about how it's going down out there, anything specific?"

"No and that's the problem. I have info coming from all over the place that says there's a bilateral, trilateral or even quadrilateral build-up of naval hardware going on. There's more Kilo class sneaky boats out there than you can throw a stick at, there's shit going down with the

Americans and in the last month alone two of their somewhat expensive shiny destroyers have been dented and they've taken a lot of casualties. One of their carrier task groups is wandering around trailing a red cape almost daring an attack as it sails through water claimed by China. The recent incidents point the finger and the whole fucking arm at China and to top it all we now have a Chinese SAG heading down towards the disputed end of the South China Sea. And of course we have two of our own ships snooping around there, so my trouble antenna is going like the clappers."

"You think they'll have another go at Ocean Guard?"

"Dunno. They will obviously be aware she isn't what they thought she was and König Marine is the only pro-active anti-pirate mob with armed ships. It won't be long before they piece together what happened and who they are dealing with, and then we'll see."

"Be nice if we knew who we were dealing with too. I read Simon and Jonno's reports on what's been going on and maybe the finger is pointing at the Chinese because someone else wants it to. Still, with so many different Kilos around the place there are three, four or five countries possibly in the frame for the attacks on both us and the Americans."

"Not quite that broad a field actually Andy."

Jake pulled two images out of a portfolio.

"These two may look the same but they are superficially different. One is a project 877 Kilo and the other is a project 636 Kilo or Improved Kilo. This one," he held up the image of the 877 original Kilo. "is what Iran and India and all the others have got."

He held up the second image.

"This one however is only possessed by China and Vietnam. Looking at the images from the laser, ours are pictures of Improved Kilos, they haven't got these external protrusions." He indicated a couple of places on the Kilo's hull where there were slight differences.

"If that is the case then boss, it has to be Vietnam doesn't it, since they are the only other lot around here with improved Kilos, in which case they're trying to stitch up the Chinese to have a punch up with the Yanks."

"Or they may actually be Chinese. I expect the likes of Miles Carson are turning themselves inside out trying to count Chinese Improved Kilos to see if there are any missing, likewise Vietnam."

"Yeah I can imagine, whatsisface? Vern weathers wasn't it, the NSA bloke?"

Jake nodded.

"He'll be moving satellites all over the place trying to find out who's short of one."

"Yes, I'm sure you're correct Andy."

Later that afternoon Jake transferred to Bismarck along with Andy, Tetsunari and Granny Smith. To Jake and Granny it was like coming home, a few of the faces had changed and but others hadn't. The new faces replaced comrades who'd been killed during the Caribbean operations or drafted elsewhere and would have had a difficult time to fit in with the seasoned hands that remained. It wasn't easy being a newcomer, Jake remembered all too well.

The expected ambush site was around fifteen miles west of the platform that Andy was expecting to be targeted. Unusually for him he was tense as the time drew near and the furthest drone picked up two inbound boats.

Chief Petty Officer 'Taff' Elias, or CHOPs to everyone not in the OPs room, was shaking his head as he watched the screens light up now that Bismarck was radiating with her main search radars.

"The silly buggers have still got their masthead radar reflectors on." He was referring to the aluminium, often ball shaped objects, like the old fold out Christmas decorations with lots of metal surfaces to reflect back radar emissions. These made it safer for yachts and merchant ships to work in foggy or low light conditions. They also made it easy for a warship's radar to see them. There were a few chuckles at Taff's information. Now it would be child's play to get all the data they needed to work the angles on the ambush.

Bismarck speeded up in response to the course changes from the OPs room and the two RHIBs were contacted and given their intercept instructions. It wouldn't be full dark for another half hour or so but the white bow waves of the two inbound mischief makers were visible from five miles away using the low light cameras mounted high on the forward superstructure.

At last the time came and on command the lights split the gathering darkness like it was midday. There followed the sound of heavy feedback as Reiner began his speech and Bismarck turned to reveal its side view before stopping completely.

At deafening volume Reiner's voice carried the two hundred yards or so to the boats which had both immediately slowed right down. Something about orders shouted in German makes you want to comply.

"Attention in the boats! Stop engines. You are surrounded. Lay down your weapons!"

Non Germans and Germans alike understood the orders without any effort, you didn't need the language skills to hear the menace they conveyed. The two men manning the big machine guns mounted in the bows stepped back from them like they were hot to touch. The other four members of each crew dropped whatever AKs they were holding like they were in competition with each other to see who could disarm fastest.

The two RHIBS, both with their spotlights still belting out intense light, rumbled closer to the boats and Andy's security teams, all geared up to fight WW3, got ready to board.

That was it. The captured men were plasti-cuffed and taken to Bismarck where they sat on the fo'c'sle under the long barrels of Anton and Bruno turrets whilst security staff pointed weapons at them. No one spoke again. The lights went out and those who had been deliberately not exposed to their brilliance now took over from colleagues who would be seeing white dots for some minutes to come.

The journey back to the platform was uneventful and after communicating with government officials at Moroni it was decided that Bismarck herself would take the prisoners to the capital the following morning.

Part of the reason was that Jake had decided to continue his plan to steal Bismarck for a few weeks as he'd said, but also that it would send a message to any watchers both of Comorian origin and any who might be representing vested interests in Mozambique. The message was simple, it said 'don't fuck with the big boys'.

Crowds had gathered to see the awesomely impressive Bismarck as she sailed slowly into the harbour with a deck party in tropical whites as well as the anchor party in their usual blues. She was dressed with a Caymans flag at the stern and a Comoros flag at the starfish mast. The ship's horn sounded a single long blast, repeated each minute until alongside, to indicate her presence to any craft about to put out to sea but who may not be in sight at the time. Thousands of birds rose screaming from their roosts all around the port as the deep basso profundo blasts rang out.

The Comorian police also made a big deal out of the event, shackling the prisoners like a chain gang before marching them awkwardly down the gangway from the

Bismarck's decks to a waiting police van. Of course the local media were there recording it and spinning the scene just as the President wanted. Everyone came out of this looking good except the Mozambique cartel. President Assoumani switched his TV off smiling to himself as he considered the effect of this in the polls. König it seemed was a man of his word, and therefore he, the President, would make absolutely certain none of his people came to harm at the hands of any hotheads.

Bismarck sailed on the tide, again with much foghorn use as she backed out of the berth and into the main harbour before rotating to point towards the harbour entrance. Reiner reflected how Steerpods took the hassle out of leaving harbour, but also the skill out of the seamanship to some extent. A step forward, or a step back? I bet the old sail ship captains used to say that about steamships, he concluded.

Checking all around from the bridge wing he waved self-consciously to the huge crowds gathered to watch their departure. Spontaneous musical performances and dancing had broken out along the dock area lending a festive note to their departure.

Bismarck turned into the swell and headed west until way out of sight of land, as if heading back to the rigs, then Reiner ordered a new course of north then and hour later north east.

23rd October, Trade Secretary's Office, US Embassy, Singapore

Miles Carlson studied the high and low detail photographs again. He even tried to identify the name badge of the naval captain on the ultra-high resolution shot as he stood in front of what was supposed to be his ship's company. The angle was awkward but the man was clearly saluting the satellite. No doubt about it, this was a message.

He put down the magnifier, sat back and stared up at the slowly revolving ceiling fan. Miles Carlson knew very little about international trade, except in arms, money and information. What he was looking at now was, in Monopoly terms, the 'Get out of jail free' card for China. But it was also someone else's 'Go to jail, move directly to jail, do not pass Go and do not collect $200' card. He looked over to his colleague Steve Nolan.

"If I live to be a hundred those fuckers will be surprising me on my very last day." He sighed mightily. Were they being played?

Miles continued.

"The navy guy downstairs is a submariner. He spent all yesterday examining every boat to see if they were trying to slip in a ringer somewhere. As far as he's concerned it's the most Improved Kilo class submarines he's ever seen in one place. He wanted to know if we could slip a few Tomahawks in there now, just to save having to sink 'em later."

Nolan laughed.

"He has a good point, I like his style. You do know the ambassador will go apeshit when he learns you've been passing stuff over the back fence again Miles?"

Steve was referring to the fact that in Singapore the embassies of many countries were co-located, to the point where the back fence of the US embassy was next to the back fence of the British embassy and the Chinese embassy as well as the Australian embassy. It was great; they could talk and trade information without going out the front door even.

"Yeah, I just hope he'll fire my ass back to Langley. However since this shit could avert a war between the US and China, my guess is that Foggy Bottom won't really care whether it came over or under the wall, or was beamed through by Captain Kirk."

Nolan smiled, his older colleague, 'the dinosaur' as far as the ambassador was concerned, just did his job anyway he could. He broke whatever rules he felt were necessary to get the job done whenever he felt it necessary to break them. That didn't mean he was out of control or a whacko like in the films, it was just that Carlson saw the end point and worked towards it. If that meant kicking chairs out of the way and overturning desks then fine he'd do it, but if it meant being charming and erudite he could do that with equal facility.

Nolan and the other two CIA local operators lived in awe of him and had learned so much over the last eighteen months that they almost believed that he was there on a Senior Officer's rotation to the field. That's what he'd so say arrived for. But they all knew it was to keep him out of the way after what he'd done in the Caribbean. He was so damned good you just didn't know what he was going to say or do next and how serious he would be when he said or did it.

"So are they for real then? Does this really mean the Chinese are in the clear over the Simmons?"

"Steve, as you know nothing is ever quite what it seems, well usually. However in this case the Chinese have been set up and they want us to know they know it. So they have gone to the unprecedented length of proving it by lining up all ten of their Improved Kilos in a single place where they know our satellites do a regular pass as well as their own, only five minutes between them so I'm told. Then they went further, they got all their crews in dress blues or whatever they call 'em, and lined them up on the jetty next to the boats. Then, unable to resist giving us the bird, they have them come to attention and salute when the satellite passes over. Guess it's a good way to catch our attention. Then they hand the photos taken by their sat-bird, to me. They know we've got them in the US but they know things can go missing so they spread it about a bit. My bet is that our embassies in half a dozen countries have received copies of these and I expect Moscow and India have them too, just in case. So yeah job done, well done Mr Chinaman, what next?"

A frown crossed Nolan's features what was the old man going on about now?

"What do you mean, what next? You think it's not over out there? The word is out Miles, they'll just fold up their tents and go home surely?"

Miles put on his best condescending half smile, a crusher.

Nolan was crushed.

"Of course it's not over Steve. The Chinese want to have a poke at the people who set them up so there is still a battle to play out. When have you ever known a politician anywhere give up on a piece of insanity before the body count gets high enough?" The last was said with real venom as Miles rotated his memories through earlier screw ups which could have been prevented if the right information had been given and shared with the right people.

He relented, Nolan was a good troop and a fast learner it's just that they turned them out of spook school nowadays as if all they'd learned there was following protocols and making sure the expenses receipts were in order.

"Look, there are still some good people in harm's way through no fault of their own, our people and friends of ours. So now we have to work towards getting this 'end play' finished with as few lost on our side of the park as we can and if that means letting certain people know for sure they've been set up and by whom, then that's what is needed."

"I'm still not happy about giving them classified information Miles, really that goes against the grain."

"Yeah I know, but its information they have in different bits, they already know who tried to drop them in it. All we are doing is putting it all together, making sure they draw all the right conclusions and point their anger in the right direction, whilst making sure Uncle Sam doesn't get blamed for anything else."

"I kind of see that but hell, it just seems, well I don't know how it seems Miles, but shit..." He trailed off.

Miles waited a few seconds.

"We are the good guys, right?" He got a nod.

"We don't always get it right do we?" Another nod.

"Sometimes we fuck up badly don't we? Like the Ukraine for example. Uncle Sam has finger prints all over some of that shit and everyone knows it. The spinners spin their lies and throw doubt on stuff but everyone really knows we fucked up. Makes us look like the bad guys. Mostly it's when some politician at State, who should never have been given the keys to the stationary cupboard never mind the State Department, issues instructions which the guys on the ground have to turn into action. Some guys interpret the instruction as doing irreparable harm to the image of the US and they get in the way as much as they can, others have been sucking on the liberal teat since they were born and they are zealots in the execution of these plans. So what I'm saying is you have to think for yourself, think things all the way through before you do something which could make people think the US of A is the bad guy. We owe our allegiance to the US, not to some global ideal dreamt up by liberal ex-hippies."

Nolan looked up. Whatever you said about the dinosaur, he had a way of cutting through the crap and getting right down to the nitty gritty.

"Thanks for your patience Miles, it isn't easy to separate all these threads out, you know?"

"I know all too well Steve, but if it's any consolation, you're doing just fine."

24th October, 06:00. Hood, Search Area One.

There was a bit of a buzz about the place Roby noted as he took his command chair early. He'd strolled from stern to stem with a steaming mug of coffee before heading for the bridge and the refill pot. Passing the galley area he'd noted a louder than usual buzz of chatter along with several outbreaks of laughter. Nice to see everyone in good spirits, he decided, might be because the buzz is that we'll find something today or it might be that they knew this was the last day of wandering around the South China Sea. He did a double take when he walked past the security room and saw Mr Crause smiling as he listened to something Arkady Zotov was saying, he tried to think of the last time he'd seen Crause smile and couldn't. It wasn't that Crause was heavy handed or a big and obvious disciplinarian, but he was damned if he could remember the last time he'd seen him smile.

Wandering past the drone workshops he could hear Chief Mackenzie supervising the movement of a drone on to the rails that would lead it out on to the launch platform, he too sounded cheerful and the laughter that came back from his partner wasn't forced.

So Jon Roby arrived on the bridge with a smile on his face, which then became the subject of a buzz later in the morning, about what was likely to happen today because the skipper obviously knew something they didn't yet.

At 07:00, Roby nodded to Julius Kopf who touched his mike twice and said 'Shipwide'.

"Hands to flying stations, hands to flying stations. Prepare to launch drones."

The kick-off. Everything was now protocols and procedures as the drones were lined up ready, with a recon bird off first for a good look around as it spiralled slowly up to five thousand feet and its optimum altitude. The OPs room personnel watched the LIDAR returns and moved the cameras, zooming to the horizon before doing a full 360 degree sweep. Kiwi McClean up in the MGCC watched the video relay and moved all four main turrets slaved to the bird's camera. As it reached its operational height the drone caught sight of Ocean Guard some twenty miles to the north as she too began the process of launching her birds. Lt Bianchi zoomed in using the incredible optics until the Ocean Guard's stern seemed only yards away, then he settled back to minimum, released control to the CMS and watched it switch over to small racetrack patterns and motion detection. Almost at the same time, Ocean Guard's just launched recon bird became their responsibility and for the next five hours at least.

Next off after ten minutes was the first laser bird and then five minutes later the second which were handed on to Ocean Guard to monitor. This was the plan that he and Simon had worked out, Hood was to look after the recon drones for both ships while in the air and Ocean Guard would plot courses for and look after the laser searching drones. The final drone was undressed at the moment; she could have either of the packages, anti-surface or recon loaded as required.

All was routine until 14:30 hours. Then everything changed and events moved out of randomness and into action and reaction mode. Just after lunch the most promising search areas in area one were exhausted without result so one of the two assigned drones carried on looking at the much less likely locations and the other was brought down to Hood for a refuel and a quick check over. A twenty minute turnaround, pit stop style and she was off again to search area two, then the second was brought down to refuel.

A couple of minutes later the newly refuelled laser drone from Hood began to search an area close to a two-atoll group almost at the top of search area two, it appeared to have an significant oval shaped deep water section between the two islets. The search coordinator on Ocean Guard plotted-in an almost north south track which would allow two runs to cover the majority of the area with a further two parallel north east to south west diagonal runs to ensure nothing was missed. He hit the enter key and the drone began obeying the search pattern. He watched for a few seconds before turning his attention to the second of Hood's drones which would be handed on to Ocean Guard a couple of minutes after take-off.

Then the alert beeper sounded. He automatically cancelled it and then it sounded again. Once more he cancelled it but this time turned his attention to what might have set it off. He wasn't expecting anything, the alert had sounded a number of times before and a person naturally stops getting excited after the first few false alarms. So he began the procedure to rerun the appropriate segment on his screen. Meanwhile the alert sounded again.

Ayize Mopantokobogo was in Hood's OPs room at that time and rather bored until the alerts started sounding. He was sat looking at the holographic display when the pings began to sound and he noted their position on the map. So he plugged in to the software console that Hood used when running her own laser drones. He watched exactly the same images as the operator on Ocean Guard and arrived at the same conclusion at the same time.

"Shit, it's them." His big voice cut through all sound in the OPs room and staff monitoring the recon birds turned at his announcement.

He tapped his mike twice.

"Captain." Click then.

"What is it Ayize?"

"Your bird just found the missing ships skipper."

"On the way."

Then Simon came through on the command channel.

"Hood, we have bottom contacts which match the parameters of some of the missing ships."

Roby walked in and answered as he made his way to the holo display.

"Yes I just heard from Ayize. How many have you found?"

"Eight so far I believe. Can we have a recon bird down on the deck in the area to spot any oil traces or debris on nearby shores?"

"Good idea." He nodded to Lt Bianchi who was coordinating the recon birds for both ships. "Is there anything on the atolls nearby? Bianchi have one point its camera over there please and zoom us in."

They both watched as the camera on one of the recon drones pointed that way and began to zoom. It stopped zooming when each frond on the various palms could be counted.

"Out a bit please." Asked Simon watching from his end.

The camera panned back a little and began to play along the land. It passed over what looked like a series of dilapidated and clearly deserted huts. One or two looked quite large.

"Lot of huts on there." Commented Roby.

"Yes, perhaps they used them for fish drying or even smoking?"

"Maybe. No sign of anything larger than a lizard."

"Put it on the second atoll Bianchi please."

"Aye Sir." Bianchi nimbly manipulated the camera joystick and the picture moved to the second atoll, also horse shoe shaped with the open end directly opposite the other, like twins.

"More huts. Hang on a sec pan back a little and get down to the shore line."

The camera moved back and pointed at the beach opposite one of the large huts.

"That looks like someone's pulled a boat up there recently, the track seem to go all the way up to the hut." Simon pointed out.

"Mmm. Perhaps someone stayed the night or something before moving on. You'd want to have your only means of leaving close by wouldn't you? If I was a fisherman I can't imagine I'd leave my boat at the water's edge, just in case it went wandering on the next tide."

"Me neither, still that's about the only thing that appears to suggest anyone has visited in the last hundred years."

"We'll continue looking for the other four then. We shall need to keep a sharp lookout and a good listening watch. We don't know who the hell did this but we can be sure they don't want it publicised. We'll probably find they've stripped the ships bare of anything of value, had all their POLs pumped out then sunk in place." Roby speculated.

"Yes, I'll get these vids off to head office pronto then the cat will be out of the bag whatever happens. I'll take Ocean Guard up that way and deploy divers with cameras too and the ROV. Then the whole sorry mess will become public."

"OK Simon, let us have one of the laser birds looking in my secondary areas just to rule them out. We'll chug up there slowly too. Well at least Lloyds will have a partial answer; the big problem is ownership of these waters. If the Chinese are serious they'll be all over this as soon as it gets out, or sooner if this is their doing. If it's just a bunch or more organised than usual pirates, I hope they do rock up and have a moan at us being here."

"OK, I'll be in touch when I've got more."

Roby turned to look at the big Zulu engineer.

"So what can your birds tell us so far?"

Ayize turned his screen so Roby could see it. Then pressed play on the video screen. The images had been cleaned up by the software and as the clip played the unmistakeable shapes of human constructed artefacts became first visible, then when the clip was speeded up and the image matched against successive tracks to produce a full picture, the outlines of a number of ships became clear. Clear enough to match the sizes and hull shapes against the records.

"Good Lord. That's as clear as a bell. The ROV piccies will be interesting."

"Yeah, look how they've lined them up. Damn, like there's only five metres or so between them and they all point the same way for fuck's sake. Jees, whoever organised this is either military through and through or an obsessive compulsive, ya know, the kind who would come in your house and straighten a picture on the wall."

"Yes I see what you mean Ayize. Now where are the others?"

"Can't help with that one skipper but I can tell you why they aren't here."

"Oh, why would that be then?"

Ayize fast forwarded to the end of the recording and froze one frame.

"Look, our anally retentive fella ran out of room to play in."

Roby looked where Ayize was pointing. The depression in which the ships had been deposited started to shallow up and ran into some coral heads.

"Right. We have to assume they thought they would carry on collecting ships up until they ran into Ocean Guard that is. So the other place they've found is likely to have more storage space than just for four ships. We can rule out anything undersized because our organisational freak wouldn't allow them would he?"

"I think you may be right Captain." Said Ayize thoughtfully. "I'll get on to the searchers on Ocean Guard and get them to size up how much room this guy would take to place four ships at least, then get them to filter out smaller places. It should considerably reduce our search areas."

"Sounds like a plan." Said Jon Roby, feeling quite cheerful for the first time in weeks. Even if they couldn't find the others then once it became public there'd be people swarming all over this area demanding searches. They'd be out of here in 24 hours anyway.

Two and a half hours later Simon McClelland steered the viewer back to the atoll on the right. Something niggled and nagged at him and he was damned if he could think what. They were now in the bay to the south of both atolls and astride the narrow channel which led into the oval seabed depression between them. He had one team of four divers for now; there was another on Hood they could use when she got here. The ROV was going to slow manoeuvre in the west first then they'd swap with the divers and switch to the east. The idea was that the ROV would be able to map the silhouettes so they could get an id on the sunken ships if there were no names or registry evident, the divers would be looking for cargo, for evidence of what happened to the crews and anything else of interest.

"ESM. Anything at all, and I mean at all?"

"Last thing we had was racket on the same bearing as the starboard atoll when we were about two miles away. It was a single burst transmission but it could have been anything between zero and ten miles away, maybe more. But, I'd guess the closer end. It was very brief too. Like we'd do a sighting report would be one way to describe it."

"Thanks Marshall."

Simon's mind went into overdrive. The niggle returned and he pushed it aside for a moment, all the while he was flicking between screens noting the lead diver's camera view then the ROV's view then outside view, all around and finally recon view. Flick, flick, flick.

Then as usual it all clicked into place and he froze in fear.

"Dive lead, return to ship."

"We've only two left to search." Came back the distorted voice of the lead diver.

"Dive lead, this is the Captain. Immediate recall."

"Aye, aye sir."

"ROV control, bring it in now, not in five minutes but now, standard speed."

"Martin."

"Yes Sir?" Turner was as amazed at the sudden orders as anyone else but of all else on board he had seen Simon's hunches, intuitions, instincts whatever you call them. He'd seen them work out more often than not, much more often and he was thoroughly alarmed now.

"Take in the anchor as discretely as possible but keep it just below the surface until I give the order to move, and keep us here on station keeping. I'll explain in a minute."

"Aye, aye Sir." Off he went more puzzled than ever.

Simon's next call was to the security team leader.

"Murphy OPs room please, immediately."

"Aye Sir." Came the surprised reply.

Simon went back to checking the viewers. He was particularly interested in the huts on the atolls, the OPs staff noted.

"How long before the dive RHIB is aboard?" He asked the question of no one in particular but the senior OPs rating was immediately on the VHF to the RHIB with the dive team which should be heading back to the ship right now.

"Not able to contact the RHIB Sir." He gulped before he committed to his next sentence. "VHF, HF, Inmarsat, are all being jammed Sir. Source is on the starboard Atoll."

Simon swivelled to the viewer and trained it on the RHIB with the divers in it and zoomed in. The last one it seemed was just flopping into the boat. He panned back and moved to the view to the huts on the right. Nothing. Huts on the left. Nothing. The security TL arrived at the rush.

"Get your team geared up to fight. Everyone, armed to the teeth and deploy them bow and stern but stay out of sight from the land. Engage any hostiles without further reference to me. Clear?"

"Aye, aye Sir. You're clearly expecting trouble. Mind telling me who from?"

"Not sure but you'll know them when you see them, they are currently jamming our radios from that atoll on the right. Probably the same mob that visited in the night."

"Right, on the way."

"Martin we set?"

"Yes Sir, anchors in and station keeping is in charge."

"Right. Go to 'Q' stations please Mr Turner." He made the formal statement. "I believe we are about to come under attack. These atolls are not as empty as they seem."

Turner was taken aback but like the good officer he was, he immediately began to issue orders and made a general broadcast.

Simon spoke into his mike.

"Roby." Click then.

"Hi Si, what's happening?" He knew Simon hated being called Si and wondered when he was going to get annoyed enough to say something.

"The atolls are not empty. We are currently being jammed on all radio frequencies except of course our discrete link. Source is the starboard atoll. ESM picked up a racket on that bearing when we first arrived. Something was different about the atolls, I noticed earlier but I couldn't see it for looking. When we saw the marks on the beach I spotted it but didn't realise what I was seeing. Absolutely no plastic bags or plastic bottles on the shoreline or higher up, none. On every other place we've visited there has been the usual random assortment of human origin debris. Blue plaggy bags, old coke bottles, bits of polystyrene. Every single one. But not here. I've recalled the divers, the anchor's aweigh and as soon as everyone is on board we are out of here and heading towards you."

"Anything moving on the islands yet?" Answered a thoughtful Jon Roby.

"No. Bugger all. I'm hoping we'll be gone before whoever is the owner can release their quick reaction force once it's obvious we're actually going. My rationale being if the owner is our nocturnal visitor's boss, he's not going to miss this opportunity to put us to sleep permanently. My worry is that he's already called the cavalry but hasn't done anything overt yet because we appear to be here for the duration and haven't apparently communicated with the outside world."

"When did the jamming start?"

"Not much more than a minute or two ago. Full spectrum of standard comms. He's clearly not aware we have military grade kit."

"Why then? Why a couple of minutes ago and not an hour ago?"

"I see what you mean." Simon paused and then it hit him. "Fuck! The cavalry is close by, the bastard started jamming because he doesn't want us broadcasting a mayday or setting off our GMDSS alert. Right. We're out of here now."

"I'm on the way Simon, we are less than thirty minutes away. I'll give you back your recon drone and march mine over too, move yours a bit north and east and I'll go north and west."

"Roger that. Speak later."

Roby hit the action station alarm.

"Action stations, action stations. Assume condition one Zulu throughout the ship."

"Officer of the Watch full ahead please. Steer a safe course for Ocean Guard, I don't want to be on a coral or a sandbank when they need our help."

"Aye, aye Sir. Full ahead steer for Ocean Guard Sir."

Now Roby addressed the OPs room.

"Lt Bianchi, move our recon bird to the north and west of Ocean Guard."

He didn't wait for a reply just spoke into his mike.

"Mackenzie."

"Aye Sir." Answered the drone chief immediately.

"Fit the anti-surface package to number four and recall the two laser birds, re-arm for ASuW, thermobaric and flechette on each."

"Aye, aye Sir. Do you want number four up as soon as it's ready to go?"

"Yes. Do it chief, in record time if you please."

"On the way Sir."

Roby sat back and let his mind walk through a few options. The re-armed drones would give him a light but quite lethal surprise assault option. The AT-9 'Spiral2' anti-tank missiles they carried had glass tubes which were discarded on release from the underside of the wing and

244

the encrypted radio guided missiles could be operator controlled out to just over three miles from the drone itself. He had been mightily impressed with the loadout options too. High explosive and fragmentation but also the third generation thermobaric or fuel air explosive variant which Jake assured him gave lots of 'boom' for its size.

He doubted he'd be up against large fleet units so the drones could, if the opponents were small, do great damage or even sink them. Even frigate sized vessels being fragged would have their radar and comms gear screwed up. The thermobaric option though could sink small vessels easily with the massive overpressure they generated. All in all a pretty neat and nasty surprise since the launch platform would be undetectable and the missiles would appear out of nowhere.

He didn't doubt for a minute that Simon's assessment was correct, he just hoped what they'd now set in train would outflank the enemy, whoever the buggers were. They were starting to really piss him off, he misliked all the secret bloody squirrel stuff. Sneaking around causing all sorts of shit, clearly trying to provoke a war or something. Bastards.

*

Simon willed the dive boat to open his throttle but it didn't. Bugger it, he decided.

"Hoist flag Papa and sound the horn to draw their attention."

Turner broke in from the bridge.

"Won't that let them know we've sussed them Sir?"

"Yes but if they have units already in our area we're going to be in the shit anyway if we don't get a wiggle on."

"Right Sir, flag Papa it is." He quickly sent a lookout rating to the flag locker, when it was bent on he gave the instruction to hoist it and then sounded the foghorn once.

Simon grabbed a viewer and focussed on the RHIB. He could see the helmsman crank open the throttle but the RHIB was heavily loaded and although it speeded up, it wasn't exactly riding the wave tops. One more thing, thought Simon.

"Joshko."

"Yes Captain?"

"Get the gas turbine flashed up and get ready to give us everything you've got."

"Aye Sir, gas turbine up and engines ready for full speed."

The starboard lookout spotted the first movement, a thirty something German from nowhere near the sea in Augsburg, Bavaria; Hans Kassel just loved being at sea and when he'd come to the end of his twelve years in the Deutsche Marine, he decided to join an old friend then serving on Bismarck. Now he saw movement, out of the ground it appeared, a sponson with a heavy machine gun suddenly started rising into view, at the same time hut walls were suddenly dropping and dark clad men were racing down the beach hauling camouflaged canvasses off what looked like RHIBs, two of them.

"Aufmerksamkeit auf das Recht!" He shouted forgetting to use English.

It didn't matter in this case since people were already looking that way.

"Smith, batteries released. Get that fucking gun first!"

"Aye, aye Sir." Answered the gruff voice of Chief Gunnery Instructor Scouse Smith, ex-RN and former field gunner to boot. Complete with broken nose and a voice that could be heard through a force ten gale, he was someone you never considered ignoring.

Right now he dropped the plates shielding the two starboard AK630 Gatling guns and using manual control trained them on what looked like a 20mm auto-cannon which was rapidly turning towards them. Then he pressed the tit and the weird sheet ripping sound of the AK630 mini turrets commenced followed by the now expected vibration while they began chugging out rounds at 4000 per minute. The Chief Gunner automatically corrected as the first shells fell short and walked the rest straight in to the cannon. The bits flew in all directions and the mount toppled over without having fired a shot.

Simon moved the viewer to check on the dive boat. It was still only halfway to the Ocean Guard and Simon was certain the newly launched attackers would easily get them. He refocussed on the two enemy RHIBs both of which appeared to be attempting to mount a mini-gun machine gun on a bow platform. Fortunately their own motion wasn't helping, but once past the surf it would flatten out and then the dive boat would be for it. Clearly the Ocean Guard RHIB driver had seen the attempts to mount the guns too so he started start to zigzag which of course slowed the boat and made the distance that much greater. He should have waited. Should have got someone to spot. Should have, would have, must do….all useless thoughts.

Oh fuck, he sighed. One of the two now had his min-gun in action and Simon saw a line of splashes to the right of the wildly gyrating dive boat. Throw the fucking cylinders overboard for God's sake he mentally urged them. Then someone on the RHIB had the same idea and the splashes of air cylinders disappearing over the side were apparent.

The dive boat slowly increased speed as it got lighter which meant that the attackers weren't gaining as much if at all.

"Move us slow astern Martin. Chief can you get a clear shot with either gun?"

Chief Smith grunted and switched to single weapon flicking between them as he tried to get at least one to bear on the two attackers. Then it appeared the RHIB driver had an idea, he must have seen Ocean Guard go slow astern so he swerved towards the bows clearly intending to round them and put the ship in between them and their attackers, which opened the arcs for the gunner.

"Got 'em." Shouted Chief Gunner Smith." The viewers showed the aftermost AK630 zoom in on the leading enemy, flashes visible from its bow mounted gun. Then mayhem went out to play and the boat, plus crew disappeared in pink mist and black rubber pieces as the heavy 30mm bullets chewed them apart.

"One down." Said Chief Smith gleefully. He slewed the gun around and found the second RHIB which was unsurprisingly no longer interested in their dive boat and was now swerving wildly, trying to avoid what they knew was coming next. Another series of ripping sounds with accompanying vibration and the second boat disintegrated too.

Simon sickened, looked away from the high magnification monitor. It was different when they weren't exactly pirates. He had no problem killing pirates. Pirates were scum. Those guys were probably ordinary soldiers or sailors on duty. Someone had sent them to kill his men he knew, but it still didn't seem quite right.

Time for a call to Hood, but before he could tap his mike the OPs room chipped in.

"Bridge, OPs. Opening shared channel." Came the call from Robin Howes one deck below as he switched on the shared open link.

"Go ahead." Answered Captain McClelland.

"Active radar transmissions at three five zero, range two zero miles Sir. Classified as Mike Romeo 352 Positive-

E, NATO classification, 'Cross Dome'. CMS suggests most likely Vietnamese. 'Molniya' or 'Gepard' class ships!"

Simon answered automatically whilst his mind processed the information.

"Acknowledged. Stay passive for the moment but keep a close eye on the ESM array, those little things carry a major punch. Let me know why CMS suggests Vietnamese."

He turned his attention back to the outside.

"Get that RHIB aboard pronto and let's get out of here Gentlemen, they've made it plain we aren't welcome."

Vietnamese? According to OPs only Vietnam was operating that radar type around here and only Molniyas and Gepards had it. The computer had very low odds that it was either Russian, Indian, Greek or Ukrainian, the other users of the same system. So really what must have happened was 'the base' had whistled up support hence the transmission when they arrived, and only Vietnam had answered the call. Ergo, it was a Vietnamese base in Chinese held waters which is why they most assuredly wanted it kept quiet.

His thoughts returned to the Molniya or Gepard, the plot repeater gave out the vessel's speed and that made it the Molniya because it was cracking on at over forty knots. They could launch their SS-N-25 *Switchblade* missiles now or even out to a hundred and sixty miles if they were the new ones. His ship would be in surface radar detection range very soon. They must have other ships in the area too, he decided, or they would likely have launched a bearing only shot relying on the terminal homing radar. Perhaps their captain wanted a visual sighting before firing?

"Jonno, where are you?" Simon wasted no time on the usual pleasantries.

"Err, we're about twelve miles South South West of that atoll cluster you were going to be searching this morning. Why? What's happening?"

"Well apart from there being a base UNDER the damn atoll, its Vietnamese I believe, link should have our contact report."

"Link is intermittent at the moment." He said disappearing briefly in static before the frequency agile link reconnected. "Maybe their jamming is getting more effective."

"Shit, that's all we need. Anyway they fast-launched a pair of armed RHIBS to get our dive team, they opened fire immediately. No attempt at parley at all. So I opened fire on them, both destroyed, no survivors. Now they seem to have whistled up support that's way out of my league. A Molniya. At least one may be more. Just under twenty miles at three five zero degrees."

"Shit. They are wicked little buggers I recall."

Roby turned his attention back to Simon having quickly reviewed the spec of the Vietnamese Molniyas.

"As I thought they are wicked. Sixteen SS-N-25s, Uran-E hopefully, not the new SS-N-27 Club missiles anyway, but even their AK176 would make mincemeat of you. Have you recovered the RHIB yet?"

"Just coming aboard now. I'll go to full speed and head towards you. They're using ECM to jam VHF and our nav radar but our datalink should be fine the closer we get. Don't know why they haven't started shooting yet. They don't appear to have anything active in the air either for guidance. I'll go active in a minute, that's when they'll shoot I think. They're probably wondering what kind of 'Merchie' can shoot back. I expect messages are flying to and fro to the mainland. Even the Viets might be reluctant to fire anti-ship missiles at a merchant ship."

"Not when they're certain that the base commander isn't smoking dope. They'll shoot then."

"You're probably right. I've got my ass pointed at them and we're speeding up now, so I have them in the best defensive quarter for the ship. Doubt they'll launch sixteen at once against this little thing, so I might get a few before they decide to volley fire."

"OK Simon I concur. I reckon they'll fire as soon as they are cleared to do so. They're still uncertain of your capabilities and identity; we can hope that uncertainty lasts. The link's clear now so we're getting your passive picture." He looked slightly left at the nav indicator. "I'm up to thirty three knots now and we are only about fifteen degrees off a straight line to the Molnya with you as the middle point. We won't be able to offer cover for missiles until we're only five miles away as you know. Erm...roughly seven minutes by my SWAG calculations Simon."

"I'm impressed Jonno. Yeah I make it about seven minutes until you can deploy the 'anti-shit' umbrella. I'll move a drone to spot for you and then I'll get on and inform Jake as soon as the ECM has diminished enough. He's going to be as pleased as punch after all the shit we got him into with the Iranians and the Indians. Can't imagine the PM is going to be too chuffed either."

"Righto, I've got one ASuW drone on the way and two more will be available over the next ten or fifteen minutes, but they need to close to about three miles from the target. Incidentally you know he could have fired those missiles already. They could be on their way to you now since you aren't radiating."

"Of course. The perennial game of hide and seek. When my son was three, he got the idea of hide and seek. So when it was his turn he just sat there put his hands over his eyes and said, 'right you can't see me now Dad'."

Roby laughed out loud.

"Good tactical awareness at an early age. Obviously takes after his father. Well it's up to you old son when you switch on, keep your bum cheeks tight."

"Will do. Speak later." Simon McClelland closed the connection and turned his attention back to the viewer. He decided it was time to check out the Holo picture and what the drone could see. Evening was fast approaching and he wondered if that would make things better or worse.

The two ships were now closing at a combined speed of sixty nine miles per hour. Hood's specially shaped hull combined with the use of carefully placed air ducts which blew air underneath to cushion her and keep the quarterdeck and after-parts above the water, made her a stable and fast accelerating ship, it had been a problem with the original Hood apparently.

Roby removed himself to the OPs room as well, all the while ruminating on the recent events; they were starting to accumulate some serious baggage which must mean by the law of averages, they'd be taking casualties soon. That is unless whoever was stirring the shit had a sudden attack of common sense. The secret was out, what was the point now?

The simple fact though was that politicians of whatever stripe could never ever admit they were wrong and would never ever pull the plug out on their crazy schemes in time to avoid needless death. The EU was a case in point, past its 'best before' date by two decades at least and it still staggered on trying to steamroller over individuality, supposedly for the greater good.

He had no real idea of the motive behind this particular game being played out, but odds were it was going to be money or revenge. Or maybe both.

Simon McClelland looked over to his OPs Chief who was desperately willing his boss to allow him to go active.

"All right Chief, light her up. Let's see what the bastards are up to."

"Aye, aye Sir." Answered Pete South.

A panel slid back toward the rear of the Bridge superstructure and up from below deployed the kind of radar antenna that would only be found on a warship, which of course was why it was hidden most of the time.

The Sea Giraffe 1X looking like a wide screen, flat panel TV and rotating once a second, is a full 3D AESA array in the X-band. Exactly why it was perfect for anti-piracy work in all weathers and especially littoral seas. But it had been designed for small surface combatants which was good news for Ocean Guard at this moment in time. As It rose to its eight metre deployed height the antenna began its work. Two seconds later it had twice scanned the airspace around Ocean Guard out to a surface distance of twelve miles and increasing out to sixty miles at higher altitudes. It could detect objects as small as a tennis ball and now it did its job.

"Vampire, Vampire, Vampire." Announced the CMS with a calm female voice similar to some Sat-Nav systems. Pete South's screen border flashed red with the word Vampire in the centre.

"CIWS to Automatic. Cancel?" It now asked.

Pete hit the 'NO' button on the screen nearly pushing his finger through it.

"Shit. Contact, bearing 348, range two three miles course is 168 degrees, altitude ten metres, speed 600 knots. CMS to auto fire. CIWS deployed. Contact designated sierra 1."

The rumble of the deck plates sliding back both above and to the side of the four cannon

"Time to engagement zone?" Snapped Simon.

"Err one minute forty three Sir."

Simon nodded. His vessel wasn't expected or designed to fight incoming missiles however the radar, CMS and 30mm auto-cannon were. The only thing they lacked really was some chaff. One minute and some more seconds countdown to the last frantic fifteen seconds when those multi-barrelled cannon outside would either keep them safe or fail. Waiting is the worst part so the cliché went. It may be a cliché but it's true, he decided.

They were heading almost due south and the missile was coming in slightly to starboard of their stern which would allow two cannon mounts to engage it. There would likely be more attacks so he needed the magazine crews to be prepped to replace the exhausted or part used four cassettes which contained 2000 rounds, each of which weighed nearly three quarters of a ton.

"Martin have the ammunition party standby to replace the starboard cassettes if we use more than ten percent of their load on the first one. If we do that, have them remove any remaining rounds and feed them into a new cassette."

They had ten cassettes and a further 20,000 rounds which could be loaded into them when empty. Enough for months of anti-piracy work but they could be gone in a few minutes on anti-missile work. A crew of three men worked the hydraulic lifts and placement gear for replacement cassettes.

"Aye Sir." Acknowledged Martin Turner from his action station on the Bridge.

"Now is the time Chief when we discover how well you polished those little perishers when you were feeding them into the cassettes."

There was a subdued chuckle from those around, everyone knew the Chief Gunner personally examined, wiped and inserted every one of the fourteen ounce shells as well as personally cleaning each of the six barrels on each mount. He might one day let someone else do it under supervision he'd said, but since these guns were the only real weapons they had and he was the only real gunner then what was the problem?

He spoke into his mike.

"Roby." Click.

"Yes we have it on link. The picture gets better for every yard you move away from that jammer I reckon. Three minutes before the umbrella comes out, we have the new San Shiki shells to try out. Looks like they'll get a baptism in the traditional way."

"That's great Jonno, love being a guinea pig."

"The way it goes Simon, those are the umbrella. Just using fused HE at that range isn't going to help much."

"Refresh my memory, just what is inside those things?"

"Well let's see. They are 5.1" shells containing seventy steel stays and seventy incendiary tubes filled with rubber thermite. They have a delay fuse set by the fire control system that detonates where the computer calculates a best chance of hit. When it explodes, the steel stays and the incendiary tubes are ejected in a 10-degree cone forward; with the shell fragments from the explosion itself further increasing the amount of debris. The incendiary tubes have drilled holes along their length and ignite about a half-second later and burn for five seconds with 16 foot long flames at 2500C. It breaks up into about 2000 fragments which will have opened up to a fifty yard cone if they don't hit by a thousand yards."

"You swallow the data sheet Jonno?"

"No, I'm reading from it. Look, the tests we did off Little Cayman six months ago were pretty awesome to see and they got hits on nine out of ten targets. A missile's body only needs a fraction of a second exposure to the thermite, to burn through."

"Thirty seconds Sir, he's gone active, X-band." Came the voice of Pete South in Simon's background.

"Have to go Jonno, less than thirty seconds now."

"OK. Nothing else to say."

Simon looked at the countdown clock. The auto-cannons would open fire five point three seven seconds before the missile reached the engagement zone then they would pour whatever was left in their cassettes into the air until they hit or the missile hit. He just hoped the Chief hadn't wasted too many rounds on the RHIBs. Damn, I should have turned so the port batteries were exposed. A quick look at the ECDIS told him he couldn't have anyway because it shoaled there.

Then it started. Two sets of ripping sheets and mega vibrations.

Simon, calm to all around, reached for a viewer and pulled it towards himself hoping no one would see the tremble of his fingers. He was just in time to see two lines of green tracer cross each other and then there was a dirty puff of smoke and debris rained out of the sky, the sheet tearing stopped. Thank God or perhaps thank Mikhail Knebelman who designed them.

The respite was shorter than he'd hoped as less than a minute later the CMS piped up again.

"Vampire, Vampire, Vampire!"

"Error. Mount two not available, engaging with mount one only."

"Fuck, what's happening?" Said Simon in a voice which betrayed his nerves.

The Chief Gunner was listening on his headset.

"Right. Double to it then." He closed the connection.

"Bit awkward getting the second cassette locked in place Sir. They've done it now and it's running through its reset. The CMS will add it in to the calculations as soon as it's cycled."

"Right Chief."

"Vampire, Vampire, Vampire!" Then five seconds later. "Vampire, Vampire, Vampire!"

The CMS was still on auto so Pete South just acknowledged the report before turning to Simon.

"Three more Sir from the same bearing. Same flight parameters."

Simon stared briefly at the deckhead. Bloody marvellous. About the only good thing was the interval he supposed. If the CIWS managed to kill the first within five seconds it would be able to engage the next at maximum range and so on. Until it ran out of ammunition.

A beep in his ear. Incoming transmission.

"Simon, we're opening fire in less than a minute old son, the Chief came up with an extra knot or two."

"Thanks Jonno that's bloody good news. I expect we'll have to duck when you let your fireworks off, they're going to be flying over my ship with inches to spare."

"Good point, I'll make sure they don't fuse them to explode before they pass you, wouldn't be polite to singe your backsides on the way by would it?"

Simon's imagination conjured up seventy Catherine wheels whizzing by at nearly two thousand miles an hour and shuddered. He looked at the countdown clock. Forty seconds for the first. That would likely mean they had that one to themselves.

"How's the link Chief?" Simon was wondering whether the ship to ship link was fully operational yet or whether the jamming was still impeding it.

"In the green Sir. Shall I hand over to Hood?" The ability of networked ships to remotely operate sensors and weapons wasn't new but it had improved massively with the advances in computer technology, allowing millions more calculations per second to be made and enabling commanders a far greater awareness of what was going on outside by taking information from other platforms including the drones.

"We'll take the first one then hand off I think. Did you catch that Jonno?"

"Yes, fine. We're standing by. Just getting preliminaries from the drones now. I'll let you deal with this first one then we'll sort the rest in this batch. Then we can have a chat."

"Roger that. Speak later."

The countdown clock was below twenty now and Simon braced himself not to flinch when the six barrelled monsters started again. He drew the viewer to his face and slaved it on to the firing bearing of the guns.

"He's gone active now Sir."

Once more the harmless looking green lines reached out to something he couldn't see and once more there was a dirty puff of smoke when they'd crossed, like Ghostbusters he thought irreverently. Then they flicked over to a new bearing and stopped.

Almost above their heads there was a loud crack like a particularly vicious summer thunder clap and Simon nearly wet himself. Dear God, he thought. Almost immediately afterwards, the viewer dimmed slightly as a series of intensely burning objects became visible and zoomed towards the horizon. He looked up alarmed. No sheet tearing sound. Had they got it then? Another thunderous crack and more intense light whizzing by down range. By all the Gods, those fucking things are dangerous!

In the background he vaguely heard Chief South confirming hand off to Hood. It's like being on the firing range he thought, at the wrong fucking end!

He chanced a glance at their small version of the holo table and could see icons where there'd been none before. They bore red chevrons with a directional stalk pointing southwards. There was a little information block next to it.

He climbed out of his command chair and sat next to the hologram, one by one he brought up the icons with the information tabs attached to them.

Three Molniyas in a rough 'V' formation. Two other contacts further back with amber icons because they hadn't been positively identified yet. Speed logged at twenty eight knots. Must be Gepards then, more bloody SSN-25 missiles, he thought gloomily. It really is only a matter of time.

Hood's OPs room was in full session with all stations manned and information arriving from Ocean Guard's radar, the drones and electronic intercepts. The big surprise for the Vietnamese was going to be Hood. If they thought Ocean Guard was going to be hard to kill just wait until they try us, Roby fumed. He was grimly determined to rescue his partner ship. The gap was closing now, they would pass on reciprocal courses in about a minute.

"Mr Kopf, can we have someone with a lamp on the port bridge wing please and I want a single long blast on the foghorn when we pass."

Julius Kopf smiled. This was as exciting as it had been on Bismarck when she'd gone into battle that last time in the Caribbean.

"Aye, aye Sir. What message by lamp?" He wasn't puzzled by the request, despite the fact that the Captain could just talk to Ocean Guard over the data link. This was a seaman's moment and was as much for Hood's crew as anything else. He was almost sure he knew what the message would be too.

Simon McClelland felt a lump in his throat and had to cough slightly before he could answer Martin Turner's shouted message telling him what Hood's lamp signal said. It had simply said 'You are relieved Sir'.

"Answer. 'I stand relieved.' Add, 'Good Luck'."

"Aye, aye Sir."

Sod it thought Simon.

"I'm going to the bridge."

He stood on his own port bridge wing as the Hood charged by at less than a cable's distance, her foghorn blaring a single mournful note.

"Sound the foghorn in answer, two short blasts."

Even though it was nearly dark now the moon was up early and he could still make her out clearly. A great white bone between her teeth and a rooster tail at the stern shone with a white radiance as she swept by at over thirty five knots with her guns trained slightly to port. God she looked magnificent, he thought, wondering if he'd ever see her again. At a combined speed of sixty nine miles per hour the moment was brief and he turned to watch her disappearing northward with a sudden belch of dark smoke from her forward turrets but no flash. He looked over to the nearest viewer set to OPs. More little red chevrons inbound in a stream. Bastards. How he wished he was back on Bismarck where he had something to shoot back with. They would keep their own radar on for as long as it was useful to Hood, probably another five minutes or so. Until that time they would be the only visible target for the bad guys.

Roby concentrated on the high resolution chart of the next three miles for a few seconds while marvelling that Simon's recent mapping of the area was now incorporated on his own systems. It was clear they hadn't an awful lot of manoeuvring room until they left the channel they were currently driving up. Then about three miles short of the suspect atoll it opened out. He'd decided to put down some HE on the atoll to kill the jamming and stop any further observation by laser, IR or TV. Simon had mentioned what looked like thin masts rising apparently from a palm tree, not visible on radar so probably carbon fibre or anti-radar paint. They could have all sorts of optronics mounted on them and were likely over the horizon systems too. They'd know soon enough if there were laser designators on them, their own laser ranging detectors would activate an alarm. Didn't matter though, there was all sorts of stuff they could mount on them nowadays, with the advent of fibre networks so much more was possible.

A shout from Lt Bianchi.

"Six more vampires inbound, same profile as before, not targeting us yet Sir."

"Very well, take them down with 3" and the AKs if you can, save the San Shiki's for a rainy day." He looked at the bulkhead clock and under his breath mouthed, 'like in about another hour or so'.

He was between a rock and a hard place. If he stayed close to Ocean Guard the missiles would keep coming until they started to get through. If he closed with the missiles shooters he was heading into the unknown and straight towards trouble. He really had no choice.

"Have one of the recon birds move north in an arc from west north west, to north east. Move it twenty miles further out than now, I don't want any more surprises. Have the other recon bird do a sky scan every second cycle, have the Lidar concentrate towards," he paused and checked the chart again. His finger traced a line to the air base at Bien Hoa and then over to Thanh Son Air Base. "the north west in one cycle, and north in the next. Where are the three armed birds?"

"They are manoeuvring to come in from the dark side Sir, currently six seven and eight miles east south east of the nearest Molniya." Reported Ringbolt Langford who was looking after them while the drone Chief and his partner prepped another bird.

"Do we know which Molniyas have already fired?" Roby asked, there was no point in targeting a ship which had already shot its missiles.

"Err yes Sir. We cannot be 100% certain because they may have swapped positions after firing and before we had them all on the Lidar, but I'm fairly confident. The trailing ship on their port side, we think is the one who has not yet fired at all, the far side has fired eight of sixteen and the lead has fired eight too. All told from this group we could face another thirty two missiles, then there are the following Gepards to deal with."

It was clear to Roby that his OPs team had been plotting and planning while the action was happening and had neatly brought their three armed drones into a position to attack the most dangerous of their immediate opponents. The others would be in gun range very soon.

They had no idea how good the Vietnamese point defences were, it was known that apart from their 76mm deck gun they two of the single mount AK630 Gatlings as well as up to twelve Igla-M, MANPADS. So there was no point in firing the AT-9 Spiral2 weapons singly or in pairs, it would have to be all six to have a serious chance of one hit. Unless. Unless he took a leaf out of Reiner Krull's book of tactics. He recalled how Reiner had caught the attention of the terrorists in the Mediterranean incident so they wouldn't see the initial flame from the launch tubes. It was likely the Vietnamese would have a pretty alert crew and MANPAD operators perhaps scattered around the bows since the AKs were at the stern. Or maybe they didn't expect an air threat at all.

"Have we good IR images of our first target ship? If so, zoom in and see if they have people on the bow deck or out on the missiles deck."

It was dangerous to wander around a warship at action stations when weapons systems could train and fire without warning. These little buggers had a 76mm automatic gun on the bow and two noisy AK630's on the stern. He didn't fancy being a MANPAD operator in close proximity to either.

"Zooming in now Sir. No one starboard side that I can see, one man on the main deck aft the missile batteries. I think he's sat down. Anyway he's not doing a good impersonation of a super sailor."

"Right. Kiwi, on a countdown I want you to shoot an illumination round as far to their starboard as possible, give us the countdown to detonation then Mr Langford here can launch three Spirals at the target ship, have them go low and fast please."

"Aye Sir. Illumination round to THEIR starboard with countdown." Answered Kiwi McLean up in the gunnery control room.

"Aye Sir. Shoot three on countdown at first target." Answered Ringbolt Langford manning the AT9 controls.

"Correction. May as well take advantage of this. It probably won't work again so target the remaining three on the group leader and bring the birds around so they are almost head on to the ships to mask their CIWS, see if we can knock another eight off. Time to gun range on THEIR starboard vessel?

"Err, that would be one minute and thirty seconds Sir." Answered McClean on the ball as usual.

"Right as soon as we initiate this we'll begin a turn to port to let all main guns have a go, then continue the turn all the way until we are on zero nine zero. Then we'll have the drones back and reloaded. They will of course guess there's a new player out in front of them."

He spoke into his mike.

"McClelland." Click then.

"Yes Jon?"

"Can you risk turning around and giving us a bit more of your radar coverage? It's just that they haven't got us yet and although they'll know there's another player out there in a couple of minutes we still won't be easy to pick out in the clutter of these little atolls even when they get in radar range."

"Glad you asked, yes we can do that. Did you know that Bismarck passed a Slava, intermittently active, at a range of three miles without being spotted?"

"No I didn't. Bloody hell. Well I think our RCS isn't much different and I can get the deck coolers going to keep us hidden from IR detection if they use it. Thanks Simon." He deliberately used Simon's full name, the time for winding up friends was long gone.

"No problem, but you'd better shut that jammer down pronto, we are at the edge of Link usefulness now."

"Yes, it's on the list." Simon missed the sardonic tone in Roby's voice.

The Hood sped towards the Vietnamese ships on a shallow intercept course and Roby waited it out, he wanted everything to go dark for the following Gepards, all at once. He wanted them wondering what the fuck was out there when all they could see was a single merchant ship.

The last light had gone, it was now as dark as it was going to get until the moon set in about three hours. Visibility was about three miles. Time to start things decided Roby.

"Standby Gentlemen."

Everyone made ready.

"Guns ready." Answered Kiwi McClean.

"Missiles ready." Answered Ringbolt Langford secretly happy that Chief McKenzie was going to be royally pissed off that he didn't get to do the shooting.

"Helm ready." Answered Geordie Moore, praying that he didn't fuck up the turn or put them on some pinnacle, as happened to one of his mates on HMS Nottingham back in '02.

"Standby."

Roby looked at the bulkhead clock, then wondered why it mattered.

"Guns shoot." There followed a thump as A turret fired a single illumination round. The countdown clock started.

"Standby Langford." Langford grimaced. The boss must be tense he thought, since that was the most unnecessary order he'd ever been given. Twenty five thousand yards. Time of flight twenty six point nine seconds. Seemed like ten lifetimes. Then it was time. The clock dropped to zero, then plus one. He clicked the fire command.

"Firing." Now six missiles sped towards the oncoming ships, almost head on.

Somewhere over to the west of the enemy ships, an illumination round had popped in the sky, all eyes turned towards it and many shouted exclamations followed. No one on any of the three ships saw the six AT-9 Spiral 2 missiles ignite and leap from their glass tubes. The three firing drones turned away and dove for the deck and a course back to Hood.

The port side Molniya's NATO code 'Bass Tilt' fire control radar picked up the inbound missiles on its next sweep and immediately alerted the operator who was concentrating on the main 'Cross Dome' search radar. With an irritated glance he looked over to see what was happening and turned white. Recovering himself he hit the 'auto' button on the two AK630 Gatlings on the after deck, then realised the ship would need a radical turn to get them to bear. The clock was ticking. Fired at a range of three point five miles but immediately dropping to the deck, the time of flight for the six missiles was eleven point five seconds. With six missiles inbound and four AK630 guns capable of engaging them, there was little chance that all six would be taken out in the short time available. The problem for the Vietnamese, and to some extent all navies, is that they don't like to have the automatic cannon, on automatic engagement -in case they start shooting at seagulls or even their own ships or passing aircraft which aren't squawking. People just don't trust them.

Consequently the time it took to recognise the threat, to activate the system to deal with it and then the time it took to get the bridge to commence an emergency turn to starboard so the guns would bear, ate up nearly all of the flight time.

Thermobaric charges are horrible weapons. In the case of these Spiral 2s, they were popped up thirty yards into the air some sixty yards short of the target, then the missiles split open dispensing the fuel in a cloud carried forward by its own momentum. After a short pause to allow dispersal, the initiators sparked and the resulting triple explosion was dreadful. Even on such a small weapon as this, the 'bang', the fire and the overpressure were equivalent to a much larger charge of TNT. One might have been survivable but three most definitely were not.

The sailor on the port side with the MANPADS had stood up to look where everyone was pointing at the illumination round. He focussed on the bright white light and just had time to wonder where it came from when he heard the second warning and turned to look forward. Suddenly aware of the danger he snatched up the launcher tube, activated the infra-red seeker and brought it to his shoulder just as the ship heeled over in its desperate attempt to unmask its point defence weapons. He heard a brief tone indicating a lock, then overbalanced as he tried to keep turning with the ship. A microsecond later he was gone in a burst of flame which sucked the oxygen out of the air around it.

Thermobaric weapons are most effective against buildings and tunnels, they also invade ship's compartments with equal facility, then they detonate. Anyone inside or outside a structure will be killed instantly if they are within the cone of effect.

The two Molniyas were immolated along with their crews as secondary explosions in the superheated missile bins cooked off the remaining shots finishing the work of the Spirals.

The third vessel had little time to ponder where the missiles came from or what the illumination round was all about as Roby ordered it destroyed.

"Guns, open fire on the last vessel."

"Aye aye Sir." Responded Kiwi Mclean having already programmed the shoot.

"Engaging now." Range was down to ten and a half thousand yards, six miles. 'A' turret left gun, then right gun, followed by 'B' turret left gun, then right gun, then back again to the beginning. The Hood began to turn and 'X' turret got in a couple of shots before rounds started landing on and around the last Molniya.

Back on the last surviving Molniya the horror continued in slow motion as out of nowhere, giant white fountains of water appeared off the bow, tracked towards them, and then the hits started.

Nearly four seconds in flight, the shells began arriving almost in pairs, following the ill-fated ship as it began to turn under emergency helm. The drones recorded the event in full HD quality, for the observers on Hood it was over quickly, but for the crew of the last Molniya the awful progression of white spouts followed by tremendous explosions as they caught up with her lasted their lifetime. In fifteen seconds A turret fired nineteen times, B turret fired sixteen times and X turret four. Hood had put down thirty nine 5.1" shells in the firing time with no effort to break records.

In the OPs room they all stared at the screen showing the mayhem they'd caused. Roby spoke up.

"Bit overzealous with the ammunition there Mr McLean. Much more of that and I'll be taking it out of your wages." A couple of chuckles followed as Roby then ordered them to turn about and head back towards Ocean Guard, he didn't want them dwelling on what they'd just witnessed.

He switched comms to Simon listening in on the Ocean Guard.

"Simon, you may want to shut down your active suite at the moment, no one got a reading on me and the Gepards are still too far for me to shoot at. Perhaps they'll 'dwell a pause of two marching paces' to try and work out what just happened. All the Vietnamese know for sure is that they fired a shed-load of missiles at an apparently armed merchant ship, and it shot them all down as well as sinking the three shooter vessels."

"Sounds like a plan." Said Simon reviewing the latest data from the recon drones. "I wonder how far up their chain of command this goes? Could it be a local senior commander doing his own thing?"

"Well if it is he'll be shitting himself by now. How the hell could he explain the loss of three corvettes and their crews?" Added Jon Roby.

Fifteen minutes later the drones observed two newly arrived Vietnamese ships stop and begin rescue OPs.

"Well it looks like there are some survivors, the Gepards are picking folk out of the water as we speak." Noted Jon Roby over the open connection. "It can't stay secret for long. Unfortunately, whether it's local or not, they are in a shit or bust situation. They are three down, a base discovered, sunken ships discovered next door to it, and bugger all to show for it."

"Yes, it does sound pretty dire." Simon concurred. "They have two choices as far as I can see. They can either quit now and blame it all on an overzealous local commander, or they can keep pushing to see if they can get something out of this to save face."

Roby thought for a few seconds.

"OK. On that basis if it's a local guy only, he'll quit now and be shot later anyway. He might be able to get his family out before the net closes, if he hurries. If it's a politician, we're in for more shit because they aren't in danger themselves and they don't know when to stop. They will be wanting something to come away from the table with or they will be in deepest darkest shit with their colleagues for fucking up; so they'll keep throwing the dice whilst someone else's life is on the line or until someone with enough clout pulls the plug."

"Such a cynic." Said Simon. "However a very likely scenario. There was me thinking I was the only cynic in this outfit. OK. So we'll turn about now and wait for you to catch up, then we'll head down to Labuan area again?"

"Righto. Be along shortly I've just got to drop a few bricks on their base to keep their sensors offline."

Hood came level with the occupied atolls five minutes later, she turned onto a course which took them past but allowed all four main turrets to engage, and slowed down to a leisurely ten knots.

"Right Guns, walk a line of shells along the spine of both atolls starting with known locations and working out. Drop a barrow load on that bit with the masts. Use standard rounds, no need to bother with flashless for this one."

"Aye, aye Sir." Answered Kiwi McLean flexing his hands before giving the gunnery system its commands.

Then he spoke over the main broadcast.

"This is Guns. Shoot commencing in two zero seconds. Will be using standard rounds so look away if you need night vision."

Twenty seconds later the tinny sounding fire gong repeated through bridge and OPs room. They didn't need such an antique notification system but Roby liked it.

All eight guns fired together then again and again. Each time the night sky was ripped apart by eight blinding flashes and the crash of thunder rolled back to them even from these low lying islets. Simon's bridge wing lookouts some miles away could hear the thunder quite plainly and the northern horizon flashed like summer lightning.

Skilfully McLean began to walk the rounds along the low lying dunes; any human structure got extra attention just in case. Then he switched to the other atoll and repeated the performance. Some secondary explosions were apparent, one fuel and another clearly ammunition cooking off.

Finally the turrets ceased firing and returned to their fore and aft position. The buffer would be pleased anyway, thought McLean, since this system retained the fired shells rather than having them eject in every direction, taking chunks out of the deck and knocking anti-rad paint off everything they bounced off.

A number of the bunkers on the atolls caved in, some unfortunate enough to be filled with an inrush of seawater not sand. Minutes after the last shells had landed, shocked and injured survivors began to gather above ground, wondering just who would come and rescue them since all their communication gear was smashed into fragments along with all those who knew how to use it.

Roby scanned the two target areas intently using his viewer's IR add on.

"Good show Guns. Secure and then re-stock, I don't think it's over yet."

24th October, 22:30. South China Sea, 300 miles East of Cam Ranh.
USS Nimitz Carrier Task Group 11.1

Admiral Summers sat with his senior commanders and reviewed the latest intel from all sources. The Chinese SAG would pass them at a range of one hundred and eighty miles sometime in the early hours, if everyone held their course. They were pretty well north of his task group paralleling the coast of Vietnam. Twelve ships he noted, possibly two SSNs below them. Centrepiece was the new type 095 destroyer Shanghai, then five type 52D destroyers, Kunming, Changsha, Yinchuan, Nanjing and Taiyuan. The interesting thing was the last two were transfers over from their East Sea fleet. After them came four type 54A frigates of the Jiangkai II class and finally a fleet oiler and a general fleet replenishment ship. The admiral looked up.

"It's a fucking cruiser at thirteen thousand tons. Same as the Zumwalt is. I don't care what any pencil necks calls them and I don't care that the Chinese call destroyers after cities, a thirteen thousand ton warship is a big cruiser, a heavy cruiser in fact. Why do people have to change stuff?" It was a rhetorical question as everyone knew so they all sat and listened attentively while their admiral went off on his hobby horse about what was a destroyer and what was a cruiser.

"Anyway what is interesting is there's no carrier so to my mind they are not wanting a fight with us. Yeah sure they have hundreds and hundreds of SAMs and SSMs in those ships but they aren't looking to fight us. Given where they are and where they appear to be headed they can't rely on land based air support, so we aren't an item of interest as far as I'm concerned."

Jose Maringa, Commander Air Group went next.

"Pretty powerful SAG though Admiral, that new destro....cruiser has some pretty impressive gear on board and they're using cold launch as well. Maybe they are getting safety conscious at last?"

There were a few murmurs of laughter at the CAG's little joke. Bull Balfour put his two penneth in then.

"The message they are sending to my mind is this. We aren't interested in the USN, but don't fuck with us. That's why their latest and greatest cruiser is the centrepiece, and has the top of the range destroyers to keep them company AND the top of the stack frigates to watch over them. The Virginia says she's had trace on one possibly two Shang class 093G types she thinks. She is deliberately staying at arm's length to avoid pissing them off if they trip over her. My vote is that these guys are heading towards our friends in the Hood, now what they will do when they get there is in the realms of crystal ball work."

"Anyone think anything different?" The admiral looked around his senior commanders noting the senior OPs officer had said nothing yet.

"Jonny, what's eating you?"

Commander Jonny Molinsky was legend in the USN, he was the one you didn't want to come up against in the war games. A 'total geek', envious colleagues called him, and sure enough that's what he looked like, a college professor with the barely legal eye glasses and bald head even though he was only thirty seven. What was left was salt and pepper, more salt than the latter too. He was skinny and lanky but he was truly a 'geek' when you used that word to describe expertise.

"Nothing much Sir, I concur with what I've heard but I'm looking at what may go down where Captain Balfour thinks they're headed. I'm not sure but given that Hood and its partner are operating in what the Chinese designate is their territory, I wonder if they aren't going to make an example of her, because really, will they care if the Caymans kick off for losing their ships? It's just live weapons drill for them against two ships but it will serve as a message to anyone, including us, that there's a price to pay for operating in these waters."

That was like dropping a cup of ice cubes down the back of their collective necks. Balfour chipped in again.

"The reports from the Simmons and WS Churchill were glowing to say the least. Simmons temporary Captain had nothing but high praise for the bravery and professionalism of those who came over to help. He's pretty sure that without those generators and pumps, she'd be on the bottom by now. How many of her wounded would not have made it through the day is a wild guess but for sure some of them wouldn't if they had not been operated on there and then. There is no doubt in my mind we owe them big. But we can't do a damned thing if that's what the Chinese are heading down there to do."

No one spoke, it went against everything they thought or represented as officers and men of honour. You just didn't leave friends and allies in the shit. It was like being saved by a passer-by from a mugging, only to watch them get the crap kicked out of them ten yards further on and walk away.

Admiral Jamie Summers stood up and walked to the nearest scuttle and gazed out, he remembered all those years ago in Copenhagen when he, as a Lt jg, and some of his own guys were ashore after a particularly tough three week exercise in shitty weather. He never knew how the bar fight started but he knew they were in deep shit, outnumbered and taking casualties. Then the door had burst open and half a dozen British officers had come in, already a little worse for wear. Sizing up the situation a tall British Lieutenant had shouted, 'Come on chaps, the cousins are in a bit of bother' then he led them in the attack shouting 'STANAVFORLANT to the rescue'. That was how he met Jon Roby. Roby should have just got his men back outside and called the shore patrol or police. He didn't, he did what was right not what was legal.

He turned back to face the table, decision made. There goes my third star.

"We can give them intel, we can give them EW support we could even put a CAP over them and shoot as many missiles down as we can. We won't be hitting the Chinese. CAG, can our guys take out their anti-ship cruise missiles with AMRAAMs?"

Marenga looked uncomfortable. Fuck. What was the old man thinking?

"Err yes Sir the AN/APG-79 AESA on the Rhinos can track and target inbound missiles. The Growlers can make the electronic picture awkward for them too."

He referred to the EA-18G Hornets converted for Electronic Warfare which had taken over from the original Growlers, the EA-6B Intruders.

The admiral thought for a few seconds.

"Bull, you remember that exercise we had planned, the one where we defended an allied airbase against attack?"

Bull looked thoroughly confused for a second or two then the light bulb went on.

"Oh that one, yeah we scoped out as the final exercise for this deployment. But Sir you wanted to keep it secret."

"Yeah I know, I've changed my mind. Let's say one of these iddy biddy atolls is the air base we are defending against seaborne attack, what do we need to do for a twenty four hour cover?"

Jonny Molinsky was polishing his glasses furiously.

"Err I wish you'd brought me in on this earlier Sir, I've a couple of plans partially complete for similar events. I think I can work you one up in pretty short order. Let's assume this is the atoll we are defending." He pointed to the digital chart some thirty miles south of Long Hải Island in Vietnam, right next to where Hood and Ocean Guard were operating.

Jose Maringa looked around him thinking they're all fucking mad. They are really looking to intervene here. This exercise shit is as transparent as a pane of glass. If we lost a single plane or sailor the stripes and stars would carpet this floor....after they'd been torn off the sleeves and collars. I can't believe they're even considering this.

"Err Sir, really is this wise?"

"What having an exercise CAG? We do that all the time."

"With respect Sir that is not what you are talking about here and we all know it."

"Jose you are correct. Sometimes doing what's right comes before doing what the book says you should. But hey, I will write my own obituary clearing everyone here of complicity, so your stripes will be fine."

"Don't exclude me Sir." Said Bull Balfour. "I'm not after any more stripes or stars, I'll stand for what is right."

Jose Maringa looked even more incredulous and annoyed.

"It isn't about my stripes Sir, they and my life are always on the line every time I take off and every time I tell my people to shoot or not to. I'm thinking about what the Chinese might do if we interfere, I know they have no fixed wing over them but they have literally around a thousand SAMs available if they get pissed off enough to use them Sir. I'm thinking about my people!"

"Enough Commander!" Bull Balfour wouldn't have anyone raise his voice to the boss.

"No he's right Bull. OK, Commander think of it like this. Your guys and gals can sit back ten miles from the 'atoll' and still have thirty miles worth of firing range. The Chinese will be anything from a hundred and fifty to three hundred miles away when they fire. They haven't got any SAMs that will go that far to my knowledge. They will need to use a helo to give mid-course guidance to their anti-ship weapons I'm guessing as well, since they aren't going to fire blind. But we don't have to do anything about that. The Hawkeye can give us long range warning of inbounds and the Growlers can see if they can confuse them, no one gets in person to person range. Great test of our systems wouldn't you say?"

Maringa was quiet for a moment.

"OK Sir, I'll play along but with one proviso, if the Chinese ships close to SAM range we bug out."

"Done. Now get me get some planning done."

A messenger stuck his head around the door.

"Sir, the vessel Ocean Guard has just gone active with a Sea Giraffe 1X radar, it appears to be heading due south away from a small atoll cluster and there's a racket to his north which appears to be a Vietnamese Molniya class missile corvette. Oh and the Chinese have slowed to nine knots Sir."

"They are way out of Vietnamese territorial waters. What's happening down there? Why have the Chinese slowed down? What the fuck are the Viets doing poking around there? I need some answers people. Move a Hawkeye over that way so we get some data on what's happening."

*

Miles Carlson Bowed slightly to his oriental counterpart who smiled and did the same. With permission from Foggy Bottom, the Chinese could sort their differences out with the Vietnamese with no interference from Uncle Sam. That was America saying 'fuck you' Vietnam, you caused massive damage to one of our ships and killed a load of our guys and girls you treacherous bastards. And really, Miles decided, they only had themselves to blame for the 'ass whupping' the Chinese were going to give them for trying to stitch them up.

As long as it was done quietly and well away from the western media, then no problem. The last part was easy for those in the orient, of a communist persuasion that is, less easy in the west but really all they needed was another anti-Trump story circulating and the silly retards of the Washington elite wouldn't even mind if someone pulled the plug in the South China Sea or it evaporated suddenly. Boy did they hate that guy, he reflected, just because he wasn't 'one of them' he could do no right at all. Well, he decided, the President can be a useful distraction for what needs to happen down here.

The fact that both he and his opposite number both knew that nothing was resolved between them in regard to the disputed seas, played no part in this little quid pro quo.

America was going to watch the Chinese test a few of their platforms and weapons on the Vietnamese, and hoover up as much information as it could to help for the time when they themselves had to take on the Chinese –if they did. Be interesting for the armchair strategists he supposed. A last wave to Mao or whatever the fuck his name was today, and then through the back door once more to receive the ambassador's wrath. Fuck him. He'd go straight to his prison cell on the fifth floor, he needed to brief Vern over at NSA so he could then tell the Nimitz group commander what was actually happening and get it moved a bit closer so their EW and AWAACs could pick up all the gen on what was going to happen. He stopped in his tracks. He'd forgotten all about König's band of Robin Hoods. He smiled at his own pun. Hood. He really did hope they pulled through though, and the fact that they'd apparently found eight of the ships meant their justification for being there was very strong. His local navy guy had given it a less than evens that both ships would come through given what the Viets had heading their way. Pity he couldn't drop König the nod, or maybe he could?

*

"Jamie, I was just going to give you a call, we've made some progress. But you first." Said Jon Roby, somewhat surprised by the call.

"Err Jonno we are wondering whether that Chinese SAG is going to come down there and kick your ass. It will pass us tonight and is less than four hundred miles from you at the moment. I've ordered the group make up, course, speed and current location sent to you."

"Thanks Jamie, I really hope they don't because we've enough problems with the Viets."

"The Vietnamese?"

"Yes I was just about to tell you that we found most of the missing ships. Eight in all. Two of them were US flagged, so I thought I'd better let you know. So it stands to reason that the Kilos belong to Vietnam too and that they did the hijacking as well as torpedoing your ship. Best guess, they wanted to set you and China at each other. Reason? Buggered if I know, probably money or revenge or both is our best guess."

"Damn me you did it. So what is the problem now?"

"Aah, they objected to us discovering the ships they stole. They tried to take Ocean Guard again but once more Simon's boys took care of business. Then three Molniyas objected and fired a load of missiles at him, he shot several down and we arrived in the nick of time and shot the rest down. There are more ships on the way though, we have eyes on two Gepard class frigates just over the horizon, but they may not be the only ones. At the moment I've sunk all three Molniyas and bombarded the atolls that had been occupied, now I'm heading south and west out of the way." He went on to describe the discovery of the ships and the response from the atolls.

"Jees you don't hang around do you Jonno. I'm moving my guys over your way a bit just to keep an eye on things, I'll get them to give you the IFF codes for tonight so you don't accidently obliterate my air wing, there's other stuff been going on in the background that is so, what do you guys call it? Hush hush?"

"Err if you mean the kind of info you get shot for even thinking about, then yes, Hush, hush does the job."

"Well anyway, there may be more fireworks on the way but not necessarily aimed at you. Can't say more right now. I've given my boys and girls permission to engage any hostile missiles that approach your position, the AWAACs will find you soon, or at least Ocean Guard."

"Well thanks a lot Jamie. Hope you won't get into any trouble over this."

"Nah, I'm due retirement soon anyway." His lie didn't convince either Roby or himself.

"Well thanks again, I'll make sure to meet up in Japan in a few weeks then."

*

Admiral Jamie Summers looked again at the communication in front of him. Dammit, not the Chinese, Roby was on the mark it seems. He looked up at the knock as his senior command group filed back in, despite the late hour most seemed fresh.

"Gentlemen, our favourite spook has been busy again and I just got off the phone with our Caymans allies. Get this, we are certain the sub was not Chinese, all of theirs are accounted for. Can you fucking believe it? They lined them all up together along with crews for the passing satellite to snap as it went by –before you say anything it's been verified by Naval Intel. In addition it seems there's been some background manoeuvring going on. It appears as if the bad guys are actually the Vietnamese and this little plan of theirs has backfired spectacularly for a number of reasons. First, Jon Roby and his merry men have discovered the location of eight out of the twelve missing ships, including two US flagged. They were lying in a neat line on the bottom of the sea next to an atoll pair which was supposedly unpopulated but just happened to have flak cannons and special forces teams on it. OK. Then they were attacked by three missile corvettes which they put down and apparently there's bigger fish heading their way."

He looked around at their faces which varied in expression from relief to deep concern and ploughed on.

"Next we have the Chinese SAG, I have it on good authority that we should standby and monitor what happens when a Chinese SAG administers punitive punishments to the representatives of countries which cross it. Foggy Bottom says they can kick the crap out of any Viet forces they fancy and we just watch and learn. In addition we have open season on any detected Kilos." He saw their surprise.

"Well we know they won't be Chinese because they told us." He added with a big smile. "Hope for their sakes they aren't lying because right now we are tracking two. So we're going to move a little closer by going south west near to the end of the abyssal, we'll have one Virginia ahead of us, in fact," he looked at his watch. "She's on station as of now. So we'll watch and learn and anything that flies our way can legitimately be shot down."

24th October 23.55. Hood, five miles South of disputed atolls.

Roby sat in the bridge command chair and brooded. It wasn't that they hadn't performed extremely well, they had. However they did have surprise on their side so they should have won, but there was just the nagging doubt that they may have missed something. He looked at the bridge chart viewer, about a mile to starboard was another weird horseshoe shaped atoll, the last in this particular chain. It was still relatively shallow here just 94 feet, the South China Sea seemed to drop away to his port side in a series of steps down to the abyssal a hundred or so miles away. If you drained this pond it would look like a giant's staircase, 164 feet down to 328 down to 656 then 1640, all in nicely defined contours, plenty of hiding places for ships.

"Torpedoes inbound bearing 30 degrees off the starboard bow!"

The shouted warning shook him awake. Ah yes, that was it, the bloody Kilo.

"Range is just seven hundred yards Sir, they just appeared from behind a shoal near the atoll to starboard."

Roby looked at the flashing OPs repeater. Fuckit they've done it again, sneaky bastards.

"Starboard 30. I'll give you an exact course in a second."

"Guns have you anything that will train and fire HE closer than 500 yards?"

"Aye Sir." Came the answer from the Assistant Gunner, Leading Seaman Fred Delderfield. Which side Sir?"

"Port. Start dropping HE in the water fine on our port bows, range four fifty yards. Keep them going and listen to the torpedo range on the OPs channel. A ten degree arc. Need them to explode in the water."

"Aye, aye Sir. Ten degree arc at four fifty."

No more than three seconds later the forward port twin 3" begin pumping out rounds fused to explode below the surface.

"Slow to fifteen knots." Enough for good manoeuvring but not too much if they copped one or two even, which it looked like they would. Depends if the torpedoes are impact or proximity fused where they will explode, he mused.

"OPs, update?"

"Sir." Answered Ringbolt Langford. "Two torpedoes range five hundred yards, speed fifty five knots." Roby wondered if anyone had ever tried this for real. Probably not, he decided, it's not in the book.

"Clear the for'ard compartments back to delta section please Mr Kopf."

They would probably take at least one hit. Being of shallow draft meant the torpedoes too would need to be less than ten feet below the surface if they were going to hit. So the chance that a high explosive shell detonating nearby may set them off was real? No idea.

The seconds ticked by with agonising lethargy. Then a cheer went up. He looked at the viewer in time to see an eruption of white water ahead.

"Good shot Delderfield, bet you're the first Killick sailor ever to shoot a torpedo with a three inch gun!"

The voice of Lt Bianchi brought them back to reality like a bucket of ice cold water.

"Second one still running straight and true Sir, it's gone active."

Roby looked at the chart again. The water to starboard was getting uncomfortably shallow.

"Under the arc now Sir." Came the disappointed voice of the Assistant Gunner.

"Very well, good try. Sound the brace for collision Mr Kopf." He could not turn either way now, if he did then the torpedo would impact further along the hull and quite possibly do very much more damage and he had no countermeasures.

"Aye, Sir."

The noise of the collision alarm was incredibly loud against the background steady voices and beeps in the OPs room

"Do you hear there. Brace, brace, brace. Damage control parties standby."

The impact was greater than ever he feared. Roby knew that if he hadn't been sitting down he'd have been knocked off his feet. It was like running into a wall. The whole bow rose up along with a massive eruption of water like those old movies show when depth charges go off. Alarms rang out and were silenced.

"Stop engines. Casualty reports and damage control reports as fast as you like." He said in a matter of fact voice sounding like he was just mildly irritated at the interruption.

The water had subsided now and in the darkness it was impossible to see the extent of the damage. For one wild moment he hoped that the hit had been right on the bow with its super tough Titanium alloy at eight centimetres thick.

The first report came in from the Chief Engineer as he expected.

"Lt Braime Sir. The impact was seven feet from the bow, port side Sir. There's a hole through and through for Alpha section, completely flooded. Bravo section, the for'ard bulkhead has buckled and is leaking badly, we may make some progress with the flooding in there given time but at the moment its gaining fast and I've ordered it sealed back to Charlie section which the barbette for A turret divides. Bravo section is quite a sizeable space Sir. She's down by the head and getting lower. No casualties reported or encountered."

"Thanks Chief, do what you can."

"Mr Kopf, go and inspect the bow section from the upperdeck, don't worry about showing lights we should be well out of sight of the other atolls."

"Aye, aye Sir." Answered the First Lieutenant practically bounding off the bridge where he'd witnessed the explosion first hand.

Julius Kopf touched his mike. "Crause."

"Sir!" Came WO Crause's instant answer.

"Bring two men and torches to the fo'c'sle. A couple of ropes too." He added as an afterthought.

Down in the OPs room Roby fumed and stared intently at the chart, particularly the depth at the entrance to the lagoon between the horseshoe shaped atoll ahead. It shoaled all the way up to the arms of the horseshoe then got just a bit deeper once passed the entrance and on the inside. If it became necessary he'd beach her within those arms which, given the shallowness of the water, would make it impossible for any submarine to approach submerged. The more he looked at it, and the creeping inclinometer on the bulkhead, the better it sounded. He supposed they could surface and try a few more torpedoes but the moment even a napkin showed above the water a rain of five inch would reduce it to scrap in seconds. Hope they don't stand off and try their bloody missiles though.

He tapped his mike.

"Chief, I want to beach her in a lagoon, about half a mile away. I'm going to reverse her in. I'll need some counter flooding and serious good luck to get over the bar at the mouth. Can you sort that?"

The Chief Engineer was standing in ankle deep water watching the damage control party finish shoring the

Charlie section bulkhead. The weeping had ceased for now which was a relief. He blew out his cheeks and put his fists on his hips before running his hands through his still coal black hair and answering his Captain.

"Have to be sooner rather than later Sir or it won't have any effect, or rather enough effect; and if we leave it 'till later we won't get over the bar even if we do counter flood, we'll be drawing too much."

"Right. Better get cracking then."

"Aye, aye Sir, I'll head back to DC1. Give me a minute. I'll run the for'ard pumps at max too Sir."

"Right you are Chief. Helm, Steerpods to full port turn, ease off when the stern is getting lined up with the entrance to the lagoon which is at this moment just off our starboard bow. The idea is to back us into that lagoon Moore. Go slow astern and wait for further commands. Got it?"

"Aye, aye Sir. Steerpods to full port turn. Easing as we line up with the lagoon entrance then slow astern."

"Anything on the screens Lt Bianchi?"

"Just the two Gepards, they've finished rescue OPs and are just stooging around at present Sir. There was a racket from the north I'd estimate way beyond where we sank the Molniyas but that was five minutes ago. There's a US AWAACs astern, about three hundred miles, he's heading this way steadily, transmitting all the time. Probably got some little friends with him. I have the IFF codes by the way. Nothing in the direction of the Chinese SAG."

"Right."

He tapped his mike.

"König." There was a short delay as satellites routed and re-routed the call and encryption systems did their bit.

"Yes Jonno what can I do for you? Have you found the rest of the ships?"

"Err no Sir. We found an UGST torpedo though, or rather it found us."

"Oh bugger, how is the ship and what casualties have you taken?"

"Casualties are zero at the moment Jake but both Alpha and Bravo sections are fully compromised. Charlie is holding, we're still filling though so I'm going to beach her in a lagoon. I have a feeling this chap will try again if he gets a chance. Oh and Leading Seaman Delderfield gets a very big gong. He shot a torpedo with a three inch gun."

"Jesus, that's a new one on me. OK, give him a pat and tell him he just earned a 10k bonus. You certainly don't let the grass grow Jonno. I've only just put down the report from your earlier escapades. What of Ocean Guard?"

"She's heading slowly away. I told her to keep going, she can't help much in this game and she is relatively visible. We'll need a deep lifter and possibly a couple of tugs to get Hood out of this mess, but of course that can only happen when there's no submarine threat. I'm going to get a couple of drones up looking for this guy. My bet is he's the same one who tried it on with Ocean Guard. The Americans now know it was the Vietnamese who attacked them so if we find the Kilo that attacked us they might wish to tell 'someone' they know where another of the buggers is lurking."

"Funny you should mention that Jonno, just had a very cryptic message from Miles Carlson, that Yankee spook chap. He said the Chinese know, and Uncle Sam will do a Nelson when *they* do something."

"Aah. I expect he dreams in in cryptic clues. Yes, I spoke with Jamie Summers again, he sort of hinted that the Americans told the Chinese what had happened and who dunnit. So the Nelson bit would seem to indicate a blind eye to whatever the Chinese do."

"Right. Do you think Simon could find somewhere not too far away and hunker down as the Cousins say? She could be a haven of last resort or she could just keep cycling the drones."

"Good points boss. If he stays twenty miles or so away from us he might stay hidden enough, don't know off hand if there are any atolls in that direction that he might get close to, and then go quiet. We'd still have the link or a drone relay if the there's no more ECM, so he can still see what's happening. I don't thinks it's worth him switching to another AIS persona since no one uses this area, bit off the beaten path."

"I'll speak to him direct, you get on with conning her into that lagoon and getting the DC sorted. Keep me informed Jonno and keep a good lookout."

"Certainly will. No one takes me by surprise twice."

"Hope not Jonno, hope not. Oh and I'm going to try to ring someone high enough up the Vietnamese food chain and get this shit stopped."

Forty tortuous minutes later with the Chief pumping out Bravo for all he was worth and counter flooding near the stern until the bow was over the lip of the coral, Hood eased her damaged bow into soft sand at the western end of the lagoon. There were some small hillocks on this islet along with palms and no mud huts or human habitation signs at all this time, but of course it was dark, low light and IR could only do so much.

Roby stood up and stretched.

"Let's get a diver over the side to bring back some nice piccies of what's left of her bow. The rattling as we moved here tells me there's more damage than we're aware of. Everyone else stay alert for the slightest sign of those frigates or anything else that might want to interfere. I think our persistent submariner hasn't gone away yet, he's bound to want to check his handy work. I'd like very much to give the bugger all eight barrels and a reload."

He left the bridge to a chorus of Captain's left the bridge and Officer of the Watch has the conn, and headed down to the OPs room, no sooner had he arrived than Ringbolt Langford piped up.

"Racket bearing 285. Short transmission on a military frequency Sir. Very close, I reckon it's on the island or just beyond."

"Could be our wily submariner reporting in, or...have security do an all round sweep of the island but from the upper deck. Maybe this bloody place isn't as empty as it looks again."

A few minutes later Arkady Zotov and four of his security team were deployed at strategic points around the beached ship. Roby noted them when he checked the viewer. As he was just about to look away another figure emerged from the superstructure. Everything looked out of proportion, he was wearing dive tanks which looked tiny and a tiny diver's knife sheathed on his right thigh. Roby squinted and then suddenly realised the diver was Ayize the rather large Zulu chap, good choice he supposed since he was a marine engineer. Looked like Chief Braime was accompanying him and relating last minute information given the rate at which his hand gestures were coming. The fiery Breton held no man in awe despite the fact that Ayize was over two feet taller than him and twice as wide.

He walked out on to the port bridge wing and watched as they walked by, the Chief still going at it hammer and tongs, and smiled. They were a good crew he was proud of them all and his adoptees, Ayize and Arkady, both singular experts in their fields. He turned to go back in just as the OPs room came on again.

"Sir, ESM reports we are being laser designated."

"Fuck. Active now." He instructed Lt Bianchi and the Sea Giraffe radar surged into life, painting the sky for hundreds of miles with discrete pulses of microwave energy, getting a full picture update every thirty seconds now it was on high PRF.

"Arkady, any sign of the bastard?"

"Sweeping again with IR Sir, he's well-hidden is all I can say."

Roby descended the steps into the OPs room and walked over to the Holo display map. Now they were active every military unit for two hundred plus miles would know it and exactly where they were, but likewise they would know too what was around too, but not nearly as far out as they could be seen.

"Vampire, vampire, vampire. Four missiles bearing 235, range fifteen miles. Altitude one hundred thirty feet. Speed 0.8 mach. In trail. Single launcher. Seekers are now active. CMS says NATO classification SS-N-27 Sizzler and the 3ME1 variant." Came Lt Bianchi's voice pitched higher than normal, Roby noted.

"Fuck a stoat. Caught us again." Roby managed before the portside three inch guns began firing.

"Chaff?" Asked Roby to the OPs room in general.

"Too close Sir, not enough wind either." It'd probably blind our own sensors as much as anything." Answered Ringbolt Langford through the corner of his mouth as he juggled his ECM array hoping to blind the radar seeker but discovering it was frequency agile and damned hard to pin down.

Bright green lines shot from four barrels as the two turrets with twin Gatlings began correcting their aim. The AK176 twin turrets also began to crack out their much larger rounds at the phenomenal rate of 120 rounds per barrel per minute, some using the highly successful Pre-Fragmented, Directional, High Explosive Canister PFDHEC or 'PC' for short. Similar to the San Shiki shells they'd used earlier these 3" shells were like shotgun shells. Perfect for when the target was heading straight for you, be it a missile or plane. They were ideal in this instance when all the missiles were essentially following the same track, a single shell may hit more than one and aim correction was easy because they were all on nearly the same bearing.

Ringbolt Langford mused quietly that it was probably a good job they weren't the 3M54E variant which accelerated to Mach 2.9 when close to target, otherwise, this close, we'd never have got more than five rounds off.

Roby was somewhat detached from the activity around him because his well-trained crew were doing their jobs and needed no input from their Captain at this time and he too had the opportunity to muse about what might or might not have been. At least the Kilo had fired its full load, no more from that direction. Did the fact that he had fired his missiles mean he had given up on the torpedo option?

The first missile exploded in spectacular fashion almost as soon as it came in range, so that was one to the 3" system. The second clearly fell to a 3" PC canister shot. At this point the forward AK630M2 demanded a reload and they were down to just the one AK630M2 and the three twin 3" inchers.

But time was running out for the defenders as the third missile blew apart, killed by the AK630M2, the last was inside the minimum range for the 3" guns and the remaining AK630M2 now demanded a reload as well. The twenty foot missile flew wide of the main superstructure and dived into the bow. The four hundred plus pound warhead blew with a blinding flash and a tremendous thump which threw the ship over to starboard briefly.

The OPs room was a hubbub of noise as OPs staff cancelled alarms, checked and cross checked sensors and readouts.

Roby left them to it and pulled a viewer over to him to check out the bow. Had the Zulu gone over? What of the Chief and the security personnel? Slowly calm returned and reports began flowing again.

The Chief came up on the net to report that he and Ayize were safe; they'd had enough warning to get in the shadow of 'A' turret.

One of Arkady's security guys wasn't so lucky. He'd been right on the bow when the hit had occurred, probably thinking it would be the last place the missile would hit. In normal circumstances it would have been, for sure. Roby had a sneaking suspicion that from an inbound missile's perspective the bow would look like centre mass given that the torpedo explosion had probably removed a significant amount of anti-radar paint.

Arkady reported that his man a fellow Russian by the name of Maxim Golvanov, had died of his injuries before the medics could get a line into him. Arkady kept the gory details to himself. It wouldn't help the Captain to know that Max had been ripped apart by the blast and only his Kevlar vest with his name stencilled on the back had allowed instant ID.

He moved to the top of B turret and began to scan the shoreline then back further up to the crest line for the dunes. He completed each sweep twice, once in low light and the other in infra-red. He was keen to get ashore and find the bastard who was designating, then he'd personally gut him. Max had been an old and reliable friend way back even into the bad old days. *There*! He almost missed it.

In low light viewers, movement was quite stark, even dark clothing reflects light of different intensity and someone who appears perfectly blended into the background will stand out massively when they move. He briefly sighted his long gun, a Swiss Brügger & Thomet APR308, to get the location nailed before he rested it on its bipod on the turret roof. He got his laser range finder positioned and focussed it on the bowl of a tree near to his now stationary target; he needed a decent reflection to get a good reading. Range 807 metres, now he waited. Low light switch, on. Wait for another movement, there. Line up. Breath out, squeeze to first pressure, hold breath, second pressure and the kick. The target was thrown backwards over the dune crest. No more laser designators from him, bastard. He began scanning again and spoke into his mike.

"All Security units. Max is down. I need another man on top, bring your long gun, I just popped the bastard that lined us up for the sub shot. At least I hope it was him. Be aware, we are now in hostile territory, anything that moves out there, slot it and report after."

Single clicks of acknowledgement came back through the radio from his team positioned around the upper decks. Time to visit the armoury and see what goodies Andy Evans ordered for the deployment, he decided after another minute or so scanning the islet. Where there was one Viet soldier, there were bound to be more and we are sitting on a large stationary target, he mused.

The shit just hasn't finished pouring down the back of my neck yet decided Captain Jon Roby gloomily. He was now ensconced in the OPs room and staring intently at the holographic dome looking for clues.

Continuously the radar and other sensors, as well as the recon drones added their own pieces of information to the overall picture; with each update he was hoping that the enemy's next intentions would suddenly become clear so that for a change, he could be in the driving seat instead of having to react all the time. It so went against the grain, and all his training, to be 100% defensive. He just had no fucking idea who or what was lurking outside range of his radar and drones. Like shining a torch in the dark, you only knew what was in the illuminated area everything else was guesswork.

He tapped his mike.

"WEPs." Bungy Williams answered huffing and puffing.

"How long until the cassettes are reloaded?"

"'bout another minute or so Sir. One of the buggers is more awkward than my mother in law." There was a known glitch with the forward AK630M2 cassette loader Roby knew. That would be on the replacement list if they got home...when they got home, he corrected mentally.

Roby smiled at Bungy's non PC mother in law reference and moved on down his checklist.

"Crause." He waited for an answer.

"Aye Sir."

"Any chance of getting some anti-radar paint on the bow section to cover where it's burnt off? That was why the missile headed that way; it was the strongest radar return."

"I'll get it organised Sir."

Next on his list was the Chief Engineer.

"Chief." He waited for the connection.

"Aye Sir."

"What is the situation up for'ard?"

"Well that Zulu man is over the side now Sir. Been down a couple of minutes and I've seen the flashlight go on the camera several times. I expect he'll be up soon, wouldn't want to be in the water if another attack comes in. From what I can see the missile impact was on a reinforcing strut which connects the bow to the frames. Remarkably it is still intact and the explosive force seems to have gone at a tangent to the impact point; meaning it did not do further damage inside the hull. I want to examine that strut closely when we get a chance though, to see if it has been weakened. Amazing stuff this Titanium alloy."

Roby could imagine him shaking his head in disbelief.

"Well they aren't designed to be armour piercing Chief, no one has any armour nowadays." He added facetiously. "How is Charlie section bulkhead holding up?"

"Oh that's fine Sir, the fella who designed this baby knew what he was doing. There's a Titanium Diboride sandwich between each section. Acts as a shock absorber. That's what stopped the damage at Charlie."

"Good, I'll remember to send a special thanks to him if we get out of this in one piece. Keep me posted on what Ayize's pictures show."

There was a beep in his ear.

"Captain?"

"Arkady Sir. Where there's one hostile there's going to be more than one out there Sir. I've deployed extra men on the upper deck and the superstructure, I've also taken a 2" mortar out of the armoury and the gunner's assistant is having a play with it now. I've put him on the boat deck of the aft superstructure. If need be he can lob bombs over the dunes, or the mast and close to the bow, if we have anyone trying to board." He added as an afterthought. "He's got one of your chefs as a loader and we can spot for him. I had an idea to decoy future missiles Sir, we could set up a smallish mast ashore and hang a couple of your radar reflectors on it, an inbound missile would probably find them a much stronger reflection. If they use radar guidance that is, and not TV."

"Good stuff Arkady. Fine with the mortar. Not so happy about the mast ashore though. As you say if there's one out there, there will be more. I have no doubt you are correct about the decoying bit but it could cost us some men to get it ashore and far enough away to be useful. I expect we are under observation even now."

"True, but they don't appear to have sniper rifles or we'd have known by now. Big slap on the head for their QM."

"Well unless there's another Kilo around we should have plenty of warning for any further inbounds." He disconnected Arkady and addressed the OPs room at large.

"I'm wondering why the Gepards haven't fired yet people. I mean we are as visible as it is possible to get and those frigates to the north seem to be running in figure of eights at the moment. We are well in range. Ideas please?"

He had included Ocean Guard in the loop for that announcement, plenty of experience there to call on and Simon was straight in.

"Well we have to assume they have a tighter chain of command than us so there will be a fair bit of requesting orders is my guess Jonno. I expect it was a bit of a shock when you took out the three corvettes so easily. If I were on one of those Gepards I'd be trying to get some other bugger on the front line before I'd have another go at you."

"Two choices really then? Well that was more or less my take on this Mexican standoff Simon so waiting for orders or whistling up some pals to help out. Well anyway it will start to get light in three and a half hours and proper dawn is at 06:04 then we'll get a good look at where we are. With the drones providing extended surface cover beyond our radar lobes I don't think there will be any more surface surprises, what else is anyone's guess. You know I was really hoping that someone with a brain in their hierarchy would have been consulted by now and that he'd call it off." He added wistfully.

"Depends whether whoever is in charge is asking the right folk for their input. If he's surrounded by a bunch of 'yes' men he's going to be in an ideas echo chamber." Added Simon thoughtfully.

"True, true. We'll see, and thanks Simon."

"No problem Jonno. On a slightly tangential subject, you'll be pleased to know the link is working perfectly and the two CMS units are good pals. We see your damage control board as well weapons status and the usual radar picture."

"Jake will be pleased to know the kit is working well Si, you should tell him." He added mischievously.

They didn't have to wait long for the answer to become apparent and suddenly it all changed again.

"Captain, LIDAR has aerial movement to the north west at high level and to the north at low level." Reported Ringbolt Langford.

"Gepards are moving again." Reported Lt Bianchi. "Both appear to be heading our way but not at high speed yet." He noted.

Another two tense minutes followed as the systems refined the contacts and added them to the plot.

"Radar has new bogeys, bearing 320, range two hundred and eleven miles, altitude, three zero thousand feet, speed six hundred knots."

And as if it couldn't get worse.

"Captain, Arkady here, we have movement in the dunes above the beach on which the ship is sitting, I count twenty plus bad guys and they are tooled up according to my man up on your signal deck."

Fuck. It never rains but it pours, thought Jon Roby as he absorbed the details of what was clearly going to be a coordinated attack. Hi-Lo air assault and something on the ground too.

"Right chaps." He said to the OPs room, bridge and gunnery centre at large. "Are we back up to full loads on all weapons?"

A chorus of acknowledgements greeted the question.

"My instinct says we'll see a lot of distraction stuff, with a final assault from the shore. So potentially, with missiles raining down from different directions that will keep our folks off the upper decks, then they can begin an assault from the beach. So let's clear the upperdecks for a start and only have folk out there as and when an assault is detected. Arkady, get your watchers inside and plugged into the nearest viewers, and get my crew to show them how to use them to their best effect. The bad guys won't be aware of what coverage we've got so that is an advantage for sure. If an assault is picked up, we'll have Mr Delderfield outside quickly and he can start chucking mortars at them, then Arkady's chaps can take care of anyone who manages to climb aboard, but from the cover of the breakwaters and superstructure. No idea if they will have any heavier weapons than machine guns. We can but hope."

The defenders prepared themselves once more, the loaders for the cassettes containing the AK630 rounds checked and re-checked the load lifters and waited in tense silence. The men detailed to help uncase the 3" rounds from their protective packaging made slits and cut pieces away from the packaging ready to spring the rounds out as quickly as possible in order to re-supply the two hundred and fifty round ready use magazines. Those tasked with moving the seven foot monsters, which was what a five inch round with its cartridge measured, sweated and mentally rehearsed the moves to load. They had the first five as HE in A turret, the next twenty were all San Shiki and to be fired one at a time in a carefully controlled manner, there were no more San Shiki shells after that. The other three turrets had the same loadout of HE and SAP. They all stared at the deckhead above them and waited. Time passed like cold treacle running down a tin.

*

At 30,000 feet and now ninety miles away from Hood, a pair of Su-30MK2V's from the 935th fighter regiment were going through the final arming sequence before release of their Kh-31P, NATO AS-17 'Krypton' anti-radar missiles. Leisurely they manoeuvred the big strike fighters onto the correct heading for final release. The missiles would stay high for most of the ninety mile journey picking up speed to 1500mph. Homing in directly on the radar emissions from Hood they would airburst just above the target and shred the radar antenna. Even if Hood switched off her radar now, they would home in on the original location and explode as before.

On a verbal command each aircraft dropped four missiles in sequence, then turned and banked away for the short return flight to Bien Hoa Air Base. All eight missiles ignited and flashed away into the night.

Down on the deck eight old SU-22M4 fighter bombers of the 937th regiment out of Thành Sơn air base were listening in to the countdown and preparing for their own debut in a few minutes time, after the enemy radar had been destroyed. Behind them a second flight of eight, considered utterly unnecessary by the planners but there just in case, trailed them by twenty miles. The lead group went about the arming procedure for their Kh-58 EM, NATO AS-11 'Kilter' anti-ship missiles, with practiced ease but a little nervous as this was the first time any of them had fired at a live target.

Each aircraft carried four of the missiles along with a set of drop tanks. They would fire at around fifteen miles from low level, easily within the capability of the Mach 3.6 missiles.

Their RWR was twitching and showing increasing emissions from their south east, it wasn't capable enough to tell them that this was an American E2D Hawkeye AWAACs. It was just something to be aware of. Briefly for the duration of two sweeps, a fire-control radar to their east made the RWR ping again.

Simon watched in increasing alarm as the odds against Hood started to rack up. The link showed him everything that Jon Roby's radar and other sensors could provide. A high raid and a low raid. CMS identification of the pair of aircraft which had just launched eight missiles was a tentative SU-30 based on what was assumed as their cruising speed and the attack profile. The ID of the missiles was not in doubt. These were radar killers KH-31Ps. Designed to wipe out a ship's ability to detect incoming threats these were to prepare the way for the low raid, as yet only visible on the recon drone's LIDAR.

It was equally alarming that the atoll they'd run aground on was occupied by Lord knows how many Vietnamese soldiers or sailors or whatever. He and his small OPs team looked on but could do nothing to help, like spectators at an impending road traffic accident they could see what was coming down the road but had no way of affecting the outcome.

He was however intrigued by a racket that Hood had picked up briefly, it was to Hood's north and east. The CMS had tentatively classified it as a Chinese Naval fire control radar HT-233, for their HQ-9 SAMs. The other racket had got close enough now to give actual tracking data, Hood could see the E2D which marked the furthest reach of American sensor range, at a range of two hundred and ninety miles, altitude 30,000 feet and slowly moving in a zig zag pattern aimed north east. Simon knew this attitude would give the sensor platform the broadest feed of data from any targets, potential or otherwise, in the carrier group's north east aspect.

He'd spoken to Jake after Jon Roby had briefed him and had located an area twenty two miles south south west of Hood's current position. Ocean Guard was now nestled in between four small atolls laid out in a trapezoid shape. The ship was slightly west of the halfway point between them and he was certain that even a sneaky submarine would broach if it tried to pass through the myriad of channels. Jake was of course very concerned and was trying back channel diplomacy as well as getting a heavy lifter and a pair of tugs organised ready to come and get Hood out of trouble when it was safe to do so. That of course was the rub. It seemed that the Vietnamese were out for their pound of flesh and given the units involved it had to be someone high up the totem pole who had authorised this operation, maybe the Defence Minister or even the Premier himself?

"Roby." The usual connection clicks.

"Simon, I assume you're current so I won't bore you."

"Yes, watching every move Jonno, I can imagine it isn't nice being a fixed stationary target with that lot heading towards you. Anyway, two of the drones are due at your place in a few minutes, I think they should all come here for re-arming and refuelling. The Vietnamese don't know about them yet, at least I don't think they know."

Roby cursed himself, he'd completely forgotten about the drone's endurance and the ones returning to re-arm. It would also take a load off his OPs staff too.

"Yes, you're right. Forgot about them in the heat of the moment. Thank God one of us is on the ball."

"Don't knock yourself Jonno, you have been a bit busy after all. All you need to do is let me know what packages you want on them and it will be sorted. I wonder if our American friends will come good on their promise?"

"Rest assured Simon, if it is within God's grace to allow, then Jamie Summers will come through. I think in fact he's already chucked his third star away for us, poor bugger."

"That's a shame, you've known him a long time haven't you?"

"Yes, since we were both pretty junior Lieutenants in fact. Met many times over the years as we both went up the ladder, you know what it's like in the service, just because you aren't spending weekends together doesn't mean you don't think about old friends. Then when you meet again it's like it was only the week before when you met last. Different today with Facebook, email, Whatsapp and so forth. I swear my daughter thinks up a new way to communicate with me just because she knows it will be torture for me to work out how to use the bloody thing. Anyway, we shall see what we see. The Indians are gathering in the hills so to speak and the attack is under way. Thanks again Simon, been nice working with you."

"You too Jonno." Simon didn't like the sound of that fatalism. Yet when he looked at the holo display he could see why Roby might be feeling a little down.

*

Jon Roby was intently studying the holo dome, watching the inbound high missiles whilst listening to the background noises as his OPs team configured the defences. Here they come, he thought. There were four American aircraft on screen now, flying a racetrack some five to seven miles south of them now, all around 5000 feet CMS identified them as F-18E Super Hornets. Another slightly slower aircraft at twenty thousand feet ran racetracks and CMS tentatively had that as an EA-18G Growler electronic warfare variant.

Warrant Office Crause had just popped his head in the OPs room to say that all the security personnel had been shown the necessaries on how to use the viewers. Truth be told they were rather like periscopes with the handles and the mask-like viewing pieces. It just needed someone to point out that twisting the right hand grip changed the magnification and the left one changed the mode between day, low light and IR. More complicated functions like being slaved to a target, weren't necessary. Crause was in combat gear complete with Heckler & Koch machine pistol, flash bang grenades, Helmet and a sidearm. He brought with him four holstered Sig Sauer P320 side arms, just in case he'd added, and informed Roby that all personnel not engaged in fighting the ship were now kitted out similarly and were ready to fight *for* the ship as of now.

Roby hung his pistol on the back of his command chair after checking it.

"When the land attack comes in, we'll secure the hatches properly and lock them down."

"Aye Sir." Answered Lt Bianchi for them all.

The missiles were closing in at twenty five miles per minute.

"Standby on the first San Shiki please Mr McLean."

"All set Sir; turrets are now switched to auto-fire and slaved to the CMS."

He had barely completed the sentence when A turret kicked out its first round, three seconds later it fired again. All eyes were on the viewers as they locked on to the patch of sky from which four deadly missiles plunged at over fifteen hundred miles per hour. Range for the outgoing rounds was greatly diminished when they fired at a high angle, down to 8750 yards. The missiles raining down were travelling at 400 yards per second. The outgoing shells were fired to meet the missile at the edge of their maximum range and travelled at over 900 yards per second. Thank God for computers, thought Jon Roby as now the 3" guns briefly joined in followed almost immediately by the AK630M2s.

The first San Shiki shell exploded and the seventy thermite Catherine wheels blasted out, the missile disintegrated in a spectacular flash, and so too did the next just a second later. The third appeared to wobble, possibly caught in the blast of the missile exploding in front of it, the wobble increased as the gyros on board tried to correct, then it did a spiral kind of manoeuvre, smashed into the after superstructure and exploded. No time to wonder why.

The guns commenced on the next inbound and the remainder were destroyed without further problems. The ammunition parties now frantically began replacing the expended ordnance ready for the next attack. They could wait until a magazine was emptied, but it made more sense to re-stock whenever there was a pause in the action. The disadvantage of having fixed capacity magazines as opposed to a magazine and shell hoists, was now apparent.

Seven shot down and just one hit but the one hit was pretty severe it had knocked out their after radar array, yes they had two but both provided information on which the computer based its aim. The loss was bad but the loss of Fred Delderfield and Marco Galvoni, one of the chefs, was worse.

They had been sheltering in the after superstructure when the missile impacted, they would probably have been fine had the hatches onto the boat deck been closed but Fred had wanted it open so he could get his not inconsiderable bulk outside with the mortar as quick as possible, just a bloody fluke isn't much of a consolation for Mrs Delderfield back on Little Cayman with their two boys or Mrs Galvoni senior back in Tuscany.

Not much time to ponder now just time to keep on reacting.

"Low level raid has popped up Sir, they're climbing to launch altitude. Range is sixty miles, now on our radar. CMS id is SU-22 probably M4 variant, old birds but not what they carry. They'll launch any second." Lt Bianchi sounded calmer now that action had been joined, Roby supposed he had too much to think about and do to have any spare time for mundane things like fear and panic.

"Arkady Sir. Movement in the dunes they are prepping for assault."

"Have you replaced the mortar team?"

"No Sir. Only had one mortar and that looks like someone stood on a beer can. No problem though we'll be OK. That was just an extra."

Roby hoped it wasn't bravado, but then Arkady had no need of bravado, he had literally been there and done most things that people only read about.

"Vampire, vampire, vampire!" Rang out PO Langford's voice yet again. "Low raid is launching, bearing zero zero five, range forty nine miles, speed approaching Mach 3.0 and now passing. Altitude five thousand feet now descending. Count is under way. Shit. Count is thirty two. Mach 3.6 steady now. CMS has them as Kh-58UEM NATO reporting name AS-11 'Kilter'."

Shit indeed, Roby thought as he absorbed the news.

"Wind?"

"Very light Sir. Fitful at two miles per hour from the east."

"Chaff forward please. As many as you can get out in the time, we want to be longer than the Nimitz by the time they get here."

"Aye Sir. Chaff for'ard, maximum." Answered PO Cole Moscrop, their one and only Canadian and the fourth member of the permanent OPs team.

Within seconds the thump of the 57mm Super Barricade chaff rockets could be heard and felt as they were fired from their launchers on both the port and starboard sides. The pattern would be set short, medium and long range, the idea being that the plumes of aluminium foil would drift into each other making the ship appear much longer to a radar seeker in the warhead.

"Arkady."

"Yes skipper?"

"How does the chaff bloom look?"

"Err, looks good from here, the close ones are spreading nicely, can't see past them. Looks like it might reach the dunes though, hope some of the missiles drop in there."

At two thousand seven hundred plus miles per hour they only had just over sixty seconds before the first arrivals, bearing their three hundred pound warheads. It was certainly looking pretty grim.

"Drone has a second wave of aircraft Sir, trailing leaders by twenty miles."

"Oh fucking perfect." His exasperation was apparent he quickly realised.

"I was just planning to go and get a bacon sandwich and a cup of char."

Mustn't slip like that again, he chided himself, it was bad enough they were in the shit up to their necks and beyond but their resolve mustn't fade nor their morale drop.

"Even our chefs couldn't manage a bacon sarny and a cuppa in under a minute so I expect I'd better postpone it until we've got rid of these rather persistent buggers. Thank God for titanium."

It never did any harm to be reminded that your ship was one of the best protected in the world and that several inches of titanium alloy sandwiched with a composite, protected them. Several nods from the OPs team told him that they'd taken in what he'd said. Now all they could do was wait.

Another thump told him some entrepreneur had raced to the magazine and retrieved at least one more chaff rocket and manged to load it in time for the computer to decide it was worth firing. Hope whoever it was had got back into the citadel safely. He was the only one not really doing anything, how frustrating was that?

He noticed Lt Bianchi finish his touch screen typing and sit back.

"All set Alfio?" Bianchi swivelled his chair.

"Yes Sir, only a few seconds before they enter the engagement zone."

"Right you are." Nothing more to say. Fucking waiting was intolerable, he decided. There was little or no chance they'd get the lot, not from a single source now and there were so many.

Thump, out went the first San Shiki. Now time goes the other way.

"Commencing now Sir." He thought it was Langford but he couldn't be sure over the noise of the guns.

Admiral Summers paced the admiral's bridge on the Nimitz like a man possessed. He longed for the days when he could have whipped out a foot long Cohiba cigar and polluted the atmosphere, not anymore, the thought police and the health Nazis would be all over him like a strawberry rash.

Instead he paced. Whenever someone brought a message, he'd stop, read it, nod and move off again. A cold cup of coffee sat on a nearby table. Thoughts roamed his mind like a montage of his life. Waiting was always like this, waiting for the strike to launch, waiting for it to come back, waiting for an update on this and an update on that. If he forgot something his flag Lieutenant would show him on the big chart with the cellophane overlay. Then he'd be off pacing again.

"What is the position of that Chinese SAG now Miller?"

"Err eighty miles north north east of the disputed atoll Admiral."

What were they going to do? They'd been in range of the Viet surface ships for some time now. All we'd had was that brief sweep of the fire control radar.

Further south it looked like his boys and girls were just right to help Hood when they needed it. He'd declined the order to fire when the high group launched their radar killers. Jonno would have to take care of them himself his flight of four CAP had six AMRAAMs each. Good missiles and what they were firing at wouldn't be trying to dodge either. It wasn't likely they'd kill one for one but he hoped that they'd thin them down so that Jonno's mini battleship could do the rest.

Commander Jonny Molinsky had come up with a firing plan which should make the best use of their available missiles. Each hornet would fire in turn, the first at the lead missiles, second would aim back a ways, the third further back still and so on. The idea was that while they wouldn't wipe out an entire wave they would thin them down, thus easing the burden on the ship's defences. Well that was the theory, they were just about to find out the reality. The only other thing they could do was to try and burn a few with the ECM suite on the Growler orbiting high above the Hornets, there were only three frequencies these missiles used so he was pretty sure they'd jam some, just a good job they weren't the newer more capable Kh-58UShE which had a wideband seeker.

The signal in his pocket was burning a hole there like a piece of plutonium. On no account was he to interfere with operations between the Chinese and Vietnamese, he was also denied permission to attack Vietnamese assets. Was a missile an asset any more than a bullet? His interpretation was that an asset was manned by people and that was what he'd tell them at his court of enquiry anyhow.

"The Hornets are firing Sir!"

He nearly said 'thank fuck for that'. As time had passed he began to wonder whether Jamie could in fact come up with the goods, but he should never have had a moment's doubt.

"Very well. Let's hope they get one for one."

Roby watched the Holo projection as the hornet's missiles converged with and then merged with the inbound missile stream. Designated targets dropped off the screen, four here, three here, four there and finally the best, five of six. That only left fifteen. He nearly laughed out loud. Did I really just think 'Only fifteen left'? Jees I'm losing it. Four more fell to the ECM and went wandering off to run out of fuel over the horizon. Then another blow.

"Vampire, vampire, vampire. New contacts designated…..on it went. The two Gepards had fired now. Sixteen more tracks inbound, they'd moved off to the northwest in the last hour or so.

"PO Langford, I'm beginning to think you are a stuck record. Got any good news?"

Ringbolt Langford looked around in surprise.

"Err, I'll see if I can find some Sir. Then he smiled and turned back to his screens.

Then like the harbinger of doom he began again.

"Fire control radar at zero two five, wait one. Vampire, vampire, vampire. Multiple contacts bearing zero two five degrees, course is….. not towards us exactly Sir." He sounded puzzled. "Range seventy five miles. Number's going up all the time now at twenty two, three and four. That's it." His screen border flashed with an identification.

"Chinese Sir, HT-233 for their HQ-9Bs the CMS says. Course is towards the second wave of SU-22M4s Sir.

"PO Langford, you amaze me." Langford looked around with a surprised look on his freckled face. "Only ten seconds ago I asked you for some good news. Now that is an impressive response. Change their designation from vampire would you. Amazingly they appear to be friendly, if one can be friendly with a Mach 4.2 anti-aircraft missile."

Well that only leaves 31 missiles heading for us.

"Is it getting light yet?" I think I'll see this battle out on the bridge gents, you are doing an incredible job and you certainly don't need me distracting you."

With that he got up and began walking towards the bridge stairs.

The first hints of dawn, a lightening of the sky in the north east, greeted Jon Roby as he took his seat in the command chair on Hood's bridge. He'd only been there a moment when Julius Kopf arrived looking grimy and very much worse for wear.

"Shoring on Charlie section bulkhead is complete Sir, not a drop seeping anywhere. I've examined the photographs that Ayize brought back from his dive and I think it might be possible to get some softwood wedges into the damaged seams in bravo section. If we can do that we might have some luck pumping out Bravo and if we do that we could back out of here and make a tedious stern first return to Labuan if Mr König wants that is."

"That's excellent news Julius, very well done."

Kopf's chest puffed out with pride and he stood an inch or so taller as well.

"Just got to get through the next hour or so, in fact the next few minutes would be nice, I'd like you to go to the OPs room Julius can't have both of us up here when there's all sorts of stuff in the air."

"Aye, aye Sir, but shouldn't it be you to go below?"

"No, not really, it becomes quite tedious watching other people do their jobs so well. I hadn't realised how much of my concentration was concerned with conning the ship and the wider picture, now we're static it seems I have plenty of time to over think things."

Julius clicked his heels which was quite unusual for him, indicating his level of agitation, and then disappeared down the ladder towards the OPs room with a puzzled look on his face.

The guns started again. Even though the blast screens were in place the noise was still terrific. He turned a viewer in the direction the first set of missiles would arrive from, just in time to observe the explosion of one of the San Shiki shells and then another slightly to its right. The ignition of the thermite was quite spectacular and the flames generated, appeared to race through the night wildly spinning. Then Hood began her jamming too.

Whether it was the combined effect of two sets of different jamming or something entirely different, three more missiles suddenly went haywire, one in a vertical dive another turned right and the third just nosed up and headed for outer space. The San Shikis took three more in quick succession and the aim was switched further back.

Now the 3" turrets began to spit, as usual, the first five were standard HE just to allow the aiming corrections to kick in and then the PFDHEC Canister started with dramatic effect as two missiles were brought down less than a thousand yards away. Roby noted they were saving the AK630s for absolute last ditch since a thousand yards was well within their firing zone.

Then the green lines walked out into the night bringing down yet another two almost instantaneously, looks like the loss of the aft radar wasn't so critical he thought and then cursed himself as two missiles arrived, seemingly not targeted by any of the systems. Shit. He quickly looked across to the bridge repeater and noted that one of the 3" turrets had a jam on its left gun and the auto-ejection system seemed to be having problems at the same time the starboard after AK630 ran dry. Trying to compensate was taking too long and one of the missiles did its terminal pop-up and smashed down straight onto the bridge roof. The second appeared spoofed by the chaff and exploded on the sand near the bows.

Roby's ears were ringing and there was dust everywhere with smoke and flames coming from the port side of the bridge. Coughing he and Geordie Moore picked themselves off the deck and headed over there reaching for the nearest 2kg dry powder fire extinguisher bottles before taking on the fire. The ECDIS had blown up for some reason, then he looked up and could see tiny splinter holes in the deckhead. That explains that then.

At that point the missiles from the two frigates began arriving dividing the defences further. Now turrets A and B fired at the north western inbounds, X-Ray and Yankee at the last of the northerly set. The jam had been fixed by Kiwi McLean and a two pound hammer, he slammed the rear turret door flicked the activation switches and raced back for the open hatch. He nearly made it. A missile, one of the last from the first plane group got past and slammed into the starboard forward superstructure about twelve feet above and to one side of him, the gale of splinters lashed in all directions and half a dozen caught him across the back of his calves as he dived inside. WO Crause pulled him the rest of the way and slammed the hatch.

"Too slow Mr McLean. You need to lose some weight. Ach you have, from the back of your legs I see."

"Fuck off Crause. You're a shit comedian." Was the agonised New Zealander's answer.

Crause quickly applied a spray of iodine dry powder and then a field dressing over the top. Another massive explosion shook the ship and both men looked up and forward.

"Fuck. The bridge again." Kiwi struggled to his feet.

"Giz a hand mate, let's go and see what the damage is up there."

Crause was about to argue but thought the better of it. He nodded and took Kiwi's weight on one side while shouting into the mike.

"Bridge hit. Is anyone from DC up there?"

A voice from the damage control centre answered.

Mason here Sir. Answer is no, we had two hits aft, they've headed that way. I'm all that's left."

"Scheisse. OK Wilf, stay there, I'm going up there with Lt McLean he's wounded as well. Get a medic up there if you can find one."

"Will do Sir."

They made their way along the corridor past the OPs room and up the ladder to the bridge; there was plenty of acrid smoke but no apparent fire. Daylight was coming soon and it became noticeable that light was spilling in from outside, and not through any regular entry point. None of the bridge lighting was on and none of the people were apparent.

Crause went right to look for his Captain and Kiwi staggered left to look for the helmsman. The smoke was clearing slowly and Crause began searching near the command chair. The chair itself was at an angle and parts of one side of the arm rest were missing he used his torch to search beyond but the smoke still limited his visibility.

Finally he found a piece of uniform jacket sticking up through a pile of debris. He quickly and carefully cleared away the debris, slowly revealing his Captain. He found the head, charred and blackened and felt round the neck for a pulse. He tried again. With all this crap around he couldn't see the extent of the injuries, he began to get angry. Then he found it. Sweet Jesus he muttered to himself hitting the mike twice.

"Doctor or Chief Doc to the bridge. Captain is down. Repeat, the Captain is down."

Kiwi hobbled over to help.

"Moore?" Asked Crause as he uncovered more and more of the Captain's body.

McLean just shook his head and carried on helping. He had difficulty speaking at that moment because he'd found bits of that mild mannered Geordie in three different places and nearly lost his stomach contents.

A moment or so later a form bustled onto the bridge. Chief MA Sid Parker didn't say a word, he immediately took charge and began examining Jon Roby.

Crause looked at Kiwi McClean. Another explosion forward caused both men to duck then look out over the bow. Impact near the anchor hawsers. No problem.

"OPs this is Crause. Tell Lt Commander Kopf he is now Captain. And Leading Seaman Moore is dead, Lt McClean is wounded. The bridge is a wreck." He tailed off.

There was a moment of silence.

"Aye, aye Sir." Said PO Langford turning towards a stunned looking Julius Kopf.

Langford went back to his plot, the ECM emitters had taken a few more missiles down and the chaff had lured a fair number too. The last missile had just been downed by the last round in the starboard after twin 3" mount. He was absolutely knackered. The concentration levels needed for this were enormous and energy sapping over a period of time. He checked the ammunition feed figures again. With both the Gunnery Officer and his assistant out of the game Ringbolt was the main man. Frantic efforts were underway now to re-ammunition the starboard mounts which had taken the brunt of the action, because fuck knows what was coming along now, perhaps a kitchen sink or two he decided.

Next to him in the OPs room but separated by about ten feet of physical space, Lt Alfio Bianchi was checking the drone reports. Now that Ocean Guard was looking after them he only needed to check the feed they were giving and see whether they'd found the *bastardo* submarine that had put them in this position.

A knock on the hatch leading to the OPs room was answered by a challenge from Lt Bianchi. Satisfied with the response, a very welcome steward was admitted with coffee and sandwiches. The first food since an early evening meal, which seemed like an eternity ago. Ringbolt wolfed his 'corned dog' and pickle sandwich as if it was his first food in a year. Then he slurped some of the hot, sweet coffee and felt his strength returning. The bastards might think they've got us cold but we are not out of it by a long way, was his final thought on the subject, anger was simmering below the surface. Below the surface was where he needed to keep it too, couldn't do the job in a flying rage.

Surgeon Lt Keith Aitcheson stripped his gloves and stood back from his current patient. There was a troubled frown on his face.

Captain Jon Roby lay still as death, an intravenous tube in each arm as they tried to rebuild his circulatory system with plasma expanders. He looked pale enough to be dead too which is where he was headed unless he was operated on soon, in Keith's opinion. Multiple splinter fragments still inside, he'd taken out as many as he could see and tied off where he could, sutured a lobe of his liver and a section of bowel. But there was more. For every bleed he located and stopped there was another when he'd finished it. The scanner showed multiple fragments still present any one of which could cause his death if moved. When Roby's blood pressure had hit bottom he decided to gently pack the wound with Kaltostat wool to cause clotting and then lightly bind the whole abdomen to keep everything in place. The BP was coming up now but he could not give more plasma expanders, you really had to have blood to move oxygen around hence a need for transfusion volunteers.

Warrant Officer Crause looked on as the doctor finished tying the bandages that were effectively keeping the Captain's guts inside. He himself had an intravenous line running out of his left arm near his elbow, this one into a blood collection bag, he had plenty of blood and if the Captain needed a litre or so then fine. He needed to get back soon because he was pretty sure there was going to be some dirty fighting yet. No mangy *arschloch* was going to get his ship without a bloody fight.

Aitcheson noted three more volunteers waiting for their turn to donate blood. One of those was the already injured Kiwi McLean who's admonition to the doctor when he was first declined as a donor was a simple 'for fuck's sake Doc, it's my blood isn't it?' He'd then gone on to describe the partial removal of his left calf and accompanying lacerations as a scratch. The doctor shook his head. Injuries which would normally have people in a hospital bed for three or four days were mounting up in the crew and being ignored.

It seemed the Vietnamese did have a stock of rocket propelled grenades or RPGs so WO Crause had said. But they were not doing much actual damage just making it dangerous to be on the upper deck, which of course was their plan, so he understood.

Arkady Zotov waited for the right moment to peek over the damaged bows. Some of the little bastards had got right down to the shore line under cover of a half a dozen RPG barrage. He wanted to know what the fuck they were up to. An RPG exploded behind him near the base of the superstructure with a whoosh and a bang, he didn't look in the direction.

Now. He popped his head out to one side and looked over the edge of the deck towards the bows. Quick as a flash he was back.

Fuck, they'd got scaling ladders. Perhaps these buggers were SF too like the ones that had attacked Ocean Guard? He passed the information on via his headset now regretting not having the helmet mounted cameras. He unclipped a fragmentation grenade, pulled the pin and let the spoon fly off, he paused a second then leaned out and threw it towards the interlopers sixty feet or so away. A sharp crack followed by a scream of agony told him he hadn't lost his grenade throwing arm. He risked a quick burst from his HK MP5, a tried and tested weapon. Another shout of pain. Then the machine gun, or one of them over by the dune crest, began firing in short accurate bursts and he quickly scuttled back behind the breakwater whilst rounds pinged off the front of it.

This in turn led to the starboard forward AK630M2 squirting a couple of short bursts at the crest. Tit for tat. No one getting anywhere. Well that suited him fine, the longer this went on the greater the likelihood of relief in some way. The RPGs had been a bit of a surprise when they'd appeared, but only a bit. They were almost as common as the AK47s that now littered the world courtesy of his own countrymen's desire for hard currency –from anyone. He and his reduced team would have to be careful when they finally decide to come over the top. Clearly there'd be a diversion and covering fire, but what else?

The sound of someone leopard crawling towards him caused him to look back over his shoulder and then look again. Crawling towards him bearing a long gun out in front was Ayize Mopantokobogo. As he came up beside Arkady he grinned.

"Thought you could use some help keeping the bastards down, while you kick shit out of the ones by the bow. Before you say anything I do know how to use it. I spent plenty of time at the ranges in Uni, fuck all else to do 'cos I had no money and the ammo was free." He laughed.

"Besides, in South Africa if you don't live in a city with cops everywhere, you need to know how to use a weapon, lots of weapons. My people are not quite at home with freedom and responsibility yet."

Arkady nodded once. OK.

"Ayize, see if you can get up onto the signal deck." He lay on his back and pointed to a position above the bridge about ten or twelve feet under the forward radar antenna. You are really large to try and keep a low profile man, just make sure that big black ass isn't hanging out in the open again while the rest of you is hidden."

Ayize followed the direction Arkady was pointing at. OK, going to need help from the guys inside as to how to get up there, he thought to himself.

"Can do. I think."

"Right when you get there," he flicked back over on to his front and slowly raised his head until his eyes were level with the top of the breakwater but behind one of the capstans. Ayize copied the move. "Look to where the dune crest is cut by that lone palm, the one leaning right. See it?"

"Yeah I got it."

"Well there's an MG up there who's a pain in the ass. If you could spoil his day we'd be better off. Of course if any other fool pokes their head up, feel free. My range estimate is three hundred and fifty yards."

"Got it."

"Yeah. On my way." He began to crawl back the way he'd come being careful to keep his bottom low as well.

Arkady smiled. He was glad Ayize was on their side. The sight of him then with his head low and his backside sticking up had nearly had him laugh out loud. Seemed the big fella could take a hint, hence the backside dipping he'd just witnessed. He returned his attention to the threat ahead and spoke into his mike.

"Carl. Your turn for a look and a frag." He spoke to his opposite number on the port side behind the breakwater."

Two clicks on the radio was his answer.

"Hopefully we'll have a long gun above and behind us in a minute or two, wait until then."

Two more clicks on the radio gave him the acknowledgement.

Captain Julius Kopf sat for the first time in the OPs room Captain's chair. He did so gingerly, out of respect for the usual occupant as much as anything. The other members of the OPs staff looked briefly in his direction and then turned back to their consoles.

"Captain?" Lt Bianchi got the ball rolling, he needed his new boss comfortable in the role, or as comfortable as he could get, as quickly as possible.

Julius almost didn't answer, his attention was on setting up the console in front of him and the prefix Captain hadn't registered as something to do with him and then suddenly it did.

"Yes Alfio?"

"Sir the Ocean Guard has a fix on the submarine which attacked us. It is now seventeen miles north west of us and on a track which will take it to the Vietnamese island of Long Hải if it continues on course. What do you wish to do with that information?"

Sheisse. Thought Julius Kopf, what a first question. What the fuck would Jon Roby do? Why would he do anything? Then his heart slowed a little and his tactical brain engaged.

"Get that information to the Commodore pronto. I understand that he's got back channel contacts with our new and temporary allies."

Julius rationalised that if anyone could get that information into the right hands i.e. someone in a position to attack the submarine, then it would be Jake König.

"PO Langford, I will take over the gunnery station now, you can go back to your radar and ECM."

"Aye aye Sir." Said a relieved Ringbolt Langford. Doing the guns bit had been fun almost for a start, but the novelty had certainly worn off. He knew also that the new skipper had been the Gunnery Officer on the Bismarck during their extended sea fight in the Caribbean, so he should be pretty shit hot on the subject.

Julius was back in his element to some extent, there really wasn't much for the Captain to do but monitor what was happening and making sure the team member responsible was taking the correct action. So going back to gunnery for a while would be a useful distraction from the thousand and one questions and answers running around his head.

He checked ammunition feed status and grunted in satisfaction, the ammunition handlers were doing well.

"Galley." He spoke into his mike.

"Galley aye." Came back a tinny voice he didn't recognise.

"Captain here. Where is chef?"

"Gone to the head Sir. Anything I can do?"

"Sorry, who are you?"

"Steward Kelso Sir, joined in Khasab."

"Ah yes. Listen Kelso, I know the chef has been sending out coffee and sandwiches, has he sent any to the ammunition parties do you know?"

"Not sure Sir, but when he comes back I'll ask. There's two big servers of sandwiches set out in the galley and an urn of tea and coffee Sir."

"Good. Thanks for that."

"Crause." The click of connection.

"Crause here."

"WO Crause, can you go around and make sure that each section sends people one by one to get food and a drink. It's laid out in the galley."

"Aye, aye Sir. The Captain is bad Sir the doctor says he must have surgery soon to survive. I'm just giving blood at this moment. I will be through in two or three minutes."

"Oh. Erm, what blood group does the doctor want?"

"'O' negative Sir. The Captain is 'O' negative."

"Ask the doctor if he can spare Chief Parker to come up to Ops with a collection bag and kit, I'm 'O' neg."

"Will do Sir...Captain."

Julius turned his attention to the viewers and began to scan the area surrounding the Hood, light was growing in the north and east and the low light cameras were at their best right now. He tapped his mike twice

"Ocean Guard." He waited for connection.

"Julius, how is Jonno?" Simon McClelland's voice came back full of concern.

"Not good Simon. The doctor says he won't make it unless he has surgery soon. I have no idea how soon that would be but those who can are giving blood. It is a bad abdominal wound as I understand it."

"Surgery soon? Jesus how are we supposed to organise that, strap him to a drone and fly him to hospital?"

"I know. Frustrating isn't it. Listen we are being sniped and RPG'd from all around, can we get a recon drone over here so that we can see what they're up to. Arkady says they're gathering for an attack but he can't see where they are massing, how many etc."

"On the way, the drone chief has just finished re-fuelling a recon bird. If it isn't going far I'll see whether they can quickly add a couple of Spiral 2s to the mix."

"Thanks Simon we need the help." Simon heard the doubt creep in.

"You will be fine Julius, you are a brilliant gunner, a great tactician and will make a fine Captain, of that I have no doubt."

"Thank you Simon. I will do my best."

He closed the connection and turned his attention back to the battle.

"Now where are those blasted Gepards people? I can't see them on the display." Then he realised they'd been filtered out by the seat's former occupant when he was doing something else.

"Belay that. I've got them." He examined the two contacts carefully they were right on the border of a red ring on the display which marked the extreme range of Hood's 5.1" guns. He was tempted. They would certainly be in the range of the laser guided shells which had about a 30% overreach on the ordinary shells. Of course they were smaller so would do less damage and these were 2000 ton frigates, they weren't going to be stopped by a few low calibre shells. He decided to wait and see if they came closer. For them to use their 76mm deck gun they'd need to be well within range of Hood's main guns, if of course, that was their intention.

"What happened to the second wave of aircraft?" He now asked having not been in the OPs room when the Chinese launched their SAMs.

Lt Bianchi answered.

"The Chinese took them out Sir, every single one. They've just launched at the returning first wave too."

"Guter Gott they are really annoyed with the Viets aren't they?"

"So it seems Sir and if their strike rate is the same as before then this lot haven't got a chance either."

"Did no one in the second wave raise an alarm?"

"It seems not, perhaps they used IR guidance. The HQ-9B has that capability. No warning at all."

"So these are just flying back into the shit?"

"I believe so, their RWR is old, it will show a threat direction but nothing more, those Chinese fire control radars have been off and on several times now with nothing apparently happening, so maybe they just ignore them but keep a watch out that way. Their own Kopyo search and track won't look that far to the left or right."

"Then they have my blessing, I hope they shoot them all down."

Ayize was out on the weather deck close to the rear of the main superstructure. With the bridge a total mess it was deemed the external ladders would be the best way up. He slung the rifle over his shoulder and adjusted the small back pack in which they'd stuck a load of rounds for him. He set himself and put a foot on the first step. Then he heard a noise behind and without hesitation ducked and quickly spun around.

One of his massive arms, the left, connected with something solid and knocked it flying and he managed get his head round in time to see a figure lunging towards him with a knife. His right arm was just arriving in its own swing and he accelerated its motion smacking the second attacker. Out of nowhere a third appeared to his right and stabbed towards his right kidney.

Ayize could do nothing about that for the moment so grabbed the second attacker with his huge right hand. He then reversed the momentum, roaring out his anger, and still holding the hapless soldier he swung the unfortunate commando back into the comrade who had just stabbed him. The resultant collision rendered both unconscious. Without hesitation he picked both men up, raised them to shoulder level and brought them together again with a bone shattering smack, he then threw the limp bodies over the rail and went looking for the third team member whom he'd simply brushed aside. He decided to have a laugh when he found him, so he picked the unfortunate commando up and shook him until he woke up.

The poor man woke dangling in the hands of a giant black man who was smiling broadly.

"Go tell friends. This ship for giants only. Go away." All the petrified man could see was this giant black man laughing as he wafted him over the side of the ship by just one arm.

The dangling man nodded vigorously and Ayize laughing out loud drew back his arm and launched the hapless commando through the air and over the rail. He noted the splash followed by more frantic splashing as the former attacker swam away.

Ayize touched his side where the last bastard had put his knife, just under the undersized Kevlar jacket that was too small to do up. A little blood, it didn't feel bad so he decided to carry on with the job and began climbing.

"Ayize to Arkady. I just threw three of your bandits over the side by the starboard superstructure entrance. Maybe you need a lock down?"

Shit. Arkady jumped up and ran back finding a discarded assault rifle and lots of wet footprints. He looked up to see Ayize waving, and then down in the water and two bodies were bumping alongside with a third swimming for the beach like he had 'Jaws' chasing him.

"All security detachments, this is Arkady. Lock down the citadel. All outside personnel search and sanitise."

A series of mike clicks told him he'd been heard. Now was the time to start the hunting. He loosened his combat knife, stuck a new magazine in his assault weapon, took a deep breath and started looking for any of the little bastards who might be hiding or setting charges. He heard the crack of a high powered rifle and knew that Ayize was starting his own campaign.

Jake grimaced as he read the latest casualty list. Dear God why don't they give up? The game's over, it's out in the open, nothing to gain only people to lose. Idiots.

He picked out the card with Miles Carlson's number on it and dialled.

"Hi, this is for Miles Carlson. Vietnamese Kilo class boat at position..." He gave the coordinates and added course and speed. "Be obliged if you could pass on to your Chinese counterparts they've just torpedoed one of my ships. Will update if necessary."

Then he disconnected. It had two chances.

He touched his mike twice.

"Captain."

"Jake?"

"Give it all you've got Reiner, I don't care if we run out of fuel on the way back."

"Aye, aye. Sir."

*

In the lightening sky above the mayhem on the water, the returning first flight of SU-22M4's heard the cheep, cheep of their radar warning receiver indicating active radar to their north east. They were tired now, the adrenaline from the night time low level approach had all but worn off, the pop up and shooting live weapons for the first time, the subsequent high level return with all of their comrades had left them weary but exultant.

The growing light in the north east was not at all helpful. It was difficult to maintain a good night vision because looking at the approaching dawn meant they could no longer see anything over on the dark side of the sky and sea.

The Chinese had however got it slightly wrong. They had sensibly targeted the rear members of the flight first, intending to rapidly work forward through the flight and so had allotted their HQ-9B missiles in the order that the enemy planes were flying when they fired. Now due to tiredness and a drop in formation awareness, two of the aircraft had crept forward past their squadron mates and these two died in spectacular balls of flame even as other missiles reached for the rest. The most alert was the flight leader, a typical thing in communist doctrine, he was responsible and he dared not take his eye from the skies around him. He also had good reflexes. Before the explosion had blossomed to its fullest he had his stick over and was diving for the deck twisting as he went while vigorously pumping out chaff and flares to decoy something he had not seen but only imagined. His shouted order to break reached only one other set of ears before explosions took the rest. His frantic calls drew only one reply and now with just a wing man he hit the deck and put the aircraft throttle to full military power heading for the nearest friendly airfield whilst screaming out his warning over the radio.

The Chinese SAG continued its leisurely approach to the Long Hải area intending to stay well outside the twelve mile limit more because they wanted to stay clear of the shallow water than fear of Vietnamese attack. Everyone however was on full alert. The presence of the American carrier task group to their south and east was always a little distracting since there were any number of airborne plots to be tracked and identified as well as the ever present AWAACs radar washing over them.

They had noted the effectiveness of the Super Hornet's AMRAAM missiles against the missiles launched at the Gweilo vessel stuck on one of their islands. Headquarters had not yet defined their attitude towards this vessel. The Commander hoped that it would not be his duty to destroy it.

At that moment a message from fleet HQ was wordlessly passed to him. It was a Pandora's box. The message gave the position, course and even depth of a Vietnamese Kilo class submarine. It was to be destroyed using either anti-submarine helicopters with torpedoes or, they could use their new anti-submarine YU-8 rockets similar to the American ASROC. It was the on-scene commander's decision which to use.

He quickly ordered the location to be plotted and discovered it was three miles beyond the furthest reach of the missiles in even his leading YU-8 equipped ship. He immediately gave orders to detach the *Liuzhou* a type 54A frigate, and for her to close ten miles at top speed before firing. However, clearly that was the least significant piece of information in the message. What was important was that the foreigners could somehow find and track a submerged and very quiet submarine. How in the name of all my ancestors, can they do that? He asked the morning sky.

*

Simon connected to Hood.

"Drone reports two anti-submarine torpedoes from a rocket powered delivery vehicle have destroyed our persistent Kilo, Julius. Good news eh, at least the bugger can't hurt you anymore."

"Do you know who did the job?"

"Yes, from the inbound direction it's clear they came from the Chinese SAG north and east of you."

"Well I hope they don't come any closer, we're a little busy right now with bandits on board."

"Shit. Any details?"

"Only that we are in lockdown and our Zulu friend Ayize killed two and threw a third back over the side."

"Good Lord, I bet that was a surprise for them, I'm sure I wouldn't want to be on the wrong side of that gentleman."

"No, me neither. He's up on the signal deck sniping them at this moment as it happens."

"Anything else going on?"

"Well we've had an increase in the number of RPGs hitting us all over, thank God they aren't terribly accurate over a decent distance, and we're just setting up to bombard the reverse side of the dunes they're all hiding behind. Daylight will be a bonus but it's starting to mist up. I do expect a thick fog by dawn and Arkady thinks that's when they'll make a big effort. Clearly they don't realise we have low light and IR viewers."

"Right. What's your ammunition status and any more news on Jon Roby?"

"Sheisse! Thanks for the heads up Simon." Julius was annoyed that he'd made the elementary error of not checking the ammunition status and Simon had just politely nudged him. " Err as you've seen, we have about ten percent of everything left and that could go in less than five minutes. As for the Captain, the only news is that he's been conscious briefly a couple of times and the doctor thinks he will come round fully soon. Problem is that he's not any better off; that can only come with surgery."

"It's so frustrating I wish we could ask the Yanks to come and help but I know they've done more than ever they should, already."

There was a series of thumps from up above them then a curse.

"Sir we've lost primary radar. I suspect it's been hit by one of those bloody RPGs. I'll find out." Ringbolt Langford got on the internal comms and asked if anyone in damage control could safely get a look at the forward antenna. Within a minute the answer was back.

"Not rotating Sir. Ayize is about twenty feet below it and reports three close hits by RPG's, almost simultaneously."

"Damn. Right Simon, you still there?"

"Yes Julius, bad news. I'll make sure you have good drone coverage and I'll send the two Spiral equipped birds at once."

"Right. Speak later."

"Listen up everyone, I have a good picture from one of the recon birds, warn all stations I will be commencing fire with the main battery in two minutes. Mr Sharp, make a broadcast and ensure security are aware."

Steve Sharp, now First Lieutenant, tapped his mike and began to speak.

Julius concentrated on the images from the ridge line. It was clear there were designated groups of RPG firing soldiers with people tracking from ammunition dumps to resupply them. Like ants wandering to and from the nest. He continued designating spots where he wanted shells to land or air burst, whilst the two minute warning played out. Then finished he ordered Sharp to warn again.

"Do you hear there, main battery commencing fire shortly, all hands stay away from the upper deck. That is all." Steve tapped his mike to discontinue and resumed checking on the security situation. Apparently three more commandos had been discovered and despatched for just one wounded security officer. They had been in the process of laying charges to breach the after superstructure citadel when they'd been gunned down by Arkady and two of his men, one of whom took a round in the shoulder.

The seconds counted down and then all hell let loose above decks. All four main turrets began training in different directions, and as soon as they had settled they commenced firing. Most shells were HE fused airbursts ten feet above the positions to scatter death and destruction amongst the RPG teams. The other shells were ground bursts and worked their way back to the ammunition stores where there were a couple of secondary but massive explosions as they found their mark. Just thirty seconds later the guns were silent again and the firing smoke hung in the breezeless air.

Ayize coughed slightly and that caused a jarring pain in his side. He reached down and felt the injury site again. His hand came a way covered in blood. Shit.

"Ayize here, I'm going to have to get down, I've got an injury that the doc needs a look at. Maybe some help?"

"Arkady here, I'm on my way with help."

Warrant Officer Crause arrived at the rear of the superstructure at the same time as Arkady both looked up.

"Ayize, are you coming down?" Asked Arkady.

No answer. They looked at each other. Arkady walked over to the ladder and began climbing. When he got to the platform that Ayize lay on he did a double take, the light still wasn't good enough to see clearly but he had a sinking feeling as he quickly knelt to examine the big Zulu. Pulse was thready but present. He began an external examination and as soon as he moved the knee he'd been kneeling on he discovered that it wasn't shadow on the deck but blood, lots of it.

"This is Arkady. Ayize is down on the signal deck. He's out cold and has lost a lot of blood but I haven't located the wound yet. I'm going to need serious help getting him down but I need a doc to look at him quickly.

"On the way." Answered Sid Parker quickly.

Crause was thinking about getting Ayize down, must be over a hundred kilos, he thought. He looked around as Parker arrived complete with his med kit on his back. Crause thumbed upwards to Arkady leaning over the lip. Then his eye caught the crane used for lifting the drones.

He tapped his mike and said 'broadcast'.

"Crause here. I need the drone crane driver to close up and I need someone to bring an aero-med stretcher to the base of the forward superstructure NOW!"

The stretcher arrived being carried by two seamen. Crause indicated they should lift it up to Parker and Arkady. Bullets occasionally spanged off the superstructure just to remind them they were still in danger but the RPG threat seemed to have gone for the moment. He heard the electric whine as the crane started up.

"Move the hook to above the signal deck and wait until the stretcher is hooked on. I'll give you the word to lift."

"Aye, aye Sir". Came the tinny voice from the operators perch in a glass bubble at the rear of the aft funnel.

"Can't see far enough around the funnel Sir."

"Ach, I will direct you. Extend derrick. Now lift up. Enough. Rotate to port. Enough. Wait now." Crause expertly directed the crane to where it was needed.

Up on the signal deck Sid Parker completed his primary survey and having found the small entry wound in Ayize's side stuffed Kaltostat wool in it as a temporary plug. He whacked a dressing over it and then set about organising the huge man to be rolled into the stretcher bed. He shook his head in wonder as they finally managed to roll him into it but noted that Ayize's legs dangled a foot or so over the end, so Sam tied them together with a bandage and took a couple of turns around the railing of the stretcher to keep them still. He placed a Guedal tube in Ayize's mouth to ensure a good airway until he was down below. Then hooked up the helicopter strops to the crane jib and gave the signal to Crause waiting below, everything was non-standard for this lift. A prolonged burst of machine gun fire stitched its way just above their heads so they had to wait before trying again. Problem was they were getting ever more visible as the light grew even though it was foggy.

Crause ordered the crane driver to lift and retract the derrick at the same time, this raised the angle on the derrick and moved it back away from the sporadic machine gun fire. As soon as Ayize and his stretcher had cleared the superstructure Crause ordered it lowered. It took Crause and three others to lift the big man inside the citadel and then down the fortunately wide passageways to the Wardroom where the doctor had set up his triage area.

There was a commotion in the passageway outside the OPs room and Julius, irritated at the disturbance vented.

"What is going on out there? Are there intruders?"

Langford spoke into his mike to the security just outside the hatch and then went over to open it.

Captain Roby assisted by two others was helped inside and the hatch closed again. Julius sprang from his chair to help.

"Sir, does the doctor know you are here?"

Captain Jon Roby made a sound and Julius leaned in to hear better.

"Don't be silly Julius, he'd kill me."

Which flustered the current Captain even more.

"Which would be most comfortable. Your command chair or a chair near the holo table?" He asked.

Another barely above whispered response directed them to a seat near the holo table.

Julius returned to his command chair speaking into the mike.

"Mason."

"Steward speaking."

"Mason your Captain has returned to the OPs room, bring iced water and a glass please and inform the doctor."

"Aye, aye Sir." Answered a surprised and worried PO Steward.

Julius observed his Captain discretely, what was he thinking? He was in no condition to be anywhere except in

Sick Bay. The steward arrived, made his boss comfortable set the water where he could get it, cast a worried look at Julius then left.

Jon Roby sipped the ice cold water, God that was good. The pain in his abdomen was intermittent. Everything down there felt odd, numb or not quite there. He was as weak as a kitten, it was all he could do to talk into the headset and give the computer instructions to display the various facets of the ongoing battle. He was dying, he knew that from the look on Keith Aitcheson's face when he came round. The normally taciturn doctor was a good man but he had trouble keeping his thoughts off his face, made him a bad bridge player. Roby smiled to himself. The morphine helped, the doc had also catheterised him when he was out so he had a bag in his jacket pocket. According to Sid Parker they'd also topped him up with various antibiotics as well as washing out his insides with dilute morphine. Probably why it felt so funny. So it was all going to end here was it? So be it, I've had a good run. He turned his limited attention to the holographic display in front of him noting the absence of any radar data.

Some minutes later while Julius was setting up another barrage to keep back the gathering hordes beyond the dune and worrying about the diminishing ammunition supply, Ringbolt Langford handling comms as well as everything else, asked him to listen to a channel 16 broadcast supposedly from the Viet commander.

"You are in violation of the territory of the Socialist Republic of Vietnam you have five minutes to surrender or you will be boarded and destroyed. Leave your ship in the boats and come to the shore. You will be treated well. Refuse and die."

"Julius."

Kopf looked round at his former Captain.

"Yes Sir?"

"Will we surrender?"

Kopf was surprised by the question, he didn't think surrender was a viable option in all honesty, was the Captain suggesting they should.

"No Sir, I had not intended to do so."

"Good, let me answer him then.

Julius waved his arm as if bowing, indicating for Jon Roby to continue.

Roby sat up straight in the chair, a grimace of pain crossed his features. He composed himself, drank a little water and cleared his throat, then pressed the button to give himself some more morphine if the self-administrator would allow.

He turned to Julius and explained.

"What follows is part way through my mess dinner party piece, you should consider yourself lucky you don't have to sit through the rest.

Jon Roby, Captain of Merchant Protector Hood, opened the microphone connection and began speaking in a voice none present had heard before. He knew this would be his last speech and he knew it would be recorded by all listening vessels and aircraft.

"I have your answer and this is it." He drew a breath.

"Good God why should they mock poor fellows thus?

Let me speak proudly, tell the constable we are but warriors for the working day, our gaineth and our guilt are all besmirched with rainy marching in the painful fields but by the mass our hearts are in the trim. Herald, save thou thy labour, come thou no more for ransom gentle Herald they shall have none I swear but these my joints which if they have as I shall leaveth them. Shall yield them little. Bid them achieve me!" After a moment's pause to catch his breath he added weakly.

336

"This is Captain Jon Roby, RN retired, Master of this vessel and Captain in the Cayman Islands Naval Service and that is my answer."

He closed the connection and slumped in the seat, a sudden reddening of the previously white bandages indicating a new bleed.

"Get the doctor now!" Shouted Julius Kopf, current Captain of Hood.

*

"Admiral what do you make of it?" Asked Commander Jose Maringa.

Admiral Summers walked away and stood looking out of the nearest scuttle.

He could not have spoken had he tried. There was a softball sized lump in his throat which had been there since he'd listened to the message picked up by the Hawkeye and relayed back to Nimitz. The voice that spoke was weak and clearly managing with great difficulty, there were certainly more pauses than there ought to be. I'm getting damned soft in my dotage, he thought. Ignoring the background chatter he cast his mind back to a mess Dinner on HMS Cornwall when he was a guest of Lieutenant Jon Roby RN. It was a mess dinner on the 25th October, hell he couldn't remember what year, late 80's sometime, and he recalled his own ignorance of what anniversary this was.

After the dinner and the speeches, when the port had passed several times the president of the mess, an older Commander, tapped his glass with a teaspoon and introduced an 'entertainment'. At which Jon Roby had stood, finished off his port with a flourish and then made his way to the head of the table. He then gave the famous pre-battle speech from Shakespeare's Henry the fifth, in its entirety, including the last part where the French herald arrives to ask for surrender one more time.

Summers had never studied classics much but having enthusiastically cheered his friend when he'd finished his recitation, decided to educate himself in regard to this at least. Now he surreptitiously wiped a tear from the corner of his eye, drew himself up, swallowed the softball with difficulty and turned back to the officers in his cabin.

"That was Jon Roby's party piece for mess dinners, part of it at least." He hurumphed again swallowing as the lump threatened to return. "He always liked to give Shakespeare's speech from Henry the fifth on the anniversary of Agincourt, that's the last part of his recitation; it's also his daughter's birthday. He used to say to be born on that day was the greatest gift he could give her. His wife didn't agree but there it is. Anyway it's just his fancy British way of saying the same as General McAuliffe did when the Germans wanted him to surrender at Bastogne in war two, but Roby would never have been happy with just 'Nuts'."

Bull Balfour knew his boss well enough to know that he was deeply upset so he went for distraction mode.

"What's the status on the Hood right now Jonny?"

"Well as best we can tell, she's beached intact, has lost all her radar and from what some of the returning Rhinos say, is under fire from the dune areas around her, RPGs and MGs. I've had to deny repeated CAP requests to strafe. She has power. She has also taken anything up to a dozen hits from various missiles. One tough cookie though, she's still shooting back. Don't know for how long though."

"What about the Viet naval units?"

"Well there's now three Gepards hanging around, they appear to be waiting for something, we don't know what but they still have a full missile load each we think. It appears the Hood sank all three Molniyas and the Chinese took out the whole of the first flight of eight SU-22M4s and all but two of the second. Guess they're using the HQ-9 IR variants since we have no pre-hit emissions and the total surprise seems to confirm that."

"Submarine activity?"

"Well I don't know how the hell this plays out but the Chinese SAG suddenly detached one of its type 54A frigates which raced ahead and fired two YU-8 ASROC equivalents. They didn't stop to begin an ASW sweep, they didn't use a helicopter to localise before shooting and they didn't ping, they just went straight to point A and shot. Not only that but they scored too, Virginia is still shadowing and heard the explosions followed by break up sounds. That's another Kilo they've lost."

The Admiral sucked in his upper lip and pointed to Hood's position.

"Could we get a V-22 in there for SAR work Commander?"

Jose Maringa took a breath and counted to five before rushing in with an answer.

"Well they are in range Sir but it would be a hot LZ. Current CAP reports Viet tracer from half a dozen points around the ship and I really can't think of a way of suppressing that fire without direct intervention Sir, they sure as hell aren't likely to allow anything, even with red crosses all over it, to land."

"OK. How much closer to that area can we safely move the carrier? I want to be on hand when this shit is finished, I want to be around and available to help out and lift guys off if need be."

Captain Balfour did a quick calculation and put a pencil mark on the admiral's chart.

"We can move another forty miles closer Sir without compromising our ability to detect inbound submarine threats. Both Virginias and the Sea Wolf are to our north and west now, in a loose cordon around the rim where the water starts to get deep; nothing would be able to sneak past them and get close to us. As to air and surface threats, we're closer to Vietnamese airfields but they really haven't got enough to bother us and the Chinese SAG is not on our case at the moment. No air movements at all Sir, that is very unusual and I take that as a cooperative signal."

"Thanks Bull, thanks Jose, Jonny. Right Captain, take the group as close as we're allowed and be ready for some SAR work at a moment's notice."

*

"Shit. Here they come!" Arkady's voice over the net punctuated by short bursts from his MP5, told them all the next attack was starting.

WO Crause, Able Seaman Willi Bortz and Andy Millner of Arkady's security unit waited in the lee of the after superstructure immediately behind X turret. Viewers mounted on the superstructure gave a real time view of the stern area despite the thick fog, so they waited. Only swimmers or boat delivered raiders could get on deck here and as far as Crause knew there were no boats, so just swimmers. Lightly armed he hoped, and knackered after a scary swim. He nodded to Millner.

The ex-marine sprinted to the port side and dropped the grenade he'd already primed, over the side, then he ran to starboard and repeated the action before returning to the entry hatch. The twin explosions were muted thuds but anyone in the water within twenty yards or so would be hit by a shock wave and stunned. After that they waited.

The fog was as thick as a London pea-souper, so the resident cockney Arthur Clinch would have it. That he was forty years too young to have ever experienced one didn't seem to stop him claiming a proprietary interest in the phenomenon. It was thick but unlike the fogs in northern climes it was warm, which all of them on the upper deck, being northerners, thought weird indeed. Worse it was unmoving, not a ripple stirred the water of the lagoon and no breeze moved so much as a single palm frond ashore. In such conditions noises are muted until close by then amplified suddenly.

The drones switched to IR and had a perfect view of the assault group as it sprinted across the sand to the bows of the ship, the lead party carrying a bundle which they dumped on the beach while two of them ran forward with ropes and grapplings which they swung up over the bows. They began climbing. Before they reached the level of the deck both stopped and threw a rope end to the other over the bow. Then they passed each other's rope through the mooring cleats before signalling the beach party. The shore side ends were then taken up and lashed to a scrambling net which was quickly hauled up.

The two climbers swung over onto the scrambling net and started their next task. Each primed two grenades and then watching each other carefully let the handles spring out and counted to two before throwing them over the bows. They then repeated the action and lay aside as the storming party passed them with assault rifles slung.

Arkady now on the signal deck where Ayize had lain, along with a colleague on the opposite side, waited to see what the Vietnamese would do in order to get around the obvious disadvantage of having to climb over the bow. The exploding crump of the grenades gave the clue and had the watchers been behind the fo'c'sle breakwater, they'd have been minced by the fragments.

Arkady held up three fingers then two then one and the pair of them rose looking for targets. The fog obscured the bow totally but the IR goggles made nonsense of the fragile cover it offered. People began climbing up over the bow two, three, four, they were unslinging rifles when Arkady and Johan Renzler opened fire with short controlled bursts knocking them back over the bow like a gardener hosing the patio. Then both quickly stepped two paces to left or right and shrank back down to watch and wait.

More grenades arrived and exploded and then more figures climbed over to face the short controlled and deadly bursts from the two hidden gunmen. An RPG whizzed by Arkady's head.

"Cover!" He shouted and Renzler ducked immediately. Two more followed, one impacting near the broken radar mounting and Arkady felt the sting of splinters on the back of his legs.

Then the starboard forward 3" gun erupted and even through the dense fog, brief stabs of light followed by explosions showed the closeness of the detonations. This whole thing was playing out over an area no longer than a football pitch, with the distance between the penalty areas marking the open area the attackers had to cross before the relative cover offered by Hood's bows.

"OPs. We just turned back two bow assaults. Expecting more."

"Roger that Arkady. Nothing further aft yet."

Five minutes later the starboard waist security detachment were in action as swimmers using grapnels tried to board there. To be fair they were in an impossible situation, only the defenders running out of ammunition was going to allow them to get on Hood. Firing from behind a makeshift metal screen and with a piece of canvas stretched from top of the hatch to just above the metal cover, they were almost immune to grenade assault and rifle fire as the canvas just bounced any grenades back where they came from, only a lucky explosion on the canvas itself would defeat the simple but effective defence. The defenders all two of them just shot anything that stuck its head over the edge of the deck.

Down in the OPs room Julius Kopf noted the action points and responses and programmed in shoots for the main battery guns as well as the secondaries, whilst tutting over the dwindling ammunition supply and waiting for it all to end.

They had no choices left, they just had to grit their teeth and keep fighting, but it seemed the more the enemy lost the more determined he became. A ping alerted him to check the surface group position. He'd set a radius of two miles around them on the system, if any of them moved out of it, he would be informed.

There were three ships where there'd been two, the IR and LIDAR images from the drone confirmed a third Gepard had joined the other two, now they were all sweeping around and away from Hood. Opening the range? They knew he had no radar and this activity occurred almost immediately after the ship had repulsed the last ground assault. Or maybe they'd had enough? Hope surged in him briefly.

Julius noted the Gepards were now nearly seventeen miles away and slowing, then they began to turn. Shit, twenty four more missiles on the way any minute now. There'd be fuck all left of the upperworks after that. The possibility of knocking a few out was there, with a reduced hit rate because of the radar loss, but they'd never get twenty four. Despair replaced the brief surge of hope.

"Main broadcast." He spoke into the mike, had to be main broadcast because he had people out on the decks.

"Do you hear there, Captain speaking. Looks like we're in for another missile deluge gentlemen. Clear the upper decks and prepare yourselves."

He stopped speaking abruptly, wondering what the hell anyone could do to prepare themselves for what was coming. Even with help from the resident four Hornets above them there were going to be lots of hits.

"Fog is thinning Sir, it don't take long for the sun to get to work around here, it's only been up five minutes." PO Hogarth was trying to cheer everyone up Julius knew, but this was his first command and he was going to lose it soon one way or another, so the cheer was lost on him. All he could do now was release control of the batteries to the computer and hope that it could cobble together a firing solution for when the shit started arriving –and have enough shells to do it. Was there no end to this torment?

Then there was thunder in the morning. Long rolling thunderclaps. 'Wheel barrows full of bricks' type thunderclaps.

Arkady had nearly closed the armoured hatch when he heard it. Thunder like some he'd heard before, it sounded like...

"Arkady here. Artillery gunfire in the distance, lots of it, continuous it seems, difficult to tell the direction but it seems to me it's from the north west or west."

"Arkady this is the Captain, get into cover it could be coming your way."

"Think it would have been here by now if it was Sir. Now it's just a continuous rumble, sounds like heavy artillery to me, maybe naval artillery? Fog's really thinning now."

"Ship off port bow Sir. Bearing zero eight five degrees, range nine miles. It's shooting." Shouted Ringbolt Langford.

Arkady turned to look in the indicated direction, he couldn't see a damned thing. He entered the citadel, closed and secured the lock before heading to the OPs room. What the fuck was going on, were the Yanks getting in on it? Maybe the Chinese had decided to make another point. He raced through the passageways and used the intercom to get them to release the lock to get in the OPs room.

Everyone was plugged in to a viewer.

"Shell splashes and hits on and around the lead Gepard Sir, I'm moving the drone further across. We also have two Spiral armed drones on station now what do we want to do with them?"

Hell, everything at once, thought Julius.

"Have McKenzie and Hayward target the troop concentrations near the bow and beyond the ridge line. Any communication with the ship approaching?"

"Err he's gone active Sir and Chief McKenzie reports another drone in sight, not one of ours. He says it's an Arado 196 Sir!"

Ringbolt Langford jumped up and shouted.

"It's Bismarck Sir. She's knocking seven shades of shit out of them."

A smile touched the corner of Julius's mouth.

"Control yourself PO Langford and report properly please."

It was now a wide grin and everyone could see it. Through the viewer a dreadful deluge of high explosive tracked then landed on the three ships, the sheer volume was staggering.

The super controlled and taciturn Julius Kopf released the viewer he was using and jumped up pumping the air with his fist. Everyone laughed then.

Lt Bianchi plugged in to Bismarck's systems using the newly available link.

The Holo picture changed immediately and now they had Bismarck's drone picture as well as her radar too.

The Vietnamese frigates were all in a dreadful state now, one was clearly sinking and the other two weren't in much better condition, all were on fire. Bianchi whistled as he looked at the round counter on Bismarck's ammunition displays, watching it climb at a phenomenal rate as her eight 5.1" guns pumped out radar directed shells at the rate of one every two seconds per barrel, or four per second. He also noted the first shells fired were radar fused and San Shiki type. That must have scared the shit out of them, as well as shredding their fire control and search radars before they knew they were being attacked.

Firing at maximum range he calculated that roughly a hundred shells were in the air before the first hit. Each salvo corrected by the latest target data. Bianchi watched through the fish eye lens of Bismarck's drone which had clearly approached the enemy ships stealthily and quite closely. Quietly stooging around giving away target data without them even being aware. Well that's tough; they were going to kill us now they're the ones in the shit. No sympathy.

"Bismarck on the line Sir." Chimed in Po Langford glued to his screens like someone watching a favourite film.

"Captain Kopf." There was an intake of breath and a slight pause before a familiar voice spoke.

"Aah Julius, how are things?" By that Julius knew he meant the ship and then the Captain in that order.

"We are afloat Sir, only superficial damage to add to the earlier list. Captain Roby is unconscious Sir, gravely ill. He is not expected to survive unless operated on, yesterday."

"Damn. What other casualties?"

"I'll have a list transmitted Sir, we have several dead amongst the security detail as well as a number of wounded. Some needing more help than we can give here. We're just hitting the enemy ground troops with thermobarics from the drones and hopefully that will be enough. They are streaming back to the holes from which they emerged, taking their dead and wounded with them. I take it you were close enough to hear Captain Roby's answer when ordered to surrender?"

"Yes, we were in range via the drone link. It was always his party piece on the anniversary of Agincourt whether the mess he was part of were having a dinner or not, he'd dine out if necessary but always did his recital much to his wife's embarrassment."

"It would have been nice to know you were on the way Sir." The merest hint of censure apparent in his voice.

"Yes, I understand. But we had to approach totally at EMCON, just guided by the information from Ocean Guard and even that unknowingly from them. Just daren't risk the bad guys, of whatever stripe, getting wind of reinforcements. Wouldn't give much for our chances of tracking a Kilo at thirty five knots."

"I understand. I'll speak to the doctor to see if Captain Roby has regained consciousness, he'd be very pleased to know his ship is safe and that you have arrived."

"Yes do that would you. I'll see if I can whistle up a SAR from somewhere, see if we can't get the badly injured better care. Doctor Crib and Chief Coultard will be along in a few minutes we've already despatched a RHIB."

"Good, they'll be welcome I'm sure, Lt Aitcheson has done a sterling job along with Chief Parker but I'm sure they could do with the help. I'll get back to monitoring things here to see if it really is over."

"You do that, I think the naval assault is over, we had been watching them for a while and knew we had to shoot as soon as they started the turn."

"Glad you did. Perfect timing. I thought we'd had it."

"Julius we ditched everything but the chef to save weight and get here on time, and he was worried for a while too. Right, speak later Captain Kopf."

"Aye Sir." Julius was both sad and happy. The Commodore had acknowledged his brevet promotion but his friend and mentor lay dying. He'd give the chair up in a microsecond to get Captain Roby back there.

*

"Just had a request from Bismarck Sir, Commodore König wonders whether we can oblige with a SAR for the worst of the casualties now the fighting seems done. He says he's happy to pay any bill that accrues."

"They're so Goddamn polite. There are no bills for brave men. OK. Let's do it. I also want to send the Chinese a message if they are still wanting to play down there. I want a rotating CAP of at least six Rhinos over the horizon from them, I want everything in the air and patrolling around there, get the 'Death Rattlers' up there, they're marines they can put on a good show when asked. I want OVERT. They must understand or think we are prepared to go further than shooting down a few anti-ship missiles. I want intermittent active radar from all units. I want noise in the sky and get that Osprey airborne with medics on the double."

"Aye, aye Sir." Answered Bull Balfour for all of them, wearing a big grin on his craggy features.

Admiral Summers sat down at his desk, what could be Jon Roby's last words on the message slip in front of him. He carefully folded the paper and decided that if they were his last words, Roby's daughter would receive them from his own hand. What an unnecessary waste.

Epilogue - Aftermath.

The Chinese SAG took the hint. The sky was so full of 'noise' of the electronic kind that the systems operators on the flagship were awed. Their ships were painted with twenty to thirty different active radar for the next five hours as well as a double helping from the AWAACS. Also, and operating within the radius of the AWAACS, the Growlers were actively jamming and preventing any Chinese search radar from seeing even the outer screen which they were never really in radar range of, but they didn't know that.

The Chinese admiral commanding sighed with relief when HQ Southern Fleet ordered them to return, the diplomatic fallout was to be kept to a minimum. He ordered a turn away and set course back towards the Paracel Islands which China claimed quite illegally too.

With the Chinese out of the picture Summers pushed his AWAACS further north to ensure adequate warning of any further Vietnamese air or sea activity. Given the proximity to real full blown engagement for the US ships and Air Wing, he thought it was a good exercise for the crews. He didn't anticipate any further Vietnamese aggression, but he did anticipate more and more requests from CNO for more and more information on what had been going on and he knew his time as Task Force Commander was coming to an end. He had no regrets. He'd done what was right by his code of honour, in fact not as much as he wanted to do. Maybe that König fella needed an advisor of some kind?

He picked up his cap and walked out, he had a visit to make. Sailors and marines made a hole for their admiral as he went through the ship. Morale was high, he could see that just by their faces. They'd taken the losses on the

Simmons personally and now could justifiably feel they had evened the score, a bit of swagger never hurt a fighting sailor, a 'don't fuck with me' attitude was a good deterrent.

The Captain in charge of the medical section met him at the door to the compartments in which the Hood evacuees were being looked after, he had plenty of spare places in his eighty bed medical centre. He looked tired, his surgical mask hung from the two lower strings and his surgical greens were creased with sweat patches at the arm pits. Not surprising Summers thought when you consider he'd just spent the last six or seven hours patching people up.

He had no idea what he was going to find or had any heads up on the patients they'd fetched off, from what the Osprey driver had said was more like a bombed dockside than a beached ship.

The first patient was a big surprise in every way. Laid on his front with pillows under the foot or so of leg which protruded from the end of the generous bed frame was an enormous black man. He had tubes coming out of his arms both sides, and units of blood and maybe saline Summers thought, going back in.

The doctor explained that this one had taken a stab to his loin area which had punctured his kidney, he'd lost a lot of blood but would be OK. Next was an ordinary sized person, that was the best way to describe the difference that Summers brain could conceive, he was conscious and propped up with bandages around his chest. The Doctor explained that this was the Chief Medic from the Hood who had been caught in the blast radius of an RPG when he was out on the upperdeck dragging in a wounded crewman.

The doctor wagged a finger at Sid Parker.

"We pulled about thirty or so metal fragments out of his chest, fortunately he did at least have a Kevlar jacket on, otherwise he wouldn't be here. The fragments never got much more than skin deep, well most of them anyway, there were a couple which were pretty close to some large blood vessels and their doctor wisely decided he need more attention than he could give. He disobeyed the first rule of a combat medic didn't you Chief?"

Sid looked somewhat shamefaced.

"What's the first rule Chief?" Asked Admiral Summers out of curiosity.

"Don't become a casualty Sir, because you can't help anyone if you're dead or injured. An old axiom which is ignored by most medics in battle, but now I know why it's in there."

The doctor moved on.

"Next bed we have the man he was pulling to safety and who will, when he wakes up, owe the Chief his life for disobeying all the rules. He took the blast from the RPG before the one that got the Chief. His legs are shattered and his femoral artery was severed on the left, if the Chief hadn't got to him and clamped that off he be stone cold by now. We've picked out enough metal fragments to make a mess kit -and cutlery. Then we put a load of metal back in to stick his bones together, we're lucky having an orthopaedic surgeon on this rotation. Anyway this guy's X-rays look like a Metal Mickey snapshot.

Over here in this intensive care unit we have the luckiest of them all. This is Hood's Captain, he had about a thimble full of blood left in him when we got him on the table, his blood pressure was so low it barely registered, I've seen road kill with a higher systolic. His doctor took out thirty or forty pieces of metal and sealed of the leaks but the blood kept coming. Wisely he decided to pack the abdominal cavity and hope for better scanning and surgical resources. It was a gamble but one I'd have probably taken in his place too. Now he's still on the critical list but is wandering in and out of consciousness. You have exactly a minute Admiral then I'm going to throw you out."

Admiral Summers acknowledged the doctor's threat with a smile.

"I hear you loud and clear Clive."

He stepped into the ITU and was immediately aware of various beeps and clicks and machine noises. A nurse was monitoring the instruments and nodded as the Admiral entered. In a hushed tone he informed the Task Force Commander that his patient was in and out of consciousness all the time.

Summers stood by the bed for a few seconds overwhelmed by the amount of medical paraphernalia arrayed around the extremely pale Jon Roby.

As he watched Roby's eyes fluttered open and some light of intelligence appeared. His lips moved but no sound came out. Summers looked across to the nurse who promptly put the nozzle of a water bottle between his lips and gently squeezed. Roby swallowed.

"Hi Jamie. Am I on your bathtub?"

He then promptly fell asleep leaving Summers with a big smile on his face.

"He's still all there upstairs." He said to the nurse as he walked quietly out.

*

Jake looked intently at the blast and smoke stained hull as his RHIB entered the lagoon. He looked overboard and could clearly see the coral not too far below and mentally whistled as he considered how Jon Roby had coaxed his wounded and flooding ship over the ridge into the lagoon beyond.

The sparkling sea belied the rage and destruction that had been wrought all around just hours before. Until that is you took in the occasional dark mound on the sands. There were still Vietnamese military of some kind on this atoll and so the dignity of burial would be denied these men until such time as their commander surrendered or Hood left them to it.

There was a recon drone accompanied by a Spiral armed drone in low circuit above where the island's occupants had been seen to disappear. Any sign of armed men exiting would elicit an instantaneous response from the drones and from Bismarck anchored just a quarter of a mile away but with guns trained on the area under observation.

On board the RHIB with him were Lt Ian Halshaw, Bismarck's electrical engineer and Lt Cdr Oleg Scotnikov the Chief Engineer and primary design consultant for both ships. Lastly and by no means least was a heavily armed Tetsunari who looked like a one man army. Jake could have sworn Tettas had a gleam in his eye as he donned all of his 'Action Man' kit but when he looked again he was back to his implacable self. Tetsunari rode easily standing next to the coxswain, eyes roaming everywhere looking for danger to his boss.

They were met at the quarterdeck entry by Julius himself.

"Sorry for the lack of formality Sir, but everyone is trying to get us as repaired as possible before we try for the big moment."

Jake noted the now rotating after radar antenna and the crew sweeping debris off the decks with Crause supervising the litter collection and disposal. They clearly weren't intending to leave anything behind to mar this otherwise tropical paradise. Jake had already stated his desire to see the damaged bow first hand and of course Scotnikov had the same idea too. With four of Arkady's security troops deployed in an arc around the bow and

Tetsunari on the bow itself, Jake felt the risks were low enough to at least have a look. Lt Braime, Hood's Chief Engineer accompanied them, glad to see his old boss Scotnikov too.

There followed a technical discussion involving 'fothering', flotation buoys and other arcane nautical terminology, then everyone retired on board to discuss the situation.

Hood slid back from the beach with a grinding and crunching which made everyone wince. The moment she moved to deeper water the inflow to Bravo section began again. Canvas rectangles were applied to the seaward side of the leaking bulkhead seams to try and temporarily reduce the flow. With pressure from the water outside pushing the fothering canvas against the leaking seams, the pumps were at least keeping pace. The next step involved securing every flotation aid and fender that could be gathered from both ships and packing them inside the ruptured Alpha section. Where possible they were secured to the deck of Alpha and thereby became buoyancy aids. The tricky part once more was getting her trimmed so she could exit the lagoon without leaving her engines behind or running the bow into the coral barrier. This accomplished Hood slowly came about and in an undignified stern first motion approached the already sunken heavy lifter anchored and waiting beyond Bismarck. Once aboard the vessel the hydraulic pumps were engaged and Hood was lifted out of the water as the loading platform rose. Now there was simply the ten and a half thousand mile, forty day trip to Little Cayman via the Panama Canal.

Bismarck passed through the outer screen and into the centre of the Nimitz carrier task group, sailors lined the decks of the vessels they passed and cameras flashed as the famous Merchant Protector approached the giant Nimitz.

An MH-60R Seahawk lifted Jake from Bismarck's quarterdeck and landed on what would be 'spot one' on a British carrier, by the massive carrier's island but he supposed the Americans called it something different.

He was welcomed on board by Nimitz's Captain who led him to the Admiral's day cabin.

"Jonathan Henry König, as I live and breathe it is a pleasure to meet you Sir." Admiral Summers pumped Jake's hand. "I have read with interest accounts of your exploits in the Caribbean and more recently been intimately involved with your Hood. I am pleased to have been able to offer what little assistance I was allowed."

"My gratitude along with that of my men on all of my ships, is something that cannot have a limit. I am eternally grateful for your assistance." Jake replied, pleased to meet the man who Jon Roby had admired for so long.

"Well while we're back slapping you ought to know that the acting Skipper of the USS Simmons has requested a Presidential citation for Hood in gratitude for the skill of the crew and the bravery exhibited by all in hostile waters."

"That is very gracious of him, though I doubt the President would want to acknowledge much of what went on here in the last few days and there's still the thorny matter of where all the crews went along with the other four ships."

"You are probably right, politicians have a bigger picture to paint and publicly rubbing the Vietnamese nose in their duplicity won't help pick up the pieces after this blows over. As to the crews of the missing ships and reparations or salvage for the ships themselves, well I believe the State department and the British Foreign Office are already quietly reading the riot act to the their Vietnamese ambassadors. We just don't know where the people went and Vietnam hasn't yet admitted they are even complicit."

"Well at least this part should be solved without the use of weapons other than barbed words and I'm glad we have at last pulled the lid off what was going on out here. Do you have any insight as to what it was all about?"

"No more than guesswork. I suspect given the Asian penchant for bearing a grudge over many years, this had something to do with getting one back on China for the losses Vietnam suffered back in the 80's over the Paracel Islands, but I can't be sure."

"Yes my conclusion too. Silly buggers. If they had kicked off a shooting match between China and the USA there'd be a lot more dead sailors to write home about and that is just the human side, the economic disaster would be global."

"Yeah well, thanks to your guys tripping over the ants nest, so to speak, they didn't get their way." He cocked an eye at Jake. "I have a feeling though Commodore."

"Jake please."

"OK. Jake. I have a feeling you would like a visit with your sailors down in the sick bay. I won't come with you, Captain Balfour will escort you, I have a few things to pack before I leave too."

"Oh, was this as a result of the assistance you rendered us?"

"I couldn't really say at this time but I have an appointment in the Pentagon for an ass roasting I believe. But don't concern yourself over that Jake, I'd do the same again no matter what. The guys in Washington just have to do what they have to do, got nothing to do with right or wrong, good and bad."

"Well, I know what you mean on a smaller scale. I am most grateful for the help you gave and if ever I can be of assistance, you only have to ask. I mean that most sincerely."

"Well that's mighty kind of you Jake, I just may take you up on that one day. Be seeing you."

Bull Balfour had come in without Jake being aware.

"This way Commodore, I'll take you down to see your folks."

"Thank you Captain." Jake nodded to Jamie Summers and left.

Down in the medical centre people were starting to get impatient. Ayize had a plaster over his right eye after discovering that even the mighty Nimitz wasn't designed for seven foot plus Zulus. He was mobile now and itching to get off the carrier which wasn't due in to its Japanese home port for another four days.

"Hiya bossman." He Rumbled as Jake entered with one of the corpsmen.

"You come to break us out of jail?"

"Love to Ayize but the doc says you still need to stay in, blood in the urine is still an issue you can't ignore."

"Uh so he told you did he? Well it was worth a try."

"Otherwise you're doing fine so I'm told and eating four rations of steak every meal too."

"They said I needed to eat meat to get my blood back, so I'm doing as I'm told. I always thought Americans were big on steak, but they must have small cows. That's why I have to have four each time."

"Ayize, in all honesty I don't know why they just don't give you a whole cow between two bakeries."

He moved along.

"How are you Chief?"

"Fine Sir now that I've lost weight." He opened his bedside locker and took something out.

"The doc says they took this bit from less than an inch away from my aorta."

He handed over a piece of sharp edged metal about the size of an AA battery.

"Hell that was a lucky escape Sid. Glad they got you sorted. Are you mending?"

"A little sharp pain every now and then but there isn't any metal left in me so I expect it's just healing. Looking forward to a spot of leave though, the missus is in a bad way, she hasn't been right since that taxi bumped her in Georgetown."

"Yes I heard. Sandiford Roche wanted the driver in prison for a ten stretch but had to be content with five years and no licence renewal."

"Still, could have been worse, she's going to need a lot of TLC until all the bones have knit properly, hot weather and plaster casts are a nightmare."

"Take care Sid, see you back at base."

"Gregor, how are you mending?" Gregor was one of Arkady's security detachment and the reason Sid parker was in sick bay. In heavily accented English he thanked Jake.

"I tell my friend Sid there, he need anything ever, he ask Gregor. Nyet problem." He tried to laugh but gave up when he coughed in pain.

"Take it steady Gregor." Jake admonished before moving on.

He knocked on the door and a voice said 'enter'. No longer in intensive care Roby was a senior officer so they gave him his own room despite him wishing to be in the same ward as his crew.

Jake walked in.

"Jonno how's things?"

Roby looked up and smiled.

"Ah my saviour, the lads have told me that you showed up in the nick of time and took out the Gepards. You truly have redeemed the name of your ship, if it ever needed redeeming that is."

"Well I would say that your saviours were many and varied. According to Doctor Aitcheson you were like a little vampire having a pint of blood off anyone and everyone you greedy bugger."

Roby smiled and winced as he tried make himself more comfortable. Why was it you always slid down hospital beds?

"I'm going to sue you for inadequate armour plating on the bridge. I thought you told me the damn thing was bullet and bomb proof."

Now it was Jake's turn to smile.

"Well if you will test theories in person. I never had you down as a crash test dummy Jonno. By the way, I see you managed to get an abbreviated Henry five in then."

"Ah yes, I can't remember much as the morphine was kicking in good and proper then, guess not having much blood left concentrated it a bit, still it was my daughter's birthday so one has to keep up traditions."

"I do wonder what the Vietnamese Commander made of it? Probably confused the hell out of him. He asks for surrender and you quote Shakespeare."

"Serves the silly bugger right. Anyway what's the news, I've heard from 'she who must be obeyed' back home so what else is going on?"

"Well Hood is well out into the Pacific now, another twenty eight days or so before she gets home. The shit has hit the fan locally, the Chinese are talking seriously to the Philippines, Malaya and the IMO, there's been some muttering in the UN Security council but it seems that at long last a deal in the area may be on the table. Vietnam of course loses out big style. They've been quietly disposing of anyone Colonel and above who knows anything about what happened. Seems like they will just airbrush it out of their history books along with the soldiers, sailors and airmen they lost. The good news though is that the remaining four ships have been located, not far from where you found the others, better still, the crews have miraculously turned up at the Chinese border with Vietnam. China must have really twisted their arms to do that. So they are as we speak on their way to various places called home. Lastly, Lloyds are very pleased with the results of our efforts and a big fat bonus is available to all. We have of course saved them a fortune, because no doubt Vietnam will pick up the bill."

"A good end to a bad story, but we lost people once more, because of greed and revenge."

"Yes, there is no compensation for that." He paused and hesitated before continuing. "I'm beginning to think it's time to retire my warships from active service, they've not been around for long and seem to have been in the thick of it with barely a pause. I find it hard to justify the continuing losses of our people."

Roby was thoughtful for a moment.

"Your decision to build them was because they were filling a void that national navies were not. It was a good decision and the void is still there if not bigger. Their shape is irrelevant but their work has not been. Just think for a minute all of the lives we've likely saved and all the misery we've prevented; put that on the other side of that balance you're mentally weighing Jake."

He fidgeted again trying to find a comfortable position.

"Now I need some sleep so bog-off." He finished with a smile.

Reuters Newsflash November 1st

At a press briefing in Tokyo the head of König Marine Security announced today that his company had tested and deployed a means of detecting moving subsurface objects using special wavelength laser devices. He also added that the data on this technology would be made available as an open source item on the company website.

Various governments including US, UK, Russia and China called the decision irresponsible and dangerous.

If you enjoyed this book please take a moment to review it at Amazon